The Bangkok Betrayal

Other novels by Frank Hurst:

The Postmistress of Nong Khai – 2016
The Chiang Mai Assignment – 2018
Mekong Dragon – 2019
The Peccavi Plot – 2020
A Backward Glance – 2021
(a family memoir written under his own name)
The Story of Jett – how he became a secret agent – 2023

THE *Bangkok* BETRAYAL

Frank Hurst

The Book Guild Ltd

First published in Great Britain in 2024 by
The Book Guild Ltd
Unit E2 Airfield Business Park,
Harrison Road, Market Harborough,
Leicestershire. LE16 7UL
Tel: 0116 2792299
www.bookguild.co.uk
Email: info@bookguild.co.uk
Twitter: @bookguild

Copyright © 2024 Frank Hurst

The right of Frank Hurst to be identified as the author of this
work has been asserted by them in accordance with the
Copyright, Design and Patents Act 1988.

All rights reserved. No part of this publication may be
reproduced, transmitted, or stored in a retrieval system, in any form or by any means,
without permission in writing from the publisher, nor be otherwise circulated in
any form of binding or cover other than that in which it is published and without
a similar condition being imposed on the subsequent purchaser.

This work is entirely fictitious and bears no resemblance to any persons living or dead.

Typeset in 12pt Adobe Jensen Pro

Printed on FSC accredited paper
Printed and bound in Great Britain by 4edge Limited

ISBN 978 1916668 867

British Library Cataloguing in Publication Data.
A catalogue record for this book is available from the British Library.

For my remarkable mother, a unique human being, who sadly died a few days after this final manuscript was completed. She travelled much and always cherished the remarkable peoples and civilisations of the Far East.

Betty Cooper née Rawlin, born 18th April 1930, Istanbul, died 25th October 2023, Cowes, Isle of Wight.

"*Au fond de tout patriotisme, il y a la guerre:
voilà pourquoi je ne suis point patriote.*"

"At the bottom of all patriotism there is war.
That is why I am not a patriot."

Jules Renard, *Journal* (1899)

Author's Notes

Some Context

This is a work of fiction, although the central character in the novel, Henry Gough, actually lived. He was born in the London suburb of Marylebone in 1835, and was my great-grandfather. My first story in this series, *The Peccavi Plot*, shadows his early history. Research has shown us Henry's family life was both scandalous and complicated, to say the least...

We know Henry Gough was less than six years old when both his parents, Charles and Hannah, died. We know he was brought up by his grandfather, Richard, a Haymarket chaff-cutter, and there is evidence that Henry started work, aged thirteen, for a baker named James Cummings who lived appropriately in London's Upper Baker Street. We know also that Henry eventually rose from this highly inauspicious start to own a thriving business, becoming a hansom cab proprietor with stables and forty horses. He lived and worked, for the most part of his life, close to his birthplace in Marylebone. Henry Gough went on to sire twenty-one children – nine with his wife, Hannah, and twelve with his mistress, Caroline, who subsequently became his second wife.

How Henry prospered and managed his life largely remains a mystery. How he coped with keeping two families concurrently and feeding so many children, is even more of a conundrum. We can only guess.

This novel is a whimsical attempt to add further colour to his story.

Given my own working background, it was inevitable that Her Majesty's Excise would enter part of Henry's fictional story. The excisemen, policemen and War Office characters are all inventions, although, like Scotland Yard, the Excise Detective Branch at Tower Hill and the War Office Intelligence Branch at Horse Guards Avenue both existed. The Excise Detective Branch was created in 1850 to address the problem of illicit alcohol; it was the forerunner of Her Majesty's Customs and Excise Investigation Division, which has played a key role in recent years to combat drugs smuggling into Britain. The numbers, objectives and methods of the early Detective Branch are portrayed as accurately in the novels as I have been able. The War Office Intelligence Branch was set up in 1873, with an objective of better understanding Russia's ambitions in India. It had an initial staff of seven officers. This was a time, much like now, when Russia's ambitions in the world were causing concern to Great Britain.

What happens to Henry Gough in this story, set in 1880, is complete make-believe, although I have made every effort to preserve as much historical detail of the period as possible. A few of the prominent events of the time are cited, and some of the lesser characters were conspicuous in Victorian Britain.

The characters in Siam are all fictitious, with two exceptions. The story told within the novel of Sir Thomas Knox and his daughter, Fanny, is based on fact. King

Chulalongkorn, otherwise known as Rama V, ruled Siam between 1868-1910. He earned his rightful place in history as a transformational and acclaimed monarch, much loved by his people. None of the thoughts, actions and words attributed to Chulalongkorn in this novel are his. All are completely fabricated, and products of my own imagination.

Henry Gough died in 1912, aged 77, surrounded by the children and grandchildren of both his marriages. I am a third-generation product of his love affair with long-time mistress and eventual wife, Caroline. My grandfather, James, a man I much admired, born in 1888, was Henry's twentieth and penultimate child.

It has been fascinating to speculate about Henry Gough's life and utterly absorbing to write another novel with him at its centre.

FH
Chiang Mai
October 2023

Chapter One

London, Monday, 21st February 1880

Henry Gough had heard gunshots before – many times, in fact. He knew the sound of a pistol report well enough, but never in his life had he heard a volley of gunfire in South Kensington. He puffed out his cheeks, and with a weary outbreath of night air, he examined the broad, lamp-lit thoroughfare. With one boot on the step of his hansom cab, he wondered how this day, that had opened with so much expectation, could have ended like this. Not in his wildest dreams could he have imagined such events. The blood on his hands was still warm. Despite the carnage before him, there was a strange, despairing tranquillity about his bearing. The lifeless body of his passenger, head split half-open and barely recognisable, was slumped under the wheels of his cab. Folk were running hither and thither, shouting all about. Throughout this pandemonium he remained astonishingly calm, unruffled – almost serene. Henry cocked his ear to hear the clatter of a retreating horse far away along Ashburn Place. He leant over the body once more. Ribbons of crimson snaked in rivulets across the cobbles to form a pool under the hansom's nearside wheel. He concluded, with icy logic, that the fatal shot must have come from behind, such was the distorted state of the poor man's face. The shell must have escaped from between the eyes. The shocking mutilation told its own gruesome tale.

The day had started with such great promise...

Henry seldom stared into the looking glass these days. The mad rush of his busy life simply didn't allow it. There never seemed a second in his hectic existence to call his own. There were always countless problems of some sort to disentangle, a challenge to overcome, an issue to resolve. If it wasn't the horses, an unwelcome vet's bill, a carriage's broken axle, or a grievance from one of his grumbling staff, his three young sons always found ways to infiltrate any spare moments. But, on this pristine February morning, as the vestibule clock had chimed six and he was tying up his boots, his eyes had fallen on the swordstick that Albert Woodward had given him some years before. Propped in the corner of the hall, next to the honest oak coat stand, the skulking weapon, flawless of design and lethal of purpose, seemed to call out to him. On a whim, he'd reached out for it and turned it in his hands. A torrent of stirring reminiscences came flooding, whimsical and welcome, into his head. It was a strangely powerful moment, and Henry was forced to inhale a deep draught of calming air, gripped as he was by those precious seconds of icy solitude.

Then, raising himself from the battered stool into the hall's hushed embrace, his boots polished and laces firmly set, and with the house sleeping around him, he'd carefully balanced the swordstick back into its rightful place, and stood tall before his reflection in the long glass. With shoulders pinned back, spine as straight as he could manage, extending to his full height of nearly six feet, with chin raised, he'd pondered the image for a while.

'Tut!' He'd clicked his tongue and frowned into the mirror. Was that a hint of grey he detected amongst the tangle of whiskers? He was now almost forty-four, but he felt more youthful – his young wife and the babies saw to that. He looked in good fettle too, a broader waistline perhaps, but there was barely an ounce of fat to the naked eye. The gunshot wound to his side, inflicted by Dimitri Michaelov three years earlier, had healed well. True, there were twinges of pain on chill mornings such as these, but at least the scar was a constant source of amusement to Caroline and the children. In all other respects, he felt as fit as a circus flea. A few silent moments of contemplation passed. After a bout of mental self-congratulation, and freshly emboldened by his appearance, Henry had turned a lock of stray hair behind his ear, brushed his shoulders, and unbolted the catch to his front door. On yet another impulse, so typical of his character, he'd dropped his arm, and with a single pluck, he reclaimed the old swordstick, flicked it under his coat and strode out into the still, dark yard.

And now, less than twelve hours later, with several routine spells of commonplace clipping around the capital city behind him, he had somehow become embroiled at the centre of a bloody and violent crime, the like of which the good people of South Kensington must surely have never beheld.

A young policeman approached, hurrying from the east, truncheon in hand. On seeing Henry and the horrifying tableau in detail, he put a whistle instantly to his lips, and soon a shrill call for help was reverberating around the neighbourhood.

'Did you witness the deed, sir?' he barked with all his breathless force, once the piercing blast had ceased – it was an unnecessary exertion, as he was less than two paces from Henry and well within earshot.

'Yes, Officer, that I did.' Henry nodded to the uniformed interloper with the air of a man in full command of his senses. The policeman approached the body and gingerly picked up an unblemished cuff of the man's overcoat as if he were about to search for a pulse. Instead, and rather bizarrely, he commenced to examine the coat's material and its stitching.

'He's dead, Officer.' Henry spoke the obvious with a steady composure. 'He must have died in an instant, shot in the back of his head from less than a foot, if I'm not mistaken.' From a crouching position, the officer turned his glazed eyes towards Henry and seemed lost in the moment. Temporarily dumbstruck, he fumbled for his whistle again and put it to his lips. Within seconds, the sound of noisy shouting from the nearby street corner resumed, and presently the young bobby ceased his blowing.

'And you must be the fellow's cabbie? Am I correct?' the officer in blue serge stammered. He had recovered his tongue at last.

'I am, Constable.'

'When did this occur? Did you see the crime? Do you know this man? Did you see the attack? Where has the attacker gone?' The young peeler had transformed from mute to chatterbox in a few short seconds. Clearly, the man was befuddled. All his questions now came out in a flood of frenzied demands, which appeared all the more chaotic by the clouds of vapour that filled the cold air as he blathered on. Before Henry could answer even the first enquiry, the policeman added, while scanning anxiously over his shoulder, 'my fellow officers will be here shortly. I can hear them now. Please stay calm and do not move, I beg you, sir.' Another puff of fog rose from his lips and dissolved into the night.

Henry decided the best course was to heed the officer's advice rather than answer his flurry of questions. Better to wait for reinforcements to arrive before making any statement that might be inaccurately recorded by the clearly inexperienced and agitated man before him.

'I have no intention of moving, Officer. I will gladly obey your command, and I will tell all when the time is right.' Then thinking better of it, he added, 'But perhaps, to answer just one of your questions, the attacker was on horseback and cantered off that way about two minutes ago.' Henry pointed southwards towards Chelsea. 'I fear he has escaped for sure by now.'

'You have blood on your hands, sir,' the policeman observed carelessly, without a trace of accusation in his voice.

'Yes. It is my passenger's. I did my best for him – I tried to turn him over, but it was too late. His head is half blown away.'

At that moment a broad-shouldered officer of middle age slid to a halt in front of them. Much of his face was hidden behind a resplendent array of mutton-chop whiskers. The three stripes on his arm announced his seniority. Seconds later, two further blue uniforms tumbled onto the scene.

'Is this man under arrest, Constable Jones?' the large man thundered.

'No, sir, I don't believe so—'

'Have you arrested him, Jones?' the sergeant repeated, this time with an edge to his voice.

'I have called for the doctor—'

Before the young policeman could add further to the confusion, Henry intervened. 'No, Officer, I am not under arrest. My name is Henry Gough. I am merely the honest cab driver who collected this passenger.' Pointing to the corpse he added, 'I brought him to this point, I witnessed the crime, and I did what I could to defend the wretched fellow. But I regret the villain has fled the scene. I could do nothing to stop him.'

Waggling a disapproving head at his junior colleague, who by this time had shrunk back into the shadows, the older officer sighed, then turned his face back towards Henry. With a look of drained resignation, he said, 'Very well, Mr Gough. While we await the attendance of the good surgeon, pray give me your full account. Constable Fairfield!' he shouted over the head of the hapless Jones, 'take out your pocketbook and note down what is said between us.'

Henry explained that he had collected his passenger from the Langham Hotel just before five pm. It was to be his last fare before returning to his stable yard in St John's Wood.

'Was this man staying at the hotel?' the policeman asked.

'I cannot be sure. You can check. I was hailed by the doorman, and I pulled over to wait a few moments before the man entered the cab.'

'Where did he ask you to take him?'

'He did not speak to me. The fellow was of foreign appearance and maybe he wasn't able to converse openly with me. I doubt if English was his mother tongue. Instead, the hotel doorman handed me a note with the address of 21, Ashburn Place. It is the premises about a hundred yards further along, you know.' Trying to be helpful, Henry indicated down the street, but the policeman's eyes did not follow his signal. Instead, the two orbs concentrated their gaze on the witness before them – now with an ever-greater intensity.

'A foreign gentleman, you say?' The sergeant flexed his shoulders and jutted his jaw towards Henry. The officer's deep intonation and slow delivery was typical of a long-serving official of the law – it was as if the language of Whitechapel and the legalese of the Old Bailey had combined to create a most singular vernacular for the sole use of those occupying this certain rank and station.

'Yes, Officer, he was Chinese, I believe,' Henry replied at length. 'Of middle age, I estimate; small of stature, as you can see. The face is all but destroyed now, but before his accident he had the unmistakeable appearance of a Chinaman; the eyes narrow and dark, the hair black and straight.'

'Are you taking this down, Fairfield?' The sergeant addressed these words to the officer at his side without once removing his cold stare from Henry.

'Yes, Sergeant.' Reading from his notebook, Fairfield continued, '"The witness believes the dead man looked like a Chinaman".'

'So, tell me what happened at the scene.' The burly policeman twisted his moustache and resumed his exchange with Henry.

'As I turned the corner from Harrington Gardens, I rapped on the hatch to tell my passenger we were approaching his destination. The road was quiet for the time of day, but suddenly a horse approached at speed from behind us and overtook the cab. After a few paces, the rider halted his charge directly in front of my hansom, and I was forced to pull the reins quickly to avoid colliding with the animal. A man dismounted and approached the cab.'

'Can you describe him?'

'Yes, I believe him to be another Chinaman. He wore a covering of some yellow- or gold-coloured cloth. It was wrapped around his upper body, his face and neck; 'twas a warm fabric, I'll vouch, wool possibly, much like a thick cloak or scarf. He had a dark woollen hat too, with flaps which covered his ears. I called out to him to ask what business he had by obstructing my path in this way, but he ignored my entreaties and made straight for the front of the cab, where he engaged my passenger in some language which I did not comprehend. The talk was not friendly; I could tell this despite my understanding of not a single word. The intruder spoke loudly and with rage in his voice. As I started to dismount – I wanted to intervene in the ugly matter – the cab started to shake and I nearly lost my footing. I could see there was a struggle between the two men. It was a wrestling match of sorts, and I believe my passenger must have tried to escape the cab from the other side, for a second later there was a loud report. I knew straightway it was a gunshot. I have heard such cracks many times before, but this blast alarmed me so much that I feared for my life. I ducked behind the wheel, where I withdrew my swordstick – only to defend myself, you understand…' he added with a trace of diffidence.

The policeman nodded with a sagacious turn of his eyebrows. 'Pray continue, will you, Mr Gough.'

'The rogue must have spied my weapon, for he stopped in his tracks as if contemplating his next move. Then he made a dash around the hansom to where the man had fallen, and I turned to follow him. To my horror, the villain brandished his pistol and yelled something in a foreign tongue towards me. I stood my ground as he advanced closer, but then he raised the gun to fire at me. Well, I had no alternative, Officer. He was out of range of my swordstick, so diving to the ground, I rolled to the side and drew the horsewhip from my belt – I have a certain reputation, sir, for being skilful in its use…'

'Pray continue.'

'Well, with a desperate lunge of the switch and a degree of good fortune, I managed to free the pistol from his grasp and it fell clattering onto the cobbles. The villain leapt back, seemingly confused and in disarray, and in that moment the heavy yellow scarf that had covered his face and neck slipped to his shoulders and dropped into the street. That's when I saw his face clearly for the first time. I will never forget it. He was an oriental gentleman without doubt. And most shocking was the appearance of his upper body. He wore a loose-fitting shirt beneath, 'twas of thick ivory-coloured cloth, no buttons, just tied around his waist by a belt of some dark material. That is when I saw it… Below the collar line, as the shirt flapped open, I could see his body was painted all over. There was a motif, a black design – I believe it to be a tattoo of sorts. 'Twas a tiger, as God is my witness – a leaping, striped tiger that danced across his upper chest for all the world like some attacking beast.' Henry paused his account and looked carefully for a reaction from the brawny policeman.

The sergeant merely pursed his lips. 'What happened next?' he advanced at length.

'By this time, there was uproar all about, and in a flash the fellow had dropped down to collect his pistol from the street. Then he scrambled under the cab trying to retrieve his heavy scarf, but it was out of his reach, and he gave up in the attempt. The next second, he'd remounted his horse and was away in a flash before I could stop him.'

'Show me your swordstick.' This was not a demand Henry had expected from his audience.

'My stick is of no consequence, Officer. I did not use it. I keep it only to protect myself.'

'Show me your swordstick, please, Mr Gough. Such an instrument can be used to cause great hurt if brandished with malice aforethought – even when the subject is confronted by a pistol.'

Henry bit his lip and passed the stick to the officer, who examined the handle carefully. Then, with a theatrical sweep of his arm, the sergeant withdrew the two feet of polished steel from the sheath and pointed the tip into the air. 'This bears the markings of government service, unless I'm mistaken. How do you come by such an instrument?'

'Officer, are your questions strictly necessary?'

'They are most pertinent, sir. I mean no harm by them. Pray tell me the truth and I may be able to enlighten you.'

'If you insist, the stick was a gift from the Excise detectives of Tower Hill.'

'I must press you further. Did you perform a service for them?'

'Officer, I must protest. That is my personal business and not connected with the unpleasant matter before us.'

'I insist that you answer.' Turning to his notetaker, the sergeant cried out, 'Constable Fairfield, are you taking all this down?'

'I think I have most of the gist, Sergeant, but you both speak so fast.'

'Then just make sure you record Mr Gough's next reply...' He paused and turned back to Henry. 'Sir, I put it to you again, what service did you perform for the Excise detectives to earn this pretty cane?'

Henry sighed. 'I helped them trap a man called Solly Burke. He was a purveyor of white whisky who escaped from Newgate and then committed a foul murder. There you have it, Officer. I hope you are satisfied. And now, pray tell me, how does that advance your cause?' The policeman paused a while before a sly smile drew across his whiskered face.

'Because I now know who you are, sir, and I know you can be trusted. Although I feel you have not told me your full story, I confess I am mightily glad to be in your company. You are none other than *the* Henry Gough, the cabbie that my chief superintendent speaks of so often – Inspector Boscombe never tires to tell the story either. Why, it was their finest hour! The chief superintendent tells the yarn over and over to those of us still prepared to listen, and you were at the centre of it, sir! Great Scott, sir, you are none other than *the* Henry Gough who helped Mr Grieve save the life of Her Majesty at Victoria Station, no less. If you deny it, I shall eat my head.'

Henry's haughty irritation soon dissolved into a broad grin, once he knew the old sergeant meant him no harm. 'I hadn't realised my part in the recent affair was so widely known,' he offered, sounding almost apologetic.

'Come, Mr Gough, I can see you are a modest man but there is no reason to hide such a wonderful truth. I have heard also about your skill with the horsewhip – it was your account of how you disarmed the attacker today that first got me thinking. Let me introduce myself. I am Sergeant Petronius Marshall, at your service.' Instead of offering his hand to Henry, he waved it carelessly towards the other officers. 'But look, the situation here is now under our control. I see the surgeon has arrived, not that it will help our Chinaman friend in any way, gawd bless his soul. It is late and you must be tired. I thank you for your statement. Go home to your wife and children, I know you have many of them...' Sergeant Marshall gave Henry a melodramatic wink. 'If tomorrow you could find your way to Scotland Yard, I am sure Chief Superintendent Grieve will be delighted to see you. In fact, he may even wish to take you to lunch. I suggest twelve noon to give him a chance to do so.' he said with a laugh. 'I'm sure you have many things to discuss – not least this very troubling and intriguing case. When a Chinaman fights another it is usually to do with opium or gambling – sometimes it's women. I'm certain this matter will be cleared up in a flash; the perpetrator will be captured and hanged before the spring. If not him, someone will have to pay. After all, this is a civilised part of the city. We cannot tolerate foreigners coming here to break our laws, now can we, sir?'

Henry returned the speech with a bleak smile, and decided to say nothing in reply.

The silence was broken by Constable Jones who approached them carrying a length of yellow fabric in his hand.

'I found a bullet lodged in the frame of the cab, sir, and this was on the ground near to the hansom, Sergeant,' he spluttered. 'Just as Mr Gough has said...'

"Tis the scarf that fell from his face,' Henry added, trying once more to be accommodating.

'And there's more!' The young policeman's voice was showing more confidence now. In his left hand, Jones held up a highly decorated pouch of bright golden fabric. 'Sergeant, I found this on the body, before the doctor attended. I think it might be important.'

'You found this, eh?' Sergeant Marshall took the pouch from the officer's hand. It appeared to be woven from the finest silk, of intricate oriental design, and about the size of a fat envelope – no bigger than a lady's purse, in fact. He held it towards the street lamp. 'And where, might I ask, did you find it, Constable?'

'It was in the lining of the man's jacket, Sergeant. I thought the sleeve looked bulky and misshapen – I took my penknife and cut the cloth, and out it fell. From his left arm, actually.'

'Did you indeed?'

'I checked the other sleeve and the rest, but found nothing further. It looks to me like it might contain a letter of sorts. See here, it has an unbroken seal of red wax.'

'Or maybe it holds documents – secret papers – ha-ha! Well done, Jones! At last, you appear to have done something useful in the cause of London policing. You may return to your colleagues. I will take charge of this evidence now.' Turning to Henry Gough, he offered up the purse. 'It's as I thought, there are foreign symbols or writing here, do you see – on the seal? I will ensure that Chief Superintendent Grieve sees this first thing in the morning. I suspect the purse contains money, in truth, or a sample of opium, perchance.' He chuckled to himself. 'We shall get to the bottom of it, don't you worry. To have the bullet that killed him is indeed a blessing; nowadays we can learn much from that, so I am told.'

'May I respectfully suggest that the purpose of today's assault was to recover the purse from our Chinese victim,' Henry offered. 'I am no detective but it is sealed, and as you say, in a most unusual fashion. It may have more importance and bearing on the matter than we might imagine – of more substance than the bullet even. My intervention may have deterred the attacker, and he had to leave empty-handed. With the crowd approaching from all sides, is it not possible the rogue was forced to flee without his reward?'

'You may be right, Mr Gough, you may well be right… Methinks there could be deep waters that lie ahead…'

Chapter Two

By the time Henry reached St John's Wood and his rooms above the yard in Bolton Street, it was nearly eight o'clock, and a low mist had started to form amongst the plane trees that lined the mews. An hour earlier, the police had completed their search of his cab for clues, but nothing further of interest had been found. Despite not having possession of the murder weapon, they seemed content with their exhibits; the exotic, yellow silk purse concealed in the lining of the murdered man's coat seemed the most intriguing evidence of all – if only someone could unravel its secrets. There had been a lot of blood, most of which had spilled onto the street after the cab's unfortunate occupant had failed in his attempt to escape from the veiled assailant. Henry had helped Constable Fairfield examine the carriage door for traces of human tissue, and he swore it was a smattering of the poor fellow's brains that he'd cleaned from the sill. Then, after agreeing with the now most amiable Sergeant Marshall to meet the chief superintendent the following day at Scotland Yard, he was allowed to proceed, and this he did with great haste, not sparing the horse. He knew that Caroline would be concerned about his late arrival, and he was anxious to be at her side as soon as possible. These days, Henry made every effort to be a man of routine. George, his fourth son with Caroline, was just a babe in arms, and he knew she fretted for his health. The terrible, gasping death of their eldest boy, young Henry, just a few months earlier, had hit the family hard. Caroline had been with child at the time, and she'd blamed herself for not being able to nurse the young lad to recovery. Young Henry had always been a sick infant, mind, but his loss was nonetheless terrible for it. The birth of baby George had been a welcome distraction for Caroline, but her weeping at night had continued for many months.

Henry's working day began at six am and ended at the same hour each evening. He liked to take one day each week for rest, but sometimes his business demanded his attention, even on a Sunday. There was always something that needed attending to, even if he was not taking fares and driving one of his five cabs along the city streets. His business had prospered in the two and a half years since his shameful arrest by the Excise detectives and the period of high adventure that followed. His decision to cooperate with the Crown officers had been a good one, however. It had brought them some success against the illicit trade in white whisky and had saved his skin from the hideous confines of Newgate Prison into the bargain. He recalled with a wistful smile how, just as he'd been celebrating his good luck and newly found freedom, he'd been drawn inadvertently into the terrible, but exciting business of Russian intrigue and vicious plotting. The affair had consumed all his waking moments for more months than he liked now to contemplate. The drama had finally concluded with his near-fatal brush with Dimitri Michaelov alongside the railway tracks at Victoria Station. Michaelov had been a Russian anarchist, bent on revenge for alleged crimes committed by the British Raj in India. Henry's role in thwarting the man's evil intent back in '77 had been one of the most striking periods of his whole life. It had even brought him a short period of fame, which Henry now imagined had long since passed. But the matter had clearly not been forgotten by the constabulary, for which Henry found himself much gratified. With the reward money he'd been presented, and a small advance from the bursary promised to him by the head of the Excise detectives, Major Callaway – both provided to account of his "bold services to the Crown" – he'd been able to invest and grow his small business. The result was the purchase of three further hansoms, all second-hand but serviceable, to add to the two cabs previously owned, and six extra horses of better than average quality, with the promise of many more miles in their legs. Two further coachmen were taken onto the books to join old Joshua Stone, who had proven to be a solid and dependable employee these last three years. Both of the new drivers Henry knew very well. Scotsman, Keith Moore and Kentish man, David Lee had both volunteered to join his service, drawn away from his former wife Hannah's own cab business. Henry imagined the flattering newspaper reports and his new celebrity following his late part in smashing the gang of Russian anarchists had been part of the attraction, for the pair had talked about nothing else in the first few weeks of their employ. It was the incident the papers liked to call "The Peccavi Plot", and for nearly a fortnight the story was everywhere, avidly consumed by London's eager reading public.

Two stable boys and a jovial quartermaster completed the staff list. Caroline's ability with numbers had not deserted her, despite the brood of children at her feet, and she had insisted on maintaining the books and accounts for the rising business despite Henry's rather subdued – it must be said –

protestations to the contrary. His golden rule on the days he took one of the hansoms out was to take his last fare no later than six pm, so he could be home in time to see the children to bed and, if necessary, help with a few of the domestic chores.

'Oh, Henry, my precious, I've waited hours for your return,' Caroline cried as he removed his hat at the front door. 'You look tired, my dear. Come sit, I have poured some whisky for you. Tell me your news.' Today, her fussing seemed all the more impassioned.

'Are the boys asleep?' Henry asked with a slight groan as he lowered himself onto the hall stool to remove his boots.

'George has a slight cough, but I have given him a tincture against it. Walter scraped a knee today in the mews chasing a cat, but seems none the worse for wear, and Arthur is Arthur – he could slumber in a force nine gale if it suited. All are fed and sleeping soundly.'

'I have had a most extraordinary experience this day, my love.' Henry sighed as she pressed the whisky glass into his hand.

As he recounted the tale of his eventful day, Caroline sat at his side, an arm on his shoulder stroking the nape of his neck. At some points in his story, she gasped openly and made little noises of surprise with her mouth and tongue. Towards the end, her eyes widened to their maximum extent on hearing about the mysterious silk purse, but she knew well enough not to interrupt the teller until he had finished his narrative. When he had concluded and regarded her once again with a loving smile, she jumped from the sofa and cried, 'Henry, how could you let the poor man, your passenger, be killed in such a way?'

This was not the reaction Henry had expected, but he remained resignedly composed and quietly reminded Caroline that the attacker had possessed a pistol, quite probably with further bullets up the spout, and his only defence was his whip and the swordstick that Albert Woodward had given him nearly three years before. She seemed satisfied with the answer for a few seconds, but then confounded him by crying out, 'Why did you put yourself in so much danger, my darling? You should have been thinking of the boys and me at home before waving the stick and flashing the whip at him. What were you thinking? What would we have done without you?'

Henry Gough knew there was little advantage in pointing out the obvious dichotomy in Caroline's last two statements, so closely made, so he sipped on his Scotch and let the matter rest. 'I will behave better if such events repeat themselves, my dearest,' he soothed, 'and now may I make a small request of you? Another whisky before supper would greatly calm my nerves.'

The following morning, Henry woke early but rose late, spending a whole luxurious hour alone with Caroline snug between the sheets before the children stirred. She was still a beautiful, desirable and loving woman, and he always relished the short snatches of time they were able to enjoy together. After a leisurely breakfast, he wandered into the yard feeling rejuvenated and bustled amongst the stables, giving advice and offering up genial conversation to his staff and the coachmen as they embarked on their rounds. He asked his old friend and senior cab driver, Joshua, to delay his departure till eleven, so he could drive his master to Scotland Yard, and not wishing to delay Joshua any further from his profitable duties, he told him he would make his own way home once his business was complete. As Joshua clicked the horse away, and the cab disappeared, clattering down the embankment, Henry had a moment to reflect. The truth was the shocking events of the previous day had affected him more than he cared to admit. Despite his outwardly gay and carefree appearance to others, this was a day when he felt he had no energy to drive himself on. A rather ominous, lethargic mood seemed to grip him, as if the unexplained and vicious killing he'd witnessed was just the prelude to more terrible things to come. He decided not to tell the others in the mews of the events of the previous day and requested Caroline to keep her counsel, too – at least until such time as the matter had either been resolved, or his part in the affair had concluded once and for all.

The drive to the illustrious headquarters of London's Metropolitan Police took less time than he'd bargained for, and after Joshua had dropped him in front of the archway of Scotland Yard's imposing red-brick edifice, he found he was nearly twenty minutes early. Rather than hang around in the cold, Henry bade his driver farewell, reminding him not to wait or return and to get smartly about his lawful business, and made his way inside and to the broad-fronted desk where, much to his surprise, Sergeant Marshall was already stationed. As Henry approached, the policeman, silver stripes resplendent against his navy-blue uniform, hailed him with a genial and hearty wave. After a firm and vigorous handshake from his host, the two men, walking side by side, mounted the wide stone staircase to the third floor and the private office of the celebrated "great detective". This was the man who, most would say, had famously foiled "The Peccavi Plot" – none other than Chief Superintendent Jack Grieve. Henry knew the truth of the matter, of course, but he also appreciated the futility of trying to put the record straight. And anyway, he liked old Grieve, so there was nothing to be gained by rocking the boat.

Chief Superintendent Grieve was waiting for him, standing erect, hands in waistcoat pockets, feet apart, beside a huge oak desk. Much to Henry's pleasant astonishment, Albert Woodward, the senior Excise detective who had become his great friend of the last few years, was positioned at his side. After shaking the illustrious detective's hand and sharing a few formal words of greeting, Henry turned his face to the old exciseman and smiled.

'My, 'tis a great surprise to see you here too, Albert.'

'For me also, old friend. Mr Grieve and I were just discussing the trade in opium – it is becoming a problem in parts of the city. He told me you would be attending him later, and he asked me to stay and join the discussions.'

'I thought your two minds might help us solve the mystery of the Ashburn Place killing,' Grieve interjected with an amiable grin.

'It must be nearly a year since we last spoke.' Henry thumped Albert on the shoulder.

'It is ten months and three days – to be more accurate.' Albert's notorious attention to detail clearly hadn't left him. 'It's good to see you,' he added in his slow Welsh burr, which always seemed to accentuate the precision of his speech. 'How is the lovely Caroline?'

A spontaneous conversation about Henry's family and business followed, but it was very brief, cut short by the edgy impatience of their host.

'Come, there's no time for tittle-tattle,' Superintendent Grieve interrupted. 'We have most important business to discuss, gentlemen. A murder has been committed and the consequences might be very grave – I would value both your thoughts on the matter,' he added grimly. When his two guests had fallen silent, he continued, his voice displaying the same tones of affected gravity. 'To sum up... yesterday, I received news of this frightful killing, and when I learned you were attending me today, Henry, I took the liberty of asking Mr Woodward to join us as the professional bond between the two of you is known to all of us. Furthermore, in the light of certain intelligence I received last night, which has some bearing on our talks about the ravages of the opium trade, I thought it a capital idea to reunite our little band – after all, are you not part of my team? Are we not the men who solved the infamous plot against Her Majesty, our beloved queen, just a few years past? Before you arrived, Henry, I was able to give Albert all the information in our possession, bar one detail which I wanted to share once we were all together. You see, it drives us to the heart of the matter.'

'So, you know all about this murder, Albert?' Henry asked.

'Only what Mr Grieve has told me in these last ten minutes. It looks like a crime of passion to me.'

'Whatever the motive, it was a most shocking event, I confess,' Henry replied. 'To see a man cut down with such cruelty was hard to stomach, especially as I could do nothing to spare him.'

'That is where you are both wrong, my dear friends. Your intervention, Henry, has made all the difference! You may not have saved the man's life, but your actions, and the account you have given, have given us a path by which we may solve the case.' Grieve paused once more to ensure he had everyone's undivided attention. 'I can reveal now, Albert... the killing was certainly *not* a crime of passion!'

'Indeed... pray tell all,' the Welshman replied with a quizzical look.

'In short...' Chief Superintendent Grieve took a few steps away from the others and then turned to face his visitors, 'there were three clues left at the scene. One was the bullet fired to commit the deed; the second is the scarf that fell from the attacker's face; and finally, perhaps most important of all, is the silken purse secreted in the linings of the victim's jacket. In the matter of the bullet, found lodged in your cab, we have used it to identify the murder weapon. It is our belief the pistol discharged was of French design, of the type issued to French officers in the field. The MAS 1874 revolver has six chambers and fires 11mm calibre cartridges. It's quite common around the world, I am told; we have an example and a box of projectiles here at Scotland Yard. This has allowed our ballistic experts to be confident of their identification. On the whole, the pistol, while rarely seen in Great Britain, is in widespread use both in France and in its overseas colonies. Of the scarf, it's true importance lies only in the face of the man it tried to conceal, and we have Henry's account of a climbing tiger emblazoned on the assailant's chest and neck. The golden fabric itself appears to be of foreign origin and of the very highest quality cloth.' Grieve paused once again, spread his hands onto his leather-topped desk and contemplated his visitors with a bulging stare. In a theatrical tone, which the others frankly found mildly amusing, he offered up what he clearly imagined to be his *coup de grâce* statement. As Henry and Albert attempted to conceal their sniggers, he said with a flourish, 'And finally, we come to the concealed purse.' Grieve took a deep breath… 'As we are all assembled here today, I can now reveal its contents!'

Albert Woodward took advantage of the hiatus by blurting, 'Ha! I'll wager the contents of the silken purse were none other than a set of box seats for *The Merchant of Venice* at the Lyceum. I hear Henry Irving's latest performance is matchless!' It was not common for Albert to attempt jokes, and his timing could have been neater. Henry chuckled back all the same. Conversely, the policeman who held court was not amused. His brow furrowed, he inhaled deeply and his hands returned abruptly into his waistcoat pockets.

Struggling to restrain himself, Grieve decided, nonetheless, to carry on, but this time his voice was a good degree softer – the melodrama had been snuffed out. 'Sir,' he addressed Albert

Woodward directly, 'I have called you to join us because I value your skills as part of my team. If you wish to have no part in it, I have many fine officers at Scotland Yard who I can call on to take the matter up. This affair has the whiff of political intrigue and some far-flung conspiracy about it. As we have together been successful in the past investigating such matters, I wanted your opinions on my stratagem before I took the matter further. I intend to share the details with Mr Hope at the War Office Intelligence Branch once our deliberations today are complete. I would wish that you took this matter with the seriousness it deserves. A mysterious man has died in a quiet London street, felled by a bullet to his skull. That which was secreted in the purse he carried is not a cheap music hall ticket, sir. It has given us his identity *and* his nationality, no less. Furthermore, it notifies us of his high rank and' – unable to resist, he paused once more for effect – 'none other than of his secret mission to London!'

By this time, the others had ended their chortling and were now regarding their host with open-mouthed attention.

'Secret mission, you say?' Henry blurted.

'Yes, sir. It appears that our victim was not a Chinaman after all. From what we have been able to unravel, he was none other than an emissary of the King of Siam, and the speculation must be the man was in this country to pursue some hidden purpose.'

'Siam?' Henry frowned. 'Is that not from where the celebrated twins originated? 'Tis close to China, is it not?'

'Indeed, it is. And the famous twins were undeniably Siamese; they died a few short years ago, I believe. The country of Siam, as you say, is in the same region of Asia as is China. Or thereabouts,' Grieve added vaguely. 'I'm told there are many elephants there, wild creatures, and a lot of jungle. My reports tell me of a bold civilisation too, and lavish riches to behold.

More importantly, perhaps, from our limited research we have found it is a kingdom with which we have friendly relations.'

'How did you arrive at this, Jack? The idea of some clandestine mission seems fanciful to me,' Woodward observed, now fully transfixed by the unfolding conversation.

'Why, from the contents of the silken purse, of course! Therein was a parchment, an official paper it appeared to be, with a large red-inked stamp at its head. That was all. Of course, it was indecipherable to us, but Scotland Yard retains the services of a Chinese interpreter – for matters, you understand, that arise from the disorder created by the opium houses of the Limehouse community. Mr K Chow is his name and I sent officers to bring him to me this morning. His verdict was immediate. The letter is not written in any Chinese script known to him. The message therein is, in his opinion, of Siamese origin, about which he knows very little. But he gave me one piece of news which I feel is of great importance. He believed the letter was from the King of Siam himself – if not the king, from a senior member of the Siamese royal family. He said he recognised the royal emblem on the document.'

'This is most intriguing indeed,' Woodward replied. 'What is your intention? I think it unlikely that the opium trade will lie at the heart of this affair, so any expertise I might have on the subject appears to be of little use. I firmly urge that diplomatic channels should be pursued with all urgency, so the document can be translated in full.'

'I agree, Albert. The opium connection may have been a possible consideration this morning, but given the victim's apparent rank, I feel sure the motive for this crime must lie elsewhere.'

'Have you discovered the man's identity?' Henry asked.

'That we have not, and that must be our first goal. I believe we shall shortly have the answer,' Greive replied. 'Nathanial Hope awaits us at the War Office. It is to him that I intend to take the purse. And I would like you to join me, Henry. You witnessed the crime and your testimony will help us all unravel this matter. Hope has confirmed our appointment at two. He has invited another official to attend us, a man recently returned from our consulate in Siam. Together we will examine the evidence and decide on a course.' Glancing at his pocket watch he added hurriedly, 'Come, we must leave for the Intelligence Branch immediately. I'm sure Hope will be most gratified to be reacquainted with you.'

Before Henry Gough could respond, Chief Superintendent Jack Grieve leapt from the side of his vast oak desk and was soon pulling on his overcoat. Henry remained seated and with a heavy sigh leaned over to his old chum. 'It seems that duty calls once again, Albert. I had planned a quiet afternoon with Caroline to recover from the ordeals of yesterday, but it appears I am embroiled in yet another spectacle. It's just my bad luck that murder still seems to follow me through the streets of London.'

'It is the life you lead, my good fellow. In your trade you see all of our city in all its guises in a single day and much beyond, I'll warrant. Into your hansom come both the great and good, and those with evil intent. I'll be bound, countesses, clergymen, spies and criminals have all taken their place inside your cab – what other profession can say the same?'

'How true, my friend.' Henry stood to go. 'But now I must do the policeman's bidding.'

'I shall not join you. I'm no longer required. But should you need me for advice, Henry, I should be happy to give it. You know where to find me. Our offices at Tower Hill are the same, and the inns of Fleet Street are equally welcoming and still flowing with ale since the time we last supped together.'

From the far side of his office, the chief superintendent bellowed out, 'Come now, Henry, stop this tittle-tattle. We must not keep Hope waiting any longer than necessary. I have the papers in my attaché. I will send a message to you, Albert, should I require your counsel any further.'

And with that, the two were gone, hurrying breakneck down the broad staircase at Scotland Yard, Greive barking out orders as they went, to emerge into the frigid February sunshine and be carried along by a flurry of winter leaves that danced around their feet.

Chapter Three

It took less than fifteen minutes to cover the distance between Scotland Yard and the War Office on Horse Guards Avenue, close to Whitehall. The police growler selected for the journey covered the ground well enough, but Henry's professional ear picked up a grating sound from one of the rear wheels – a bearing no doubt. As the coach rounded up Northumberland Avenue, he turned his head towards his companion, thinking to raise the issue, but on seeing the troubled look on Jack Grieve's face he thought better of it, and allowed the journey to proceed in silence. The wind had got up by the time they descended the coach and their capes buffeted and gusted awkwardly around their necks. Holding onto their hats, they carefully mounted the steps and made their way into the calm sanctuary and marbled halls of Great Britain's imposing War Office building. A short while later they were ushered into the offices of the head of the Intelligence Branch, Nathanial Hope.

Hope had been the driving force behind the creation of the Intelligence Branch six years earlier, and during the intervening period the office's complement had grown from seven to twenty-eight. This flourishing force was a reflection of British concerns to safeguard their empire from foreign intrusion and the prying of others into the affairs of their colonial estates. India was of paramount importance, naturally, but as the expansion of the empire continued apace, the Intelligence Branch was front and centre of efforts to provide the War Office, the Foreign Office and government in the round, as much information as possible to help in their decision making. This intelligence was mostly gleaned from overseas sources and often involved the recruitment of clandestine agents to gather it. The reports collected enabled the state to gain a better picture of the intentions of other European powers in the helter-skelter race for new "trading opportunities" around the globe. Hope's grip on international affairs and his standing within government had risen greatly over the period of his office, reflected by the growing numbers of staff under his command. He was now unquestionably the man who knew more than anyone about Britain's competitors overseas, whether they be friendly or otherwise.

There was no doubt also, that Hope's perceived role in confounding the conspiracy to assassinate Her Majesty Queen Victoria back in '77 – otherwise known as "The Peccavi Plot" – had a hand in propelling his career. This despite the fact that the reality was somewhat different. Indeed, while Hope had led the charge, it had been a combination of Henry Gough's raw courage and the calculated efforts of the Excise detectives, with Scotland Yard hard at their heels, that had finally solved the crime and saved the day. But in the circles of high government, it was convenient to shower Hope with the accolades, the most recent of which was an offer of a knighthood. This honour, perversely to some, he turned down, thus burgeoning his reputation as a stalwart yet humble servant of the Crown. The fact was that while he played the role of self-effacing loyalty to perfection, Hope was ambitious in the extreme, and he had quietly, yet fixedly, set his eyes on an even greater state prize.

Hope cut a lean and angular figure as he welcomed his visitors with a cool smile and an open-handed gesture of greeting. Dressed in a sharply cut frock coat of the finest cloth, complete with satin lapels, high white collar and a fine silk necktie, he looked both powerful and elegant. His piercing eyes and neatly trimmed moustache left the onlooker with the unmistakeable image of a man who both exuded charm and knew he was in total control of his destiny.

'Gentlemen, this is such a pleasant surprise. To be reunited after such a long period makes for a most felicitous moment indeed.'

Chief Superintendent Grieve took the offered hand and shook it enthusiastically while saying in the slightly breathless tones of a man in a hurry, 'I hope you have received my first report on the matter? I sent it on ahead by messenger so you might be acquainted with the bare facts.'

'I have, sir. And the details have aroused my interest greatly. Pray, allow me to introduce Mr Charles Hurdus.' Hope beckoned with one hand, and a monocled gentleman of middling age with a shadowy complexion and hesitating mouth stepped forward tentatively from a corner of the room where he'd been standing in silence under a portrait of the Queen. 'Mr Hurdus has only just returned from Siam – in the last few days... Am I correct, Hurdus?'

As Charles Hurdus advanced dutifully, a pleasant, cultured face was revealed to all. He was of medium height and build; a slight paunch could be seen around an expanding midriff. A tentative smile appeared, and he opened his mouth to speak, but before the first syllable had left his lips, Hope beat him to the punch. 'You have been acting as one of our esteemed translators for many years, have you not?' Then, compounding his interruption, he turned to Henry Gough and said, 'Hurdus is an expert in the language of the Siamese, you know. Isn't that correct, Hurdus?' The translator lowered his head submissively and chose to attempt nothing in reply. Hope ploughed on, 'I took the liberty,' he continued, raising his voice slightly, 'to invite Charles to our little gathering, as I'm confident that his knowledge will unlock the secrets of the parchment you mentioned in your message this morning.' Now facing Chief Superintendent Grieve, he cried, 'Are you able to produce the document now, sir?'

'I am indeed!' With a practised movement of his fingers, the policeman flicked the straps of a small leather attaché case and swiftly handed Hope the oriental silk purse, its contents intact within. Without even a cursory examination, Hope passed the purse directly into the hands of Charles Hurdus.

'Now, gentlemen, while my esteemed colleague examines your fascinating and most noteworthy discovery, I suggest we sit and discuss the matter in more detail.' Hope led the others towards a highly polished mahogany conference table where the three took their places, with Hope at the head and the others facing one another on either side. Hurdus retired alone and silently to another, smaller table in the corner of the room, under the grand window. He opened the purse as he went. Hope tapped his fingernails on the expanse of burnished wood before him in a rhythm that suggested mild impatience. 'We have important things to discuss, and I have to say I am both fascinated and extremely eager to hear your story. Your fullest account would be much appreciated.'

Jack Grieve spoke next with a smidgen of sycophancy in his manner. 'It is indeed a pleasure to be seated around the table with you once more; I'm sure Henry agrees...' Henry and Hope nodded deferentially to one another as the chief superintendent continued. 'This is a most engaging case—'

Hope interrupted once more. 'Before you speak further on the matter, allow me to hear first the story from the man who actually witnessed the incident.' Hope turned his head and offered a thin smile in Henry's direction, who, taking the cue, opened his mouth to speak. Hesitantly at first, he commenced his account and was not interrupted for a full ten minutes, such was the interest and captivation with which his report was received. Rarely had Henry spoken so long without intermission — even wily old Jack Grieve, who had heard the story before, seemed gripped by the narrative. When he'd concluded, Henry sat back in his chair and folded his arms in a manner to indicate he had finished. There was silence for a few seconds before Hope rose from the table and walked to the vast sash window that overlooked Whitehall's impressive stone architecture.

'It is as I thought,' he announced at length. 'The two matters are surely connected.'

'Connected, you say,' replied Grieve, looking perplexed. 'What matters? Connected with what?'

At that moment, Charles Hurdus made a slight coughing noise — of the type used to attract attention. Henry had completely forgotten about the man's presence in the room, so preoccupied had he been in giving his account of the murder. But now, like a spectre suddenly given human form, here the fellow was, standing nervously before them.

'Yes, Hurdus… have you managed to decipher the holy scriptures, ha-ha?'

'I have, sir. They are in the plainest of language and easy to interpret.'

'And tell me,' Hope took a deep breath, 'do the papers mention the name Gagananga Wararit.'

'They do, sir.'

'Am I right in saying that Gagananga Wararit was none other than the man carrying the document – the man who was slain last night.'

'I believe so, sir. They must be one and the same.'

'I thought so. Pray continue.'

'The document holds the royal seal of the Kingdom of Siam. It is an introductory letter from the King of Siam to Her Majesty the Queen, requesting an audience for the king's half-brother, Prince Gagananga Wararit, with our own Prince George, the Duke of Cambridge.' Hurdus hesitated for a second, before adding, 'The duke is commander-in-chief of our armed forces, sir.'

'I'm very well aware of the Duke of Cambridge's occupation, Hurdus,' Hope replied impatiently. 'No need for such detail on my account. But tell me, do you feel the document is authentic, and if so, is there anything else of import within?'

'In my opinion, sir, the document is genuine. The parchment is of the correct and finest quality, the ink and script identical to others I have seen, and the seal appears valid. Many such documents and regal proclamations passed before me during my time in Siam, and this paper bears the same appearance. I even recognise King Chulalongkorn's signature at the foot of the page. I very much doubt it is a forgery, sir.'

'What name did you give for the king, Hurdus? My information is that he is referred to as Rama V. Am I not correct?'

'Sir, you are correct. Rama V is his dynastic title. He is the fifth such monarch from the Chakri dynasty. Chulalongkorn is his given name and the title most commonly used by others.'

'By others, I presume you mean by the likes of foreign representatives in Siam, such as us, Hurdus. Am I correct?'

'You are, sir. In fact, his people call him by yet another name – Phra Chula Chom Klao Chao…' His voice tailed off as he realised he had lost the attention of his audience.

'All very complicated, I must say.' Hope frowned. 'For the purposes of our discussions, we shall refer to the King of Siam as Rama V, as the rest of us are unversed in the local dialect.'

'And it's a lot easier to remember!' Henry advanced with a smile.

Hope ignored the intervention and turned to Hurdus once more. 'And the content? What of the substance?'

'In respect of the substance, there is very little else to say. The document carries no message other than the desire to introduce the Siamese prince to the Queen. The early script is mostly introductory praise for Her Majesty. Then there is a simple request for a private audience for Prince Gagananga with Prince George, the Duke of Cambridge, and following this, an audience with Her Majesty in person. The subject under discussion is referred to only once and is vague – the phrase used, once translated, is "to discuss matters of mutual military concern". In effect, the document is none other than a calling card, but of the very highest royal nature.'

'That is very helpful, Hurdus. You may leave us now. I will call if I need you further.' With that, Charles Hurdus nodded respectfully, handed the purse and its contents back to Hope and retreated, crablike, from the room.

Hope resumed his finger tapping and let out a heavy sigh. 'It is as I suspected, indeed dreaded. The man who fell, slain, under the wheels of your hansom, Henry, was none other than the half-brother of the King of Siam.'

'You said other matters were connected…' Grieve ventured.

'Yes. I fear so. You see, I had an appointment to meet Prince Gagananga this very morning. The consulate in Bangkok advised me of his intended visit two months ago. The consul had indicated that Prince Gagananga's journey to London was shrouded in secrecy. Even they had not been advised of its true purpose, despite urgent representations. I received notice that he had arrived on our shores on Sunday, and yesterday a telegram arrived bearing his name and wishing to attend me today at ten of the morning. He indicated he wished to deliver an important paper. Given the apparent secrecy indicated by Beaumont, I was intrigued as to the topics he wished to discuss.'

'Beaumont?' Grieve interrupted.

'Lawrence Beaumont is our man in Bangkok, the consul general. You see, Beaumont suspected that he might carry a paper, possibly containing a request to meet the Queen herself, which at the time of course we thought would have been out of the question – most irregular...' Hope tutted and waggled his head. The sound reminded Henry of the chipping of a jenny wren when calling for a mate. 'And here we have evidence that the mission was to meet the commander-in-chief, and indeed Her Majesty, no less.' Hope scratched his chin and looked all the gloomier. 'With no idea about the subject matter!'

Without a hint of warning, Hope rose suddenly from the elegant conference table and, gathering his frock-coat tails with hands entwined behind his back, he strolled towards the thin wintry light that spilled through the expansive glass at the end of the room. The others watched in silence as he glowered down at the hurrying and scurrying of Whitehall below. Allowing his jacket to descend back into its conventional arrangement, he drummed his fingers on the windowsill for a few seconds and then spun round to address the company once more.

'This has an unfortunate smell about it, I fear. I believe it must be connected in some way to the calamitous scandal that took place in Bangkok last year. The affair that brought old Knox down, and cost a man his life in the vilest of circumstances.'

The others, their frowned features displaying obvious bemusement, merely stared back, hoping for further enlightenment.

'I refer, of course, to the matter of young Fanny Knox and her Siamese lover.'

There was still not the slightest hint of comprehension from the assembly, but their hitherto blank expressions had been replaced by a clear eagerness for more intelligence. This desire could be plainly seen both in their eyes and from their now open mouths. Hope wondered if it was his use of the word "scandal", or perhaps it was the mention of a fallen man, or the despicable death of another that had sparked their interest. Maybe it was the revelation that a young woman was involved and the phrase "her Siamese lover" that had captivated his audience and left them wanting more.

Taking his cue, Hope raised his hands to his lapels as if to address a class of twelve-year-olds regarding the distinctions between the Latin gerund and the gerundive. He knew he had grabbed the imagination of his listeners and he liked the feeling of power it gave him.

'The affair to which I refer is a most terrible story, only recently concluded – just a few months ago, in fact. It concerns the King of Siam, his appointed regent, our former consul general in Bangkok, Sir Thomas Knox, and his young daughter, Fanny. Goodness! Even the foreign secretary at the time, Lord Salisbury, no less, became dragged into the crisis – much against his better judgement, of that I have no doubt.' Hope paused for effect and was gratified when the silence was broken a few seconds later.

'Pray enlighten us, sir. If this is relevant, we should both hear of it,' said Chief Superintendent Grieve. 'It is a matter that is new to my ears at least…'

Henry nodded earnestly in agreement.

'That is because it was kept under a cloak of secrecy at the Foreign Office for fear the scandal might harm our interests in the East,' Hope replied, now resuming his seat at the table. 'Very well, I shall tell you the details, but I warn you, some might find the narrative repugnant in parts. I must insist that the history I am about to impart goes no further than this room. I only speak it now because you need to know the context, and because you could both become further embroiled in the matter as time passes.'

Henry turned his head towards the policeman who sat opposite him. Grieve looked strangely uncomfortable and was shifting uneasily in his seat.

'The story starts back in '57 with Sir Thomas Knox,' Hope continued, 'an Irish soldier who served the Crown both in India and China before becoming military advisor to Siam. At the conclusion of his posting with the Siamese army, he was taken on as an interpreter at the British consulate and eventually rose to become consul, and then about a dozen years ago he was appointed consul general. During his long and distinguished tour in Siam, Knox took on a Siamese wife, a lady of high status and a member of the royal court. They had two daughters, the first of which was Fanny. In time, Fanny grew to become a very handsome woman, and last year she married a Siamese nobleman. It was not long before a child followed – but...' Hope raised his finger and paused for effect, 'the marriage had not received the customary sanction from King Rama V. The couple took their vows without the permission of the Siamese court, and most importantly' – Hope's melodramatic hiatuses were becoming annoying now – 'the coupling went against the specific wishes of the Regent of Siam, a gentleman by the name of Lord Bamroong. You see, Lord Bamroong wanted his own grandson to wed the beautiful Fanny. The whole affair caused quite a stir locally, but it only came to our attention when the said Siamese nobleman, Fanny's loving new husband, a man called Phra Preecha, was arrested in Bangkok on charges of embezzlement and then hideously flogged. But worse was to follow.

'Further charges, including murder no less, were brought against Knox's new son-in-law. The architect of these accusations, so I am told, was the regent himself. He was enraged that his grandson had been so dishonourably scorned by Fanny and unhappy with Preecha's too lenient punishment. In all the uproar, Knox lost his judgement, I'm afraid, and overreached himself. He interceded on behalf of his daughter in an effort to save her husband from further torment – Preecha was, after all, the father of Knox's young grandson. After pleading unsuccessfully before the king for Preecha's release, Knox took it on himself to instruct a Royal Navy gunboat to be dispatched from nearby Singapore to Bangkok. Apparently, he said it was "to calm the situation". Lord Salisbury was unsighted and most displeased when he heard the news. He was forced to intervene and after careful consideration, His Lordship gave orders to withdraw the gunboat. War with Siam would have been unthinkable at the time – especially over such a trivial matter.' Hope halted his discourse and took a draught from the glass of water at his side.

'But a man's liberty was at stake,' Henry intervened.

'But he was not an Englishman, sir!' Hope looked irritated.

'Neither is our good friend Albert Woodward,' Henry retorted. 'He is a man of the Welsh valleys...'

'My apologies, sir.' Hope flushed. 'By English, of course I meant to say British...' and then as if to curtail this unhelpful line of conversation, he hurried to his next point by adding, 'You see, Knox believed the charges against this Phra Preecha chap were all trumped up, false and baseless; he said the first trial was a farce, and the accused man had never even had a chance to defend himself or call witnesses on his behalf. Knox felt that as the fellow was his lawful son-in-law, he deserved the protection of the British Crown. Knox made a play also that the French were behind it all. Their aim, he said, was to embarrass the British and further their influence in the country. He even intimated that the French had secret plans to invade Siam, which would, of course, have been intolerable, but at the time we could find no grounds to support his assertions.'

'And the outcome?' Grieve asked. 'Did Lord Salisbury relent?'

'He most certainly did not! His Lordship's conclusion that this was a private matter, not an affair of the state, did not vary one iota. He would not support Knox, and when asked by him to return the gunboat, he flatly refused, thereby denying the military presence and the implied threat Knox so much desired. The matter, as far as London was concerned, ended there.'

'And the Siamese nobleman, Fanny's husband, Phra Preecha, what became of him?' Henry asked looking hopeful.

'For his first offences, he received thirty strokes of the lash.'

Henry winced. 'The poor chap.'

Grieve added, 'Punishment indeed – most agonising I'm sure, but at least that should have closed the episode and allowed him to be quickly reunited with his wife and child.'

'Unfortunately not. You forget there were further accusations…' Hope's speech was deliberate and sombre. 'Immediately after the beating, the second set of charges were brought by the regent, one of which, I will remind you, was for murder. The Siamese privy council sat in judgement once again – Knox could do nothing to prevent it – and they quickly found Preecha guilty of the new allegations. For all intents and purposes, that was the end of him.'

'The end of him?' Henry gasped.

'Why yes, Mr Gough. Phra Preecha was sentenced to death for his supposed crimes. The poor fellow was taken back to his birthplace and duly executed – publicly beheaded with a single cut of the sword. I remember it was just before Christmas when the news reached us.'

The table fell silent as this brutal piece of information sunk in.

Hope, realising the impact of his long speech, then made deliberately light of it. 'We were pleased the affair had ended,' he said with a harrumph. 'Fanny returned broken-hearted to England with her child – a boy called Spencer, I recall. Knox was withdrawn to London and asked to resign. It was all very embarrassing. Of course, we gave him a knighthood to soften the blow – KCMG – "Kindly Call Me God", no less, ha-ha-ha!'

The others looked back with vacant expressions.

'Why, it's correct title, of course, is Knight Commander of the Order of St Michael and St George. 'Twas the least we could do to recompense for his earlier work.' Hope paused to allow his customary grave appearance to reassert itself. 'But he's very much a broken man, I fear…'

'May I be so bold as to make an observation, and ask a question?' Henry ventured after the room had remained still for a few moments.

Hope grimaced. He didn't like interruptions to his train of thought, especially from a lowly cab proprietor, but in an attempt to appear cordial, he gave Henry the floor. 'By all means…' he replied as affably as he could manage.

'That was a most interesting and cruel story you have told us, but how do you connect this matter, now concluded these last three months, with yesterday's London killing of Prince Gagananga?'

'I have no proof, Mr Gough, but events spawn events... and the murder of your Siamese passenger, a man so close to the king himself, has more than a whiff of coincidence behind it. If only we knew the reason why the prince travelled so far to talk with us. The message he carried must have been of the utmost secrecy, it seems; even Beaumont knew nothing about it.'

Henry pressed on. 'While the subject under discussion between the prince and His Grace the Duke can only be guessed at, surely we could rightly assume it was connected in some way to the national security of either Siam or Great Britain. Given that our own circumstances should be well known to us, we must suspect that the military matter which the prince wished to raise concerned his own country, not ours.'

'Unless he was in possession of a dark secret that threated our empire,' Grieve interjected.

Hope rapped the table with his fingers. 'Enough, gentlemen! Conjecture is not helpful at this juncture. I know you mean well, but the first rule of intelligence is not to speculate until solid evidence is obtained. It is a lesson I have learned over many years of service in this discipline. It is facts we need. Facts will build the picture. It is proof that will shine a light on the true nature of events. Gentlemen, our first priority must be to apprehend the killer. If, as seems likely, he is of foreign stock, he will most probably wish to return speedily from whence he came. Nearly twenty-four hours has passed since he committed the crime. Enough time, I fear, to flee from our borders.'

'I have already passed word to our southern and eastern ports to guard against his escape,' Grieve announced. 'If he tries to cross by conventional means, he should be easy to detect. His description is most singular.'

'Are your procedures foolproof, sir?' Hope queried. 'What chance does he have of slipping away?'

Grieve bit his lower lip and tugged at his right ear simultaneously. 'I fear, if he is determined, the man has a fair chance of eluding us. He may have fellow conspirators who can shield him inside communities which we will struggle to infiltrate. He may lie low for a while and find passage as a stowaway. His options are plentiful if he has courage and guile. In truth, I cannot promise that our measures to halt his escape will be effective.'

'I see.' Hope rose from the table. 'I will send a telegram to Beaumont today informing him of the situation. I request that you prepare a report of the incident, which I will forward to him in due course, so he might let the Siamese know of the events and allow King Rama V to mourn for his half-brother. I suggest you take photographs of the dead man for identification purposes and inform them we have a witness who can identify the assailant. My guess is the Siamese will know who is behind this. The matter smacks of internal conspiracy to me. If they have a grip on their own politics, they will know the motives and in all probability the identity of the assassin.'

'I will have the report with you by tomorrow morning,' Grieve responded, 'however, a word of caution. I will arrange for photographs of the corpse as you suggest, but the resulting images will be gruesome in the extreme and may not advance the cause of identification. The head and face were so much blown away.'

'All the more important then, to demonstrate the hideous nature of the crime. It may coerce the Siamese to cooperate in bringing the killer to justice. Pray ensure that images are taken also of the man's clothing, and his naked corpse, front and back. There may be distinguishing features which others will recognise.'

'I will do as you say.'

'Then that is all for now. Once your report is complete, Grieve, please bring it to me in person so we can converse further on the matter.' Hope turned to look at Henry Gough. 'Henry, you are free to go. If I require you to make a statement, I will let you know. For now, you may resume your lawful occupation and leave the rest to us. You may not speak of this matter to anyone, do you understand? You are sworn to utmost secrecy. You will not speak of this to your wife or even whisper it into your horse's ear. You will be silent as the grave. Is that clear?'

'As clear as the Crystal Palace,' Henry replied, pursing his lips.

'Thank you for your attendance today, Mr Gough. If you wait outside, I wish to speak a few more words with the chief superintendent in private. No doubt he will provide you with passage home.'

Feeling mightily relieved that his ordeal was coming to an end, Henry got up to leave. 'Thank you, sir. You know where to find me should you require my assistance any further. I'll wait outside as you requested.' Henry collected his hat and left the room with a much jauntier step than had accompanied him into the meeting.

'The photographs may take a few days to arrange and produce,' Grieve said after Henry had closed the door.

'No matter. I suspect that my telegram to Beaumont today will be the first of many. But I urge haste. It is difficult enough to communicate with a kingdom six thousand miles distant, so we must ensure our work is both swift and excellent in all regards. Siam is of increasing importance to Great Britain, its riches have been hardly touched, and I wish to leave a good impression with the royal court, despite the terrible event that took place on our streets last night.' And then, as an aside, he muttered, 'One thing I'll wager – the French will have some part in this affair.'

Grieve cocked his ear. 'The French, did you say? What part could they have in this assassination?'

'You may well ask, Grieve. The French may call us perfidious Albion, but in matters of Indo-China, they play the role of villain *par excellence*. I would not be at all surprised if old Knox was right all along, and we find a Gallic hand has brushed this affair. Only time will tell.'

'But surely, by your own words, speculation of such nature is only futile. It is *facts* we require!' Grieve teased with a wry smile.

For once, an honest grin appeared on Hope's face. He knew he'd been trumped. 'Fear not, sir,' he replied at length. 'If it's facts we require to demonstrate French skulduggery, I shall obtain them!'

Chapter Four

It wasn't until the end of April that Henry heard any more about the affair. The case named variously by the press as "*The Mystery of the Slain Chinaman*" and "*The Oriental Assassination*" had gone quiet. One journal had even, completely erroneously and boorishly, headlined the case "*The Terror of the Tongs!*". But by now, the incident was largely forgotten by the general public. Even Henry had managed to put it largely out of his mind. Although haunted by nightmares for a few weeks, these had diminished gradually as his affairs started to return to normal. Over the last few weeks, news of the general election had dominated the newspapers, and Gladstone's dramatic victory for the Tories over Disraeli had aroused huge interest and speculation about the future. So much so, that the Ashburn Place murder had gone out of nearly everyone's minds.

Shortly after the hubbub of the election campaign, Henry and Albert had kept their promise to meet, and it was within one of the private rooms of The Cheshire Cheese in Fleet Street, the location of their first friendly encounter years earlier, they chose to renew their companionship. Their lunchtime parley was much lubricated by the half-dozen pints of ale they'd consumed between them – far too much for Henry, who had been following a strict diet of late, worried by the slight paunch that had started to develop around his waistline. His beloved Caroline had mentioned it more than once, at first teasing, but he sensed that she was more than a little concerned about his condition. Henry was nearing forty-four, his beautiful mistress had seen just twenty-six summers, so he'd resolved to keep as vigorous as he could for a man of his age and do his best to imitate the actions and ardour of a fellow much younger than himself.

Naturally, between their drinking, the two old friends took time to speak at length of the Ashburn Place killing and each wondered if any progress had been made to capture the assassin with the painted tiger on his neck. Neither had heard any more from Jack Grieve or Nathaniel Hope – it was almost as if the incident had never occurred. The newspapers had been full of it at the time, but the appetite for bulletins on progress in the investigation had faded after a few short days as other, tastier morsels from London's crime scene became more prominent and captured the interest of the general public. By the time the two met at the inn, the matter was already three weeks old and almost completely forgotten by the Fleet Street hacks.

"'Tis strange how quickly such a terrible event can be forgotten,' Henry mused as he drank his pint.

Albert nodded. He had seen it all before. 'Those damnable Tories have captured all the headlines,' he said sulkily. 'I expect we shall know all there is to know when the time is right. My guess is that your assassin fellow managed to creep over the Channel and he's long gone by now. Not even the outstretched arm of Jack Grieve can recover him now.' His gnarled face brightened a little. 'As a matter of fact, I will be talking with him next week. Our monthly opium discussions are pending. If he has news, I'm sure he will enlighten me.'

'I hope he makes clear what he wants from me soon enough. If I am to be a witness I shall need to know.'

Albert decided it was time to change the subject. 'I have some news that might interest you, Henry...'

'Let me guess, Major Callaway has a new lady friend!' was the laughing reply. 'Despite his advancing years, he remains so popular with the fairer sex I wonder how he manages!'

'Ha! You are no man to speak of such things. You have nothing to learn from him,' Albert replied instantly. 'He is but a few years older than you, and you have already captured the fairest of them all – you are indeed a lucky man.' The pair clinked beer mugs and snorted in unison. 'But, the news I have does concern Major Callaway by some circular route.'

'Speak, old friend. What news do you have of him?'

'He is moving from the Excise. His days as Head of Investigation are numbered. He has been offered a place in the War Office, no less, working as deputy to Mr Hope. It appears the Intelligence Branch at Horse Guards is building its strength once more and the major has been asked to lead on matters arising from the subcontinent.'

'India indeed. That will suit him well. His service during the mutiny will hold him in good stead. A good choice for sure. Maybe one day he will succeed Hope.'

Woodward nodded. 'That is his intention. He tells me privately that he wishes to lead the branch before he turns fifty. I think a knighthood is on his mind...'

'When will he move?'

'The current incumbent, an aged colonel who served in the Crimean campaign, will hold sway until Christmas. Thereafter, it will be Callaway's position, but I'm told he is expected to share duties with the man until he takes over fully.'

Henry Gough picked up his pint to drain it and asked in an idle manner, 'Who will succeed Major Callaway as head of the Excise detectives? Another military man appointed by the Excise commissioners, no doubt.'

Woodward flushed. 'That is my news, Henry... On recommendation by the major himself, the commissioners have invited me to take the appointment.'

Henry's mouth was full of beer when Albert made his utterance and he found great difficulty in not spluttering out the contents onto the cracked oak table in front of him. 'My Lord!' he replied, not quite sure whether to show surprise or elation. ''Tis good news indeed. Why! You deserve it, old comrade. Indeed, you do. This calls for celebration.' He rose to go to the counter. 'I will order a bottle of Madeira.'

By the time Henry skulked home, light-headed and woozy, Caroline had already taken the children to bed and was sitting alone by the fire engaged in sewing a patchwork quilt. She contemplated him with a benign but knowing smile as he lurched into the parlour. 'So much for your constitution and new regime, Henry. It appears you have drunk enough today for two men.' She tutted amiably.

'Much more than two, my love.' He belched. 'But I have good news. Albert Woodward is to be chief of the Excise detectives!'

'Come to bed, my dear. You look rather tired, and you're slated to take a horse out at seven.' Her tone, this time, was more reproachful.

Henry did as he was told, and did so silently. Caroline helped him with his boots and soon the house was quiet, interrupted only by the rumble of low snoring that intermittently broke the calm of an otherwise noiseless night.

A week after his Bacchanalian lunch with the Excise detective at The Cheshire Cheese, as the flurries of cherry blossoms fluttered downwards like late snow onto London avenues, and the sound of the first cuckoo could be heard in countryside gardens, Henry received a telegram inviting him to meet Nathaniel Hope immediately at the War Office. The message gave no clue as to the agenda but added that Chief Superintendent Jack Grieve would be in attendance also. It was customary for Henry to return to the mews at twelve for a light lunch. On some days this ambition was made impossible by the destinations his customers chose for him. On this particular day, he had returned to his stables at eleven, earlier than normal, as his horse was showing signs of lameness. Greeted with the telegram, which one of his staff handed him, he snatched a cup of tea and a slice of sponge cake baked by one of his driver's wives to celebrate her husband's birthday. Then he asked faithful Joshua to take him straightway to Horse Guards. He arrived just after noon and on presentation at the front desk, and after signing his name in the visitors' book, he was escorted up the grand staircase towards the office of the Head of the Intelligence Branch.

'Mr Hope is expecting you, sir.'

Hope greeted him with an exceedingly wide smile, so untypical of his perennial condescension. The open and outwardly affable welcome set Henry back in his tracks for a few moments. Hope had the look of a man wanting a favour of some kind, and this made Henry wary. He shook the great man's hand warmly all the same, making sure to keep eye contact as he did, in case any clues of his host's intent could be determined. Beside Hope stood Jack Grieve, whose countenance was an altogether different proposition. The policeman looked positively ashen-faced, as if he had just received news of the most dreadful kind.

'Please be seated, sir.' Hope was grinning like Carroll's Cheshire Cat. 'I'll arrange for some tea – cake perhaps?'

'I've just enjoyed a slice of Mrs Honeybun's Victoria sponge, sir, so no more cake for me, if you please...' Henry spoke in steady, deliberate tones, still eying his host. Never was a sentence about sponge cake delivered with such caution.

Hardly had the words left Henry's lips before Hope interjected. He sounded like a man anxious to move the conversation forward. 'Look, I won't beat about the bush, Mr Gough. I have called you here today because I – er, we...' he waved a hand airily towards Jack Grieve, 'need your help.'

'I will do what I can, as long as it is honest,' came the reply from the London cabbie. Henry glanced over to Jack Grieve who was seated now and still looking as if a passing shell had rocked him to the core.

'Well, of course it is honest.' A look of mock horror now crowded into the shrewd diplomat's face. 'How could it be otherwise? And I will add that you will be serving your country too. You have a fine record of loyal service, Mr Gough, and now your country needs your assistance once more.' Henry noted that Hope had chosen, for some reason, to use "Mr Gough" rather than previously "Henry" when addressing him, and this made him wonder all the more what the man was plotting. He decided to keep his counsel until he'd heard all the facts.

Hope continued. 'There are two parts to my request. The first is simple. In plain talking, I wish you to travel to Siam to give evidence in the trial of the alleged killer of Prince Gagananga.'

'I see, so the killer has been arrested after all,' Henry blurted, not fully appreciating what was being asked of him.

'Yes, but not by us...' The evidence, including Mr Grieve's photographs and your written testimony, which was dispatched to Siam shortly after the incident, allowed the authorities, acting for the king himself, to capture the suspect immediately the fellow set foot back in Bangkok. The accused is now in the king's personal custody and awaiting trial. All the evidence will be presented at trial, of course, but in your case, I would prefer it if you gave your own testimony in person. It is an opportunity for Great Britain to demonstrate to the Siamese how impartial justice can be correctly delivered. The king has for some time been concerned about the prejudicial and uncivilised manner in which his courts perform, and he has asked for our further guidance in the ways of the English courts. This case provides us with a perfect opportunity to show him. The recent example of the trial against Phra Preecha, in the Fanny Knox case we discussed during our last meeting, has given him food for thought. Until his arrest, Preecha had been one of his most trusted noblemen, and the man's conviction and vile beheading caused quite a stir in Bangkok, due to the court's apparent bias and lack of transparency. King Rama V tells us he wants to bring his judicial system into the modern age.' Hope rubbed his hands vigorously. 'You can help us, Mr Gough. What do you say?'

As Henry considered his reply, it was Chief Superintendent Grieve who spoke next. 'If I might add a little detail to your account, sir... It was Scotland Yard who provided the vital information to the Siamese on receiving the name of their chief suspect,' he said, chin raised with an air of distinct affectation. Reading from a typed report which he placed in front of him, he continued, 'The man in question is a Siamese personage by the name of er... Kittisak Aromdee...' Grieve got in a terrible tangle trying to pronounce the accused man's name, but in the end managed to spit out something resembling a moniker before continuing. 'Using information received from the Siamese through Mr Hope's office and the consul general in Bangkok, we commenced an investigation – I attached half a dozen officers to the enquiry, I may add. After their extensive door-to-door enquiries and on visiting hundreds of London hotels, we managed to track the fellow down. We discovered that the Siamese suspect had stayed in the Crystal Palace Hotel in Bermondsey between the eighteenth and twenty-fourth of February – at exactly the right period when the murder was committed. 'Tis a small establishment, in truth, definitely second class, but sufficiently legitimate to possess a hotel register. In it, the accused professed his occupation to be a timber merchant from Mueang Chiang Mai, which apparently is a district in a city in the northern parts of Siam.

'After that, the fellow disappeared without trace, and his whereabouts remained a mystery until our investigations led us to the shipping line P&O. They held a passenger manifest that revealed a man bearing his name – I'm sorry, I shall avoid attempting to pronounce it again – departed from Southampton on the sixteenth of March aboard the steamer SS *Ceylon*, bound for Colombo. The latest news received from the consul general is that our suspect was successfully arrested last week as he stepped ashore in Bangkok. This represents another triumph for Scotland Yard, as I'm sure you gentlemen will agree.'

'Thank you, Grieve. I speak for all of us when I express my indebtedness to Scotland Yard for their efforts in this matter...' Hope said the words through gritted teeth. 'But now, Mr Gough, what do you say? Will you undertake this journey to Siam for us? Will you give evidence at the trial of this fellow, Kittisak?'

Henry remained speechless for a few further seconds as the full force of Hope's entreaty dawned on him. Then he mumbled, 'But Siam, sir, it must be at the end of the world. How long will I be away? I have never set foot beyond these shores in my entire life. And my work? What about my cab business?'

'Although this will take a considerable amount of your time – overall, about four months by our reckoning – and the journey may be arduous, I have secured funds from the Treasury to recompense you and your business. I assure you that you will not suffer financially as a result.' Hope's eyebrow raised a smidgen. The presence of irritation was unmistakeable. He added curtly, 'Do you have any further questions?'

Henry Gough paused before replying, but when he spoke his voice was unfaltering. 'Sir, I have more questions than I care to ask… I will need time to think.'

'I need your decision today,' Hope answered with a decidedly fixed expression. 'If you agree to serve your country, which is the course I strongly recommend, you will have little time to prepare. The P&O steamship leaves from Southampton in ten days – on the sixteenth of May. Anything else?'

'Am I expected to travel alone?'

'You will be accompanied by Chief Superintendent Grieve. He will be your security – your companion, your eyes and ears. Once disembarked in Bangkok, you will be met by the consul general's representatives and they will assist you all they can. It is their job to know the country and its people.'

Henry was flabbergasted. Until recently, he had never heard of Siam and he had no appreciation of its place on the globe. He looked once again towards the policeman who was altering his position uneasily in his seat. Something was clearly making him anxious, Henry thought. 'Have I an option to refuse?' he asked at length.

'Of course, but I urge against it. No foreign court can command the attendance of a British subject to give witness of events that occurred in this country. But here, the circumstances are most singular.'

'Singular?'

'Yes – not to mince words, not only does King Rama V wish it, but we wish it also. The voices within Her Britannic Majesty's Government are unanimous on the matter. It is our desire that you attend the trial, give the evidence you have already given to others, both verbally and in writing, to the Bangkok court in person, so that they may convict the assassin and put an end to his miserable life in such civilised manner as they deem fit.'

Grieve corrected him, '*Alleged* assassin, sir. Under the law, the man is notionally innocent until—'

Hope never allowed him to complete the sentence. Cutting off the policeman, he said in a resolute voice, 'Your attendance, Mr Gough, will advance our cause in two ways. Firstly, Her Britannic Majesty wishes to see justice served in all places around the globe, and your appearance in court will demonstrate our support for this noble cause.'

'And the other way it will help?' Henry queried.

'Ah!' Hope touched the ends of his long fingers together as if holding an invisible ball. 'You see, there is another task I wish you to perform while you are in Siam. One of the utmost delicacy…'

Henry was beginning to understand the language of diplomats. His previous experiences and many conversations with Nathaniel Hope during the episode of the Peccavi Plot had tuned his ear to their style of speech. He knew that when a diplomat used the word "irritated", he truly meant "furious". When he said "delicate" he really wanted to say "difficult", maybe even "dangerous". Henry mused that it was this practised understatement that prevented men of Hope's rank and occupation from actually speaking the plain truth.

'Delicacy, you say?' he replied. 'Can you be more explicit?'

Hope lifted his chin into the air and scratched his reptilian neck for a few seconds. After exhaling loudly, he placed his hands on the lapels of his frock coat and returning his gaze to Henry, he said, 'The fact is we wish you to perform some further tasks for Her Majesty's Government while you are enjoying the hospitality of Siamese society. You have a valid reason to be in their midst. We feel there is a chance to exploit the situation to our advantage.' Sensing that Henry was nonplussed, Hope added, 'Allow me to explain...'

For the next five minutes, he treated the assembly to a history lesson about Anglo-Siamese relations since the time of the first English settler, more than two hundred and fifty years earlier, and how this mutual relationship "based on trade and trust between our two kingdoms" had of late become strained. This, Hope explained, was partly as a result of the Fanny Knox affair, but largely because of the treacherous interference by others, notably France. What had become a successful liaison, based on simple trade and the introduction of missionaries to spread the Word of the Lord, was now in jeopardy.

In conclusion, he declared, 'You see, Mr Gough, your arrival amidst these peoples of the East affords us an opportunity – access which cannot be gained by our established diplomats in that country. To be specific, sir, we wish you to keep your eyes and ears open and report back on what you see. Your exemplary performance during the recent attempt on the life of Her Majesty has shown us that you are talented in such matters. You are courageous, loyal – and most of all, you are discreet. And...' he hesitated, 'you have the benefit of low birth, no one will suspect a mere London cab driver of being an emissary of the British Crown. Don't you see, the stratagem is an excellent one!' he added in triumphant tones. Hope now had the bearing of a man with a purpose: animated, even excited.

'You have forgotten one thing, sir,' was Henry's first reply. 'I do not speak Siamese.'

'If that is your only concern, that can be rectified with ease. In fact, I have planned for it. Mr Hurdus will accompany you on your long trip. He is a fluent speaker of the language and a good teacher, I'll be bound. It will pass the time during the tedious passage most wonderfully.'

'But my family?'

'Never fear for your family, Mr Gough. They will be well cared for in your absence. You have my word, as God is my witness. You will be well rewarded too. I understand you are the recipient of a bursary from the Excise for services previously delivered. I'm told you plan to use this for your children's education – a most noble aspiration. Well, we shall double it! Maybe one day one of your offspring might even take his place at the Royal Academy, ha!' Hope's attempts at an unaffected chortle failed miserably. Yet he persevered, adding with a gleam in his eye, 'And imagine the adventure, sir. A chance to see a foreign land steeped with traditions and riches beyond your ken,' and then, his tone becoming suddenly serious, he declared, 'but above all, Mr Gough, think of it as a service to Her Majesty, whose life you once saved.'

As Hope blathered on, his voice rising and lowering in waves but all the time resonating with energy and enthusiasm, Henry began to feel moved by the man's oratory. The opportunity that now presented itself was indeed unique, and stirrings for a taste of adventure began to rumble in his heart. He had never been beyond Whitstable in his whole life and had only seen the open sea once. In six years, he would be fifty, well past middle age, approaching the grave fast, showing signs of infirmity, and possibly unable to undergo such a demanding expedition. If he was going to do it, best do it now, his heart told him, while he still possessed strength in his limbs and a sense of adventure in his head. What tales he might tell his children too! But leaving Caroline would be such a terrible wrench, he could hardly bear to contemplate it. And the thought that Jack Grieve would accompany him worried him greatly too. It was clear from the policeman's aura he wanted no part in it, and Henry knew a reluctant traveller would be no companion. The poor fellow must have been press-ganged by Hope, perhaps on the promise of some official recognition, but the appearance of the man gave the game away. His manner had been most affected from the moment Henry had entered the room, and now his eyes seemed to bulge most horribly, as if he'd seen a spectre. At length, Hope paused his speech, lifted his chin once more, and stroking his rangy neck, looked Henry straight in the eye.

'Well, what do you say? Cat got your tongue, eh?' he rasped.

'I will do it on one account. You say you will take care of my family during my absence and if circumstances prevent my return. Is that correct?'

'We will, sir.'

'You say you will set up a second bursary for my children's education and provide me with lessons in the Siamese dialect.'

'We will, Mr Gough.'

'I presume you will also give me more detailed instructions on what exact service my country requires of me.'

'Indeed. I cannot be more explicit until you agree.'

'Am I to be a spy, sir? It much sounds like it to me.'

Hope harrumphed and removed a silk handkerchief from his pocket. After wiping his mouth, he said easily, 'I would not call it spying, Mr Gough... A better description might be "a clandestine emissary for Her Majesty", perhaps. How does that suit? Of course, I hardly need say that our enterprise is one we shall never disclose outside these four walls, save to those who must, by necessity, know the facts. Your purpose will not be divulged even to Mr Beaumont, the consul general in Siam, or any of his office or followers, for fear the matter might get more widely reported. Your purpose is straightforward. We wish you to confirm certain facts which we believe to be true, but which cannot be divulged to you at this time. If you agree to my proposal and sign an official paper I have prepared, we can start today, both with the advancement of money and your first lessons in Siamese. How is your French, sir? Passable, I trust...'

'I do not speak a single word. I have drunk many times in the Rose of Normandy tavern, if that is of any value,' Henry quipped.

Hope disregarded the unhelpfulness of the reply and pressed on. 'Hurdus is a linguist, fortunately, and French comes easily to him, and there will be others on board with whom you can practise the tongue. Siamese is not a difficult language, I am assured, especially the version spoken at court and by the courts. Ha! Court and courts,' he repeated, 'most amusing... You shall see both, I reason! Mr Gough, what say you?' Henry remained silent. Seemingly undeterred, Hope rattled on. 'In the matter of languages, we shall have to redouble our efforts. It is fortuitous the voyage to Bangkok is a long one – more than six weeks, I believe. I would—'

'Enough, Mr Hope! I have said I will do it, but I have one condition. You have not asked me for my stipulation.'

'Why? I thought we had discussed your family, your business, recompense, the bursaries, your language tuition and the like – what more is there you need?'

'I will put my case simply,' Henry said. 'I will do your bidding only if I can be accompanied by my friend and old partner in crime, Mr Albert Woodward – if he is agreeable, that is. Mr Woodward is a devoted and upright detective whose knowledge will be useful if I am to be, as you say, "a clandestine emissary". He's older than me, I grant; the trip may not entirely suit his constitution. But he is a man of the world and I have recently learned he will be moving up in his profession shortly after Christmas. In that regard, the timing of this voyage could not be more perfect for him.' Henry turned to Grieve. 'My apologies, Chief Superintendent, but it's not difficult to see that you are none too excited by the prospect of a trip to faraway Siam. And I'm sure you have many better things to occupy you at Scotland Yard. Why, you have hardly uttered a word on the subject of travel since I arrived.' Returning to Nathaniel Hope, he concluded, 'Albert Woodward, in contrast, has time on his hands, he is admirable in all respects and would make a splendid replacement.'

'It is the crossings I fear most, Henry, that is all…' Grieve interjected. The lofty policeman now looked suddenly small; his face somehow shrunk into his collars. 'I took the *Empress* boat to Calais a few years back. I was sick as a dog. Three months at sea would be the death of me. What would Mrs Grieve make of it?'

'If it pleases you, Chief Superintendent, you have said enough!' Hope shook his head at Grieve in frustration. 'You have already explained your misgivings to me on the matter!'

Hope rose to his feet, and deep in thought, he paced around his desk for a few moments. After a full minute of contemplation, he reached for the communication cord and tugged it. A bell's sharp tinkle could be heard outside in the anteroom. A few moments later, Rupert Lappin entered the office. Lappin was Hope's bespectacled young protégé, a well-connected young man who had ambitions of high office. Hope had promised the boy's father, Lord Selsdon, that he would take care of his son and train him to advance within the service. But Lappin was too timid, too faint-hearted for Hope's liking and there had been many moments when the great man felt he should discuss the lad's future with His Lordship. To raise the "delicate" matter concerning Rupert's progress, or to be more honest, his total lack of it, was a daunting prospect, even for Hope, so until now he'd decided to let sleeping dogs lie.

'Sir, you called for me,' Lappin said with halting voice while balancing on one foot and then the other. He clutched his hands so tight in front of him that both knuckles had turned the colour of watered milk.

Hope came straight to the point. 'I read a report some days ago, Lappin. It contained a list of the advisors Great Britain has sent overseas in recent years to help foreign countries – mostly engineers, teachers, military men and the like. I recall seeing Siam on the list, but I need to refresh my memory on the detail. Find and bring the document to me, would you.'

'I know the report of which you speak, sir, and in the light of your current interest in Siam, I have taken the trouble to read it in depth. What information do you require?' Lappin turned his fingers through his hands once again.

Hope sighed. 'Very well, Lappin, as you ask… I wish to be reminded how many advisors we have currently placed in Siam. I need to know their occupations and if there are any outstanding requests for our services in this regard.'

Rupert Lappin's response was immediate. 'There are eight British advisors in Siam currently and a number of positions as yet unfilled. There are two Scottish engineers, one involved in the timber industry, the other a bridge-building expert; a lawyer, Mr Archbold, from Temple Chambers; a gentleman from the Great Western Railway; two former government officials advising on political institutions; one scientist – a chemist from Emmanuel College, Cambridge, I believe; and a Welsh educational specialist. In addition, King Chulalongkorn has agreed that Mr James McCarthy, the estimable Irish surveyor, will commence work on mapping the frontiers of the country early next year. As far as vacancies identified, sir, we have been asked to look for a man versed in the techniques required to capture smugglers – opium is a significant problem, apparently. The king is also seeking an expert to help him to break the trades in illicit production of alcohol and illegal gambling – the growing Chinese community is a concern to the king in these matters. The king also wishes to further centralise tax revenues and has sought our support in that regard.'

As Lappin drew his speech to a close, Hope looked on in undisguised astonishment. At length, the senior man said matter-of-factly and without a hint of charity, 'I see. Just as I thought... I have taken notice of your diligence, young man. Please prepare a note of your findings for my later perusal. Now you may leave us. I will call you if I need you.' Hope made a mental note to delay his assignation with His Lordship a while longer. Although he would not show it, his charge's performance had indeed impressed him. If only Lappin could learn to present himself with the swagger required of top government servants, the boy might yet go far. As he turned to leave, he called out, 'What name did you use to refer to the King of Siam, remind me, Lappin?'

'Chulalongkorn, sir, otherwise known as Rama V, or to his people, Phra Chula Chom Klao Chao.'

Hope nodded chivalrously to his acolyte. 'Thank you, Lappin. Chulalongkorn – yes, of course. Hurdus mentioned one and the same. Chulalongkorn will be the name on our lips from now on...' Lappin shuffled out of the room and closed the door silently behind him.

Hope turned to Gough and Grieve. 'I think we may have a proposal that might suit us all, gentlemen,' he announced. 'If the Siamese want a man to break their illicit stills and advise them on smuggling and tax reform, maybe Albert Woodward is not such a bad idea after all! He might be exactly the man we need. If he joins you on this assignment, he will have to understand the utmost confidentiality of our private agenda. Do you think he will accept the invitation to accompany you, Mr Gough?'

'We can only ask. If you offer up the same rousing speech you just gave me, sir, I think there is every chance.'

'Very well. Pray speak to him, soften the ground a little, and if he agrees we shall meet again – strictly *in camera*, naturally – back here within the next few days. I have vital information to disclose which can only be imparted once I have the promise of his and your full cooperation. Can I suggest next Tuesday morning at eleven?'

Chapter Five

The following morning was a Saturday. Before light, it saw Henry busying himself in the stable yard, performing mostly menial tasks that he could have delegated to others, had he the mind to do so. At breakfast, he made the decision not to venture out in his cab for the day. Instead, he asked David Lee to substitute for him, and after a few words of advice to his recent recruit, he watched the horse and hansom trot away towards Euston. Henry had other things on his mind, and he needed time to think. After sharing a light lunch of cockles and beer with Caroline, during which he'd manifestly failed to raise the subject of his forthcoming voyage east, he plunged his head amongst the office registers and account books as a way of diverting his mind from the inevitable conversation with her that would soon be required. He wished now he'd spoken of it the minute he'd returned the previous day. A spontaneous and enthusiastic announcement of his intentions might have allowed him to make light of it and carry her along with his excitement, but for some reason he'd baulked and could not bring himself to mention it. Now he was regretting his vacillation. The extemporaneous moment was lost and with each passing hour, the task of breaking the news was becoming increasingly more difficult. The day wore on without incident or any new ideas, and it was not long before the casement clock in his jumbled office chimed six. He peered up from his ledgers to hear David Lee arriving back in the yard once again – hooves clattering and sliding on the cobbled stones, bridles clanking, and wheels skidding as the horse snorted to a halt.

A flawless evening light streamed into the ancient mews; spring was very much in the air, and Henry's mind wandered to the time he'd first touched hands with Caroline. It had been around the self-same desk where he now sat that she had expressed her love for him, and the moment had changed his life – and hers – forever. Now they had four children to show for their union. He pondered with a wistful and contented smile that the tenderness they showed towards one another had remained steadfast throughout and showed no signs of abating. He breathed a deep and heavy sigh, and with elbows resting on the bureau, he pressed his temples with both hands. To leave her alone with his babes for more than a quarter of the year would indeed be a deep sorrow, but the more he contemplated the matter the more he knew there was no turning back. The Siamese adventure was the opportunity of a lifetime, and he should seize it with both hands.

'Good evening, sir,' Lee piped as he entered the office. 'A good day so far – I have taken nigh on twenty-five shillings since I left you. Three trips beyond Charing Cross too. Your cab ran smoothly throughout. I can tell why that particular hansom is your favourite.' He smiled. 'With your grace, I will take my rest now. Unless you wish otherwise, Hawkins will change the horses and take the cab out on this evening's run.'

'It is indeed a comfortable machine, Lee. But no more than the others, I'll vouch. As you can see from the empty yard, all our hansoms are on the road and earning their keep. I confess I wish I was amongst them as I sit here, knee-deep in the papers and accounts.'

Lee retreated back into the yard, and Henry was left with his thoughts once more. Maybe it was the fact that he had just spoken to another human being for the first time in many hours that reminded him of his tongue and the urgent need to use it to talk with Caroline. Suddenly, the preposterous nature of his self-inflicted predicament struck him, and slapping down his papers untidily onto the desk, he collected his hat, picked up his swordstick (which since the Ashburton Place incident had been his constant companion) and marched out into the yard. Less than five minutes later, he was turning the keys to his rooms above the mews.

Caroline was fussing with George when he entered and did not look up to greet him.

'My darling, I have news I must impart!' Henry did his best to create a note of spontaneity, and he wanted his voice to sound buoyant – cheerful, almost.

'Presently,' came the singing reply. 'Young George has spoiled his baby napkin.'

After a period, which seemed longer than it actually was, during which Henry tried to keep his optimistic mood alive, Caroline finally turned her head towards him, still holding young George to her breast. 'My, what is it, darling?' She smiled sweetly. 'You look most animated.'

'I have to go away, dearest. My statement to Scotland Yard has been read in the law court of Siam, and they wish me to attend so I might give my testimony in person,' he exclaimed. 'I have just a week to prepare. I leave from Southampton on Sunday.' Caroline's almost immediate reply astounded him.

'I see...' Caroline knitted her brow for the briefest of moments. ''Tis no problem, I will wait 'til your return, never fear,' she said nonchalantly while balancing the now struggling baby in her arms. 'How long will you be away, my love?'

'More than three months, I fear... maybe longer...'

'If it has to be done, if you are summonsed by the court, then it must be done. Worry not for me. We shall be here for your homecoming,' she replied without even the blink of an eye.

'But, will you not miss me, my dearest?' Henry's tone had turned abruptly from one of bold optimism to one of mild panic.

'Of course we will,' she said soothingly, 'but needs must. We shall survive. Now sit. I have bought haddock for our supper today.'

Henry prided himself that he knew the ways of women – for the most part, at least – but as he took his place obediently at the table, with his darling wife fussing around him, he suddenly comprehended that his knowledge on the subject was severely lacking.

From that day on, events seemed to move at lightning speed. With Hope's instructions ringing in his head, Henry sought an early meeting with Albert Woodward, and when it came, just the following day, it was much briefer than he had expected. Seated in a private first-floor corner of The Olde Bell Tavern in Fleet Street, with a view down the thoroughfare towards the dome of St Paul's, a pitcher of amber ale in their midst, Woodward had lit his oily briar pipe as Henry outlined Hope's daring Siamese proposal. The timeworn exciseman leaned back contentedly, drawing in the musky miasma as the project unfolded, never interrupting – just nodding wisely and muttering soft sounds as clenched teeth gripped the stem.

'You see, Hope won't give us all the facts until we agree,' Henry had concluded, 'but for my part, I am decided. I'm ready for the adventure. I can't see myself being offered such an opportunity again in my lifetime, and I dare not refuse him. Caroline has agreed to allow me a period of absence too...' he added, his voice trailing off as he displayed a guilty smile that fooled no one. Albert's eyebrows raised a smidgen as the deluded words were mouthed by his companion. 'So, what do you say, old friend? Will you accompany me on this jaunt so that together we can imitate the actions of both diplomat and sleuth?'

Albert Woodward put down his pipe and took another draught of ale. He looked as pensive as Henry had ever seen him. ''Tis a most enlivening expedition you have before you,' he replied at length, 'but I am an old salt with more than fifty years at my back. Are you sure you want me to accompany you all the way to the Orient? Is there no other man who could do this for you?'

'I will go with no other,' Henry replied simply. 'It is a condition of my involvement in the enterprise. Hope knows it and has concurred. You must concur, Albert, that travelling as an expert in all things Excise will be the perfect disguise. It is a marvellous fact that the Siamese have already requested a visitation from an official to help them – an authority in exactly your line of business; I have no doubt that you will accomplish the task with ease. Why, there is no man in London better versed than you in the ways of the moon-curser and the liquor-runner. This latest problem of opium is also one you know well. By the heavens, your arrival in Bangkok will be hailed from the highest ramparts of the king's palace!' Henry raised his jug, leaned conspiratorially towards his companion and added in low tones that Albert thought rather over-theatrical, 'And between us, we may solve the riddle of the murder at Ashburn Place.'

'Of course, I will have to ask Major Callaway first...' Albert Woodward replied at length.

'He will agree, and you know it. Callaway wants Hope's job after all, and his cooperation in this venture will surely create favour at the War Office and set him on the right path.'

Woodward gave a chuckle and took another draw from his pipe. 'You flatter me, Henry, but I forgive you; 'tis indeed a prospect to shake a man out of his lethargy. But,' he paused and took another draught, 'I expect the beer thereabouts may not be of the type I best enjoy...'

Henry looked at him reproachfully and screwed his lips into a wry smile, but before he could utter a word of mock censure, Woodward suddenly hit the table hard with his clenched fist.

'By St David, I shall do it! I shall join you on this wild goose chase to Siam, wherever that may be. And if I never return, so be it. It will be the will of God. Come, let us do this together. Tuesday, you say – a meeting with Hope? Tell him I will join his crew of misfits and can meet him any time he pleases. Why, even today if he wishes it!'

After a Sunday spent entirely in Caroline's loving company, Henry again found himself in the hallowed halls of the War Office Intelligence Branch and the sumptuous office of Nathaniel Hope. This time, Albert Woodward was at his side. Their encounter in The Olde Bell had allowed the pair to begin their preparations for the long journey ahead of them, in the knowledge that the intricate details of their mission and its objectives still remained unknown – at least for the present. Both, however, were united in their determination to see the matter to its end, whatever they might encounter. While there was an air of apprehension in their planning, the aura of anticipation for what lay ahead grew ever greater with each passing hour. By the time they joined Chief Superintendent Grieve inside Nathaniel Hope's oak-panelled domain, the mood was pregnant with tension, and the sense of veiled exhilaration was hard to miss. When Rupert Lappin pushed the heavy office door shut behind them with such a finality of purpose, it gave the impression of a portcullis slamming to bolt a castle barricade – their secret inner sanctum had been sealed.

'Welcome, gentlemen,' Hope opened with the typical affected geniality that the rest had become accustomed to. 'I have asked Mr Lappin to remain with us for today's meeting. He will take whatever notes are necessary.' The group of five took their seats silently on each side of the long mahogany table, with Hope at its head. 'I will not beat about the bush,' he announced, 'but before I commence with my brief, I need to confirm that Mr Woodward has agreed to take Mr Grieve's place on this assignment?'

Henry and Albert nodded in grim unison. The look of relief that washed over Grieve's ruddy face on receiving the news that his services in the Orient were no longer required was palpable.

'In that case, I must ask you to leave us…' Hope said bluntly, turning his face to Grieve. 'What I am about to say here must be restricted to only those who need to know. Please do not consider this a slur against your loyalty, Grieve, but you know as well as I, that this is how affairs must be conducted from now on – in the most utmost secrecy. You are free to leave us now, and thank you for your service. I'm sure I need not remind you that your future silence concerning what you have already learned of this affair must remain unceasing. On that, I must insist.'

The heavy-shouldered policeman rose to go. 'You have my word, sir. I will speak to no one.' As he gathered his top coat, he turned to the assembly and in a voice that appeared to catch slightly in his throat, he added, while facing directly at Henry and Albert, 'My last words to you two bold gentlemen, are simple: Godspeed and good fortune. I look forward to us reuniting on your return.' And with that, Lappin escorted the chief superintendent to the exit. Drawing open the oak "portcullis", he ushered the strangely stooped Grieve wordlessly out of the office. The door closed behind the retreating figure with a sonorous air of finality.

Hope smoothed his moustache. 'And now to business, gentlemen. First, the simple travel arrangements. You are booked on the P&O steamer *Verona* that departs from Southampton on Sunday, 16th May. The journey to Singapore will take about five weeks, but the *Verona* is considered, by those who have experienced it, to be a comfortable and reliable vessel. As subjects of the Crown, we have secured first-class cabins for all three of you – Charles Hurdus will be travelling as your guide and language teacher. This should allow you to study both the languages you will find useful – Siamese and French – in relative ease. From Singapore, you will transfer to a local vessel, which regrettably, I am informed, will be much less well-appointed than the *Verona*. In this craft, you will travel the final nine hundred and seventeen nautical miles to your destination – the port city of Bangkok. This subsequent passage will take another week, at least. I estimate your first day on Siamese soil will arrive before the end of June. Hurdus has made the long trip before and will be able to answer any questions you may have on the subject.

'My only advice is that you travel well-prepared for the climate. It will be hot and steamy – well past ninety degrees. The monsoon rains generally start in July. You will receive a modest allowance for tropical clothing which can be redeemed at Galt & Gieves in Savile Row – they will be able to advise you better than I. In regard to your personal security, I will speak to you later on the subject, but for now, we must cut to the quick – you need to know what I want from you...'

'I have one question before you commence, sir...' Henry grabbed the opportunity of yet another of Hope's extravagant silences to interject.

But before he could pose it, Hope snapped back, 'Pray, do not interrupt my train of thought, Mr Gough. Unless you wish to ask me if you can withdraw, I suggest you keep your counsel until I have finished. All will be revealed. All you have to do is listen. If you have any questions, you may speak once I have concluded.' Henry pursed his lips and remained silent. Hope rose to his feet and started to pace around the room, appearing to gather his thoughts. After what seemed like an interminable silence, he eventually resumed.

'I will commence with a little history – just to provide some context for the tasks that lie ahead of you.' Raising his voice slightly, in the manner of a crusty old schoolmaster, he declared, 'With the exception of Siam, the politics and destiny of South East Asia lie in the hands of the two greatest European powers. Although Great Britain possesses the lion's share of the region, France has, of late, become embroiled in its own colonisation of the region – within the area they refer to as *Indochine* – our term for it is Indo-China, of course. To the east of Siam, the French now have control in Cambodia, Vietnam and Laos, while we remain masters to the north, west and south – in Burma, Malaya and Singapore. The Kingdom of Siam sits neatly at the centre of this imperial map, currently un-subjugated, but surrounded on all sides by the dual competing empires. Siam, therefore, acts as an important buffer state between the two European powers.

'Over the last thirty or so years, Her Majesty's Government has been at pains to assure the Siamese royal family, and the peoples of their country, that we have no interest in further expanding our position in the region. And in that, we are telling the truth – to a point at least…' Hope paused and raised a glass of water to his lips. 'Until recently, this was the avowed position of Mr Disraeli's government, and our diplomatic efforts have, for many years, been to foster commerce and good relations. Both the former king, Mongkut, and the new king, his son Chulalongkorn, have been left in no doubt that our interests in their country are benign and limited to ensuring the free and fair movement of trade between our two kingdoms. Of course, the recent election here and our change of government could have changed this policy of conciliation, but I can announce happily, that it has not. I'm informed that Mr Gladstone, our prime minister of just a few days, takes much the same view as his predecessor.

'But he is more hawkish on one important point. He draws the line utterly at French interference and expansion in Siam and wishes us to do all we can to prevent it. For me, as a government servant, it is, of course, my duty to act according to the wishes of my political masters, but I will declare now that this matter is made all the easier because I support wholeheartedly the new prime minister's policy. Our new foreign secretary too, Lord Granville, is of the same mind. In a nutshell, Great Britain does not want to rule Siam, but we will do all in our power to prevent France from taking it, thereby protecting the native peoples from a Gallic invasion!' Hope paused and looked at the others for the first time in three minutes. 'I will break for questions; are there any?'

Henry was mesmerised. For some reason, the only thought that came into his head was how Hope was managing to look simultaneously gloomy and haughty as he scanned his small audience for a rejoinder. Perhaps unsurprisingly, no reply came from the assembly. The only noise in the room was Lappin's studious scratching into the large red leather-bound notebook that lay on the table in front of him.

'Then I shall continue. The French have, of late, been more troublesome than normal. News has reached us from well-placed sources in Siam that they have secret plans to overthrow the king, plant a puppet monarch in his place and create a French protectorate – much as they did in Cambodia a few short years back. There are two powerful families in Siam, without whose support the king's position would be on shaky ground. These are the Aung and the Bamroong families; they are the greatest of rivals in their quest for power in Siam. Currently the Aungs are in the ascendancy and have the ear of the king. They favour modernisation, and the idea of embracing European ideas is not entirely repugnant to them – a forward-looking position which Her Majesty's Government naturally supports. The Bamroongs, on the other hand, are more traditional in their outlook and resistant to modernisation. It is their wish to maintain the existing feudal system, which has, of course, brought them great riches over the centuries. But this thinking does not find favour with the young king, who desires change. The Bamroong family's influence has dwindled as a consequence, and their shrinking hold on power has allowed the French to sow the seeds of their dangerous protectorate.

'In short, France would oust Chulalongkorn and put a Bamroong on the throne of Siam, with all the shallow riches that accompany it. True control would belong to the French, of course. A gilded steel cord would reach from Paris to Bangkok as Siam was brought into their Gallic orbit. This outcome would be an abomination to Mr Gladstone's administration, and he has charged us with thwarting the project by whatever means available to us. Which brings us to you two gentlemen… Shall I continue?'

Hope's earlier gloom had given way to a mood of energy and zeal, and he now exuded a positive vigour, as if he was relishing the task of frustrating the French in their imperial ambitions. *The man's a veritable chameleon*, thought Henry silently, as he and Albert nodded their acquiescence.

'Very well. This is the nub of it, gentlemen…' Hope straightened his back, took in a lungful of air and said simply, 'I believe we have a traitor in Bangkok.'

For the first time, a low murmur could be heard around the room; the volume was sufficient to drown out the noise from Lappin's infernal scribbling.

Hope continued. 'We have, for some time, suspected that one of our number in the consulate has been passing our secret intelligence to the French, and possibly to the Siamese, but the fact is we cannot prove it. We have a suspect in our sights – a man who, regrettably, has been a long-time servant of Her Majesty and stationed in Siam for nearly twenty years – a fellow by the name of Horatio Chalke. What I want you to discover, gentlemen, is whether our suspicions are valid, and if so, to furnish us with proof of his guilt.' With a flourish of his frock coat, Hope resumed his seat at the table and looked intently at the others.

'I see,' Woodward said at length. 'I do have some experience in such matters. Passing intelligence to the criminal community concerning the strength of the Excise and its intentions has long been a problem for our service, and from time to time we have to draw the puss out. It is my experience that the best way to haul a turncoat from the shadows is to watch and wait at the outset, and then, when the time is right, to lay a trap for him.'

'But we don't even know the man,' Henry said.

'But you soon shall, Mr Gough. Chalke is slated to be your interlocutor in Siam – he will be responsible for your programme and act as your liaison with the courts. Furthermore, he will provide introductions and translation services for you too, Mr Woodward, as you embark on a feasibility study for the Siamese revenue authorities. You see, our delegation in Bangkok is a small one – just six British souls. We have tasked Chalke to be both your points of contact, as much by necessity as by design. And you are quite correct, Mr Woodward, a deception is the only way to trap our man. I'm sure your experience in these matters will greatly help our cause.'

'And if we are successful, what then?' Henry asked.

'To be forthright, sir, that is no concern of yours. All I will say on the matter is that Her Majesty's Government will be left with options, and you will have done your loyal duty. That is all I am prepared to offer.'

'Ha, for certain, you will have "options" as you call them,' Woodward advanced. 'If you discover Chalke is truly corrupted, you can turn that to your advantage. I have done much the same in my career. By the laying of false trails and by sharing fabricated information via your newly found traitor, you'll be able to deceive the French. It will become a game – albeit a deadly one.'

Hope frowned. 'I repeat: what we do with any information or evidence you provide will be for me and others to decide.' Hope laid his hands flat on the table with an air of finality. 'I will not comment further. If I share too much information now, you may let it slip inadvertently and sink our enterprise, so by keeping my own counsel on the affair, I am, in effect, protecting you both. It is best to keep our lines straight and simple. You both have legitimate tasks to accomplish in Siam. You should focus on performing them to the best of your abilities. Of course, the secret task I have given you is of the utmost importance to us; you must never forget it. It is your primary purpose. But by doing your legitimate duty, you will find that doors will open naturally for you, people will enter, friendships will be made, and you will learn much to our advantage. The courtroom trial will take up most of your time, naturally, Mr Gough, so go to it with a will. Do not shirk to help the authorities all you can. Help them to make their case. Show them how British justice works. And you, sir,' Hope turned his face towards Albert Woodward, 'will have your hands full with the native revenue authorities. Do your level best to assist them. Help them to solve their problems, engage with them, get them to like you. This is the way to learn much.'

Hope slid his hands sideways across the smooth table and tapped his long fingers once more onto the polished wood. 'In regard to your confidential assignment, gentlemen, keep it close. Only one person in Siam will know of your hidden agenda – Beaumont, the consul general. He is the only man I will inform of your mission, and he will be instructed to speak to nobody of it. He is an upstanding man. I know him personally, a fellow Wykehamist, and he can be trusted. But even he does not know the full picture. He's only aware of the aspects he has to know to allow our little business to run smoothly. That's the only way to conduct such an enterprise. So, you see, my friends, you are not alone in being kept in the dark on certain matters. If you must speak of it to one another, perhaps to share information and ideas or make plans, only do so when you three are utterly alone and cannot be overheard. The French have spies everywhere – including amongst our own ranks, it now appears, so you must at all times be vigilant. Is that clear, gentlemen?'

Henry and Albert nodded solemnly.

'If we have news to impart, how shall we share it with you?' Henry asked after a short pause.

'Speak to Beaumont. He can arrange it. I suggest you find a way to update him privately when the need arises. A missive dropped in a hidden place known only to you three would be my suggestion. If either of you have something for him to collect, you can use a pre-arranged signal – an unusual word or phrase, perhaps, used in casual conversation, that will alert him.'

'I am very familiar with these methods,' Albert growled. 'Why, we used a cavity behind a brick under Blackfriars Bridge to communicate with one another in the affair of that Russian assassin, Dimitri Mikhailov, did we not, Henry?'

Hope pressed on. 'Beaumont has confidential means by which he can communicate directly and independently with us here in London. Likewise, if I have news for you, I will pass it, and he will share it. Trust me, gentlemen, you will hear from me if there is anything you truly need to know.'

'There is one thing...' Henry advanced. 'You talk of laying a trap for Mr Chalke. Can you enlighten us further? Do you have something in mind?'

'I certainly do, Mr Gough. It's a little stratagem that may settle the matter. A simple sleight of hand that may draw our man out and allow us to see his true colours. In short, sir, I wish you to deliver him a letter.'

'A letter?'

'Yes, gentlemen, one that I have written, but it will not be my letter...'

Albert let out a sigh and shuffled in his chair. He planted both elbows, with a noticeable thump, onto the grand table, and opening his hands, he frowned at Hope. 'You talk in riddles, sir. Pray, speak plainly.'

'Very well, my friends. I will give your story – the story you shall impart to Chalke the minute you both clap eyes on him, the minute he shakes your hands for the first time on the steamy quayside in distant Bangkok.' Hope rose from his seat and resumed his pacing around the room. Henry and Albert fixed their eyes on him as he took each deliberate step on the patterned Persian carpet beneath his polished shoes, backwards and forwards, almost silently, both hands clasped at his back, chin thrust into the air. Only Lappin seemed unmoved, buried as he was in his pen and notebook. *He must have seen this routine many times before – of that there must be little doubt*, thought Henry.

'On your arrival in Singapore,' Hope announced, 'five weeks into your long journey to Bangkok, you will see, from the deck of your P&O steamer, two Royal Navy "flat-iron" gunboats patrolling outside the harbour. Lappin will give you photographs of the vessels in question so you will be able to describe them. The vessels are the latest the Royal Navy has to offer, and each possesses the most marvellous firepower. Am I clear so far, gentlemen?'

'Yes, all is clear,' Albert said for both of them. 'But why should we need the benefit of Mr Lappin's photographs if we are to see these gunboats in the flesh – so to speak?'

'Because, sir, you will not actually see them! Your report will be fabricated – it will be false. You see, the gunboats will not be there. But you shall report the sighting to Horatio Chalke all the same – casually, of course, as if it were just a trivial but exhilarating piece of gossip. You will say you glimpsed the two warships on the morning of your arrival in Singapore as they slipped past your own steamer, in line astern, heading north, in the opposite direction to your own. It was early – just before sunrise – but you got a pretty good view; you spotted the British ensign and all that, and you'll exclaim what a marvellous sight they were. To add colour and context, you might say you were enjoying your morning constitutional at the time, perhaps…' Hope turned and made a strange face, as if to say *"you can give whatever story you like"*.

He pressed on. 'Naturally, you will pass the excited word to your fellow P&O passengers, telling them how enthralled you were to encounter such British power at close quarters, albeit briefly, as the vessels had soon disappeared into the early morning gloom, almost as soon as they had heaved into view. My bet is the word will spread like wildfire, and suddenly other passengers will be unable to resist speaking of seeing the vessels themselves – such is the need to crow about such things amongst some of our fellow men. In short, the sighting will quickly become a fact. Next, you will comment to Chalke, light-heartedly and carelessly, of course, on the number of cheerful Jolly Jack Tars you encountered around the docks and in the local harbourside inns and hostelries. Again, Lappin will provide some images of suitable naval uniforms and the like, to allow you to better communicate your observations.'

'And then? How do you expect Chalke to react?'

'With mild interest, I suspect,' Hope replied slowly. 'He won't want to appear over-inquisitive, but the more questions he asks you the greater I shall like it. You see, the presence of two Royal Navy gunboats so close to Bangkok will rouse him, especially if he has received no prior telegrams on the subject. By this, you will be laying the ground for the letter.'

'The letter you wrote, which is not yours, Hope?' Albert advanced.

'Precisely.' Hope moved towards the desk and opened the top drawer. 'This letter. I have not sealed it because I wanted you to see its contents before you deliver it.' Hope handed it to Henry Gough, who hesitated for a moment. 'Open it. Read it aloud, if you can.' Hope was grinning all of a sudden.

Henry examined the white envelope which had been already addressed, but he could make nothing of it. The script was foreign. There were no letters or words, just a series of neat symbols drawn in blocks with a bright-blue ink – as if it were a form of eccentric calligraphy. At first glance, the contents gave him no clues either. They were written in the same hand. There was just a single sheet formed of about a dozen lines, each composed of about fifteen individual blocks of symbols, each of different lengths. He gave a blank look to Hope and passed the papers to Albert for his inspection. 'I can't make head nor tail of it.' He shrugged.

'I expect better of you than that, sir! Are you not the man who cracked the code that led us to Mikhailov? Come, look more closely. What do you make of it, Woodward? Do you see any clues yet?'

Albert balanced a pair of reading glasses on his bulbous nose and frowned. 'It looks Chinese to me. Oh!' he added suddenly. 'It must be Siamese. Am I correct?'

'For the most part – but if you are to succeed in this game, you must both learn to apply more scrutiny to each task. Look again. Take nothing for granted.'

Albert ran his finger down the line of characters and after a few seconds, he exclaimed, 'Why, I think I have it! The words "HMS *Foxhound*" are hidden amongst all the other symbols.'

'Not hidden, sir. Why, they are in plain sight!'

'I see it now, and the letter is signed "Jim" – this looks to have been written by a different hand,' Albert said, handing the letter and envelope back to Henry. 'But I fear, sir, you will have to explain further.'

'With pleasure. I arranged for one of my oriental translators to prepare it on my instructions – in the utmost secrecy, you understand. No one else knows of it. The missive purports to be a letter from a lonely English Jack Tar, whose name we have given as "Jim". He writes to "Kop", his fictional Siamese sweetheart, a young lady he first encountered during his ship's visit to Bangkok in '79. My translator came up with the name "Kop", which apparently is a common name in those parts. More to the point, if pronounced correctly, I'm told it means "frog" in Siamese, which we both thought was appropriate, under the circumstances.' A conspiratorial grin widened Hope's face. 'I should add that HMS *Foxhound* was indeed in Bangkok last year. She was anchored opposite the golden pagodas of the Royal Palace, no less. At this very time last year, too, during the dreadful Fanny Knox affair. The ship's visit will be acutely familiar to Chalke as it was the subject of such a hullabaloo.'

'And the rest of the letter... What else does this sailor, Jim, write to Kop?' Henry asked, his eyes now full of intrigue.

'To paraphrase our little communiqué,' Hope replied instantly, 'it records the fact that our lovestruck matelot is missing his Kop more than he can stand, and offers up both joyful and distressing intelligence. It reports that Jim has received a gashed and bloodied leg, which he incurred in a fall onto the quayside while painting the hull of his ship – the aforementioned HMS *Foxhound*. The Navy, he tells his beloved Kop, has decided to leave him in Singapore, to allow his wounds to heal, while his warship undergoes gunnery trials at sea, off Georgetown, over the next few weeks. The brighter news soon follows, however! You see, Jim reports that his captain has undertaken to return to collect him once the ship's cannons have been aired, and before the *Foxhound* finally heads north to its next port of call.' Hope paused and wiped his brow with a blue silk handkerchief.

'I presume you mean Bangkok will be its following destination,' Henry intervened.

'Precisely! And our letter informs young Kop that the vessel and crew of *Foxhound* have been readied for a lengthy run ashore in Bangkok on this forthcoming visit. Our lusty Jim adds that a reunion with his sweetheart will not be far distant, and she must wait for him just a short while longer.

He urges her to check for his arrival outside the bowling alley at the Falcks Hotel at six o'clock each evening, after two weeks have passed from the date of receiving his missive, and for every day thereafter, until the happy moment of their loving reunion.' Hope halted and looked at the others.

Albert spoke first. 'And what of the captain of the *Verona*? What if Chalke asks him for corroboration of the facts? Presumably, if we have been lucky enough to see the gunboats, so will he, or at least the lookout on his steamer.'

'You forget, sir. You will leave the *Verona* in Singapore and board another vessel for the journey to Bangkok. Chalke will not have an opportunity to question the captain personally, but in any case, I have thought of every eventuality and the answer is simple. The P&O captain of the SS *Verona* on this voyage is well known to the War Office, he being formerly a captain of Her Majesty's warship *Agincourt*. Captain Lancelot Canavan will confirm your story, should anyone ask. He is a man of upmost good standing and can be trusted. But you must never speak to him of your part in this. He knows nothing of your mission or the greater picture. His mandate is merely to perform this simple task for us. If he is asked by others to confirm the sighting of warships outside Singapore harbour, he will. If he is not approached by anyone for corroboration, he will remain silent on the matter. That is all he or you need to know.'

'You seem to have thought of all possibilities, Hope. My congratulations. The plan has merit,' Albert Woodward said. 'But what then? What is the next step?'

'That is a matter for us to decide. We shall take small steps at the outset. You will both go about your lawful duties. You in the law courts, Mr Gough; you, Woodward, in the midst of the royal court and amongst the Siamese revenue department's highest civil servants. Horatio Chalke shall be your interlocutor at all times. You shall see him daily. Keep your eyes open and listen carefully to everything you hear. You may ask questions too, but beware your enquiries are not transparently inquisitive. That way you may learn much. Keep your own counsel, save to Beaumont. If you have anything to impart, speak with him. If I have a message for you, he will seek you out. If any news contained in sailor Jim's message to Kop appears in France, we shall hear of it, and so shall you.'

'I take it you have infiltrated a man into Paris?' Woodward smirked knowingly as he sucked on his dry pipe.

'You should know better than to ask that question, sir.' Hope did not return the smile. 'Suffice to say, if the false news contained in this letter reaches our ears in Paris, rest assured, we shall have trapped our traitor. And you will know the instant we hear of it,' he concluded with an air of assured finality.

'Will we see you again before we depart?' Henry asked lightly, sensing the mood had changed for the worse.

'I very much doubt it. The day before you sail, I must ask that you return here. Lappin will give you the letter for Miss Kop. He will also issue you each with a Bull Dog revolver for your protection, in case the need arises – which I very much doubt,' he added carelessly, 'and a dozen rounds of light ammunition. Lappin will demonstrate the pistol's operation, if you require any instruction. In addition, you will both be given a silken pouch containing no less than a dozen fine Siamese rubies, each of a single carat. They are as good as currency in those parts, I'm told. I recommend you conceal them well. They are for use when and if you need them – but only in a crisis. I must insist on this. They are not to exhaust on mere creature comforts and must be either restored or accounted for on your return.'

'I'm sure we both understand,' Henry offered.

'Then, if there is nothing else, I bid you both farewell and Godspeed. I leave you with these final words. Your country will not forget this duty that you perform. I make no apologies if this enterprise puts you in personal danger, but I assure you we have tried our level best to find other ways to skin this cat, and there are none as suitable as this. By the very nature of your unambiguous and laudable assignments, coupled to your humble backgrounds – if I may be so bold –' he added quickly, while tilting his head strangely to one side, 'you will not be suspected as clandestine envoys of the Crown. These are your greatest assets – they will give you the essential cover to allow you to triumph in your task. Play up to them, but tell no one. I have every confidence that you have the skill and panache to succeed, and should your Webley pistols falter when the need arises, I'm certain that God himself will protect you, as it is truly God's work you will be performing on behalf of Her Most Gracious Majesty. Now gentlemen, you have no time to lose. Your ship sails in less than five days. Speak to Hurdus, prepare well and make sure you arrive in Southampton in good time. But tell *no one* – and trust not a soul!'

This final speech took Albert and Henry rather by surprise. Slightly stunned by its eloquence and passion, and now in the full knowledge of the awesome undertaking ahead of them, there seemed nothing else to say in response. Instead, they bowed their heads respectfully, shook Hope's hand, and almost noiselessly, slipped out of the room.

Chapter Six

Charles Hurdus proved to be a mine of information. When not in the suffocating presence of Nathaniel Hope, he proved to be a changed man. The transformation in his demeanour was startling. Gone was the submissive personality he'd displayed while in the great man's presence. Alone with Albert and Henry, he offered up an easy charm, a talkative disposition, and a surprising sense of humour.

A visit to Galt & Gieves was identified as top priority, and at three pm the same day, he accompanied Henry and Albert to the bespoke tailor's elegant premises in Savile Row. Here, they each had a fitting for tropical suits, shirts and assorted lightweight undergarments. Hurdus was remeasured, having complained that his existing suits felt tighter than when he had first purchased them five years previously, and after the bespectacled and sycophantic Angus Sutherland, the master tailor, had tutted amiably about his old customer's expanding waistline, it was agreed that suitable replacements would have to be custom-made. Sutherland's genial smile vanished when he was advised of the tight deadline, however. He visibly blanched on the news that he had a mere four days to prepare the garments, turning a ragged ribbon of tape measure nervously through his fingers.

'I may have to outsource some of the work, sir,' he complained, shaking his threadbare skull.

But then Hurdus had smilingly reminded the aged seamster of his firm's long service to Her Majesty's Government and the importance his office held in continuing that relationship. Only then had Sutherland given his sullen pledge that three loaded portmanteaux, containing new suits, including formal dinner attire and various shirts, for both his existing and two new clients, would be delivered to P&O in time to catch the sailing of the *Verona*.

'We'll have you both speaking Siamese in no time!' Hurdus announced with a broad grin as he shook Henry's hand on the corner of Regent Street. 'I have to hurry back to the War Office now, but please visit me if you need any more assistance before we sail. I am at your service, gentlemen. In addition to our language lessons, there will be ample time on the voyage for me to introduce you to the peculiar but enchanting ways of the Siamese too.'

'I take it from Hope's remarks that you have spent considerable time in Siam,' Henry declared.

'I have indeed. Too long, some say, but I pay them no attention. I have a Siamese wife and three children waiting on my return. The history of that country is both fierce and bloody, but I'll vouch you will find it heart-warming too. If you have a will to learn, you will be fascinated by the experience you are about to undergo. You may not be surprised to know that I have a deep affection for the people who you will shortly encounter, and I am confident you will be arrested by their charm in due course, as well. But before I depart, I have a gift for you both.'

'You have done enough for us today, Hurdus. Surely there is no need for a gift,' Henry replied with a hint of awkwardness.

'Charles, my dear chap… pray, call me Charles. We are friends now and soon to be shipmates. And to put your mind at rest, your gift is not of the material kind. *Laan gon!*' he announced with lifted eyebrows. 'There, I have given you your first lesson in Siamese!' The others looked blankly back at him. 'It means "goodbye". *Laan gon!*'

And with that, Charles Hurdus turned on his heels and marched off briskly in the direction of Leicester Square.

～:～

By mid-afternoon, five days later, Henry and Albert found themselves alongside the pier in Southampton, gazing at the long and elegant lines of the P&O steamship *Verona*. The train journey to the south coast had passed quickly and without incident. Henry had always been thrilled by railway engines; as a boy, he'd loved to watch the steam locomotives blasting their way in and out of Euston. So, the journey to meet the ship had been almost as eagerly anticipated as the looming and lengthy voyage to the Orient itself, so much so that Caroline was forced to speak abruptly to him after dinner one evening.

'Henry, when will you ever cease your talk of locomotives and steam engines?' she'd scolded him while she sided the table. 'Part of me wishes I could actually advance the day you depart for Siam. Why, you speak of nothing else! At least I will have some peace from it while you are gone…'

Henry's response had been both contrite and affectionate. 'My darling, you are right to tease me. I am such a nincompoop. You know I love you more than life itself. My jabbering is just the ramblings of a man attempting to hide the truth of the affair, as in two short days we shall be apart for longer than I care to imagine.'

Caroline replied softly, 'You must do your duty, my love. There is no escaping it, and you will do it with grace. When you return, which I fully expect you will, both strong in mind and limb, I know you will bring honour on our family and to the name Gough. I shall keep a place by the fire for you. The flames will not go out while you are absent, either in the hearth or inside my heart. When you return, our reunion will be joyous, but until then, pray, no more mention of the London and South Western Railways!'

Henry's work as a hansom cab driver had given him countless opportunities to penetrate parts of the great city which would have been almost foreign to most folk – alien districts where most never ventured. London was drawn out in his head like an exquisite map. Its thoroughfares were the arteries from which a multitude of veins and tiny blood vessels ran. He knew all its crevices and crannies, and sometimes he felt he knew its secrets too. On his rounds, he'd collected more fare-paying passengers from the city's giant railway termini than he cared to remember. Waterloo, nevertheless, was rather less well known to him, being south of the river, but he was still confident, as he travelled through the station's blackened arches, that he'd attended its fogged-up platforms more times than the majority of the folk who dwelt in the ancient capital.

Earlier that day, Henry had said his fond farewells to Caroline and the children. Caroline had put on the bravest of faces, so much so that her lack of tears made Henry feel all the more forlorn as the two disengaged hands and he mounted the hansom. Hawkins then took up the reins and clipped out of the yard to start the two-mile journey to Waterloo. But en route, Henry's desolation gradually passed as his mood lightened, and the prospect of his new adventure took its place in the front of his mind.

On arrival at the terminus, he met Albert and Charles inside the waiting room at platform four where, together, they drank cups of sweet tea while their not insubstantial baggage was being loaded onto the boat train by a pair of brawny station porters. Galt & Gieves had been as good as their word, and three individually labelled cases had arrived as promised. The train departed exactly on time, and it was not long before Charles Hurdus had started the first of many jovial and reassuring stories of his many years in Siam, while admitting he was looking forward to his return to the tropics more than he could describe. After passing through Basingstoke, they had sat together in the restaurant car, around a white damask tablecloth, and dined on dishes of cold chicken, fresh fruit, and *pâté-de-foie-gras* pie, all washed down with chilled glasses of the most delicious Moselle Henry had ever tasted.

Minutes after arriving in Southampton, the Peninsular and Orient Shipping and Navigation Company's vessel SS *Verona* lay before them, and very grand indeed did she appear as our trio mounted the gangplank. On deck, they were greeted by liveried crewmembers who took them to their respective cabins, thus adding to the other one hundred and two first-class passengers on board, most of whom were destined for Bombay. The *Verona* was a three-masted steamer, with a smoking funnel situated just forward of amidships. Almost new, she'd started life in the shipyards of Greenock and had entered service the previous year. At nearly four hundred feet in length, she presented quite an amazing sight.

'Ha, she is indeed a fine vessel,' Charles Hurdus remarked on witnessing the astounded appearance on the faces of his two new friends. 'This will be my second trip on her. I was fortunate to be on board when I last returned to England, back in February. I think you will find her most comfortable.'

'I confess, I have never been to sea,' Henry offered in a rather low voice.

'Nor I, save for the odd colliery vessel in St David's Bay,' Albert advanced. 'But I expect I shall get used to it. Needs must, I suppose,' he added rather sullenly. 'Plenty of time for that...'

'The ship will cross the oceans in no time, and I vouch you shall not be bored on the voyage, gentlemen. There is much to learn, I assure you. My Siamese lessons will keep you amused, I'll wager. By the time we approach the king's palace, I will have you speaking with confidence – after a fashion, I'll grant – but enough to have the rudiments and to enable you to converse with the natives in their own tongue.'

Henry had never occupied such sumptuous surroundings in his entire life. The first-class cabin he had been assigned had a porthole view amidships, over the starboard side, and was more spacious than his mews bedroom in Marylebone. Cottons and fine silks abounded, and it occurred to Henry, whimsically it must be said, that he had not encountered as much polished wood since leaving the office of Nathaniel Hope.

Charles Hurdus was as good as his word and proved to be a first-rate mentor. By the time the *Verona* first sighted the towering Rock of Gibraltar, as it transited into the Mediterranean Sea, Henry found he had at least two hundred words of Siamese consigned to his memory and sufficient grammar to allow a short sentence to be formed. Siamese script was becoming more familiar too, and the realisation he could read a little made him swell with pride. Henry's schooling as a child had been sadly lacking. Orphaned at just five years old, the struggle to survive had been the only imperative; his upbringing had been a relentless period in search of the more immediate needs of food and warmth. But soon after the first bristles had appeared on his chin, the appetite to learn had taken hold, and when eventually given the chance, he flourished. At eighteen, he'd taught himself to read and work with numbers, to a passable level. By the time he was thirty, he could recite the poems of William Wordsworth and lines from the books of Thackeray. The works of Charles Dickens had become a particular joy to him. His favourite characters by far were Oliver Twist and Philip Pirrip – such were the parallels to his own humble childhood. These days, after a hard day's grind amongst the city's crowded boulevards, Henry would often be found in silent engrossment, cradling a novel by the fire.

Albert Woodward, on the other hand, had received a proper education in the Welsh valleys. But the one-time scholar, perhaps due to his more advanced age, had proved to be a slow learner who struggled to absorb Hurdus' teachings. The writing of Siamese was especially frustrating for him. Albert's progress was painful to witness at times, and it was not long before Henry's abilities far surpassed those of the distinguished Excise officer. As a teacher, Charles was a hard but genial taskmaster. From time to time, much to the others' great pleasure, Hurdus lifted the monotony by giving short discourses on the history of Siam and offering up personal anecdotes, often hilarious, sometimes raucous, of his past times spent in Her Majesty's colonial service. There seemed to be an endless supply of such material, born from his over twenty years in the Orient. Each day, the trio commenced their lessons after breakfast, sharp at nine o'clock, in a private corner of the salon and continued to eleven. After a leisurely lunch, they resumed for another two hours until four pm, taking tea as they worked.

Three days after the *Verona* had berthed for reprovisioning in Gibraltar and they'd left the lofty crags of the mighty rock in their wake, the coastline of France appeared once more over the port bow, as the ancient harbour of Marseilles hove into view. Captain Canavan had announced at dinner the previous evening, in typically punctilious style, that the ship would be picking up passengers there. All on board were welcome to leave the ship for a few hours to experience what the city had to offer. Captain Lancelot Canavan was the antithesis of how most in society might imagine a seafaring man of long service to be. There was no greying beard, no voluminous moustache or expanding midriff, and in the complete absence of a booming voice or ebullient demeanour, Canavan's appearance and manner were, in every way, contrary to type. An austere, gaunt, meticulous man of late middle age, possessed of penetrating navy-blue eyes and stiff military bearing, he was a few inches shorter than average height. His sharp frame and angular limbs fitted so crisply into his company uniform of blue and gold one might have considered he had been born with it already attached. A man of scarce words and fewer smiles, it was clear to all those who encountered him that this was an officer in complete command of his nautical surroundings – a scrupulous man who could be relied on in a crisis.

'For how long will we be alongside in Marseilles?' Henry had ventured in reply to the captain's announcement.

'Five hours. If you decide to go ashore, you must return to the ship by six pm. If you do not, we will depart without you,' came the uncompromising reply. 'Personally, I would not bother. It is a port like any other. A lot of stinking fish and dissolute citizens whose tongue I have never fathomed.' With that, he patted his upper lip with a napkin, stood from the table, and bowing slightly, took his leave.

But as they approached the quay, Marseilles looked to be much more exciting than Canavan's rather cheerless description. Henry relished the opportunity to take a look at the city, and after some gentle persuasion, he convinced Albert to join him. On hearing they would be venturing across the gangplank, one of the other passengers, a Mr Stanley Barraclough – a youthful-looking cotton trader from Manchester with a broad, masculine face – asked if he could accompany them. By two pm, after gaining approval from their favourite teacher to skip their afternoon lessons and following the completion of various arrival formalities on board (including presenting their papers to a young and waxed-moustachioed French official), all three found themselves standing on the harbour wall looking back at the grand steamer that had brought them there.

'A brisk walk, gentlemen, I suggest. Let's see where it takes us,' Henry announced with a bright smile.

'Not too brisk, please; a gentle stroll would suffice,' Albert returned in a tone of mock grumpiness.

As the trio navigated past a large pile of trunks and assorted luggage neatly stacked close to the gangplank, Henry noticed a line of half a dozen bystanders who appeared to be waiting to board. One of them, a noticeably sturdy man, hatless, dark-bearded, of about forty, was gesticulating wildly with brawny hands, and spitting out incomprehensible sentences to one of the company staff. The fresh-faced officer in uniform looked distinctly intimidated by the presence of his sizable interlocutor. As they crossed in front of the small queue, Henry overheard the young officer say to the agitated gentleman, 'I will do my level best, sir, but for now, I would ask you to step aside and allow the other passengers to board.'

'Eee ave to goo,' the troubled man kept repeating in further volleys of Gallic-accented English.

As Henry and the others rounded a mountain of fish barrels on the wharf, they looked over their shoulders to see that the confrontation by the gangplank showed no signs of abating.

'A man in a rage, I'd say,' said the cotton trader from Salford. 'I've heard these Froggies can put on quite a display when they want their way. I don't know why the poor officer didn't deliver a sharp jab to old Frenchie's jaw. I'd have done so. I can't abide all that shouting and hollering, it fair upsets me. That's no way to speak to an Englishman.'

The sortie onto the streets of Marseilles was a revelation and a most enjoyable excursion. All three commented on how different it was from anything they had ever seen in their home country. Stanley Barraclough proved to be an amiable, if rather talkative, companion, and in the more than three hours they shared alone, Henry learned a lot about the cotton industry of Lancashire. In truth, he had wished it had not been so, for he'd been immediately captivated by the local architecture and would have preferred to have explored the town without a running commentary on looms and the misfortunes of Mancunian millworkers. But he allowed Barraclough his voice, and the three Britons wandered happily under the red-tiled rooves of the old city in pleasant, if at times one-sided, discourse.

The recently constructed Basilique Notre-Dame de la Garde was particularly impressive. Its dark marble arches and gilded mosaics were lavish in the extreme and from its lofty parapets, marvellous views of the rust-coloured city were spread beneath them. At some distance, they could spy the *Verona*, tied up and silent, its graceful stern proudly facing the harbour wall, amongst a line of other visiting shipping which Henry supposed were far less pleasing to the eye. Much to his surprise, Albert had not complained once during the near five-hundred-foot climb to the mount on which the magnificent cathedral sat. As the towering basilica bell tolled four o'clock, and the heat of the day had begun to subside, Albert announced it was time for all to return to the ship. By five-thirty pm they were safely back and Henry for one, was lounging on his bunk, shoes discarded, with a copy of *The Woman in White* in his hands, when there was a sharp knock on his cabin door. It was Albert.

'Come in, dear friend. I trust you are none the worse for our little jaunt this afternoon.'

'A little foot-sore perhaps, but nothing more,' Albert replied, absently rubbing his knee. 'But I have not come to speak of my aching bones, Henry. I feel we should make ourselves better known to the captain. I have a mind to bring him into our confidence a little.'

'But you know Hope spoke to us about such things. He was against us talking to anyone. Do you have any reason to go against his instructions?'

Albert looked hesitant – a little anxious even. 'You see, Hope never instructed us how to communicate with him during our long voyage. Maybe this was an omission on his part. Of course, Beaumont will fulfil this role on our arrival in Bangkok, but what if there is something to impart during our travels? The captain seems a fair man, a little brusque perhaps, but if he can be trusted by Hope to lie for us about the non-existent gunboats we are shortly to "encounter", then it seems to me we might draw a little closer to him. I have a further reason too...' Albert paused and appeared diffident once more. 'I should like to send a confidential telegram to Hope, and I believe the captain has the means to do this while we are in port. You see, I have learned of something which might be of interest to Hope – it's probably nothing of importance, in truth, but I should like to seek his opinion, and that of Captain Canavan too, as he may be able to cast some light on the matter also. If, in due course, the captain agrees to send a telegram, at least it will demonstrate how we might communicate should something of real urgency arise.'

Just then, there was a loud rap on the cabin door which made them both start. A shout of 'all aboard – we are about to depart,' soon followed. The voice of the steward trailed away along the narrow passageway as the sound of his knocking diminished with distance.

'A confidential telegram? Intriguing!' Henry patted Albert on the shoulder and with a curious smile added, 'It seems we are about to shove off, so if you wish the captain to oblige us, I suggest it may have to wait until we reach Valletta. Perhaps we can discuss this after dinner. But for now, join me on deck. I should like to see the ship embark as I expect it will be quite a sight. The harbour is in such a bustle and full of wonders to behold.' Henry threw on his shoes and top coat. 'Come quickly, Albert, I can feel the ship shudder. I promise we shall talk of this after we have eaten. We can return to your cabin, where we will have privacy and you can tell me your story…'

Chapter Seven

Dinner on board the *Verona*, especially in first class, was always something to look forward to, and on this, their first night since loading fresh provisions in Marseilles, the head chef was able to create a menu of true delight. Henry, Albert, and Charles usually shared the same table with five other passengers, all of whom had proved to be excellent company on the voyage thus far, perhaps with the exception of Miss Dorothea Skinner, a young schoolmistress from Cheltenham Ladies' College who suffered terribly with seasickness and was often too indisposed to join the others in the dining salon, preferring to take her meals in the privacy of her own cabin. With the coast of France almost still in sight, they dined on fresh oysters, poached eggs in clear chicken soup, roast beef and asparagus, vol-au-vents laced with bechamel sauce, and a juicy cherry flan. The selection of French cheeses was unlike anything Henry had ever seen or tasted. Cases of the most excellent claret had been shipped aboard, and the port was as superb as ever. By ten o'clock, as he rose from the table, Henry sensed he was not only replete but also as mellow as he had probably ever been. He thought of Caroline and a slight feeling of melancholy overtook him. How he wished she could share his bed that night.

As some of the others retired to play cards, Albert approached him and said in a low Welsh whisper, 'Don't forget. We have certain matters to discuss...'

'Of course. Please allow me ten minutes. It is a lovely clear night and I should like to promenade on deck a while for a smoke. It will help me digest all that delectable food. Goodness, the beef was better that I have ever tasted in England!'

'I shall not join you, Henry. My limbs are still stinging from our tramp to the basilica. I'll await your presence in my cabin. Pray don't dally. I have a mind to sleep well tonight.'

A pleasant and warming sea breeze greeted Henry as he arrived on deck. Gazing at the stars, which were as brilliant as he could ever remember, he started to stroll aft along the port side of the ship towards the mizzen-mast, where he knew he could find a place to smoke in peace. But suddenly, he found that his ability to stare at the constellations while simultaneously walking in a straight line had become peculiarly impaired. As the vessel rolled and pitched slightly, he was thrown off balance and had to seek the support of the rail to keep him from tumbling onto the wooden deck. It never occurred to him that he had drunk more in the last hour than was good for his constitution. Instead, he blamed the *Verona* for his unsteadiness.

'Damn ship,' he muttered as he regained his stance.

The evening was indeed crystal clear. When he arrived at his favourite spot at the taffrail, above the giant rudder and churning black sea, he looked upwards again and wondered at the multitude of bright points that appeared to hang, like glittering ornaments, above him. Standing alone, it felt as if the sky had been created just for him. How spectacular it all was; how marvellous he felt at that moment. He knew little of astronomy, but enough to recognise Venus when he saw it. There it was! – glorious and brilliant, dipping purposefully towards the western night. He wondered what Caroline was doing at this hour. Asleep, no doubt, he mused. Alone in the bed they shared, or maybe one of the infants had joined her for succour. He sighed gently and reached into his pocket for his pipe.

As he put the stem to his mouth, he imagined he heard a disturbance coming from behind him – a movement of boots on the teak decking, perhaps. He turned his head slowly, fully expecting to see an impatient and irascible Albert, who, having decided he could wait no longer for their much-anticipated conversation about telegrams and the like, had sought him out. But no, this wasn't Albert… A much bigger man loomed out of the darkness, now moving almost silently towards him. Then, Henry recognised the figure. The advancing shape, stark black against one of the ship's lamps, revealed a heavy beard sprouting from the head. In an instant, Henry knew who it was – none other than the strong-looking, argumentative French fellow from the dock – the man who had argued so passionately in broken English with the company officer at the gangplank.

Henry removed the pipe from his lips and lifted his hand in a gesture of greeting to the approaching figure. '*Bon soir*, sir. 'Tis a very pleasant evening, I'm sure you agree—'

Quite what happened next Henry could not fully remember. Suffice to say, seconds later, he found himself staring, face down, at the hard-scrubbed planks of the *Verona's* deck, his solar plexus smarting, breathless and winded. Whether he had been dealt a blow to bring him down he could not be sure, but as he struggled to regain his composure, he felt his whole body being physically lifted into the air, and as the view of the deck receded, so an expanse of black ocean greeted his eyes. The stern taffrail was less than four feet high, but now he felt its hardwood edges pressing sharply against his hip. He tried to fight back; he flailed his arms, but his feet were off the deck and he could get no purchase.

'Whoa!' Henry screamed as hard as his exhausted lungs would allow. The assailant's heavy beard now came into horrible scratching contact with his face and Henry could smell the reeking sweat of his adversary. The Frenchman towered over him, heaving, pushing, straining for all he was worth, now panting heavily in his efforts to lift Henry higher still. It was clear his purpose was to tip his quarry over the side and into the foaming Mediterranean Sea forty feet below. Soon, the sheer brute strength of the monster was becoming impossible to resist. Henry yelled at his attacker once more, but the effect seemed only to increase the force pressing onto his throbbing body. He managed, somehow, to grab the taffrail with one hand, and this appeared to stem the advance for a few seconds. At one point, Henry felt he had even pushed the brute backwards slightly, but soon his fingers began to sting and slip against the railings as his head and shoulders were pressed ever further backwards. The sheer fury of the Frenchman was approaching irresistible, and Henry, now balancing precariously halfway over the side, knew it was only a matter of seconds before he lost his grip and tumbled into the watery abyss.

As his resolve to resist reached its lowest ebb, there was a loud thump that seemed to come from above. At first, Henry thought it must be a roll of thunder. It's strange indeed how a man's head works in a crisis, for despite all his peril, Henry's mind coolly reminded him that the night was flawless, so the dull sound he'd heard could not possibly have come from the heavens. As he juggled with the weirdly convoluted messages his brain was sending him, he suddenly felt the pressure on his frame had miraculously been released. In an instant, the grip had been freed and he could see the sky clearly once more. He took in a lungful of precious air and did his best to stand again, but his left foot was caught between the rail posts. He felt a sharp pain in his ankle as his body twisted sideways and he toppled head first, only to find himself staring into the grains of the wooden decking for the second time that evening. When Henry finally looked up, he saw, to his relief, that his adversary was now lying on the deck beside him, apparently stricken by a blow. Then, much to Henry's surprise and great joy, he recognised Charles Hurdus standing astride the fallen Frenchman, a wooden oar wielded in both hands.

'My God, Charles! You have saved me from this wretched beast,' Henry cried as he scrambled to his feet. 'I thought I was about to meet my maker.'

'I once rowed for Cambridge, you know,' Charles replied with a note of triumph in his voice, 'and played a spot of cricket too! One swipe from this and I've knocked the blighter for six. I'll vouch I caught him full square on the side of his head.'

Henry exclaimed, 'But look, he's beginning to move once more!'

The bulky Frenchman had indeed started to recover his composure and was making an effort to stand. He grunted loudly as he managed to get on one knee, with both hands on the deck. He gazed up at the two Englishmen, and with a calculating and chilling smile, he commenced to pull himself up.

'Hit him again, I pray,' Henry cried. 'Put him down. If you don't, we'll be the worse for it. The fellow has such strength!'

Charles needed no further entreaty. He withdrew the oar to high above his head, and like an axe, brought it slicing down towards the half-prone figure. The Frenchman raised a hand in self-defence and with an extraordinary feat of strength and dexterity, he managed to grasp the plummeting wooden club before it could reach its target. Charles made a frantic effort to pull the oar from the Frenchman's clutches, but to no avail. The oar was ripped out of his hands with ease, and within a few short seconds, the tables had been turned. It was now the assailant who possessed the bludgeon, and he took no time before advancing towards them. Then, just yards away and holding the oar like a pike, he made a headlong charge at them. Henry and Charles retreated, stumbling backwards desperately, but the pair soon encountered the taffrail at their backs. There was nowhere to go, save the sea itself, as the French bull gained speed towards them. A second later, he was on them. Instinctively perhaps, Henry and Charles ducked in unison, and in the same movement, they parted sideways. The Frenchman's rushing "lance" slid harmlessly between the two of them, it's carrier soon crashing into the rail and releasing the oar as his midriff hit the barricade. The oar flew into the darkness like a lost arrow soaring over a clifftop and disappeared into the night.

Henry seized his chance. With his attacker now reeling and off balance, and with his back to him, Henry got under the man's knees and pushed for all he was worth, hoping the force would shift the mass sufficiently to consign the villain to the deep. Charles soon picked himself up also, and quickly realising what Henry was attempting, he added his own weight to the other leg, and between them they managed to lift the giant off the deck. The Frenchman must have been six foot three inches, at least, and probably weighed in at eighteen stone. But the strength of two grown men will always eclipse a single combatant in a hand-to-hand struggle, and it was not long before the balance had indeed begun to shift. With the weights starting to tip in their favour, and the Frenchman's massive thighs six inches above the height of the rail, gravity was beginning to assist the couple to push the bull over the parapet. One last agonised grasp at the rail, a slither of fingers followed by a muffled groan, saw the end of the matter, and the dreadful sight of a human being cartwheeling downwards into oblivion was something neither Henry nor Charles would ever forget. There was not even the sound of a splash as the body hit the water. It was as if their adversary had disappeared into a void of blackness – a never-ending fall towards the centre of the earth.

The pair remained breathless and speechless for a while as they contemplated what they had just done. It was Charles Hurdus who spoke first.

'By all the angels, 'twas lucky I decided not to join the card group this evening in favour of a solitary smoke,' he gasped at length.

'The fact that you did not play bridge tonight saved my life, sir. I will be eternally in your debt. Charles, you are a brave man indeed to have confronted that animal single-handed. Where did you acquire the oar, may I ask? It's not a common item to carry around after dinner!' Henry tried a smile.

'It was one of many in that lifeboat.' Charles pointed towards a nearby white wooden-hulled vessel fixed to the deck. 'When I turned the corner and saw you struggling with the fellow, I grabbed what I could. It was the first thing I saw and luckily it was easy to wield.'

'A mighty shot indeed. You near flattened him with a single blow.'

A strange stillness fell on the pair, as if the full enormity of their actions had finally sunk in. Only the rumble of the engine, the vague creaking of the ship, and the fluttering of canvas disturbed the uncanny calm.

'Who was he?' Charles broke through the silence. 'I had never clapped eyes on him until just now.'

'He only boarded the ship in Marseilles today. Albert and I spotted him as we embarked on our short sightseeing trip this afternoon. But I have no idea who he was, and I can't even guess why he might have wanted to kill me. I believe him to be a Frenchman, or French-speaking at least. He appeared a most angry individual when we first encountered him. Perhaps he is merely a madman – a poor fellow who has lost his senses through drink or unrequited love. I have encountered the like before, during the many hours trotting my horse through London's crowded streets. That is all I can offer on the matter – and the fact that I have never confronted such sheer brute strength in a man in my whole life.'

'I suppose we shall have to report the matter to the captain so it can be investigated in detail. There will be a list of all passengers. We will learn much from that, I'll warrant.'

'I believe so,' Henry replied. 'There can be no way to disguise such an awful event. But if it pleases you, I should like to speak with Albert first. He wants to get to know our captain better, and I'm sure he can advise on a proper way to proceed. Will you allow me an hour?'

'Of course. What I require now, more than anything, is a tumbler of finest Scotch. Look, my hands are shaking.'

'Oh, poor fellow…' Henry patted Charles comfortingly between the shoulder blades. 'You have been a true hero this night. How can I ever repay you? I will meet you in the salon in an hour.'

⁂

When Henry had finished explaining to Albert the events of the previous twenty minutes, he was greeted with a mixture of dismay and awe, followed shortly by a curiously knowing smile.

'I knew I should have told you of my concerns when I had the chance,' he said.

'You spoke of no concerns, Albert, save your desire to test the method of communication with Hope. Some talk of a telegram you wished to send to London, and enlisting the help of Captain Canavan.'

'Ah, I chose a bad moment to raise the matter with you, you were distracted by the departure of the ship. But at least my worst fears have not been realised, although had it not been for Charles' timely intervention, I would have never forgiven myself.'

'You do not speak plainly, Albert. What was it that gave you concern?'

'Put simply, the arrival on the ship today of the man who you have just sent to the bottom of the Mediterranean Sea. I smelled something wrong – his angry mood and deportment were most unusual. Call it my revenue nose, but the circumstances around his boarding were remarkable. After we had returned from our on-shore adventures, I sought out the company officer, the one, you recall, who spoke at length to our irate visitor at the gangplank. He was most illuminating.'

'Pray go on.'

'The young officer, Bernard, is his name, a very intelligent fellow, I might add... he informed me, discreetly, you understand, that the man in question, the creature who tried to kill you, was one Monsieur Henriques D'Argent, no less. Your would-be assassin apparently presented a paper, on arrival at the ship, identifying himself as a replacement passenger for another French gentleman who had been previously booked to our next port of call, which, of course, you know is Valletta, not only the capital of Malta, but home to one of the finest harbours in the world. The other gentleman, the passenger who had stepped aside, a Monsieur Jules LeClerc, is a regular traveller on this route and known to the line, being the currently serving consul for France in Malta, with specific accreditation in Valletta.'

'Go on.'

'Well, you see, my curiosity got the better of me. I wanted to know why Monsieur D'Argent had flown into such a fit of Gallic rage. Young Bernard described how he had informed the aforesaid gentlemen that the vessel was full in first class and it was irregular for last-minute ticket changes of the type he proposed without the physical presence and consent of the correctly manifested passenger. That's what caused D'Argent to fly into a rage. He declared that he was a servant of the French state and a close associate of LeClerc who, due to ill health, could not be present. The quarrel continued for some time, but when Bernard offered to speak to Captain Canavan and seek his personal approval for the transfer of tickets, the hulk that was D'Argent seemed to take fright and then took a different tack, becoming suddenly apologetic. He asked if there were cabins available in second class which he could purchase on the spot. There was a spare cabin, close to the steerage, as it happened, and Bernard agreed to arrange a ticket there and then. That was how the matter was resolved, and that is why we did not see D'Argent at dinner tonight. If he ate at all, he must have dined in the second-class salon.'

'But what of your concerns? You said you wished to send a telegram to Hope in London.'

'Foremostly, I wanted to bring the whole matter to the captain's attention, as something rankled. I could not exactly put my finger on what worried me. My suspicions, such as they were, ill-formed and without corroboration, I freely admit, lay with the fact that a member of the French Diplomatic Service had apparently given his place to the brute you just encountered. If indeed D'Argent had been a colleague of LeClerc, I suggest he was from a very different branch of the service. The man did not look like an envoy to me; he more resembled a dock worker than a diplomat. Listen, Henry, on this assignment we have been asked to keep our ears and eyes open, especially in view of the alleged French involvement in the matter. This is why we have had to endure hours of those dismal French lessons each day from our new-found hero, Charles.'

Henry smiled and scratched his chin. 'Old Charles is indeed a dark horse. I will pay more attention during his next lessons – you have my word! But pray continue. There is more, I'll vouch...'

'I was only doing what I thought was right,' Albert continued. 'I imagined that passing the details of our new French passenger and the circumstances of his arrival to Hope would have allowed the War Office to conduct a little research – maybe there is a list of all French diplomats and secret service personnel filed in Hope's office somewhere. As to why this monster, D'Argent, wished to take your life... my only conclusion is that for some nefarious reason the French do not want you to give testimony at the Bangkok trial. Our hidden agenda is known to no one save us two, so in French eyes, your voyage is solely to attend the court case. Maybe your evidence embarrasses them somewhat; maybe they are trying to protect the accused from a guilty verdict that surely must follow if you give first-hand evidence that the man you watched shoot Prince Gagananga in cold blood is none other than the same man standing in the dock; or otherwise, of course... your evidence could even acquit the accused. Either way, don't forget your testimony is unique, Henry. You are the only man alive who saw the incident and can identify the killer. This truth has the power to have a man beheaded. Think of that. If such a verdict is unsavoury to the French, that might account for their attempts to silence you tonight.'

'If what you surmise is correct, it adds much danger to our mission. No wonder Hope issued us with pistols and rubies. I will carry my Bull Dog wherever I go from now on. I never thought to wear it tonight. Who could have imagined an attempt on my life after such a fine dinner, eh!' Henry muttered.

'You have Charles Hurdus to thank for your life. We may not be close enough to save you next time, so be cautious. Take every care. If there is one of us who is in most danger, I fear it is you, Henry. But we cannot withdraw now. We have given a solemn promise. Just remember, trust no one; if we speak, we speak alone.'

'What of Captain Canavan? Charles and I agree we must inform him of tonight's mishap.'

'I concur wholeheartedly, but I suggest, as there are no other witnesses, we describe to the captain a suicide rather than a manslaughter. It will keep things trim. The last thing we want is for difficult investigations to result. At the very least, they may delay us — worse is possible. If he asks you to file a report when we arrive in Malta, you shall, of course, cooperate, but first you and Charles must get your stories right. Do you think Charles will agree to it?'

'I do. He is as deeply shocked by this as I am. I'm sure he will understand that it's best to remain tight-lipped, at least until we reach Bangkok.'

'Good, then bring him to me. Where is he?'

'Sipping Scotch to calm his nerves.'

'Please fetch him. We shall all discuss the report you both shall give to the captain, but hurry, we cannot leave it too long. D'Argent's disappearance will be noticed soon. It's imperative you recount the matter before the news spreads around the ship. Your stories will be simple. You and Charles were enjoying a smoke under the mizzen-mast when you saw a large man jump into the sea. The captain may order a search but, given the conditions and darkness, we all know it will be futile.'

Chapter Eight

Captain Lancelot Canavan had to be roused from his sleep to hear the report of the apparent suicide of one of his passengers. He listened without any protestation, and with his customary unruffled aplomb, as Henry and Charles gave their accounts, and generously consented to permit Albert to join the group to listen also. At the conclusion, and without asking a single question, he called for the officer of the watch, James Watson, to attend his cabin. All sat in awkward silence until the officer arrived which, mercifully, took less than a minute. Watson stood to attention as the captain explained the situation. Captain Canavan gave instructions to turn the ship around and retrace its recent passage for the next two hours, in the hope of sighting the stricken passenger. He ordered lights to be shone from both sides of the hull and gave instructions that all able-bodied men should join in the search from every available lookout point.

'If there are no sightings after two hours, we shall conclude the "man overboard" measures, resume our south-easterly heading, and continue steaming to Valletta. Is that understood, Watson?'

'Aye aye, sir.'

After the officer of the watch had left the cabin, the captain turned to the others and spoke to them for the first time. 'Of course, we shall never find that man – you realise that, I take it, gentlemen. Even if it were not pitch black out there, the odds of recovering a madman bent on killing himself are practically nil.'

'It is as we feared,' Henry replied. 'The poor fellow must have had his mind unbalanced by some event or events unknown to us.'

'This sort of thing happens quite frequently, you may be surprised to know. I lost count of the number of such incidents during my service with the Royal Navy, and more recently, with P&O. More common in the Navy, I'd say, from my experience. If I have any news, you will be the first to know, gentlemen, and now if you will excuse me, I must prepare a telegram to send to the company on our arrival in Valletta, informing them of the occurrence. They will advise the French authorities as a matter of course. It's possible that they may wish to commence an investigation. The Maltese may want to ask questions also. The island may be under British rule, but I can't predict what course of action the local authorities may decide to take. If the French press for an inquiry, who knows where this might lead us.'

'May I suggest a telegram to the Foreign Office might serve also,' Albert advanced. 'You see, as we three are on government service, on our way to Bangkok, as you well know, and as two of our number have been witnesses to this dreadful event, I suggest our masters in Whitehall should know of it.'

Captain Canavan looked even more sombre than usual and adjusted his posture slightly to sit straighter in his seat. Then he cleared his throat. 'You mean Hope, when you talk of the Foreign Office, I take it, sir...'

'I do, Captain.' Woodward looked at him with a knowing expression. 'I suggest you provide him with as full an account as possible and furnish him with all the details your company holds on the lost passenger, Henriques D'Argent, now presumed drowned, and this man Monsieur Jules LeClerc whose place he took on board. Hope may have knowledge that could illuminate the situation – for all of us...'

Captain Canavan pursed his lips, and for the first time, a glimmer of recognition crossed his face, as if some inner deliberations that had been troubling him for a while had suddenly become clarified. It was as if a veil of doubt had suddenly been lifted, and a hint of a sideways smile accompanied his next words.

'I will do as you propose, Mr Woodward. Hope shall know of it as soon as we reach Malta. I will send a separate telegram and share with him all the facts we have. If we receive a reply from him, you shall hear of it, and please, if you have any concerns on any matter whatsoever, please don't hesitate to speak to me personally. That goes for all three of you.' It was obvious that the captain was doing his best to project a friendly demeanour. 'After all, we are all serving our country in one way or another, and I am most happy to be at your service.' He stood up abruptly, indicating the meeting had ended, and extended his arm. He shook each of his visitors by the hand. 'I'm sure we shall gather again soon, gentlemen, preferably in happier circumstances,' he said, coughing affectedly as he completed the sentence.

The remainder of the voyage to Valletta passed without notable incident. After the D'Argent episode, Henry found himself to be on respectful nodding terms with the captain, and this gave him some comfort as the ship drew ever closer to the island of Malta. Only then would he learn whether the Maltese authorities desired to question him on arrival in port. He need not have worried, for shortly after docking, it became thankfully apparent that the local police had no wish to pursue an investigation. The event had not occurred within their jurisdiction, after all, and in the absence of any request from the French to take the matter up, the police must have decided they had many more fruitful ways to use their time... All concerned were much relieved, but remained distinctly taciturn all the time the *Verona* continued to be tied up alongside. The stopover in Valletta was blessedly brief, less than twelve hours, but long enough for Henry to take another run ashore, had he wanted. On this occasion, however, all three decided it was prudent to remain in their cabins, just in case the authorities had a change of heart. The last thing they wanted was to be subjected to the various embarkation formalities, thereby parading their presence to any inquisitive inhabitants. So, an opportunity to sample the delights of the city was missed. The giant harbour presented a spectacular sight from the ship, in any event, despite the strange lack of birdlife overhead that became evident after a while. Henry learned from one of the crew that the shooting of birds was a particular pastime of the locals, and this accounted for the lack of screeching gulls.

Once safely departed from Valletta, the ship continued across the Mediterranean towards the coast of North Africa, bound for Egypt. Henry found he was becoming ever more relaxed with each nautical mile that passed under the keel, carrying him and his comrades inexorably away from France. He even began to enjoy the company of some of the other passengers, a number of whom were full of lively stories about former oriental travels, while others, mostly those on their first journey east, tended to be fretful of what might await them. In Port Said, a few agreeable hours were spent ashore by many of the passengers, Henry, Albert, and Charles included, but it was their arrival in Suez that impressed Henry the most. He enjoyed passing through the magnificent canal more than anything, marvelling at the engineering feat that had connected two giant seas.

On leaving the Red Sea, the climate gradually got hotter and stickier, but the mostly gentle breezes on deck provided a degree of comfort against the harsh elements. In Aden, the steamship bunkered, taking on sufficient coal, Henry was told, to take her to Bombay and well beyond. It was not long before the ship had rounded the Horn of Africa, and after entering the Arabian Sea, it turned its bow almost directly east. Now the *Verona* had set her course, arrow straight, directly for Bombay.

Henry's knowledge of India was limited to various newspaper accounts he had read and those provided verbally by a number of his erstwhile hansom cab passengers – those who had spent lengthy periods on the subcontinent, usually in Her Majesty's service. One such passenger was the likeable and much-lamented Colonel Charles Coghill, who Henry had witnessed being brutally cut down outside his villa in Marylebone, just a few short years previously. This had been an incident of huge significance in Henry's former life, which had proved to be the turning point that enabled him to unravel the secrets of the now notorious Peccavi Plot. Colonel Coghill, who had served the British Army in India for so many years, had always spoken highly of Hindustan, as he insisted on calling the country. The tales of his many exploits, and his telling of the charm and mischief of its peoples, spoken confidently and colourfully through the hansom's hatch, were manifold, and although oft repeated, were much enjoyed by Henry, who had felt privileged to have become the old warrior's regular cab driver for so many years.

But now, as dawn broke and Henry peered towards the palm-tree'd coastline of the Arabian Sea, lit by rafts of slanting morning sunshine, he started to pick out the teeming quayside, dotted with what seemed countless ragtag members of humankind, scurrying and hurrying amidst the ancient and often ramshackle godowns of Bombay's famous harbour. He paused to wonder what he might actually find when he took his first steps ashore. The layover in Bombay was scheduled to last a whole day, including one night alongside, so he hoped he'd have time for the country to reveal itself, even in some small measure. He was thrilled at the prospect of finally seeing the Hindustan that the old colonel had blathered on about so good-naturedly for all those years. Henry intended to make the most of his brief stay. Albert, as before, was initially reluctant to go ashore, but he eventually succumbed, and with a sigh and knowing shake of his old head, he agreed to join his friend within an hour of the ship's berthing. Charles, on the other hand, was adamant. He said he wanted to lie low and refused point blank to join their little band. He had seen the sprawling metropolis before, and explained how on the last occasion when ashore at Juhu, he'd had his pocket watch pinched. While advising the pair of the risks, he urged them both to take every precaution and to keep all valuables close at hand.

Almost as soon as the gunwales of the *Verona* had nudged the pier, a hoard of half-naked porters scrambled onto the ship, running hither and thither, seeking out passengers who wanted their baggage brought ashore, and in that moment, it seemed that India had come to Henry rather than he to it. He stood back and watched the commotion with growing curiosity, tinged with a slight apprehension, resolving only to go ashore once the hubbub on deck had ceased. The majority of passengers were leaving the ship here, and Henry bade farewell to some of his new-found friends, those who he sadly expected never to see again. Stanley Barraclough approached him with a beaming smile and an outstretched hand.

'It's been wonderful to sail with you, Henry. You have been such good company – all those yarns of London's streets and the villainy you have encountered there. I have enjoyed hearing every single tale, and no mistake. Why, you have enjoyed quite a life, my friend. But now, it is time for me to make a name for myself. The cotton mills of Manchester have put their trust in me, and I must not let them down. Farewell old pal, and Godspeed to Bangkok, where I am sure another adventure awaits you.'

As Henry made ready for his first steps onto Indian soil, there was a rap on his cabin door. It was Albert.

'Ahh, I was just about to come to collect you. Are you ready to meet Bombay?'

Albert entered the cabin without invitation. He was carrying a paper. 'You had better read this first. The captain just gave it to me. It's a telegram from Hope.'

Henry took the dispatch from his old friend. It was addressed to:

```
CONFIDENTIAL FAO GOUGH AND WOODWARD
ONLY - PASSENGERS ON SS VERONA BOMBAY
```

The message inside read...

```
HENRIQUES D'ARGENT OFFICER OF DEUXIÈME
   BUREAU <STOP> BRANCH OF FRENCH
  MILITARY INTELLIGENCE <STOP> LECLERC
   SUSPECTED OF BEING SAME <STOP> TAKE
   EVERY PRECAUTION <STOP> IMPERATIVE
 PROCEED PLAN AS AGREED <STOP> SPEAK TO
   BEAUMONT ON ARRIVAL BANGKOK <END>
```

Henry read the telegram, looked briefly at Woodward, and bent to read it again.

'It's as I thought,' Albert said, breaking the silence. 'The French wish to put their claws into you, Henry – and perchance into me too, for all we know.'

'Deep waters indeed,' was Henry's first hoarsely given response. 'The Deuxième Bureau, is that part of the French Army, Albert?'

'More than that, Henry, it means the man you tipped into the Mediterranean was assuredly a French agent, perhaps a spy. He may have been just an assassin, of course – or both...'

Henry gasped. 'Do you think we should go ashore today, in the light of this intelligence?' he asked quietly, his throat catching slightly.

'I do. I have given it some thought. If the French mean to stop you, they have fluffed their lines. Their best chance was in Marseilles. We have been in British-controlled territories since then, save for Port Said, which is effectively much the same. I feel we should be safe now until we arrive in Bangkok and can seek the advice and protection of Beaumont at the consulate. I believe that by hiding in our cabins, we will serve only to draw attention to ourselves, especially amongst our fellow passengers. And a run ashore will recharge our batteries and allow us to practise the art of self-preservation a little before the serious campaign begins. What do you say?'

Henry merely scratched his cheek and turned the telegram over again in his hands.

'If you are with me,' Albert pressed on, 'I propose we disembark after speaking to the captain and bringing him into our confidence. It is important he knows of our conceivable exposure. He may be able to provide some counsel, and although he knows nothing of our secret purpose, he is not a fool either. I feel as sure as eggs are eggs, he understands we have some hidden intent on behalf of Hope. Why, it was he who spoke the man's name in the first instance. If he knows

Hope, he knows his business, I'll be bound. An alliance with Captain Canavan can only work in our favour. Forsooth, he does not need to know all the facts. The knowledge that we might be prey to foreign forces, for whatever reason, will energise him to our cause. He is a man of long military service, and a patriot. Of that I'm certain.'

'Very well,' Henry said at length. 'I need a walk on dry land besides. My sea legs need some gentle exercise. I will be guided by you, and naturally, I'll put the Bull Dog into my coat.'

An audience with Captain Canavan followed shortly after, and the old sea dog did not disappoint; his humourless bearing was peculiarly reassuring on this occasion.

'I fully understand,' Canavan said slowly, after Albert had finished his speech. 'It is as I suspected. How Monsieur D'Argent met his end is not my business, I will not interfere, but I know Hope, and I know his purpose. The French can be devils, at times, and if you have aroused their wrath, for whatever reason, good luck to you both, I say! May God help you too. Hope has already asked me to vouch for you in Singapore, if the need arises. I did not question the reasons. For me, such an invitation to support his aims is just cause enough. I will do what is in my power to protect you while you are on my ship. I will scan the passenger list and alert you to any concerns we may have. Many have left the *Verona* today, but we have twenty-three newly arrived passengers for our onward journey to Singapore. All of them, save four Americans, three Malays, two Swedes and a single Dutchman give their nationalities as British. There are no French-speaking nationals on our onward passage east, so I am optimistic of a safe and peaceful crossing.'

Finally, Albert and Henry's trip ashore could go ahead, and it proved to be more cosseted than either of them could have imagined. On advice from Captain Canavan, they took a company cycle rickshaw to the recently opened and rather grand Bombay Gymkhana. Located in the Fort area, it was just a short ride from the port. The captain sent word on ahead to introduce the pair on his behalf and to allow them admittance exceptionally as one-day members; such was his influence, the club had submitted to the request. Henry and Albert spent most of the day enjoying the lush grounds of vivid bougainvillea and sweeping lawns, and its graceful reading rooms. It was a time for them to forget their recent anxieties, relax, and prepare for the tests that lay ahead. They dined at the club too, taking both lunch and dinner on the veranda of the elegant restaurant.

But the moment of serenity was not to last, and soon it was time to return to the ship. Exhilarating pulled rickshaw rides followed this time, at Henry's suggestion, provided by two *lungi*-clad locals, each drawing their own high-wheeled machines as they ran, bumping and weaving through the wild side streets of the old city. The experience might have been further enlivened by the extra glass of port they'd consumed at the Gymkhana, which had lifted their dispositions sufficiently to threaten accepted propriety. In marvellous high spirits, they'd hollered out loudly as the rickshaws fell into competition, throwing them from side to side in a race to reach the ship before the other. Henry and Albert emptied their remaining Indian currency into their respective charioteer's grateful outstretched hands, receiving huge smiles in return. As Henry bade farewell to his driver, he remembered, with a wince of guilt, his own gruelling vocation of carrying folk across a teeming city. He reflected sombrely how hugely fortunate he had been that, as a hansom driver, he always had a horse to pull the heavy load. By ten o'clock, the bibulous duo were safely back on board the SS *Verona* and sleeping off their exertions in the comfort of their respective cabins.

The voyage from Bombay to Singapore took eleven long days, and on every one of them, the Siamese lessons from Charles Hurdus continued apace. Henry's grasp of the language had improved greatly during this intense period of instruction. Even Albert had shown some improving skills but his performance still fell way below his younger friend. Henry felt that Charles had taken a little longer than he had to recover from his confrontation off the coast of Marseilles, perhaps because of his gentler disposition. Both he and Albert had been concerned for a while, but now their tutor appeared to have returned to full form. It was obvious to all who spoke to him, the day Charles returned to his beloved Siam could not arrive quick enough. In fact, there was a veritable spring in his step by the time they had entered the Strait of Malacca and encountered the coastline of Malaya for the first time.

A day before their arrival in Singapore, Captain Canavan invited Albert Woodward into his cabin and informed him that onward passage to Bangkok had been arranged on a vessel with the queer name of *Alligator*.

'Don't expect too much from her,' he advised gravely. 'She's nothing like the *Verona* – much smaller, more a local tramp ship, I should say – but she'll get you there, and the good news is that she leaves only a day after our arrival in port, so you won't have long to wait before you embark. The passage north should take four days. You three are the only passengers transferring to the *Alligator*, so you should find you have the ship to yourselves. You may also discover that the Gulf of Siam can be a bumpy place at times, especially on board that old tub, but I fear you will just have to wear it. The company has arranged accommodation for you all in Singapore. You will be staying at the Tanglin Club. I'm a member there also and will be joining you while the ship remains in port.'

'As we are in private, I should like to broach something with you, Captain. It's a matter of some sensitivity, but I doubt what I have to say will come as any revelation to you.' Albert lowered his head slightly as he spoke.

'You can speak in confidence,' Canavan replied curtly.

'Tomorrow morning, Henry Gough and I shall be taking an early morning stroll on the deck, and shortly thereafter, we shall be reporting to you that we have sighted two British gunboats steaming past the ship heading north towards Malacca—'

'Hope has already signalled me,' the captain replied in an instant. 'There is no need for a reminder. I know my duty. If asked, I shall corroborate your account. Is that all, sir? I have pressing matters to attend to.' The captain's mood had swung suddenly. He clearly took exception to being reminded, however subtly, of the concern that he might not support the false account Henry and Albert were about to propagate around the ship. Taking this as a cue that their meeting was ended, Albert turned and with a look of mild embarrassment, he returned to the dining salon, where he knew lunch was already being served.

The following morning, half an hour before daybreak, Henry and Albert slipped out of their cabins and took a gentle stroll aft towards the mizzen-mast and stern taffrail. Each time Henry had passed the same point since the dreadful incident off Marseilles, the image of the tumbling Frenchman had come back to haunt him. The inevitable effect was to cause him to cringe slightly and to feel the hairs on his neck tremble in its sickening remembrance. This consequence appeared even more noticeable on this mild tropical morning with its cooling airs. Henry's cringe turned into a full shiver, and he was forced to cover his shoulders with his hands to alleviate the discomfort.

'We need not stay here long. Once the sun is up, I suggest we return to our cabins,' Albert said. 'All we need to do is stay long enough to ensure the coast is clear on deck, so no one can disavow us of our future testimony.'

Henry remained silent, absorbed in his thoughts.

As the first flickers of full sun caressed the elegant lines of the SS *Verona*, the pair set off to return to their cabins. Much as they had hoped, they encountered a fellow passenger in the companionway. Herbert Collins, a man in his late fifties, portly about the waist, of scarlet complexion, and slippery lipped, was a former employee of the East India Company. After its dissolution six years previously, Collins had moved to Singapore to set up a trade in gemstones. His story was known to all on the *Verona* because he had rarely spoken of anything else since leaving Southampton. Collins was returning home from a lucrative sales trip to Hatton Garden, armed with new profits and fresh finance for his future Eastern investments. He was the ideal man to stumble upon at that moment as he was a notorious gossiper and a barefaced show-off, to boot – a most unlikeable man in many respects who found multifarious ways to boast about his wealth and conquests in business (and in conversation with fellow men, of his comparable triumphs with the fairer sex). His constant talk of the huge profits that could be made with "clever hands", as he was wont to say, made him not only a dreadful bore, but in Henry's eyes, a despicable boor, also. Thus, the opportunity to lie to the man was most welcome and not to be missed.

'Ha, gentlemen!' Unsurprisingly, Collins was first to speak. 'Enjoying the sunrise, I see, and why not indeed! Not for me though... The morning tea and cake in the salon is enough to have me waking early.'

'A shame, Collins,' Albert replied. 'You have missed quite a sight.'

'Goodness, yes,' Henry cried. 'A most impressive and unexpected display. One I'd never thought to see so far from Portsmouth.'

'You intrigue me, gentlemen. Pray, tell me what has excited you both so much?'

'Why, the sight of two of the finest British warships I have ever seen, sailing in line astern, massive grey hulls, and at great speed too,' said Henry.

'They flashed past in an instant, but the unmistakeable white ensign was plain to see, as were the magnificent guns they carried on deck,' said Albert.

'They were the same class of vessel, I'll warrant,' Henry added knowingly. 'They looked most modern and untainted by rust in any way.'

'Well, I'll be damned!' Collins retorted. 'I expect they are on their way to blow up some foreign potentate! What! Ha ha ha... Well, I must be gone. The cakes await me and I must make the most of them. This is my last day before the toil of remorseless business must regrettably resume... I bid you both good morning, gentlemen.' And with that, he scurried off in the direction of the dining salon.

'I think our work here is done,' Henry said with a chuckle. 'I see no reason to mention this again. By the time we berth in Singapore, the whole ship will know of it.' And so it proved...

Chapter Nine

The port of Singapore was crammed with shipping as the *Verona* plied her way with utmost caution towards her eventual berthing place. Never in his life had Henry seen more small boats in one place, most with low triangular awnings of bamboo to protect from the blazing heat. Many of the craft were arranged in long ranks that resembled canvas tents lined up on a battlefield, while others moved industriously about their business amidst a clamour of noise and shouting. There were no signs of British warships however.

Henry and Albert reflected with satisfaction at breakfast that morning – all the talk was of the Royal Navy gunboats seen, apparently by many, earlier in the day, in the strait off Singapore. As predicted, the word had got around. The fool, Collins, had unwittingly done their work for them, so they smiled on hearing the description of events from the others and nodded politely, without adding further fuel to the fire.

As Henry was packing his belongings for the transfer to the Tanglin Club, one of the ship's boys brought him a sealed telegram. It was from Hope. It read as follows…

TRIAL OF SIAMESE ACCUSED FIXED FOR
FIRST JULY <STOP> CHALKE WILL MEET
YOU ON ARRIVAL BANGKOK <STOP> SPEAK
BEAUMONT ASAP <END>

Henry put the telegram into his pocket and made a mental note to show it to Albert at the first private opportunity.

Captain Canavan, appearing to revert to type, maintained his distance during the time they spent at the Tanglin Club. The following morning, as the cart arrived to take Henry, Albert, and Charles back to the docks and their new ship, he approached them for the last time. Their exchange was brief and to the point.

'Good luck, gentlemen. I trust your time in Bangkok will be well spent,' he said without a hint of a smile.

'Thank you, Captain. We have been most grateful for your good services,' Albert replied for all of them.

The *Alligator* was, if anything, far worse than Canavan had described. In comparison to the *Verona*, she was extremely poorly appointed. There were no fellow passengers either; Henry learned at the quayside that the ship had been dispatched from Bangkok, with a native crew, specifically to collect them. So, in the absence of fellow travellers, the three had pretty much the run of the ship.

When not on deck taking the air or sitting in the cramped salon receiving his final language tuition, Henry spent most of his time in his rather poky cabin reading a book lent him by Charles Hurdus entitled *History of Siam in 1688*. The author, Marcel Le Blanc, had been a French Jesuit who, nearly two hundred years previously, had been invited by Narai, the King of Siam, to promote the studies of mathematics and astrology. Henry found the story fascinating. He read that Le Blanc had arrived in Siam during a most calamitous period of the country's history, eventually becoming embroiled in a coup d'état to overthrow the king. Le Blanc's account of the besieging of French forces, and their eventual flight from their forts in Bangkok and Mergui was all the more remarkable, as the author had witnessed the events first hand and had only made his escape from the country with the backing of French troops. The narrative, although difficult to understand in parts, served to reinforce in Henry the reality of France's close involvement with the peoples of Siam over many centuries. It heightened the notion that France's interventions had been, for the most part, intrusive and meddling.

'Perhaps Hope is right,' Henry confided to Albert after the pair had assembled in the salon on their last night at sea. 'Given their history in the region, France may indeed have modern designs to conquer Siam once and for all.'

The journey to Bangkok soon passed and on the morning of 25th June, the *Alligator* crossed the bar at Paknam and entered the wide reaches of the Chao Phraya River. As the khaki-coloured river narrowed, signs of habitation began to emerge; rustic dwellings perched close to the mudbanks, most on stilts, and small fishing boats started to appear. Low-slung canoes with waving occupants passed the starboard beam, and then a series of high sails announced a line of rice barges that soon drifted by. As they drew closer to the main port, steam launches and towed barges could be seen chugging gently forwards in the early morning heat. By the time the golden glint of the city's temples hove into view, the river was a mass of congested shipping of all types. From amidst the throng, a small red-painted vessel pushed through, sounding its warning klaxon as it approached. The polished brass and the streaming Union Jack announced it to be the British consular launch.

'Ah,' Charles cried, pointing to the oncoming boat, 'it appears that Hope was right. Chalke has come to meet us in person.' As the encompassing open boats gave way, the launch ran up alongside and threw a line to the *Alligator*. A ladder was quickly lowered and soon our trio of comrades were standing on the narrow deck of the British vessel.

'Welcome to Bangkok!' A smiling besuited man of young middle age was there to greet them as they boarded. 'Mr Woodward and Mr Gough, I presume. Horatio Chalke, at your service,' he declared in bold and confident tones as he shook each vigorously by the hand. 'And welcome back, Charles,' he added warmly. 'Why, how we have all missed you these last four months. 'Tis but a short journey to the consulate. I have arranged for your baggage to be sent on to your accommodation. A bungalow in the grounds of the consulate has been prepared for your stay.' Chalke gave a brief hand signal to the skipper and the launch's engine fired into life once more.

As the slim red vessel turned to head upriver, Henry marvelled at the crowded quayside, piled high with wooden crates, dark boxes, and hessian bales filled to bursting – the array of fragrant local spices and other exotic wares interred within them could only be imagined. In the distance he could see plumes of dark smoke announcing the industry of the city. These, he later learned, were the bustling rice factories and the giant sawmills that remained churning at almost every hour of day and night.

'This is certainly not what I expected...' He turned to Albert.

'Nor I! A village by a dark-brown river is more what I had in mind. This is indeed a city of some size, and thriving, by the look of things.'

'Gentlemen, I have arranged for you both to speak to the consul as soon as we land,' Chalke announced above the din of the steam engine. 'I shall attend also, and we can then set out our plans. I trust you had a good journey. Such a long voyage, but I'm sure it will be repaid in spades by the experience you shall have while you are here.'

'To speak for myself, I had a most enjoyable trip, sir. I have seen things I'd never thought imaginable,' Henry replied with a broad smile. 'Although, I confess to being rather anxious about my forthcoming attendance at the court.'

'Oh, there is nothing to be concerned about, Mr Gough. I shall be there to guide you. I have been appointed as your guardian angel by the consul general, and it will be a great honour.'

The British consulate lay on the banks of the Chao Phraya River, a short distance upstream from the Grand Palace. This vast bastion of the reigning monarch, Rama V, King Chulalongkorn, dominated the eastern banks of the sacred river, the glittering tops of its golden pagodas and high battlements being a glorious and potent reminder of the king's power. It was visible for miles around. On the opposite shore stood Wat Arun, the Temple of Dawn, majestic, mysterious and magnificent, a startling blue-grey edifice and symbol of the sway of Buddhism over the peoples of Siam for more than two hundred years. Henry's first impression of the consulate, as the launch tied up against its private pier, was of an amalgam of East and West. Constructed almost entirely of wood and raised high on stilts, it was laid out on three floors. The spacious and elegant building owed much to its Siamese design, but equally, the property would not have looked utterly out of place on the Surrey bank of the River Thames. The sweeping lawns that led directly to the water, the pretty jetty, the neat paths, the trimmed shrubs, and the abundance of fruit trees, gave the onlooker the distinct impression that this was not only a magical and wonderous spot, entirely in keeping with its natural surroundings, but also wholly fitting as a comfortable and graceful residence and place of work for one of Britain's senior diplomatic officials overseas.

Henry and Albert bade farewell to Charles Hurdus at this juncture, on the promise of reacquainting themselves as soon as circumstances permitted. Henry clasped Charles' hand to his breast as he said his goodbyes.

'I shall never forget what you did for me, dear friend. I hope, one day, I can repay you.'

"Twas nothing – a few lessons in Siamese, that's all…' Charles quipped. 'As to the other matter, I have tried to forget that night. You owe me nothing, Henry, save your friendship. May God bless your time in this fair country.' And then, with a throng of porters lugging his baggage towards a nearby cart that waited outside the main gates of the residence, Hurdus hurried away to reclaim his own property – the house that had lain dormant, in his absence, these last four months.

Henry and Albert looked wistfully after the retreating figure for a few seconds before turning their attentions to their newly discovered nursemaid. Horatio Chalke was a man in his early to mid-forties, of medium build and searching eyes. Possessed of a high forehead and a heavy moustache below a thinly constructed nose, he had bushy side-beards that extended towards a prominent, confident chin. His engaging manner gave the impression of a man who knew his business – and knew also how to deliver it.

'If you'll follow me,' he said as their shoes touched lush grass for the first time in months. 'Mr Beaumont will be waiting for us in the drawing room.'

Clunking up a short flight of wooden steps onto a spacious and chair-strewn veranda, the foursome soon arrived outside a large well-appointed room, shuttered against the midday heat. The door was wide open. Horatio Chalke halted briefly at the threshold and peered in. After receiving what must have been a signal from the interior, he silently invited the others to enter ahead of him. The room was most comfortably furnished, with glittering pieces of oriental art suspended from walls, rested on various wooden tables and amongst the ornate bookshelves. There was a scattering of carpets, each of intricate design, that covered most of the polished teak floorboards. A portrait of Queen Victoria stared down imperiously towards them as they made their entrance, hanging, as it did, in pride of place, above an opulent stone mantlepiece. As they adjusted their eyes to the new light, a diminutive gentleman with grey receding hair cropped short, who Henry judged to be in his late fifties, rose stiffly from a richly embroidered armchair to greet them. Lawrence Beaumont was impeccably attired – a dark frock coat of light material wrapped around a crisp white shirt, complete with starched high collar. A stylish maroon silk necktie finished the picture.

'Pray be seated, gentlemen. I expect you must be tired after your arduous voyage. We are just short of six thousand miles from our homeland, as the crow flies, you know,' he announced, his voice rising slightly. 'Nearly double that, if you count the distance you have actually sailed since leaving England, but all the same, we shall do everything in our power to afford you as cordial an English welcome as you might receive anywhere on the globe.'

'It was certainly further than the voyage I once took from Pembroke to Swansea.' Albert laughed.

'I expect so…' Beaumont replied drily, and then realising that Woodward might have been speaking in jest, he offered a smile of sorts. 'Ha ha ha, yes, of course – I've never been to Swansea however…' At that moment, a turbaned Sikh in full livery entered carrying a tray of tea. A man of great stature, Jasvinder Singh had a commanding and powerful bearing. He salaamed gravely and left them, almost without making a sound.

Clearing his throat, Beaumont sat back into his plush armchair, clapped his knees and said brightly, 'Now, we have important business to discuss.' For the next ten minutes the consul general outlined the programme for each of them, while Chalke took notes.

'The trial of Kittisak Aromdee starts in six days, Mr Gough. It is expected to last less than a week. You are one of nineteen witnesses, though I venture yours will be the testimony all will want to hear. Then the Privy Council will retire to consider their verdict. You will be expected to remain here while they do this, as they may seek clarifications or maybe even further testimony from you. The whole process could take us into September, perchance beyond. But you should have every expectation of returning to your homes by Christmas. Of that, I am confident. Horatio will go through the details in private with you. My only advice to you is this... Tell the truth, and be not swayed by those who might urge you otherwise.

'I am sure the experience will be most enlightening. Since the dreadful events surrounding my predecessor's daughter, Fanny Knox, and the horrible injustice that was caused, we have been doing our level best to encourage the Siamese to adopt a different approach to the law. In particular, we seek their adoption of a changed system in the way their courts could work in future – a gentler style, a more modern approach, might I say, one which is more evidence-based, more objective, an arrangement that provides the accused with some rights – a chance to defend himself, so to speak. To that end we have appointed, with the approval of the king, naturally, a legal advisor, a most eminent Queen's Counsel from the Inner Temple, a grandson of the great John Archbold, no less. Frederick Archbold has been advising the Siamese for five months and during our regular audiences, he tells me progress is indeed forthcoming. This trial will be a test, not only for the accused – about whose guilt I have little doubt, incidentally – but we shall see at first hand how far we have come since some of the brutal prejudices of the past. Do I make myself clear, sir?'

'You do, sir,' Henry replied in a level fashion while all the time wondering at the contradiction his host had just espoused. Beaumont had clearly reached his own verdict without hearing all the facts. Where was the objectivity in that?

Henry added, 'I will do my best to be informative to the court and I will do my duty by the law, sir.'

'Good man! And as to you, sir,' Beaumont turned towards Albert Woodward, 'you have a most interesting task ahead of you. Intriguing may be understating it, in truth. For you have just two months, maybe three, to find a way to prevent the scourge of opium smuggling, eradicate the manufacture of illicit alcohol, set the Chinese gambling community back on their heels, and design a plan to centralise tax revenues. A tall order, what! The best I can say is, good luck to you, sir!'

'I will do what I can, Your Excellency. I can do no more. But I request to be home by Christmas too. I have an important assignment awaiting me in London, as I am slated to become the master of Her Majesty's Excise Detectives immediately after the festive season has ended.'

'Indeed – a great honour, I expect. Never fear. I will have the pair of you back in the bosoms of your families before Christmas. You can only do your best while you are here. Horatio will make all the introductions for you.' Turning to Chalke, he said, 'You will translate and interpret for them both too, won't you, Horatio?'

'It will be a privilege, sir,' Chalke replied with a respectful smile.

'Excellent. And now, Horatio, while I offer some essential reading material to these newly arrived gentlemen, taken from old Knox's excellent library, I request you attend to that matter we discussed earlier – concerning Mrs Chaldecott. I presume her husband remains missing in the forests of Chiang Mai?'

'We are doing all we can to find him, sir. The local population have been scouring the timberlands these last four days.'

'Speak to her, would you, like I said. Poor woman was near hysterical when she called on me yesterday. Her husband's a drunkard, of course. My guess is he's found a native woman and thrown in his lot with her. The blighter will surface soon enough, once the drink wears off, sadder but probably none the wiser, I expect. This sort of thing happens frequently to these jungle and logging types upcountry, I'm afraid. His wife will stop her crying soon enough, and then, I expect, there'll be hell to pay.'

'I will seek her out this instant and provide you with the latest reports.'

'Perhaps I could make a request of Mr Chalke, also,' Albert intervened.

'By all means, I am at your disposal,' Chalke replied.

'I have some correspondence which needs to find a home.' Albert pulled out the handwritten letter given to him by Nathaniel Hope over six weeks before. It looked suitably rumpled and ragged, having travelled so far. 'You see, we bumped into a sailor in the service of one of Her Majesty's gunboats in Singapore. On seeing we were about to embark on the *Alligator*, he approached us on the quayside and asked if we could do him the service of delivering his letter to Bangkok. What was his name, Henry? That jovial young chap with the terrible limp.'

'I recall he told us his name was Jim,' Henry replied. 'The fellow seemed most animated and implored us to carry the letter for him to the Falcks Hotel – the name is the only thing legible on the envelope, as I fear the remainder must be in Siamese. He said it was of great importance to him, and he didn't want to trust the scoundrels on the next mailboat to deliver it.'

Albert passed the shabby document to Chalke, who took it from him with an easy smile. 'I have no idea what it contains,' Albert said, 'but the Falcks Hotel is unknown to me. To save me the trouble of searching for it, perhaps someone could arrange for it to be sent on.'

'Of course,' Chalke said smoothly. 'I would be happy to arrange it for you. The Falcks Hotel is a well-known establishment hereabouts, and it will be easy to ensure its safe delivery.' Chalke glanced at the writing. 'It appears to be addressed to a lady – a Siamese lady unsurprisingly.' He sighed. 'I suspect it's a love letter of some kind. Leave it to me.'

'The poor matelot seemed most anxious,' Albert added with a raised eyebrow.

'From the Royal Navy, you say?' Chalke enquired.

'Yes, young Jim was a crew member of a vessel called *Foxhound*, so he said,' Albert replied. 'Apparently, he'd suffered in some accident or other and was waiting for his wounds to heal before the ship returned to collect him.'

'I believe we saw the ship, as a matter of fact,' Henry said with a hint of excitement in his voice. 'It must have been one of the pair we sighted – almost definitely, I'd say.'

'You saw a gunboat in Singapore…?' Beaumont interrupted in a surprised tone.

'Not one, but two! They steamed past us in the strait on the very morning we arrived in the harbour. A magnificent sight, if ever there was one. One of the other passengers quipped they must have been on their way to blow up a local potentate!'

'Ha ha ha – well, I'll be damned! At any rate, I'm sure your letter will find a safe home. Horatio will see to it.'

Chalke made a light bow, and placing the envelope into his pocket, he turned to leave.

After the door had closed with a gentle click, Lawrence Beaumont looked wisely at the others. 'Pray follow me, gentlemen. I have something to discuss with you both in the privacy of my study.'

Chapter Ten

The next hour in Henry's life proved one of most revealing he had ever experienced. Beaumont ushered his guests up the stairs to the first floor, where he kept his study. It was replete with bookshelves, most of which were bursting with volumes of all sizes; his wide teak desk, strewn all over with papers, stood under the window. He shut the door smartly behind them as they entered.

'A telegram has arrived from the War Office. It is for your attention, but is addressed to me personally, so you can be sure no one else has seen it. It concerns your visit, gentlemen. I suggest you look at it before we talk further.' The telegram read...

```
    HENRIQUES D'ARGENT CONFIRMED LOST
   PRESUMED DEAD <STOP> WHEREABOUTS OF
  LECLERC UNKNOWN <STOP> REPORTS REVEAL
     D'ARGENT STAYED IN LANGHAM HOTEL
    LONDON AT TIME OF PRINCE GAGANANGA
   KILLING <STOP> D'ARGENT DEPARTED DOVER
    24 FEB BOUND FOR CALAIS <STOP> LIKELY
```

D'ARGENT ASSISTED ASSASSIN TO ESCAPE TO FRANCE <END>

When they had absorbed the message, Beaumont said, 'I assume this means something to you.'

'It does, sir,' Henry replied. 'You see, I was attacked as we departed Marseilles by this man D'Argent.' Henry indicated towards the telegram. 'I was very nearly killed. Had it not been for the intervention of your translator, Charles Hurdus, I would be at the bottom of the ocean by now. D'Argent lost his life in his attempt to take mine. Hope has since discovered he was an officer of the Deuxième Bureau – a French agent, so to speak – sent to kill me. He believes France would prefer me dead rather than allow me to testify at this trial.'

'Ha!' Beaumont cried. 'It is as I thought. The French are up to their old tricks again. They have designs on this country, of that, I'm now certain.'

'But why should the French rail at the thought of me giving evidence against a Siamese accused of murdering the king's half-brother? It makes no sense to me.'

'Nor I,' Albert added with a solemn shake of his head.

'Pray be seated, gentlemen. I have a theory. Allow me to espouse it to you.' After they had settled on the divan, he continued. 'Tell me, has Hope spoken to you of the two rival families here in Siam – the Aungs and the Bamroongs?' The pair nodded their affirmation. 'Very well.' Beaumont leaned towards them. 'It is my belief that the king's position here is under threat. I believe Chulalongkorn to be a great moderniser, a man Britain can do business with, a king with whom we can trade, a monarch we can help to bring his country into the nineteenth century. But there are others who wish the opposite. These are the Bamroongs and their supporters. The king, I fear, is still king in name only. His regent, an elderly nobleman of very great power in Siam – who goes by the name of Lord Sirrichi Bamroong – holds the true authority, even now, since the king has come of age. But the regent is now realising that his power, and that of his family and descendants, may be coming to an end and must surely one day slip from his grasp. As King Chulalongkorn grows older, so his confidence has increased, as has his strength. The king favours the Aung family who are modernisers, like himself. The two share the same ideas, but the Bamroongs cannot abide it, especially the regent, who wishes to retain the old feudal ways from which their riches flow.

'It is now my firm opinion that Lord Bamroong has sought the protection of the French, in return for putting him on the throne of Siam. My spies tell me a coup d'état is looming – maybe before the end of the year. The French have done this kind of thing before, you know. Oh, yes!' Beaumont had a tendency to speak in higher tones when getting agitated. 'As long as two hundred years ago,' he continued, his pitch rising once more, 'they became entangled in an uprising to displace the then King of Siam, and now I'm positive they wish to expand their borders once more. This time, the thrust will come from Khmer, or Cambodia as we term it, where they have already installed a puppet monarch. King Norodom is merely a pawn in the game the French play, and I have little doubt that Regent Bamroong will go the same way, if invited. He will accept so-called French protection in return for the kingdom, if in name only.'

'But what of the trial? I see no connection,' Henry replied.

'Aha! There's the rub. You see, the king trusts no one, least of all the French, but nowadays neither does he favour us either. The fact is there are certain intimacies he has shared with the consulate, concerning his fears for his country and his desire for Great Britain to be steadfast against any threat, that have found their way into French hands, and he no longer trusts me or any of my staff to keep our discussions confidential. It is my belief that the king felt the need to send his personal envoy and half-brother, Prince Gagananga, to London to speak directly with Her Majesty in search of Britain's pledged support, should the French decide to depose him in favour of the regent. I should not be surprised if the French, on learning of the thrust of the message – there are spies everywhere – wished to prevent the communication from getting through. Such a tactic would keep Britain on the back foot and gain the French, and the regent, sufficient time to put their wicked plans into practice. I deduce that, in cahoots with the regent, it was the French who sent Kittisak to kill the king's messenger. I cannot be certain, of course, because the exact nature of the prince's mission to London was not shared with me, regrettably, on account of the king's trust in this office being much tested of late, and the fact that my own spies have failed me – not for the first time, I might add.'

Henry broke in. 'The presence of the brute, D'Argent, in London during February, at the time of the killing, and his residing in one and the same hotel as the murdered Siamese, seems to bear out your theory, sir. Perhaps the French appointed D'Argent to protect the assassin and aid his escape.'

'I agree,' Albert added. 'For France to send one of their own to kill a foreign prince on the streets of London may have been too perilous, even for them. Should he be discovered, a full diplomatic incident between Great Britain and France would have ensued. Better to offer clandestine protection to another than to actually fire the fatal pistol shot.'

'So, you believe the king wants our help, but does not trust Britain either. 'Tis indeed a strange state of affairs.' Henry looked perplexed.

'It is this *office* he does not trust, Mr Gough. In Great Britain, I have no doubt, he still has faith. With Her Majesty and her ministers, I feel sure, the king believes he is amongst friends. But since the debacle with my predecessor, Knox, who undoubtedly overreached himself with the king, our currency at the consulate has been of diminishing value to Chulalongkorn. I have done my best to stem the tide of mistrust, only to discover all these new betrayals. It is a very poor state of affairs we find ourselves in, for sure. The fact that the king has decided he must appeal directly to Her Majesty for assistance – monarch to monarch, so to speak – only demonstrates we are not pulling our weight here at the consulate. I might add, however, that while our value may be less than it once was to His Majesty, I know as a fact he despises the French – and fears them too. Perhaps we are the lesser of two evils, in his eyes.'

'Be assured, Your Excellency, we will do our best to provide you with evidence to end this matter once and for all – evidence in the courts and evidence to snare your snake in the grass,' Albert offered.

'There is one fact that plays to our advantage, which may allow us a little more time before the French make their move,' Beaumont resumed. 'I believe it to be a blessing. You see, it was the king who ordered Kittisak's capture – 'twas the minute the wretch set foot back on Siamese soil, in fact. He must have received intelligence and evidence from his agents that Kittisak was the true killer and when informed of the man's imminent return to Siam, the king took decisive action and ordered his immediate arrest. Since his seizure, the fellow has been in the private custody of the king's personal guard at the Royal Palace. I'm told the king will let no one else close to the accused, least of all the regent's men. The king wants retribution for the killing of his half-brother;

that seems clear. A fair trial and a true conviction will send a message to his people that he wishes to bring change for the good to his nation. It will also provide an opportunity to turn the tables on the regent and finally break the ugly bonds between them.

'Furthermore, the accused is no ordinary thug. Although Kittisak Aromdee is a man not much known in these parts – apparently, he has never once met the king – from his base in Chiang Mai, he has become one of the wealthiest timber merchants in all Siam. His visit to London indicates he is confident around westerners and the ways of foreigners which, in turn, suggests intelligence and an education, of sorts. Word is, Kittisak has benefited greatly over the years from the regent's largesse in obtaining logging licences in Chiang Mai, which have made him rich. Ordinarily, Kittisak would expect to receive protection from the great man, but at this moment, locked, as he is, in the king's embrace, Lord Bamroong cannot give it. My intelligence tells me this has made the regent all the more fearful, and he has been witnessed flying into violent fits of temper when not in the king's presence.'

'So, the trial may be a turning point for Siam... do you believe a guilty verdict against Kittisak will strengthen or weaken the king's position?'

'If Kittisak is indeed the regent's man sent to kill the king's half-brother, which all of us, including His Majesty, must suspect, then with the consequent execution of the traitor, the king will have wreaked a minor revenge. But then what? We could see a civil war. The king must see this possibility – hence his desire to reach out towards Her Majesty for support. I have told Hope as much. Sadly, I believe he pins his hopes for a successful outcome on you two and your ability to get to the truth of it. Personally, and please don't take any offence, I believe it will take much more than anything you can achieve during your brief time here, before we see a way clear though this tangled web.'

'I take no offence, sir. You are right to be pessimistic perhaps, though we shall do our level best.' Albert changed the subject. 'Would it be impertinent for me to ask your excellency when was the last time you had an audience with King Chulalongkorn?' he asked in low tones.

'It would, sir. But I shall answer all the same. I have not seen His Majesty these last three months. I am embarrassed to say he refuses my advances. My intelligence comes only from members of the court, and as such, I accept it cannot be entirely trusted. The truth of the matter is I know nothing for certain, but it appears that the king has finally got the bit between his teeth, and even at this eleventh hour, he is preparing to make a stand against his mentor. If his move backfires, the whole pack of cards may tumble and allow Lord Bamroong and his French friends to seize power. These are troubling times indeed.' Beaumont gazed out of his study window onto the curving river and the canal that connected to it at the corner's edge of the consulate's extended lawn. A family of boisterous monkeys could be heard chattering within the branches of a mango tree that spread its long boughs almost to touch the fast-flowing water. 'Do me the honour, gentlemen, to pledge you will repeat none of what I have told you under any circumstances,' he said, his voice breaking slightly.

'You have our word, sir,' Albert replied.

Henry nodded in agreement. 'Yes, sir.'

'All this brings me to the true reasons why each of you are here,' Beaumont continued after another moment of reflection.

'To smoke out the traitor you believe to have in your midst, Your Excellency...' Woodward replied slowly.

'Indeed – and in my judgement,' Beaumont lowered his

voice to a conspiratorial whisper, 'the man responsible for this betrayal has just left our presence. None other than Horatio Chalke. Everything points to him. He is at the centre of all things that affect the court of Chulalongkorn, and is, to boot, overly friendly with *nos amis, les Français*. Hope has sent you two here to prove it. Chalke has been in Siam longer than any. He has a memory like an elephant, and I know him to respect and honour the regent. He speaks often, in terms most flattering, of the support Lord Bamroong once provided to Chulalongkorn as a young man.'

'We may know soon enough,' Henry advanced. 'If news reaches Paris that HMS *Foxhound* has orders to visit Bangkok, Hope shall hear of it, and we shall have our man.'

'I don't understand, Mr Gough...' For the first time the consul general looked confounded.

'You see, the letter Albert just gave to Chalke is a test. It contains spurious information about the imminent deployment of a gunboat to Siam. By passing him the letter, we have given your suspect a tempting opportunity to acquire intelligence from a Royal Navy source, however lowly. It is in his hands, as we speak. If he opens the letter and reveals it to others, he is your turncoat, sir, and we shall have the proof.'

Beaumont's eyes widened. 'But what of the gunboats you have described to us today. I was most interested to hear your account, for no communication has been received from London on the subject.'

'That is because the gunboats do not exist, Your Excellency. Our accounts are false, only provided as eyewitness confirmation to Chalke that Britain's military activity in the region has been suddenly stepped up. 'Tis another trap laid to catch your man. The sighting of the men-o'-war locally deployed will support the facts he will read in the letter, should he open it.'

'I see, devilish stuff. A dirty trick indeed... Most ingenious, I must say.' Beaumont tutted at length. 'Let us pray we shall have our answer soon...' he said with the tones of a man increasingly weary of his charge. 'Before you leave me, I have one further item I wish to discuss before you depart to your bungalow...' His facial expression changed in an instant, chameleon-like, from one of sheer gloom to a visage of optimistic cheer. The widest smile yet witnessed by the others soon followed. 'Gentlemen, you have both been invited to a reception tomorrow night – at the French consulate, no less.' Still smiling broadly, he added, "Tis irony indeed, that we must keep up the niceties of diplomatic life, given all our open skirmishes and hidden prejudices, and there is no better example of this dance of duplicity and distortion than our relationship here with Monsieur Pierre Corbin, the loathsome French consul general, his pretentious lady-wife, Marie-Claude, and his mostly degenerate staff...'

For a moment, Henry and Albert were utterly lost for words. They shuffled uneasily on the wide couch they shared together as Beaumont ended his surprising outburst with another bright grin. Henry wondered whether long hours under the Asian sun had somehow affected His Excellency, for this was a most unusual eruption and from a long-standing diplomat, it was all the more surprising.

On seeing the mild shock on the faces of his guests, Beaumont sought to allay their fears. 'Ha. You see, gentlemen, not everything here is what it may seem at first glance. My little speech just then was designed to jolt you slightly, to remind you both to be on your guard at all times. Not all of what I just said was entirely truthful, perhaps with the exception of my description of Marie-Claude Corbin, who I find more condescending and haughtier than any words I can ever express. Remember, we are here – all of us – to do the Queen's bidding, never forget it. There are many who would proffer help to us, but there are others who abhor Great Britain and all it stands for. And now, gentlemen, I feel tired.' He rose slowly from his chair. 'I take it you both have evening dress. The reception will be formal and attended by many, no doubt, but it will be followed by a private dinner, hosted by "*Les charmantes*" Monsieur et Madame Corbin... These events are only for a select few, you understand – especially the last. You two gentlemen are invited to both.'

Chapter Eleven

Just after eight the following morning, as Henry and Albert sat on their bungalow's pretty veranda enjoying a breakfast brought to them by a pair of delightful young Siamese ladies (servants at the consulate), they looked up from their tea and eggs to see Horatio Chalke approaching in long, purposeful strides across the damp lawn. There had been showers of light rain during the night and a wonderful smell of jasmine filled the air.

From their veranda vantage point, the two recent arrivals had a direct view onto the broad and bustling Chao Phraya River which, even at this early hour, was jammed with all manner of waterborne traffic. The lack of proper roads in Siam – there was just a single six-mile stretch, named, fittingly, New Road, that passed outside the main gates of the consulate – meant that the river provided the main artery by which most of the city's transport flowed. Leading from the river were countless canals, known locally as *klongs*, which carried people and goods in smaller craft further inland, towards the shops and dwellings that sprawled all over the metropolis. The growth of Siam, since ancient times, had taken place along the banks of the country's extensive network of major rivers, streams and tributaries. Between the rust-red Chao Phraya towards the west and the mighty Mekong on its northern and eastern fringes, the country's abundance of water had, for millennia, provided the peoples of the region with their staple foods of rice and fish. Fuelled by the abundant monsoons that brought fertility to the land, this web of water provided the lifeblood of the country from which all prosperity stemmed. From Bangkok it was possible to reach northwards by boat right into the heart of the teak jungles and the ancient Lanna cities of Chiang Mai and Chiang Rai, and to travel eastwards into the vast labyrinth of rice fields and cultivated land in Isaan.

'I see you are fascinated by the river,' Chalke said as he drew closer. 'I still marvel at the industry of these people,' he remarked, waving his hand carelessly in the direction of the Chao Phraya. 'As soon as the sun is up, so are they! Good day to you, gentlemen. I trust you both passed a peaceful night in your new surroundings.'

'Good morning, Chalke.' Albert stood and offered his hand. 'For my part, I could still feel the ship moving under me; 'tis a strange experience to be back on dry land after so long being tossed around by the ocean.'

'Well then, I hope you will not be displeased with what I have to announce,' their visitor said cheerily. 'I thought I'd take you on a little boat trip this morning – to show you the lie of the land which, strange as it may seem, is best viewed from the deck of the consulate's river launch.'

Henry replied in an instant. 'We should be delighted.'

'I shall return for you in an hour then.' Chalke turned to leave but suddenly stopped in his tracks. 'Ah, yes, I nearly forgot… The letter you gave me yesterday is safely delivered. It was conveyed to the Falcks Hotel last night. I did it myself, in fact, as I had other business to attend to nearby. I'm sure the lady in question will be thrilled to receive it,' he added with a wink and an amused dip of his head.

Later that day, as Henry and Albert returned to the landing stage from their brief cruise, the pocket watch which Henry retrieved from his coat showed it was nearly four o'clock. Their time on the river had flown past so agreeably, and as is often the case when enjoying oneself, swiftly too. Both offered their hearty thanks to Chalke for his trouble and for laying on a most appetising picnic of local fruits, shellfish, and beer. Despite their secret suspicions of him, their host had proved to be a man of great charm, knowledge, and eloquence, and his clearly expressed love of Siam shone through with every word he spoke.

'A most delightful sortie, Chalke.' Albert smiled. 'I suspect your knowledge of this country surpasses anyone, save the Siamese themselves.'

'Charles Hurdus has me beaten in that department. He's been out here longer than any – nearly a quarter of a century, by all accounts,' Chalke replied.

'We have thoroughly enjoyed our day, sir, but now we must prepare for what the evening has in store,' said Henry.

'Ah, yes, the reception tonight with Monsieur Corbin. I shall see you there. My wife and I are invited too. I expect it will be a big gathering. The French do like to host such large affairs. If you will allow me, I'll seek you out and endeavour to make some introductions for you. The Siamese will be there in force too, although it's most unlikely that the king will attend. I will see if I can present you to the head of the Privy Council, who will be conducting the trial next week, Mr Gough.'

'You have been very kind today, sir, but I suggest my meeting with the head of the Privy Council might be unwise so shortly before I have to give evidence to his court. It could create suspicion that my testimony was tainted in some way.'

'Ah, yes, my apologies. You are correct, of course. In that case, I shall do my best to steer you away from him.' Turning to Albert, he added, 'The man in charge of the Revenue Service will almost certainly be there also, Mr Woodward. Surely there is no harm in you two meeting.'

'None at all.'

'Excellent. I think you will like him. He speaks good English, and a very jolly chap he is indeed, one who so likes to watch the European ladies, you know – he has a great affection, he tells me, for their pale complexions. They remind him of elephants, for some reason, creatures of which he is mightily fond.' Chalke let out a little chuckle.

'Will you be attending the dinner afterwards?' Henry asked casually.

'We will not. My wife and I are excused. I think it will be a more private affair – just a dozen, twenty perhaps. I don't always enjoy such events, to be truthful; I have attended so many during my near twenty years in this country. But your presence will certainly enliven things, I'll wager. New faces with the stories they bring are always refreshing.'

'Your wife… has she enjoyed the experience of the Orient?' Albert asked. 'It must be quite a demand on a woman, to venture so far away from home for such a long period. Why, it's almost a lifetime.'

'Ah, no… ha ha! You misunderstand. Perhaps I should have told you…' Chalke held up his hands. 'My wife of the last twelve years is Siamese. We have two children together – both girls. My wife, Kanchana, comes from a noble family and is very much at home here. It's my return to England she dreads the most! I doubt it will ever happen though. I am wedded to this country as much as I am to her.'

Although Henry and Albert had become more comfortable in the wearing of formal attire due to their recent period aboard the *Verona*, they decided to prepare well in advance in case of any last-minute hitches and were suitably garbed well in advance of the appointed time. A carriage had been arranged to collect them at six thirty-five pm precisely. Their dinner suits from Galt & Gieves had survived the rigours of their long sea crossing with only minor blemishes, but as the pair sat on their veranda, smoking quietly, the night buzzing with the sound of insects and the piping of tree frogs all about, there was little doubt that a sense of apprehension hung in the air. In truth, they could have walked to the reception, for it transpired the French consulate was just a short stroll along New Road from its British equivalent. The carriage had been running to and fro, ferrying others since six pm, and they were slated to be amongst the last to arrive. Only Lawrence Beaumont and his wife, Elizabeth, would reach the reception later than them.

As they stepped down from the coach, Henry was struck by how similar the consulate, as a symbol of France in Siam, was to its British version nearby. The style of their architecture and proportions were roughly equivalent, the French being perhaps the larger of the two. As they entered the flower-bedecked atrium, they were each announced in turn, and with some trepidation, they joined the throng. Most of the guests had passed through the hall and were mingling in the gardens beyond, where lighted lanterns had been hung from trees and attached to tall posts. As they followed the others and stepped through a set of wide French doors into the night air once more, a wonderfully cool breeze greeted them. The gentle wafts of air created a most pleasing shimmer on the rippling shallow waters close to the banks of the great river. There was music too. The sound of a flute accompanying a gathering of stringed instruments floated dreamily into the balmy evening. Henry and Albert cast their eyes about. Almost instantly, amongst the fireflies darting all around, they were gratified to see that Horatio Chalke and a petite Siamese lady of considerable beauty were approaching them, each with a glass of champagne in their hands.

'What-ho, gentlemen. May I present my wife, Kanchana.'

During the introductions, Henry found he could not take his eyes off the lady before him. He was instantly struck by her exquisite smile as she greeted them. He judged her to be in her early thirties. Her raven-black hair was tied into an ornate bun, exposing her long, elegant neck to the soft lighting. Chalke's wife was indeed a beauty of the first order. A waiter brought a tray and Henry took a glass of champagne.

'So, you are the star witness we have all been hearing about.' Kanchana spoke with an almost perfect English accent.

'Ha ha ha, I am but a humble driver of horses, madam. A man drawn into circumstances beyond his control. This is such an occasion as I have never witnessed before.' Henry soon found the lady a fascinating conversationalist, with no airs and graces, and as Albert was ushered away by Chalke to meet Luang Phitisak Rattana, the head of the Siamese Revenue, they were left alone to chat together contentedly on subjects that Henry found easy to discuss. Kanchana was not only beautiful, but she had a knack of putting a man at his ease. He wondered idly how she and Chalke had met as he reached for his third glass of champagne. Just as he was enlightening Kanchana about how he'd met his own wife, Caroline, another lady approached them from the side. Equally vivacious but much taller and with more European features, the interloper drew closer, and without saying a word, embraced Kanchana as if she were a long-lost sister.

'Mr Gough, can I introduce you to Mademoiselle Françoise Mielette. She is my cousin, just arrived from Cambodia. I have not seen her in nearly two years.' As Henry made a slight bow of greeting, Kanchana cried, 'Where have you been all this time, Françoise?'

'Kanchana, it seems like only yesterday. I have been visiting Europe for Papa, but now I'm so happy to be back.' Mademoiselle Mielette gave a radiant smile.

Henry was enthralled. 'I am honoured to meet you, mademoiselle,' he said. 'I am Gough, Mister Henry Gough, at your service.'

'A handsome man, at last, and English too!' Mademoiselle Mielette giggled. Her soft French accent was as delightful as Henry had ever encountered. 'But please, call me Françoise. I have been so bored up to now.'

'Oh, Françoise!' Kanchana exclaimed. 'You are such a talker. Ignore her flattery, Mr Gough. She has always been a little wild, ha ha!' Turning to speak directly to her cousin, she said, 'When did you arrive, and was the journey arduous?'

'Last night, and yes! The trip from Battambang was as tedious as ever. I hate boats at the best of times, but Papa insisted on it, so here I am. We all have to do as Papa says – sometimes, even King Norodom, ha ha ha!'

'Your lovely papa? Is he still advising the king?'

'*Assurément.*' Françoise slipped into French and let out an affected yawn. With Hurdus' language lessons turning somersaults in his head, Henry took her to mean "most certainly".

'I'm afraid I speak very little French, mademoiselle,' he advanced cautiously.

'Well, I must teach you then.' She laughed. 'The first word you must learn is "Françoise". Now repeat after me: *Françoise*.' Her lips parted deliciously as she mouthed her name to him.

'Françoise,' he echoed obediently.

'*Parfait!* Now, I don't want to hear any more of the mademoiselle *absurdité*. If I do, I am not going to talk with you!'

At that point, Horatio Chalke appeared. 'I'm sorry to intrude, but may I borrow my wife for a while? General Thonkham is an old friend of ours and would like to speak with her...'

Suddenly Henry and Françoise were alone. A whirl of people surrounded them as they laughed and chatted together. As if in a trance, Henry found he could hardly discern any others but her in the entire lamp-lit garden. Only when another guest made accidental contact as he shoved past the couple was his attention jarred briefly away from the mesmerising female with whom he now conversed – and she spoke with such a passion! Henry had not tasted the fragrance of women for nearly six weeks and was suddenly aware how much he had missed the company of the fairer sex. Françoise was simply riveting. She was perhaps a year or two older than her cousin. Her height, the tinge of auburn in her black hair, her fuller figure, and her sultry French tones gave her European blood away. But the high cheek bones, dark eyes, wide mouth, and narrow waist announced her Asian ancestry too. Henry guessed she must be one of the celebrated Eurasian beauties he'd heard so much about from the likes of Charles Coghill. Now he could witness at first hand what the old trooper had tried so hard to express. The effect was intoxicating. He knew he wanted to know her more.

'So, what brings you here today?' His opening gambit had been pitiful, and he knew it. But he had to say something, and in that moment, it was the best banality he could muster.

'As I said, my father sent me.' She smiled back.

'He is French, I take it.'

'Oh, how did you guess? Quite the detective!' she teased. 'Yes, Papa is in the timber trade. Actually, he *is* the timber trade, certainly as far as Cambodia is concerned!' She raised her hand to cover her mouth as she let out another infectious giggle. 'Papa has asked me to attend to some business for him... it concerns certain delicate legal matters. Tomorrow I will have an audience with Monsieur Corbin to discuss the affair – much good that will do me... I don't wish to speak ill of my countrymen, but the man is a fool... and as for his idiotic wife... well, words fail me!'

'You speak near-perfect English, Françoise, if you don't object to me saying.'

'Certainly not. I love compliments more than...' She paused and offered up another glowing smile. 'Well, shall I say, most things – but not all...' Had Henry detected a gesture of pure decadence flash across his companion's face in that instant? 'I learned to speak Siamese from my mother; my French came from Papa; and my English was gathered in Chiang Mai. My cousin and I attended the same school. We were the very best of friends – like two baby seeds inside a giant jackfruit. Kanchana's mother and mine were sisters, you see – from a very noble Siamese family, I might add. Aged twenty, my mother met a young Frenchman who had started a logging business in Chiang Mai. The pair fell in love. There was a scandal, naturally, but it soon passed and eventually my Siamese grandparents allowed the union. I lived in Chiang Mai until I was eighteen, and then my father fell out with some of the English community and decided to cross the border to Cambodia. He knew he would have a warmer welcome on French soil, for at that time, the English seemed to be in control of most of the logging factories in Siam. So, for Papa, it was time to "leave them to it", as you English might say.'

At this point, Henry, although he didn't know it, had fallen totally under her spell.

'A romantic story – to end all love stories, eh?' She giggled again. Oh, how Henry loved to see her giggle. 'That was my darling Papa, of course, although I could happily strangle him at this moment.' Her laughter seemed to light up the night. 'But meeting you is a reward for my long journey. These events at the consulate are supposed to be the highlights of the social calendar, but in truth, I find them so dull, so pretentious. I'd much rather be riding my horse now than sipping champagne with all these high-society dandies.'

'Horses. You like horses?'

'They are my passion. I adore my horses. Though they're not my only passion…' she paused deliciously, 'but certainly, they are one of them.' Did Henry detect that hint of fire once more?

'I have lived and worked with horses all my life. In truth, they are more than a passion for me – they are my work, my livelihood – but I love them all the same.'

At that moment, Chalke returned, this time with Albert at his side.

'I'm sorry to barge in, but I think it's time you and Mr Woodward met Monsieur Corbin and his charming ladywife. Would you mind if I dragged him away, Françoise? You both seem to be getting along so famously.'

'We were talking of horses,' Henry blurted. 'It seems Mademoiselle Mielette and I share the same passion for the creatures.'

'How interesting…' Chalke said without really thinking, 'but now, if you'll excuse us, I really think you should meet our host and hostess. You can resume your discussions over dinner, perhaps.'

Henry and Albert spent the next hour being paraded in front of the great and the good, including foreign diplomats and weighty figures from the Siamese court. There was a host of uniformed military men too, festooned with their medals, that added a dash of colour to the proceedings. Contrary to Henry's expectations, Monsieur and Madame Corbin were very gracious indeed and seemed most interested in his mission in Siam.

'Ze death of ze king's brother – *c'est une affaire* most terrible,' Corbin opined. 'I 'ope ze killer receives ze full force of ze law.'

Madame Corbin, a large lady with dyed hair and heavily rouged cheeks, shook Henry's hand with the light touch of royalty, and with a regal tilt of her head she offered Henry a pursed-lip smile and wished him *"bonne chance"* with his forthcoming court appearance. There was no doubt in Henry's mind that all in the room knew of his reason for being in Siam. He imagined it must have been the subject of gossip for many weeks and the main reason for his exclusive invitation to dine at the consulate after the reception.

Henry counted sixteen at dinner. The seating plan had separated him from Albert, and he found himself placed towards the middle of the table, next to the wife of the German consul. Much to his joy, he found that Françoise had been positioned on his right side. The meal was elaborate and consisted of six courses. Asparagus soup, frog legs in garlic, poached red snapper fish with lemon sauce, and roasted pork preceded an assortment of fruit and French cheeses. Finally, a most delicious crème caramel was presented. A selection of French wines was served with each course. Frau Weidenbach had leered civilly at Henry as they took their seats but then proceeded to ignore him. For most of the dinner she engaged in conversation with the American consul general on her left. Henry was delighted, as it allowed him to chat uninterrupted to Françoise, who had been equally shunned in her case by the Portuguese consul, who preferred to chat amiably to another diplomat's wife at his right. Opposite Henry sat Beaumont, next to the American consul's wife, who had Albert on her right side. There were only three Siamese at the table, all military men, and all positioned close to the French contingent. It was clear they were the true guests of honour, Henry mused. This surprised him somewhat, but he gave the matter little thought, so engaged was he in talking to Françoise.

As the long evening drew to a close and the string quartet played 'La Marseillaise' for the final time, Henry reflected that he had learned much from his enchanting consort. She'd revealed she was unmarried, having turned down many disappointed suitors over the years. Her character, she told him, was driven by a sense of adventure and the desire to demonstrate that a woman was "more than equal to any man alive". Kanchana had described her cousin as "a little wild at times", and as Françoise set out her life and dreams, Henry could see first hand why this description was so apt. But by far the most striking revelation was her last. She told him that the reason for her long journey to Bangkok was to give evidence, on behalf of her father, in the trial of Kittisak Aromdee. Henry's eyes widened further with each passing sentence as she revealed all the details to him.

'My father believes him to be guilty, of course, and has sworn a statement speaking to the man's bad character. Kittisak was once my papa's good and dear friend, but towards the end of Papa's time in Chiang Mai, the man took against my father, siding with the English timber merchants. He threatened Papa with a gun on one occasion and swindled him out of thousands of francs, besides. My father has not spoken or complained of his treatment at Kittisak's hands until now. He has preferred to let the matter lie, in part because he feared the rogue's bitter reprisals. But now Kittisak has been arrested, he feels he must speak up. According to Papa, Kittisak Aromdee is a man of bad moral character and violent temperament. It is this I must tell the court, as Papa is too sick to attend in person. He has appointed me as his proxy.'

'You know I am here to give witness against him, also,' Henry said softly, so the others might not hear.

'Of course! I believe everyone in this room knows of your purpose here in Siam,' she laughed, 'but, unlike the evidence I shall give, which seems to have been broadcast to all and sundry, I'm told that there is no one hereabouts who truly comprehends what you will actually say that will help us to convict the villain. Your future testimony is a secret to all. You are indeed a man of mystery, Henry Gough.' She giggled.

As Henry started to form his reply, the words of Superintendent Grieve suddenly sprang into his head – "*speak to no one*". Restraining himself, he continued thus, 'Unfortunately, my future testimony is something I may not discuss with you now. Much as I would like to clarify matters to you, I'm told my evidence must remain confidential until I am asked to give it by the court. I shall speak it in good time, no doubt, and then all shall know.'

'But I hear rumour that you actually witnessed the crime. Is that true?'

Henry hesitated. 'That is true, Françoise, but it would be improper to divulge anything further. My day in court will come in a matter of days. I shall tell all then.'

In return, she offered him one of the sweetest smiles he had ever seen and with a reluctant shake of her handsome head, she said, 'Of course, it is most improper of me to ask, but the damned Kittisak is much in my thoughts. How could he cut down the half-brother of the king, no less? He must have lost his senses.'

'Or was driven by some cause unknown to us,' Henry replied slowly.

'I should love to know what you actually saw. I'm sure it would be most enlightening.' And then, her head lowered and lips puckered, she added reproachfully, 'Pray, offer a poor girl a tiny morsel, a hint of what you experienced that day – it must have been quite thrilling. Just a snippet to arouse my imagination.'

Henry smiled back. 'Why don't you attend the court and hear for yourself what I have to say?'

'Ha ha ha. That is impossible. No one, save the council, will witness the trial. Neither of us will set foot into their presence until the moment of our own testimony. All is kept under the strictest confidence.' Her mood steadied suddenly. 'But now, enough of courts and the like, would you like to take a trip with me to see the *klongs*? I believe I can acquire the services of Monsieur Corbin's launch and a pilot to guide us. I should love to show you some of the ancient temples and tiny villages that lie inland by just a few miles.'

'Why, I should love it. But Mr Chalke has already taken us on a river cruise.'

'Oh, the river itself is dark, wide, and ugly. The *klongs* are much different. Particularly at dusk. They are intimate and *pretty*...' She emphasised the last words with a theatrical, but all the same alluring, flutter of her eyelashes that made Henry chuckle. 'It would be a pleasurable diversion, Henry. I crave something to relieve the boredom. This would be such an adventure – just the two of us, mind, save for Khun Wun, who I will ask to take us. What do you say? I have to meet with Monsieur Corbin tomorrow, and I have an engagement the following day, but can we agree on the day after that? I can pick you up at the British consulate's landing stage at five in the afternoon.'

Chapter Twelve

The following morning, two days before the commencement of the trial, Henry asked Albert to take a stroll down to the Falcks Hotel, where Charles Hurdus had told them they could receive a passable lunch. It was an opportunity to escape the relative opulence and mild stuffiness of the consulate and witness what Bangkok had to offer first hand. But most of all, Henry wanted to seek his friend's advice. A short walk from their bungalow across the trimmed lawns took them through the gates of the residence and onto New Road, where their journey started in earnest. The sun was already high in the sky when they set off, and soon the intense heat could be felt burning through the fabric of their coats onto their shoulders. It was not long before their exertions caused beads of sweat to appear and drip uncomfortably past their collars. A pair of empty rickshaws drew alongside, their scantily clad owners waving urgently towards the couple as they dragged their machines to keep pace with the progress of their prospective clients. Henry and Albert nodded in unison. Walking was such hot work; the time had arrived to allow others to take the strain.

'*Quok lau bai Falcks Hotel*,' Henry shouted, for the first time using his recently acquired Siamese. To reinforce the message, he gesticulated with both hands as he spoke. Much to his surprise, the rickshaw pullers, each wearing straw cone hats against the sun, seemed to understand immediately and soon had them ushered aboard their chariots, rumbling towards the bazaar. The Sampheng Market entrance was breached within five minutes, and the couple dismounted, paying their bedraggled chauffeurs in a few coins of local currency which Chalke had given them as petty cash. Within seconds, they found themselves amongst a host of bustling, jostling people crowded around the tiny stores of all descriptions. The shops, that mostly faced the canal, seemed to cover every inch of ground, looming as they did from all quarters of their vision. Fruit and vegetable stalls abounded, as did those displaying bright-coloured spices and acrid-smelling herbs. There were insects too, drawn in, no doubt, by the glut of overripe produce. The flies buzzed and weaved all around their heads and onto the faces of small children playing amongst the puddles at their feet. Larger premises now hove into view: silversmiths, their wares protected inside glass cabinets; blacksmiths noisily banging out their clanking beat; basket weavers; and medicine men peddling bottles of murky-coloured potions. The place was alive with a fizzing commotion. It was a well-natured throng too. Those folk who noticed the strange Europeans meandering uncertainly through the market put up their hands to offer the traditional Siamese *wai* in warm and cheerful greetings. There was laughter, moreover, and the sound of friendly chatter as customers bartered happily with shopkeepers. Henry knew the markets of London better than most but in his life, he'd never encountered any such as this. The assault on his senses was profound.

On reaching the Falcks Hotel, they paused briefly before entering. The place was much less imposing than they had imagined, even though Charles Hurdus had described it to them once as "no more than a bowling alley and a billiard saloon – a place where marooned seamen come to drink and sleep". They entered cautiously and were greeted by a pigtailed Chinese who pointed towards a corner table. 'What you want?' the waiter said in harsh single syllables.

'Two cold beers...' Albert replied, more in hope than expectation. To his surprise, the Chinese waiter nodded he understood and departed without saying anything further. The room was cheerless and unattractive, with the stale smell of past-cooked food hanging in the air. One corner was dominated by a long wooden dining table, at which sat four European men and an elderly American lady. They later discovered she was a missionary from Ohio. As Albert and Henry took their seats, the quintet interrupted their conversation to gaze enquiringly at the new entrants. After a few seconds of cold staring, they nodded their acceptance and resumed their debate. As the tray of beer arrived, Henry spoke to the waiter.

'Perchance, do you have a private room in this establishment?'

'You want loom? Come with me.'

A short distance along a teak-lined passage, an inner sitting area, complete with table and a handful of chairs, appeared. A bird-stained window opened onto the river, where half a dozen fishermen could be seen in the distance, wading in the shallows while casting bamboo-framed nets into the soft-brown water. When the Chinaman had departed, his black pigtail flicking onto his shoulder as he left, Henry turned to Albert.

'I have something I have been meaning to tell you since last night. It concerns the French reception,' he said, talking softly even though there was no one to hear them.

Albert Woodward looked at Henry much as a father might a child who was about to make a confession. 'I have a notion of what you wish to discuss,' he said in benign tones.

'You do?'

'I'll wager it is connected with that French beauty you were salivating over at dinner. The fact you had eyes for no one else in the room did not go unnoticed, you know – at least not by me.'

'You know me too well, old friend. 'Tis indeed the matter I wish to thrash out. I'll admit she was a most charming companion. We have much in common. It seems we are both to be witnesses for the prosecution; we have a deep love of horses; and her desire for adventure struck a chord with me too. All this made for a most pleasant conversation.'

'You are a married man, Henry. Married to one of the prettiest girls in all of London. Beware what you seek now.' Albert's voice was mildly judgemental, and Henry's face blushed noticeably on hearing his friend's counsel.

'I'll warrant I find her most attractive,' he said, his brow puckering, 'and your fatherly guidance is well received. But it is not about that I wish to speak. You see, Françoise told me her father was once a personal friend of Kittisak, the assassin. But then, she said, Kittisak and her father fell out – Kittisak swindled and threatened him, nearly coming to blows, apparently. She says Kittisak is a man of heinous character and she is here to testify to it.'

Albert made a deep sigh. 'Why that is most interesting… but it is also of no concern what she, or for that matter her father, thinks. I sense there are powerful forces at work here. Why, I expect we know only the half of it. What can she do anyway? There is something in her manner I did not like, Henry. I smell a deception of some kind, and I fear your judgement may be clouded by her beauty – undoubted as it is. Tell me honestly, did she press you to speak about your testimony?'

Henry swallowed hard. 'She did, if you must know... She pushed me to speak of what I'd seen that night in Ashburn Place. I refused to answer.'

'Good. I had an idea she might question you on that subject. I should leave her well alone, young man.' Albert harrumphed.

'I have agreed to meet her tomorrow evening...' As Albert's eyelids broadened, Henry pressed on. 'She wishes to show me the canals and has offered to collect me in the French consul general's launch an hour before dusk. I have a mind to send word that I am indisposed, but something in me speaks against it. You see, I sense this might also provide us with an opening to find out more of what she knows – what her intentions are also, maybe even some insights into how the French view affairs. For me, it is too much of a coincidence that she and I should meet under these circumstances. I, like you, suspect there is a game of some kind afoot.'

'I don't like it, Henry.'

'Are we not here to unearth a traitor, Albert? Françoise's association through marriage with Chalke seems all the more suspicious in the light of current affairs.'

Albert took out his pipe and sucked on the stem. At length he replied. 'If you have agreed to see this woman, and you assure me you are not blinded by her charms, then I concur. 'Tis indeed an excellent opportunity to further our cause. But first, I suggest we speak to Beaumont. These developments may be cause enough to send our first telegram to London. Hope may be able to shine some light on things. And now, please call for Mr Pigtail. I am starving hungry and am anxious to see what this menu has in store for us.'

Beaumont was in his study, drinking milkless tea while poring over a clutch of yellowed documents, when Henry and Albert were ushered into his presence by the statuesque Jasvinder Singh.

'Ah, I am glad you gentlemen have come. I was going to call for you myself, in fact. I have received news that Monsieur Corbin's launch will be visiting the landing stage at five pm tomorrow, and Mr Gough will be a passenger in it when it leaves shortly after.'

'It is about that which we wish to speak, sir,' said Albert Woodward

'I see no harm in it, if that is your issue. I have already given my permission for the launch to berth, but I wanted you to be aware that the lady in question, a most vivacious person, I may freely add, Mademoiselle Françoise Mielette, is related by marriage to Horatio Chalke.'

Henry recounted his conversations with Françoise at the French reception and the more recent discussions he'd had with Albert on the subject. The consul general listened intently throughout. Henry concluded by saying, 'If you have no objections, I should like to take up her offer, sir, as I feel it may advance our cause. I may learn something if I proffer my questions with finesse.'

'I have no objections,' Beaumont replied. 'Quite the opposite, in fact. Pray proceed, but beware the wiles of a woman – and a French woman at that! They can be the most beautiful and scheming as any I have ever encountered. And I knew plenty of them during my service for Her Majesty in Vietnam in the years before I took up this position, I can tell you.' Beaumont paused and then let out a peculiar strangled hoot. 'Ha ha! Not in the biblical sense, I might add. Ha ha!'

'Do you think this warrants a telegram to the War Office, sir?' Albert asked.

'Certainly. I think Hope should know of it. Pray, do me the service of drafting it for me. When you have completed the task, return and we shall dispatch it together. The time for sending and receiving telegrams each day is between three and five o'clock, which is between eight and ten in the morning in London. The ones we send to London are dispatched first, so pray do not dally, as we must have our text prepared before the deadline. It will give me the chance to show you how the new private telegraph system functions. It has recently been installed on a trial which, if successful, will allow further machines to be more widely spread in whatever countries the Foreign Office wishes. It's important you know how to use it, as I may have to travel upcountry after the court hearing, and I could be away a while. You may need to send a private telegram to Hope in my absence.'

Beaumont indicated the pair could leave. As they rose to go, he added bitterly, 'It's this wretched Chaldecott business that calls me away. I will do all I can to resist, as it seems they have found the absconder at last – drunk, as I suspected. The problem is the blighter has been accused of assaulting a local woman, and I'm informed that only my personal attendance will sort matters out. Hopefully things up there will quieten sufficiently to allow me to delay my journey a while longer. But the truth is I have been due a visit to Chiang Mai for a while now; I've not been to the northern borders since I arrived…' He shook his head gloomily.

~:~

After a second meeting with the consul general an hour later, during which the telegram to Hope was successfully dispatched within the deadline, Henry and Albert were shown how to use the private telegram machine. When all was understood, they found Horatio Chalke, who escorted them along the vestibule, past the grand polished staircase, into the rather cramped office of Frederick Archbold. Archbold had, for the last six months, been the legal advisor to His Majesty Chulalongkorn's most excellent Privy Council. Chalke made the excuse of some pressing engagement and left them alone with the lawyer.

Frederick Archbold's bond to his illustrious grandfather, and part-namesake, was a subject he was eternally reluctant to discuss. Such was his relative's eminence, Frederick was asked about the connection often, especially by others in the legal profession, and each time the matter was raised, he dismissed it from conversation as quickly as he could manage. His grandfather had been a celebrated barrister and writer of legal textbooks in his day, the author of a host of criminal law treatises, which made him famous in the courtrooms across the land, and to a lesser extent, in distant America also. Although the great man had been dead for nearly a decade, the memory of "pretty Archbold" lingered doggedly on through the multitude of volumes he'd bequeathed to the legal profession. As an aspiring but much less talented lawyer (although he would never concede it), Frederick found the reputation that had gone before him both insufferable to bear and difficult to shake. In fact, it had become a positive sack of potatoes to his forward progress – a weight he had to carry into every trial and in front of every grinning judge in England.

'Oh, Archbold, indeed – no need for me to lecture you on the law,' they'd guffaw. Oh, how Frederick hated them for it.

When the Foreign Office approached him with a chance to ply his trade in far Siam, it had not taken him long to make his decision. He was going nowhere in London – barely treading water – so an opportunity to practise in a foreign land, where few knew of his distinguished ancestor, was one not to miss. Archbold, still a fairly young man at twenty-eight, had no wife either, which proved to be another factor in his favour. He could spend a few years gallivanting in the Orient and return home richer, both in pocket and mind, and with fresh vigour to take on the establishment that had once so cruelly treated him.

It was approaching dusk by the time they entered the lawyer's domain, and lamps had already been lit. 'I have been looking forward to meeting you both,' Archbold exclaimed cheerfully as he rose from his planter's chair to greet Henry and Albert. 'We have much to discuss, and I fear some of it may make unpleasant listening.'

Frederick Roland Archbold was a slender man of strangely pale complexion, considering the climate, who, due to both his attire and slightly swaggering manner, was instantly recognisable as a man of the law. Even without his wig in place, Archbold cut the unmistakeable figure of a fellow who knew the Inns of Court better than he did the inns of nearby Chancery Lane.

'It's a pleasure to meet you, sir.' Albert Woodward beamed. 'I am a regular delver into the works of your father. A veritable mine of information for a man in my profession, I must say.'

Archbold did not correct Albert's familial error. Many had made the same wearying mistake in believing him to be the son of the great man. Instead, he coughed lightly and said, 'Come, sit at the table, and I will do my level best to enlighten you to the mysterious and unyielding ways of the Siamese judicial system.'

'I am told you have been in Siam but a short time, sir,' Henry ventured as they took their seats.

'Short it has been, I'll agree, but some days I feel I have been here a millennium. Whatever time served it has actually been, I fear none will ever be enough to fully comprehend the practice they call justice in this country.' Henry and Albert did their best to look sympathetic. 'But not all is gloom and doom, gentlemen,' Archbold raised his voice, 'as I'm pleased to report there are some nascent indications that we may, at last, be leaving the days of the Star Chamber behind us, ha ha!'

'The king desires it, as I am led to believe,' said Albert.

'Then you are well informed, sir. The king is indeed a reformer, of that there is no doubt. He wishes for so much, in truth, but merely wishing it does not, in itself, allow the changes to occur. Each has to be fought for, and in Siam the pace of reform, as I well know from bitter experience, can be piteously slow. The trial in a couple of days of Kittisak Aromdee is a case in point. The man is accused of murder, a crime for which the death penalty is all but mandatory. The stakes are high but, even as we speak, I have been given no assurances that the accused will be permitted to call witnesses in his defence, let alone speak on his own behalf. Tell me, are you familiar with the case of Phra Preecha?'

'We are, sir. A man who lost his head for the love of an English woman,' Henry replied.

'Indeed – there was a little more to it than that, other charges were brought, but you have the gist of it. Preecha was a man of noble birth whose activities, including his marriage to the former consul general's daughter, Miss Fanny Knox, drew fire from one of the most important families in the kingdom. To put it bluntly, his trial was a farce, and his beheading was the cruel upshot of a legal process so weighted against him as to have been nothing more than a sham. My calling here is to ensure that such a miscarriage of justice cannot reoccur, although I'd be lying if I told you this was an easy task.

'However, I'm pleased to say the trial of Kittisak Aromdee will be conducted rather differently. I have obtained the agreement of the king to allow prosecution witnesses to be cross-examined by counsel for the defendant. That, at least, is progress. But whether Kittisak is permitted to take the stand himself and speak against his accusers is another matter. I have asked it; I have explained to the king personally the rights of the accused and their importance as part of a civilised and forward-looking way to decide a man's guilt. But, as I sit amongst you now, with less than forty-eight hours before the trial commences, no approval has yet been forthcoming.'

'I am told the king wishes to convict,' Henry said.

'That may be the case, and from the evidence I have seen, including your own, Mr Gough, the verdict seems little in doubt. This is precisely why I have canvassed His Majesty so ardently on the matter. In my view, whatever Kittisak says in his defence will make no material difference to the outcome. He will lose his head, and that'll be the end of it. So, I say, why not let him speak to the court? I am concerned the king is fearful of something. I hear that there are factions who may wish to depose him. These are mere rumours, which do not concern me as a man used to dealing in truths. But if the gossip is true, then all the more reason to spike the opposition's guns by showing his people they have rights – they can expect a fair trial in future. This way, the king must surely gain the support of his subjects, once the news is broadcast in the land that he is both merciful and just.'

Archbold stopped as if to gather his breath. 'But enough of this, we must return to your part in this trial, Mr Gough.' Addressing Albert he added, 'As a man no doubt used to giving evidence before the magistrate, Mr Woodward, I expect you will also be interested in what I have to say.'

'I most certainly would be, sir. Your report thus far has been most enlightening.'

'Very well. The first thing you must know is there will be thirty judges, all privy councillors, each personally selected by the king on advice of the regent, Lord Sirrichi Bamroong. The trial will take place in the Privy Council Chamber, a most venerated part of the Royal Palace. There will be no plea. Witnesses for the prosecution will be called in turn. There are nineteen slated in all – you, Mr Gough, will be the last. The evidence shall be heard in private. No other personage will be allowed to witness the proceeding. The king will not be present, although I'm informed that the regent may attend for all or part, as suits him. Important for you, perhaps, may be the news that as legal advisor to His Majesty, with no material part to play in proceedings, I have been granted exceptional permission by the king to observe the trial. I will have no right of audience whatsoever within the chamber, of course, and I will not be able to advise you once proceedings commence.'

Henry nodded, feeling the anxiety mount.

'Each witness will be summoned in turn,' Archbold continued, 'and then, after questions put to them by Kittisak's defence lawyer, a man by the name of Boon Nam Chaidee, which as I mentioned is the major concession I have obtained from His Majesty, they will be dismissed. In this way, no witness shall hear the other's testimony. When it is your turn to speak, you must speak clearly and answer the questions put directly. The questions and your responses will be translated for you by one of the consulate's linguists, a man you know, I believe – Mr Charles Hurdus.'

On hearing that Charles would be at his side, Henry felt much lifted. 'Charles became a good friend during our voyage from Southampton, so I am most pleased to hear he will be present in court.'

'Excellent, but in view of your amity, I think it's best you make light of the matter, if you are pressed. Such a beneficial association may be considered inappropriate in some circles.'

'What do you expect I will be asked, sir?'

'Ha! Apart from your name, I doubt you will be asked many questions at all, maybe just one, in fact. For sure, I certainly do not expect you to be in the witness box for very long!'

In return, Henry's frown spoke volumes.

Archbold thundered on. 'It's likely you will be asked to recount what you saw that night. Make sure your answer is delivered at a steady speed to allow Mr Hurdus to translate. But, the single question, sir, the only one on which the verdict shall hang must be this...' Archbold took a deep breath and in the tones of a high-court judge said, 'Do you, Henry Gough, recognise the defendant as the man who brutally murdered Prince Gagananga Wararit, half-brother to His Majesty, in cold blood, on the night of 21st February, in London, as you went about your lawful business?'

'I see,' Henry said quietly.

'The other witnesses are but fluff compared to your testimony.'

There was silence for a moment. At length, Henry asked, 'Will the verdict be reached as soon as the last witnesses are heard?'

'I very much doubt it. Notwithstanding the matter of whether Kittisak will be allowed to enter the witness box, the king has granted closing arguments on both sides. In Kittisak's case, these will be in mitigation, for sure. His counsel will plead for mercy, identifying whatever extenuating circumstances he can muster, but it will be to no avail – of that, I'm sure. The council will retire to consider its verdict. A month's deliberation is typical, during which they may wish to recall witnesses. But this case is most singular, so a judgement may be reached much sooner.

'After the guilty verdict is reached, the sentence will be announced, which the Council of State must then confirm.

And finally, the king himself will have to endorse both verdict and sentence. That will be a formality. Chulalongkorn may want to appear wise and merciful, but he will not wish to be seen as weak. That would be considered as taking matters to the extreme. After the royal endorsement, I doubt if Kittisak will keep his head for a further week. In some cases, it is customary to transport the accused to his place of birth, where the execution will take place. If that is decided, there may be some delay, born as he was in Chiang Mai. A journey of over four hundred miles may take another ten days or so. Whatever the pronouncement, it will end soon, and I'll wager you shall be home for Christmas.'

Chapter Thirteen

On receiving Beaumont's telegram from Bangkok, Nathanial Hope, Head of War Office Intelligence, called Rupert Lappin immediately into his Whitehall office.

'I don't like the look of this,' he said, passing him the message. 'I want you to research our files – see if you can find some record of the lady. There is something about this Mielette woman that strikes a chord. Send a telegram to Sir John Lester in Paris – ask him to find out what he can. Lester runs a tight ship; one of his people will know, I'll wager. Speak to Graham Clubb in the Asian section, also. Ask him to concentrate on what we have from Vietnam, Cambodia and Laos. I'm sure I've read something in some papers or other. If only I could remember...'

Lappin looked up from the telegram. 'If I may be of assistance, sir, I think the lady in question may have surfaced in Malta about a year ago.'

'Speak, Lappin. Spit it out!'

'Well, sir, if I'm not mistaken, a woman answering to her description is mentioned in a dispatch from Caruthers. She was in the brief employ of the French vice-consul, a Monsieur Jules LeClerc. She caused quite a stir locally, apparently. The name we have on file is different, of course, as I believe the lady went by the alias of Helene Bonsoir. The file records her description in detail: a Eurasian beauty, in her early thirties, recently arrived from Cambodia to assist Monsieur LeClerc in his duties. That is a telling set of facts, I would suggest. I don't believe coincidence can account for it...' Lappin paused, and seeing the first signs of recognition sweep over his master's face, he added for good measure, 'especially as we now know of LeClerc's true credentials and his connections to *Le Deuxième Bureau*.'

'My God, Lappin, I think you have it. There cannot be many French-speaking women of that age, description, and background in our files.'

'Precisely, sir. I recall Caruthers met Mademoiselle "Bonsoir" on two occasions. First, at a reception, and he was quite taken by her, but she asked too many questions, and he became suspicious of her intent. Hence his report.'

'Good for old Caruthers! It's not like him to turn down the advances of a beautiful woman, even for Queen and country – ha ha! Do we know what became of the woman?'

'I can check for you, sir.'

'Yes, do – and please double-check the files and speak to the others, just in case they have more material on the woman. Send a message to Caruthers too. Maybe he can confirm our suspicions. My God, Lappin, she's a damned spy, I'll be bound, brought in by the French to loosen Mr Gough's tongue. If I'm not mistaken, she is laying a veritable trap of honey for him!'

'I agree. No doubt to prevent him from giving witness, sir. Mr Gough has already had one attempt on his life. The incident off Marseilles testifies to that, and we know LeClerc was involved in some way. Why shouldn't they wish to try once more. Clearly, the French believe his testimony will cause embarrassment or derail their plans – whatever they may be.'

Hope brought his hands to his face as if in an act of prayer and flicked the tips of his fingers together. 'Very well, Lappin. Before you commence your further research, please take this down. I have to send a most urgent telegram to Beaumont in Bangkok…'

~:~

The next day, as the French river-launch drew alongside the jetty, its red, white and blue tricolour fluttering proudly at the stern, Henry realised, with some frustration, that he'd been waiting for nearly fifteen minutes. Albert had hoped to see him on his way but had made his excuses. A meeting called at short notice by the head of the Siamese revenue office, evidently. It had been unavoidable.

Arriving a full five minutes before his assignation, Henry had taken what shade he could from the little pontoon's bamboo slanted roof and gazed towards the west, where the sun still blazed over the glinting river. As he'd counted down the minutes, he'd watched the fiery ball continue its slow descent across the ink-blue sky in the direction of the distant horizon. *Trust a woman to be late*, he mused.

His first glimpse of Françoise as she stood amidships, the flicks of hair around her neck fanning gently in the breeze, soon washed away any pent-up aggravation. She was dressed in a loosely fitting cotton skirt with matching white blouse. A hint of ankle could be seen, and for the most part, her neckline was bare, save only for the low-cut cuff of her chemise. Despite the free nature of her attire, the figure of a svelte and lissom woman was clear to recognise, even under all the covering fabrics. She greeted him with a hallmark radiant smile, taking his hand in hers as they boarded. Soon the small craft, with Khun Wun (a servant of the consul general) at the helm, was turned towards the centre of the river, on its way towards Wat Arun at the other bank. They fell rapidly into such animated conversation that Henry never even noticed her failure to apologise for the late arrival.

'First, we will visit Wat Arun,' she beamed, 'it's at its best before the sun sets. We need a little light to appreciate its full majesty.'

Wat Arun, or the Temple of Dawn, is arguably one of the most imposing sights in all of Siam. At nearly three hundred and fifty feet tall, the original construction had started over two hundred years before, but final completion of the main *prang*, or spire, was only finished thirty years earlier. As the launch drew closer, Henry was captivated by how the glinting evening sunlight reflected so magically from the thousands of pieces of coloured porcelain embedded into its massive structure. A congregation of saffron-robed monks, their heads shaven, passed noiselessly through the neatly manicured gardens that adorned the base of the huge erection. As they passed Wat Arun, the boat skirted past an array of houses and shops, most on stilts, some which floated – attached freely to deep poles embedded into the riverbed which allowed the dwellings, their inhabitants included, to rise and fall in unison with the water as the great river moved through the cycles and rhythms of its life. Françoise told him that these floating homes could be unhitched and moved up or downstream whenever the residents desired a change of scene. The notion made him smile – how happy he felt.

'Veritable caravans of the water,' he replied, laughing.

From the wide river, the launch turned into one of the narrow *klongs* that spread from it. Here, navigation had to be managed with caution, as the waterway was many times tighter that the Chao Phraya, even though the level of boat traffic seemed even greater. It felt crowded and alive as the busy vessels passed within inches of a collision. Khun Wun, a Siamese who Henry imagined was much heftier than most of his countrymen, lit some oil lamps as the light faded, and the little ship chuntered slowly ever westwards towards the reddening sky.

'Would you like to try a local delicacy?' Françoise asked as the boat rounded a bend in the *klong*. 'A short distance from here is a place we can drink *lao hai*. It is worth trying, if only once.'

'Low high?' Henry asked.

'You are nearly correct.' She laughed. '*Lao hai*.' She mouthed the words slowly, her red lips pouting most agreeably. 'It is alcohol, but it won't do you any harm. Trust me...'

'Very well. But it is nearly dark, should we not be getting back?'

'Ah, no. Of course not!' she protested. 'The evening has hardly begun.' There was that smile of enticement once more.

'I have to attend the court tomorrow. I must ensure my mind is clear...'

'Oh, you will not be asked to attend until they are ready to hear you,' she soothed, 'and anyway, I'm slated to go before you. That may not be for many days. Come, enjoy the evening! Listen, Henry...' she threw her hands into the air, as if in delightful submission, 'I promise I will have you home and safe in your bed by ten o'clock. How does that suit? We will have arrived back on the other bank in less than an hour, and when we do' – she gave him a coquettish smile – 'I have something important... and private... to tell you. In order to do so, I would like to invite you into my little bungalow.'

Henry wasn't prepared for such an invitation, and his blustering response proved it. 'But... Aahh,' he struggled for the right words, 'don't you think that is rather irregular?

I mean, what of chaperones and the like? Your man, Khun Wun, is here to witness I am a gentleman, but who will speak for me if we are discovered alone in your bungalow?'

'I shall, Henry! Goodness, this is Siam – in the reign of King Chulalongkorn! We are not bound by such meaningless conventions here. I am a woman who can take care of herself! Trust me. The fact is I have a sensitive matter to broach, some business to discuss. I believe it will help you, as my news points to Kittisak's guilt.'

'You know we shouldn't be discussing the trial.'

'Why not?' she fired back. 'The whole of Bangkok speaks of little else!'

'But I am a witness, as are you.'

'Ha, but it is what *you* will tell the court that is the subject on everyone's lips.'

'My evidence is quite simple. I will tell them what I saw that night.'

'And you will identify Kittisak as the killer, too, if I'm not mistaken.'

'Of course. I got a very good look at the man. I will recognise him when I see him. Don't fret on that account.'

'I see...' She paused, and looking suddenly thoughtful, she put a finger to her lips and sucked gently. 'My evidence in proxy merely speaks to historic events. My father hates the man, and it's revenge he seeks, that is all. As for me, I have never even met Kittisak, but from speaking to Monsieur Corbin yesterday, I am now convinced of his guilt. I can explain, if you give me the chance. I have seen surefire evidence that he conducted the murder.'

'Can you tell me now?'

'It is noisy here, and besides, we are supposed to be enjoying an evening together. I will reveal all later,' she teased. 'It will not take long, I promise...'

This extraordinary revelation from Françoise did little to improve Henry's already bewildered state of mind. But the tantalising prospect of learning something that drove deep into the heart of the trial would be difficult to ignore. He also knew that an accusation of impropriety could be levelled against him if he succumbed to her bold offer to meet alone – and at night, to boot. In the end, his instinct to gather intelligence got the better of him.

At length, he said, 'Very well. Providing Khun Wun can return me to the British landing stage by ten o'clock, I will come and hear what you have to say.'

'Excellent!' She gave a little jig. 'But first, we have to taste the *lao hai*.'

As the launch nudged the bank and came to a sliding stop, Henry could make out a low hut on the shoreline, about ten yards from the water's edge. Oil lamps hung from the beams and braces of the building, which to Henry's eyes mostly resembled a large potting shed, constructed as it was, entirely of wood, with dried palm fronds spread aloft to provide some shelter from the elements. The dim yellow lights cast shadows onto an area of mud-caked ground, where he spied four or five men squatting on their haunches. At the centre of the little group, lay a pair of large earthenware jars, both light brown in colour. As they approached, with Khun Wun hovering behind, Françoise whispered to him that the jars were filled with a local brewed fermented liquid, mixed with sodden grains of brown rice. The smell emanating from the concoction offered up an extraordinary mix of aromas – in part pleasant, but otherwise most alien. Through long homemade pipes of bamboo, the men drew contentedly from the ugly mixture, their heady smiles revealing a state of gentle intoxication.

Françoise signalled to one of the men. '*Chan dong ghan dermm lao hai.*' She spoke the words with loud confidence, and the eldest of the men beckoned her forwards. She pressed some coins into his hand. Passing her a tube of bamboo, the imbiber pointed towards the jars, and with a brief gesture of his hand and a shake of his head, he indicated they could partake. The others withdrew their pipes and stood back.

'Are you sure about this, Françoise? Have you drunk this liquor before?'

'Oh, many times, since I was a child. The drink came from Laos originally. It's a kind of rice whisky. Pregnant mothers swear by it during childbirth, and it is always served at feasts and during ceremonies. You must take a good pull and swallow in a single gulp. It is considered bad luck to do otherwise. Watch me, I'll go first.' And with that, she crouched low, planted the bamboo straw into the glutinous brew, and took a long, noisy suck. Withdrawing the pipe, her mouth now filled, she swallowed everything in less than a second. Wiping her lips as she looked back at him, she raised her eyebrows and took a deep sigh. '*Zut alors!* That is a good brew indeed. Khun Wun,' she raised her voice, 'you have done well to bring us here.' The big Siamese nodded subserviently and handed Françoise a fresh pipe of bamboo, which she in turn gave to Henry. 'Come, try – you will have never tasted the like before.'

Gingerly at first, he raised the tube to his mouth and once inserted, he plunged the other end into the mixture. Taking a deep breath, he repeated what he had seen. The liquid tasted distinctly bitter, but not unpleasantly so. It felt warm in his mouth – warmer still as he threw his head back to gulp down its contents. His throat stung, and his upper chest seemed to catch fire as the liquid seeped slowly into his stomach.

'One more and that will be sufficient,' Françoise called, and together, each taking turns, they repeated the process. Any anxiety Henry had felt in taking his first drink was now gone, and the second shot tasted better than the first. A sense of mellowness enveloped him, and he became conscious of a waving line of tall trees against the dark sky, whose jungle fronds seemed to circle easily about his head. As he made an effort to stand, he missed his footing and slipped back onto the caked earth.

'Whoa, Henry, perhaps we have had enough. Time to return to the boat, I think.' She called out to Khun Wun, '*Allez!* Help my friend. He is a little shaky, I fear... Help him to the boat, Wun. We must leave immediately.' Françoise now spoke in French; her voice was cool and assured.

Despite Henry's unsteadiness, he still had the wits to understand her commands, and much to his surprise, he found himself answering in the same language. '*Je me sens malade,*' he croaked. With Khun Wun adding his considerable support, Henry managed to walk the short distance to the waiting launch. His senses all at sixes and sevens, he stepped obediently into the unsteady craft and slumped into one of the canvas chairs by the stern cockpit, where he noted with mild interest, that the tricolour had been lowered from the now naked flagpole. Khun Wun cast off, and the boat turned to head back down the *klong* towards the dark expanse of the mighty river.

Henry closed his eyes; there was no pain, just a feeling of mild euphoria as a heady warmth enveloped his body and made even the smallest movements difficult to perform. The soft lulling passage of the boat added to an ambiance of unfamiliar tranquillity. He could hear the noises of other boats passing and the echoed shouts of people calling out into the night. The engine thudded its steady beat and they motored on. A thought that he would feel more comfortable asleep entered his head but just as the idea gathered its appeal, the launch jolted and scraped as it hit a piece of passing flotsam. Henry's eyes opened wide to see Françoise, looming and blurred, above him – all out of focus, but unmistakeable in her beauty.

'It's fine, Henry,' she soothed. 'We will have you home in no time. We will be entering the river soon and 'tis but a short distance from there.'

'But...' He started to struggle to his feet but his shoulders would not take the burden. He slumped back; his body, like a dead weight, slid from his perch onto the damp deck. He heard Françoise's voice once more. She was yelling in French to Khun Wun. This time, he could not understand the meaning, but her tones had become barking and strident, and he realised she was giving out orders. In that moment, a sudden fear gripped him, irrational perhaps, but an inner voice told him he must, at all costs, keep his eyes open.

Now the waters had become choppy once more. The sounds of other boats faded into the distance; it was noticeably quieter and darker. Gazing upwards, he found he could detect the pinpricks of stars overhead. Then, as the boat buffeted, he realised they must be crossing the Chao Phraya once more, heading back to the opposite bank. He made another attempt to get up.

'Let Wun try to help you,' he heard Françoise say. This time her voice sounded gentle. 'Help Mr Gough, Wun. Help him to get up.' She extended her arm to help. As it wrapped around his elbow, he could smell her. The scent of rich French perfume was suddenly intoxicating. Just as he regained his stance, the deck heaved and he was thrown to the rail. The image of Henriques D'Argent falling in a death spiral over the side of the *Verona* absently came to him, and in that instant, he realised he was in mortal peril. A second later, he felt Khun Wun's strong arms against his neck, and he knew for certain the Siamese meant him harm. Henry made a dreamy effort to resist, but his limbs felt like blancmange, and his mind was all haze. Then he fell...

As the water enveloped him, a strange sense of relief swamped him, for the sharp hands that had just pinioned his neck were released. Next, a cool stream caressed his face, as if to soothe him, as he sank into the river's watery embrace. He opened his bulging, smarting eyes but only a bible-black void greeted them. There was no sound, save the gentle chugging of a motor retreating from the abyss. Then he was on top of the water once more, floating. He gasped some air into his lungs before rolling back onto his face and sinking again. This time, he felt his arms flail. He hadn't consciously tried to move his limbs – it was instinct perhaps, and then, for another few seconds, he could see the stars once more. But soon, he felt his boots, heavy at his feet, dragging him down, down... One final involuntary struggle and he was back on the surface. He imagined he saw the moon, for a bright light so blinded him he shut his eyes against it. Immediately, there was sound – the noise of men shouting. Something hit him square on the head and slipped, floating, into the water beside him. He heard his name being called, as if in a dream, and spat out a mouthful of river as he tried to call back.

'Hold fast, Henry. Take the ring. Hold fast, dear friend!'

A second voice could be heard. 'I have a rope.'

Then the first shouted, 'Quick man, before he sinks again.'

There was a loud splash next to him, and black water fell in waves into his gasping mouth. Henry felt sturdy hands around his neck, and imagining it was Wun returned to hurt him again, he struggled to loosen the grip. But the fingers were too strong, the grip too intense, and his feeble resistance lasted but a second.

'Bravo, Singh! You have saved the day.' This time, Henry was able to distinguish the ethereal voice. Lifting his dripping head from the deck, he saw the indistinct but instantly recognisable image of Albert Woodward standing over him. 'You are a brave man, sir, indeed, to enter the river on such a night.'

'Only my duty, sahib,' the powerful Sikh replied. 'I am glad to be of service.'

Just then, Henry produced a mass of liquid from his abdomen. He heaved and sputtered again and again as the contents of his stomach, a mixture of river water and *lao hai*, erupted from his mouth onto the narrow deck of the launch.

'Best to let it out, Henry,' Albert said, trying to sound soothing. 'Whatever it is, it looks damned ghastly.'

Chapter Fourteen

'We thought we had lost you,' Albert exhaled after Henry's paroxysms had ended and the launch gathered speed towards the eastern bank of the river. 'We came as soon as we received the telegram.'

'Telegram?' Henry wiped his mouth.

'A message from Hope, to warn us about Mademoiselle Françoise, arrived in the five o'clock dispatch. The lady is known in London to be an officer from *Le Deuxième Bureau* – she is a spy, by all accounts, who used to work with LeClerc. I had just returned from the revenue department when the news reached us. Naturally, we feared for your safety. Beaumont and I ran to the landing stage but we were too late. Had you waited another five minutes, we could have prevented the whole affair. Then we spotted the French launch in the middle of the river, heading towards the other bank. Beaumont fetched Singh, who fortunately has experience of driving the consulate's launch, and together we set off to find you. We realised you must have taken one of the *klongs* close to Wat Arun, but there are so many, and we could not be sure which one, so we resolved to patrol the river until you appeared once again, hopefully intact. As darkness fell, we nearly gave up on you, but Singh insisted we carry on until our fuel was exhausted. We had been scouring the Chao Phraya for nearly two hours before we sighted the French boat again. It was Singh who recognised it first; he discerned the silhouette, even though for some reason, best known to the frogs, the vessel bore no flag – no tricolour to identify her by.'

'Did you witness what happened? Could you see me?'

'It was too dark to recognise anyone on board – all we could see were dim shapes moving against the shore lights – and as we got about a hundred yards from her, she turned away from us. Then Singh thought he saw a splash and something fall from the starboard rail. It was you, of course. By the time we reached the area and had slowed, the French were long gone. I thought finding anything thrown overboard in the dark would be near impossible, but suddenly you bobbed to the surface, and then we made sure we never let you out of our sights.'

'What a mess I have made of things,' Henry said morosely, shivering in his wet clothes as cooling gusts crossed the foredeck. 'I should have taken your first advice and made my excuses to the lady. I fear she has poisoned me too. I remember drinking some foul liquor with her at my side, and the next thing I knew, I was in the water.'

'Probably a sedative to make you more compliant.'

'But I saw her drink it too.'

'She may have slipped something into yours. I have learned she is quite a *femme fatale* in all respects. When you have fully come to your senses and Dr Billingshurst has seen you, I will tell you more. But for now, we need to get you back to the consulate as fast as we can.'

'You saved my life, Albert.'

'Not me. You should be thanking the brave man who now

pilots us homewards. A finer act of heroism, I have yet to encounter.'

Henry looked towards the cockpit where Jasvinder Singh stood rigid, tall and dignified at the tiller. He made an impressive sight indeed. At over six feet two inches in height, his fine torso was displayed in all its hirsute glory. Having divested himself of his *pagri* and outer garments to allow them to dry on the taffrail, the strands of extended hair and beard fluttered magnificently in the breeze. He was naked, save for an improvised *lungi* around his waist.

'We shall be at the landing ground in five more minutes, sahib,' the imperious figure announced.

~:~

It was past ten pm before Henry had changed from his wet clothes and joined Albert in the consul general's private study. Although the effects of the noxious mixtures he'd ingested had begun to wear off, he still felt decidedly groggy. His attempts to step into a fresh pair of trousers had seen him tumble against the washstand, but the collision with the soap and towels had caused him no further harm – other than to his vanity. Shortly after, the rather stern Dr Billingshurst had paid him a call. He asked Henry lots of questions, felt his pulse, and listened to his breathing. Eventually, the medic pronounced him fit to carry on.

'I suspect a camphorated tincture of opium has been administered without your knowledge. *Lao hai* alone could not have produced the effect you have described. It is fortunate you inhaled half the Chao Phraya, for without its impact on your digestive system, the toxins might have caused greater harm – death maybe. It appears you have discharged most of the contents of your stomach, which is indeed a blessing. I recommend warm milk. And do not dally long with Beaumont – the man can be a veritable debating machine, at times. You must rest, do you hear? You will be fine in the morning.'

Lawrence Beaumont greeted Henry with wide eyes and open arms as he entered. 'Such an ordeal! Mr Woodward has told me the story. Come sit. By all accounts, you are most fortunate to have kept your life.'

'He has Singh to thank for that,' Albert reminded the consul general.

'Indeed, I will make sure the Sikh is mentioned in my report to London. But now, we must regroup. The trial commences tomorrow. There is much at stake.'

'We should lodge a complaint to the French as soon as possible,' Albert remarked.

'I think that would be most unwise,' Beaumont replied with a loud tut. 'The best course of action is to do nothing.'

'Nothing!'

'Actually, I agree with you, sir.' These were Henry's first words since joining their company. 'To do so would merely draw unwelcome attention to our situation. I cannot see what it might achieve, other than to make the French all the more aggressive.'

'You will make a diplomat one day, I'll be bound, Mr Gough. You are, of course, entirely correct. Better to keep 'em guessing, what! It is clear the blighters wanted you dead, or at least that devil of a woman did. Whether old Corbin knew of it is another matter. When you appear in front of the Privy Council at the appointed time, we shall all watch their reaction with very great interest. I suggest we tell no one of your terrible experience, not a soul, not even Archbold – certainly not Chalke. Singh knows, of course, but he will be as silent as the grave. I trust his discretion above all. But for now, you must lie low, Mr Gough. Do not leave the confines of the consulate. I will inform London of events, along private channels, naturally. Thank goodness Hope's office had the wits to warn us of this woman Mielette's bad character – and just in the nick of time too!'

'If you say so, Your Excellency.' Woodward nodded grudgingly. 'But we must ask ourselves the biggest question of all. Why should the French want Henry dead? My only conclusion is that his testimony will convict a man they are trying to protect. But that begs a further question. Why should they want to protect Kittisak?'

It was Henry who replied. 'I would propose, if it was indeed the French, in collusion with Lord Bamroong, who sent Kittisak to London to do their bidding, they now have a responsibility to protect him—'

'But everything they have said up until now suggests they want justice to be done and Kittisak to be convicted,' Albert interrupted. 'Even Corbin himself told us so. And according to your own account, Henry, Françoise spoke of nothing else. Why, she is even giving evidence for the prosecution too.'

'I happen to agree with Mr Gough on this,' Beaumont replied. 'Ha! Mademoiselle Mielette cannot even be trusted to tell us today is a Saturday...'

"Tis a Sunday today, sir,' Henry said with a knowing smile.

Beaumont harrumphed. 'Never depend on the French. Their words are spoken to deceive us. Of course, our French friends will say in public they wish a conviction. We would do the same, I'm sure. But 'tis a ruse to mislead us, sir. It is clear to me now that the French want Kittisak acquitted at all costs; he is their man, after all. Between them and Lord Bamroong, they have made him promises of protection. Even the French have been known to show some fidelity, at times. And furthermore, what stories might the man tell before he has his head removed? Surely, once he knows he is to be executed, he will tell all and implicate others – and a most unhappy outcome that would be for all of the others concerned. This they cannot tolerate.

'Archbold says the evidence of other witnesses in the trial is mostly hearsay and testimony of bad character. This prosecution might appear, at first inspection, to be just a sham to please the king by securing a conviction, but I suspect with the other forces at work, the opposite must be true. We cannot be certain what any fair-minded judges within the Privy Council might make of it either, especially if they are presented with only unsubstantiated rumours with which to convict the killer. The problem is that most of the evidence against Kittisak appears to be so weak, circumstantial at best. According to Archbold, in a court of law in England it would not stand – there must be a risk it might not stand here either. If there are sufficient dissenters, or worse still Lord Bamroong's acolytes, within the Privy Council, this will create doubt, at the very least. The French must have realised, as we all have, that the conviction they so much fear relies on your evidence alone, Mr Gough. It will be your damning first-hand account of events which will actually send Kittisak to the executioner and confound all their efforts to save him. They can't risk it. He is their agent, after all, and a man who they have sworn to protect. This can be the only reason why they have attempted to silence you – on two occasions, no less.'

With a most thoughtful look, it was Henry who spoke next. 'I have to agree. The French and the Bamroongs must fear Kittisak if he is convicted. They must dread what he might say about their conspiracy with him. If Kittisak knows he is going to die, he will speak freely of the plot – let the cat out of the bag, so to speak. That would put Monsieur Corbin and the French mission in a very bad light indeed.' Henry paused and after some further thought, he added, 'The only other available course of action for the conspirators would be to kill Kittisak, but he is locked away in the king's private custody and may not be reached. I'm told not even Bamroong's men can get close to the accused.'

'Precisely, Mr Gough. You have it! Why, it could be war!' Beaumont exclaimed. 'My father experienced it with the French back in '55 during the Crimean campaign, even though the gadflies were supposed to be on our side! And he was right. I know. I have worked amongst them these many years. They would do us down at every turn, especially when it comes to Siam. Their avariciousness knows no bounds...' Beaumont continued in this detrimental and gloomy vein for some minutes, while Henry and Albert were forced to listen. Eventually, and mercifully for the rest, he changed the subject and turned his attention to Albert. 'As for you, Mr Woodward, you must go about your business as if nothing has happened. How have your meetings with Luang Phitisak been thus far, by the by? I'm sorry, I have failed to ask you before.'

'The revenue department's officials have been most gracious, sir, and so has Chalke, for that matter. He has attended every meeting and seems most interested in our project to help the Siamese in their struggles against the ravages of alcohol and the vice of smuggling. I have tabled some ideas novel to our hosts, which require further discussion. I believe we are making progress, if that is answer to your question.'

'Very well. But keep your eyes on Chalke, at all costs.' Returning his gaze to Henry, he continued, 'Now we must wait for the Privy Council's call. Archbold will attend proceedings at the outset, and I shall expect him to inform me in due course. I have decided to assign Singh to chaperone you, Mr Gough. From now on, when you are required to leave the consulate to do your duty, he shall be at your side.'

The following day dawned hot and humid. The smell of rain was in the air as Henry washed and shaved. He carefully laid out the clothes he would wear when called to give his evidence, and with nothing else to do, he returned to his bed with the copy of Brontë's *Wuthering Heights*, which had remained largely unread since his last day on the *Alligator*. Albert had left earlier with Chalke to attend the office of the revenue service. The rest of the morning passed slowly, with no news. He took lunch alone on the consulate's veranda. Singh brought him a plate of kedgeree, a boiled egg, and some cold chicken. Much as he would have liked a glass of something stronger, common sense told him to settle for tea, which he drank without milk. Overnight, he had slept very badly, in part due to some discomfiture in his diaphragm, but in the main, owing to his racing brain that seemed full of remembered visions of his near drowning and expectant images of his future day in court. After he'd eaten, he remained on the veranda, marvelling at the sights he beheld on the busy river and reading in patches. But the afternoon heat made him feel sleepy, and following a tray of tea, he retired to his room, lay on his bed, and opened the book once more. Just as he'd reached the point in the novel where Heathcliff had eloped with Isabella, there was a knock on the door of his bungalow. It was Daeng, one of the young servant boys under the command of Singh. The smiling lad made a polite *wai* and handed Henry a note. It was written in Beaumont's hand and read simply, *Come at once to my study.*

A clash of thunder overhead announced the much-awaited rain as Henry hurried across the grass towards the main residence. By the time he stepped onto the consulate's broad loggia, it was falling in noisy, heavy droplets that seemed to make the slanted roof of tiles sing out in pain. Rain in the Orient fell faster and heavier than anything Henry had ever encountered, and this downpour was no exception, accompanied as it was by violent gusts of wind which blew the branches of the tall palms flying onto the pristine lawn. Above the furious rain, the dark clouds announced the first signs of dusk. Henry's pocket watch told him it was five-thirty as he mounted the stairs towards the consul general's office.

'A telegram has just arrived from Hope.' These were the words that greeted him as he entered. 'It seems your ruse has uncovered our traitor. Look, you can read it for yourself.'

Henry took the paper from Beaumont's hand.

```
PARIS W/O SOURCE CONFIRMS FRENCH KNOW
OF ERRONEOUS SIGHTING OF TWO BRITISH
   WARSHIPS IN STRAIT OFF SINGAPORE
  <STOP> CONCLUSION MUST BE CHALKE
 HAS TAKEN BAIT OFFERED <STOP> W/O
 CONSIDERING NEXT COURSE <STOP> STAND
     BY FOR INSTRUCTIONS <END>
```

'Am I the first to see it?'

'You are. Your accomplice, Woodward, is still with the revenue people.'

'Do you know what Hope will do?'

'If I knew what these intelligence chaps got up to, I'd be a much wiser, but probably sadder, man. I don't know. Call for his arrest, I suppose... Send him back to London under some false pretence, perhaps... Push the blackguard quietly into the Chao Phraya at midnight, maybe – that seems to be the fashionable way to dispose of problems these days.'

'Or we could bide our time and play Chalke along. If we truly believe him to be the collaborator, we can feed him with spurious information to pass to the French. That way, an advantage might be gained.'

'Not only are you a budding diplomat, Gough, but now it seems you have the wherewithal to be a spy, also. Let us wait and see. As soon as Mr Woodward returns, we can discuss further *in camera*. We will not know any more from London until at least this time tomorrow. By then, we shall have their reply to my telegram informing them of your clash with Mademoiselle Mielette. That should make interesting reading… I vouch there will be much to mull over.'

There was a knock on the study door.

'Enter,' Beaumont called.

It was Singh. 'Mr Archbold is here to see you, sir. And Mr Woodward awaits outside also.'

'Pray, let them both enter.' As Singh departed, Beaumont turned to Henry. 'I think it best we all hear what our learned friend has to say about proceedings at the Privy Council today.'

Archbold took no time to get to the point. With the others listening intently, he launched into an account of his day in court.

"Tis indeed a grand affair, Your Excellency,' he started. 'The judges, all thirty of them, sat at eleven this morning, entirely raised up, lined in two rows on a dais above the rest of the congregation in the chamber, with the chairman placed at the centre. After initial pronouncements – these I understood to be the reading of charges and a declaration of the court's authority on behalf of the king – the accused, Kittisak Aromdee, was brought before the panel, his feet and hands bound in chains. I have to say, though dressed in the finest of fabrics, no doubt procured for the occasion, he looked a most dreadful sight – pale-faced, with dark, sunken eyes and a most subservient manner. I sat at the rear with Mr Hurdus, who translated events the best he could, given he was able to speak only in whispers so as not to distract the council from their lawful business.

'Then, the first witnesses were called. On instruction from the chairman, for there is no counsel for the prosecution, each gave his or her testimony. This consisted, in every case, of the reading aloud of a sworn statement, most of which were mercifully short – "I saw the accused hit a poor man in the street" and "I know the accused has a pistol" or "I was witness to the accused striking another in a fight over money" – et cetera, et cetera... When each had concluded, the members of the council were free to pose further questions, but most remained silent. Once this process had been exhausted, Boon Nam Chaidee, the defence lawyer appearing for Kittisak, rose to ask each witness his own questions. This practice is new to the council and caused some confusion at first, but after some discussions amongst the councillors, the chairman granted audience to Chaidee, who was permitted to continue. This, as you may recall, is the process I persuaded the king to adopt as a first step in modernising the way that trials are conducted. I regret to say that Chaidee failed to take full advantage of the opportunity to interrogate the witnesses, other than to ask them to confirm that what they had said was the honest truth. This made me rather vexed, I'll admit, as I have been trying to school Chaidee in the art of cross-examination these last two months. In this predictable manner the hearing continued throughout the day, with witnesses coming and going every quarter of an hour or so, until five o'clock when the session was adjourned for the day. We commence tomorrow again at eleven.'

'But the evidence sounds weak, Archbold!' Beaumont exclaimed. 'Did any of it hold even a jot of substance?'

'I fear not. 'Twas as I have described, and no more than I expected, sir. Mere fluff... Testimony that would have been ruled inadmissible at the Old Bailey. For the most part, it consisted of allegations of historical bad character. Not a single witness gave any direct evidence to demonstrate that Kittisak was even at the scene of the crime, let alone that he was the killer. Some proof that Kittisak may have been in England at the time of the murder was brought. A witness testified to seeing him board a vessel for Singapore in December of last year. Another recounted an alleged conversation he'd had with the accused in which Kittisak told him he was travelling to London. But that is all – circumstantial fluff, I regret to say. But no matter, at least it lays the foundations for the coup de grâce that Mr Gough will deliver with his singular eyewitness account.'

'And when will that be?' Henry asked nervously. 'Do you know when I might be called?'

'Oh yes, Mr Gough… It will be tomorrow, without any doubt. Sixteen witnesses have been heard thus far. Tomorrow has been set aside to hear the evidence from those they call *farang*. First, the court wishes to hear the report from Scotland Yard that confirms the accused had been staying in a London hotel at the time of the murder, and departed by boat to France. Charles Hurdus has been asked to read it in English and then translate it to the councillors orally – quite improper, of course, but there you have it… Then the court will hear a further account speaking to the bad character of the accused. This will come from Monsieur Emile Mielette, delivered as a sworn statement read by his daughter, Mademoiselle Françoise Mielette. Another monstrous hearsay, if ever I heard it. And following that…' Archbold paused and looked Henry straight in the eye, 'we shall finally turn to some evidence of substance; it will be your moment to enter the fray, Mr Gough.'

Chapter Fifteen

It was still dark when Henry woke the next day. Unable to sleep any further, he dressed in light clothes and strolled into the gardens just as the sky announced the beginnings of another day with a wash of yellow ochre above the eastern horizon. He felt the cool dew on the lawn as he trod barefoot towards the river, where a chorus of tree frogs were piping their nocturnal refrain from amongst the still unseen foliage. A pair of rival cockerels screeched in distant competition from one of the outlying villages that faced the wide Chao Phraya. Adjusting his eyes to the ever-brightening sky, he fumbled for the garden seat, which lay under a broad-boughed and morning-fragrant frangipani. Here, he sat and lit his already prepared pipe. After a couple of puffs, and much to his surprise, he suddenly became aware of footsteps padding across the grass towards him. Alarmed at first, he peered wide-eyed in the direction of the residence, from where the slightly tottering yet familiar figure of Albert Woodward loomed out of the dawn, complete with nightcap, silhouetted against the gilded sky.

'Good morning, Henry. I heard the door close and thought I'd find you here. I have brought my pipe too. Great minds, eh! A quiet smoke before I once again do battle with Luang Phitisak at the revenue will do no harm...' He chuckled.

'I could not sleep.'

'I used to fear my court appearances,' Albert replied sympathetically. 'You know, when I was a young man, I used to be nervous as a kitten sometimes, hardly able to mouth a word to the magistrate. But then, I realised 'tis no more than theatre, if you learn your lines well and speak them boldly. I latterly found the experience to be quite agreeable, in fact. A game of cat and mouse, no less. Well-armed with the true facts as you are, Henry, your role on stage today will be to play the cat. Once you comprehend that, you will appreciate that it is you who has the upper hand. Then, I swear, you will feel more at ease.'

"'Tis not so much the court I fear, old friend, it is what I shall say to Françoise when we shall inevitably meet once more. She is slated to give evidence directly before me. It will be a most awkward reunion, I'm afraid.'

'You should say nothing, of course, but I doubt you shall see her, in any event. My deduction is she is on her way back to Cambodia by now – or wherever *Le Deuxième Bureau* may decide to send her. If the stories we have heard are true, which I believe them to be, she will presume her assignment is completed, you have been silenced, and it is time for her to move on.'

∾∾

For once, Albert's hypothesis proved to be utterly incorrect. For later that same morning, as Henry's covered coach pulled up at the gates of the Royal Palace, the woman he had come to fear more than any other could be seen chatting gaily, less than a hundred feet away from him, to members of the French consulate. As she mingled happily, apparently without a care in the world, with the group of French diplomats ahead of them, Henry wondered if it was mere ignorance or pure audacity that had brought her to the portals of the Privy Council that day. Then she was gone, disappeared under an elaborate archway decorated with fearsome painted dragons and other terrifying figures from Siamese folklore. How apt, Henry thought.

Albert was right about one thing – this was theatre indeed. Henry was accompanied, in force this time, by a small entourage consisting of Singh, Charles Hurdus and Frederick Archbold. Nonetheless, a feeling of utter dread swept over him. Sensing his heart miss a beat, he watched in awful anticipation, from the immediate privacy of his carriage, as the retreating figures of Françoise and her French acolytes vanished into the inner sanctum of the palace. The others seemed not to notice – neither the presence of the French, nor Henry's sudden discomfiture. Because the events of the previous day had, on Beaumont's explicit instructions, been kept secret from the rest of the British consulate, of his three companions, only Singh knew of Henry's recent perils. But if the Sikh had noticed Françoise, he never showed it. His bearing of dignified silence never changed one iota. How Henry wished he could seek Albert's advice at this moment, but it wasn't to be. So all he could do was to take his instructions from Archbold and do his duty by his country. He stepped out of the coach into the blinding sun. Two Siamese guards, dressed resplendently in the king's livery, were there to greet them.

'Follow the guards, gentlemen,' Archbold barked. 'There is an anteroom not far from here, where we shall wait to be called. It will be much cooler in there.' He turned to Charles Hurdus as they walked. Speaking hurriedly, the lawyer said, 'You shall be the first. I will join you inside when you are called... You have the statement from Scotland Yard, I take it?' he fussed.

'I do. I have prepared a written translation also, so all should go smoothly,' came the genial reply.

'Excellent,' Archbold replied carelessly. Henry detected some nerves in the lawyer's voice. Archbold looked in more of a bluster than he had ever seen him, in fact. Perhaps courtrooms had this effect even on distinguished barristers, he mused.

As they turned a corner of the sun-baked yard, the guards stopped abruptly. Directly before them, waiting at the entrance to the Privy Council anteroom, stood Françoise and her coterie of followers. On hearing the clattering of the approaching group, the French party looked up, and with wide smiles they greeted the party of Britons. Did Henry distinguish a rather disdainful element, an air of knowing arrogance hidden in their outwardly friendly salutation? Amongst those whose instinctive beams greeted the new arrivals, was the striking figure of Françoise. Henry could not speak for the expression on his own face as their eyes met, but for her part, the sweetest of smiles that played across her face never wavered an instant.

The sound of keys jangling in an ancient lock broke the spell, and as the door to the anteroom was thrown wide open by one of the guards, both parties began to enter in single file. Henry held himself back and was the last to walk through the doorway. Upholstered chairs, on which the others had begun to take their places, were arranged inside the room. The antechamber was about half the size of a lawn tennis court; it was magnificently furnished in an elaborate fusion of polished woods, intricately painted murals, and an abundance of gilt and crimson fabrics. In the distant corner of the chamber, Henry could see Françoise still in animated conversation with one of the French diplomats. But this time, he noticed a markedly confused look on the face of her interlocutor. A conversation then followed with one of the Siamese guards, who obediently opened another door that led into a teak-lined corridor, through which Françoise and her confidant walked, leaving their two colleagues sitting alone and looking puzzled. As she left the room, Françoise turned to look at Henry once more. The laughing smile was still there for all to see, but Henry imagined it had changed somewhat. There was the tiniest of head gestures too, one of grudging approval, of recognition, perhaps – as if she were complimenting him on some deed he had recently performed.

'I don't know where they think they're off to...' observed Archbold drily. 'The door into the Privy Council is on the other side.' As Henry speculated on what their sudden departure might mean, Archbold added, 'I have to go into court now. When the council is ready, you will be called in order. You will be the first, Charles, then the French woman, and lastly you, Mr Gough.' As he departed, he bade them both good luck. 'The ordeal will be over in a trice!' he announced with a winning smile.

Shortly after the door closed behind him, the other door, through which Françoise had earlier departed, opened once again. There was the sound of Gallic whispering in the far corner of the room, and the remaining pair of Frenchmen, looking even more nonplussed than earlier, left their seats and departed from the chamber by the same door. Suddenly they were alone.

'What do you make of that, Singh? A strange business, indeed.' Henry shook his head.

'I could not say, sahib.'

'I thank the Lord that you saved me from that French vixen, Singh. I have never encountered such a witch. Had you not pulled me out of the river last night, she would have done for me, and I would not be here now to see true justice done. And the creature still had the nerve to sneer at me as if nothing had occurred. I have never seen such barefaced gall in all my life.'

Singh's brow furrowed slightly, but he made no reply.

Two loud raps from the inside of the Privy Council door announced the arrival in the antechamber of a tall Siamese guard, immaculate, wielding a golden mace of exotic design. In a most unusual voice, he announced "Sharrs Whooduss" which the others took to be the cue for Charles Hurdus to rise to give his evidence.

After Charles had entered the main chamber, there followed a period, which to Henry seemed like an eternity, of sitting in reflective silence, before the Privy Council door thumped from a further two strikes of the mace.

'Mamsan Francur Moylit,' the spectacular-looking sentinel announced solemnly, reading from a paper held in one hand.

Singh then rose and spoke a few words of Siamese to the guardsman, and after a brief exchange, the attendant, whose air of gravity had altered to one of irritation, returned his eyes to the document before calling out, 'Middur Henly Goose.'

A few short steps took Henry into the adjoining chamber, where two lonely wood chairs stood at the centre of the room. The hall of the Privy Council was about twice the size of the anteroom. It possessed high internal walls reaching towards a vaulted ceiling decorated in intricate designs, and with a host of carved wood effigies – all painted in bright colours, with golds, crimsons and emerald greens predominating. A huge portrait of King Chulalongkorn dominated the room, fixed to the wall behind the elevated dais on which the thirty councillors were seated, all raised up, in two neat rows. At the centre of the front row, on what passed for a grand ornamental throne, the chief councillor looked exceedingly imposing, dressed, as the others were, in the traditional costume of Siamese noblemen. Collectively they made quite a sight, and Henry found himself bowing towards the assembly, as he was ushered by the mace-bearer towards the centre of the grand chamber and to one of the vacant chairs.

At this point, the good-natured Charles Hurdus was brought forward to stand at his side. The two nodded amicably as they met. Henry took a moment to look around. In one corner of the room, a life-size statue of Lord Buddah stood, glinting gold, complete with the slightly elusive, yet whimsical smile that Henry had come to recognise was reserved by artists to depict the gentle benevolence of the spiritual teacher's enlightened countenance. To the side of the room, facing the assembly, stood what appeared to be a caged box, in which Henry could distinguish the shape of a seated man, his head lowered and hands chained in front of him. At each corner of the cage a liveried guard was positioned, all with gleaming swords at their sides. The poverty and coarseness of the barred cage looked completely out of keeping with the splendour all about, and it occurred to Henry that the prison box must have been wheeled or carted into the chamber specifically for the occasion. At the rear of the room, on a row of shallow benches, a group of men sat, who Henry imagined to be selected observers or court officials. Amongst them, Henry was pleased to see the supportive face of Frederick Archbold.

The chairman addressed the courtroom in Siamese. Struggle as he did, Henry picked up just a few recognisable words, two of which were his name, in the midst of the speech. At the end, Charles Hurdus merely said, "'Twas an instruction. The Privy Council has given you permission to sit down, if you wish.'

'I'd rather stand, if that meets with their approval.'

Hurdus translated and the chairman acquiesced without saying a word. In this manner, with questions asked, replies given, and translations offered, the proceedings continued. Henry and Charles had spoken in advance how together they might present the evidence, and it was agreed that Henry would pause after each sentence to allow the Siamese version to be given to the court.

After giving his name, his age, his nationality, city of residence, and occupation to the court, Henry was asked to recount the details of what he had seen on the night of 21st February. Because the account was necessarily stilted, due to Hurdus' regular interventions, Henry found he had time to collect his thoughts before speaking. This had the effect of crystallising his evidence, and he imagined it would be all the clearer to understand as a result. He started at the beginning, by explaining how his cab had been hailed by the porter at the Langham Hotel, who asked him to take a man, who he now knew to be Prince Gagananga Wararit, to number 21 Ashburn Place. Then he recounted the arrival of the mysterious horseman, and with his audience showing mounting interest, even excitement perhaps, he reached the part in his testimony when his passenger had been brutally cut down – shot in cold blood by the man on the horse. He revealed to the court how he had defended himself from an attack by the same assailant and how he'd managed to flick the pistol from the murderer's hand with a strike from his horsewhip.

Much as Albert had predicted, Henry began to feel that he held the court increasingly under his sway, eager as they were to listen to more fragments from his sensational experience. *Wait a little longer*, he mused – *the cat is about to pounce!* As he concluded the evidence of the incident, he glanced over to the boxed cage, where he could see its occupant once again. Kittisak was now standing, leaning his head into the bars and staring intently at him with bulging eyes, as his bruised and manacled hands gripped the iron rails.

One of the council members then asked a question, and

Hurdus said, 'He wishes to know if the accused hurt you in any way.'

'Not at all, sir. There was blood on my hands, it is true, but it came from the body of Prince Gagananga as I tried to revive him. As soon as I had disarmed the attacker, the man fled on his horse. Then the police arrived and pronounced my passenger dead.'

Another of the council posed a question, which Hurdus translated. 'He wishes to know if you took the photographs that he has seen of the dead prince's body.'

'No, I did not. I believe it was Scotland Yard who arranged for those to be taken.'

There then followed much muttering and chattering amongst the assembled nobility, while Henry stood silently erect and waited for the next question. Taking a brief look at Kittisak, still shackled in his loathsome cage, he could see the man appeared to be in much distress. From his iron box of confinement, the staring eyes seemed to be pleading to the whole courtroom.

Then Henry listened while the chairman spoke once more. After he had concluded, Hurdus said, 'The council would like you to formally identify the accused as the man you saw that night.' As Hurdus translated the question, the cage door flew open with a crunch of keys and a loud metal clang. Out stepped Kittisak Aromdee, unsteadily at first, into the well of the chamber. His feet were fettered also, and his uncertain gait made a horrible jangling sound on the stone floor. An image of Marley's ghost came uninvited into Henry's head. As the accused shuffled forwards, all in the room could see, perhaps for the first time during the hearing, how afflicted he appeared. Despite the undeniable quality of the long-cuffed clothes he wore on his back and around his neck and waist, none of this faded finery could disguise the man's stricken condition.

Kittisak looked gaunt, grey, unshaven and ill-kempt. There was bruising and cuts to his wrists and ankles caused, no doubt, by the brutal service of his abrasive restraints. Henry thought he could see dried blood matted in the mass of tangled hair.

Kittisak reached the centre of the room, halted, and meekly turned to face Henry. He opened his mouth and started to speak – in English, Henry imagined – 'I wooo...' But as the first syllables emerged from his lips, the guard at his side struck him behind the knee with a wooden truncheon – and with such a force, too. The accused man buckled instantly and tumbled, crying, out onto the cold flagstones. The guard grabbed his arm with another vicious movement to drag him up. Then, Kittisak was made to shuffle further forwards. After a few agonising steps, he halted to face his accuser once more.

Another speech from the bench, this time angrily delivered, followed quickly. And then another question...

'The council chairman asks again if this is the man you saw, Henry Gough? The man who shot and killed Prince Gagananga?'

Henry gazed into the eyes of the dishevelled figure before him and blinked. At length, and much to his surprise, he found himself saying out loud, 'I cannot say to be sure.'

The noise of muted grumbling started to grow from the raised bench, even before Hurdus had completed his translation. Amongst all those in the chamber who looked flabbergasted was the translator himself. Open-mouthed, Hurdus gesticulated with hands and eyes for Henry to elucidate.

Henry waited a while before answering. He reminded himself he was in court to do his duty. His purpose was to convict the man that stood before him – with strongly spoken words if necessary. But the truth was, as he tried to conjure up an image of that cold February night and a picture of the killer's appearance, something told him all was not right. He looked Kittisak hard in the face – there was something that nagged... Firstly, he remembered the assassin to have been a much younger, more agile man – or was that Henry's imagination playing tricks in a vainglorious attempt to bolster his own heroic part in fending off the attack? He recalled how the assassin had worn a woollen hat with ear flaps that night and a gold-coloured woven cloth that covered his face. Maybe the sight of Kittisak's tousled and bloodied hair was confusing him. The two were of about the same size and build, of that there was no doubt.

Henry had to think fast. The silence in the courtroom was now deafening, as the assembly waited with shocked expressions for him to speak. Should he perform his avowed duty, even though he had such doubts? That course would surely be the easiest. Then the matter would be settled in an instant, and everyone would be much relieved – bar the French perhaps, who surely wanted the accused to be acquitted. The agony was becoming intolerable. The French – what of the French? A final look into Kittisak's beseeching eyes reconciled the matter. He could not send a man to a most awful and violent death unless he was absolutely certain.

'I cannot be certain, for it was quite dark,' Henry replied at length. 'One and the other look much the same, I'll admit. They are of the same height and build. But there is only one way I can confirm it for definite. If it pleases the court, I should like to see the bare neck and chest of the accused.'

Hurdus sucked his teeth before translating Henry's response, which in the end, he did marvellously, in ever steadying tones. As Hurdus spoke, Henry tried to gauge the reaction of the court to his singular request. He detected a shuffling and harrumphing from behind him amongst the bank of observers and court officials. He turned his head to see Archbold staring back at him with an amused expression and a pair of distinctly raised eyebrows. When Hurdus had finished, the chairman, who had listened intently to the entreaty, started to speak in Siamese to his fellow privy councillors. Clearly, some were against the proposal and declared as much in raised voices to argue their case. But others, the majority, Henry conceived, appeared content with the idea. After about five minutes of cross-talk and vivid debate, the chairman called silence, and turning to Henry and Charles, he directed his speech once again to them, which Hurdus then translated.

'He has approved your request in principle,' Charles said at length, 'but the council wishes to know why you wish to see the man's neck.'

'Because it will either prove his guilt or his innocence,' was Henry's simple reply.

The chairman looked distinctly frustrated by the answer, but all the same, raised his hand to the guards to order them to proceed. The courtroom fell into an extraordinary hush as Kittisak's hands were freed. Looking as bewildered as any in the room, he started the process of unravelling his upper garments. It did not take long for Henry to realise he knew the truth of it. As the outer jacket was removed and the inner shirt, all stained with God knows what, fell to the courtroom floor, he had his answer. He took a deep breath before he spoke next.

In a raised voice, and with each word spoken most deliberately, Henry announced, 'The accused is *not* the man who killed Prince Gagananga in London six months ago. I am sure of it. 'Twas another man. I am utterly convinced of it. A younger man committed the crime, a man who I would surely recognise if he was presented to me now.'

The courtroom erupted. Some on the panel must have understood English, for Henry had been only part-way through his statement before he noticed the reaction to his words. The rumbling hubbub grew louder with each word he spoke, so by the time Charles Hurdus had commenced his speech in translation, the room was already full of chattering voices. A small section of the thirty privy councillors seemed to be mostly responsible for the babble, indeed a few had become extremely animated, while others on the dais had retained an air of quiet composure. Kittisak fell to the ground where he lay prone and sobbing on the courtroom floor. A door at the rear of the chamber could be heard slamming as some of the official spectators decided to leave in a hurry. When the disturbance in the room had finally subsided, after an appeal for quiet from the chairman, he turned his attention to Henry from his high-throned position. Much to Henry's surprise, His Lordship spoke in near-perfect English.

'We need a further explanation from you, Mr Gough. How have you reached your conclusion that the accused, Kittisak Aromdee, is innocent of the charges brought against him?'

Henry's reply was swiftly delivered. 'The man who killed Prince Gagananga had the tattoo of a tiger about his neck, chest and shoulders. When the golden scarf he wore around his neck slipped during our struggle, the distinctive design was revealed to me. I will never forget the sight. It is imprinted on my mind. 'Twas as if a great leaping tiger danced around his upper body – for all the world like an attacking beast!'

Chapter Sixteen

'Well, sir, to say your cat has jumped amongst the pigeons would be an understatement,' Frederick Archbold roared. 'I have never seen such a reaction in a court of law as the one I witnessed today.'

Henry, who sat opposite the lawyer in the man's constricted paper-strewn study, looked morose. Propping his elbows on Archbold's desk, he put his head in his hands. 'I am as surprised as the rest,' he replied with a brooding sigh. 'In truth, I thought my testimony would be a mere formality. But when I saw the accused, so pitifully presented before me, I realised that I had to be certain.'

'You did right, Henry, by Jove! You told the truth. What more can a court ask than that? Kittisak's life hung in your hands at that moment, and as God is my witness, your evidence today may have even spared it.'

'*May* have spared it?' Henry was incredulous. 'But surely, the councillors cannot convict the man after what I have said.'

'Ha! You may think that. I may think that. Kittisak may only hope it, however. The ways of the law courts in Siam are sometimes difficult to fathom, even for me.'

'But my statement to the police made mention of the killer's distinctive tattoo. How could the Siamese have arrested the wrong man?' Henry cried.

'That is a most important question. Why indeed?' Archbold looked thoughtful. 'As far as I know the evidence was presented to the king's court via the correct diplomatic channels and in the proper manner. It is conceivable, however, that your original testimony has been tainted or abridged in its passage by some person or persons unknown… that would be a very grave accusation, of course.' Archbold cleared his throat. 'If that were the case, it would mean poor Kittisak was destined to end up behind bars whatever the evidence against him. Who knows the true way of court politics? Perhaps some vile conspiracy has been playing under our noses all the time.'

'You mean Kittisak could be an innocent dupe who the king wishes to convict in favour of the true guilty party.'

Archbold lowered his voice. 'You may be right, but for what it's worth my money would be on the regent being involved if there is any substantiated shadiness abroad…' He breathed the words through fanned fingers. 'I am led to believe that Lord Bamroong had the principal hand in Kittisak's initial arrest, if not in his subsequent incarceration. And don't forget it was the king's half-brother who lost his life in London – a man of the king's own blood. My instincts tell me the king would be anxious to capture the right man for such a crime, don'tcha know? *You* would, wouldn't you? Deep waters, eh?'

Archbold stood and stretched his arms towards the window and the flowing river beyond. 'But whatever the reasons, dark and dangerous they may well be, you have done well today, Henry. No doubt all will out in the end. The hearing is now adjourned. It may be a while before the councillors come to any decision, and I just hope they are wise in their judgement. No doubt, we will receive the verdict soon enough,' he added lightly, 'but in view of your testimony, the process may take longer than we had first imagined. I'm sure the king himself will soon get to hear of today's dramatic developments, as will the regent, of course. The court may call for further proofs, as is their right. For Kittisak, the waiting will be a terrible ordeal. For him, the problem is a simple one. To describe it is easy, but 'tis near impossible to resolve. You are the only witness, thus far, to speak in his favour. What he lacks is corroboration, an alibi even, but regretfully this is impossible as you were the only human alive who witnessed the actual crime.'

'Can Kittisak address the court, to speak for himself?'

'In a word – no! So far, my pleadings to His Majesty to allow it have fallen on deaf ears. For some reason, which I cannot quite place, the king's advisors are against the idea. I suspect the regent is pulling the strings.' Archbold shook his head and sighed. 'Lord Bamroong is a man who, at the very least, dislikes change...'

'Either that, or he is afraid of what Kittisak might say in open court if convicted.'

'Why, Mr Gough,' Archbold leered, 'you are developing quite a cynical nature... Welcome to Siam! Of course, our suspicions may be valid. There could well be forces at work which we cannot comprehend. Who can tell what lies at the heart of it?'

'Or which person is pulling those strings,' Henry replied quickly.

Archbold frowned. 'But whatever the reason, and speaking as a lawyer who deals only in facts, I fear it is most unlikely that Kittisak will be granted a public audience at this late stage.'

'What if we could find others to speak in his defence?'

'But who?' Archbold looked flustered. 'I have just reminded you, sir, that you are the only man alive who saw the murder.'

'What if one of us could talk to Kittisak in private – to hear his story? Perhaps he could point to witnesses who might support his account.'

'It would be quite irregular for you to speak with him, if that is your suggestion. Or me, or Hurdus, for that matter – as we have all played our part in the proceedings so far.'

'Would you consider asking his lawyer, Khun Chaidee, to ask him some questions? Perhaps we could prepare them in advance.'

'I'm afraid to say, though Chaidee is an amiable sort, he is out of his depth and lacks the moral courage to challenge the court. His performance thus far has been submissive, to say the least... most disappointing,' he muttered with a rueful shake of his head.

'Then, if not me or the others, what about Albert Woodward? He is not connected to the case. He is a most experienced and skilled detective, from the much respected Excise, no less. The methods and wiles of interrogation are known to him as completely as the streets of London are imprinted in my own brain. He will know the right questions to ask and how to ask them. It appears to me, if we can bring forth evidence Kittisak was elsewhere at the time of the killing, this might give him sufficient alibi for the councillors to acquit him.'

Archbold returned to his chair and thought a while. 'Why do you do this, Mr Gough? I was given to understand that you wanted the man convicted at all costs. To give evidence to support him is one thing, but to actively fight for his freedom is another matter entirely.'

'I thought as much too, but now I grasp that my conscience cannot be assuaged. I am convinced of the man's innocence. What more can I say?'

'Very well.' Archbold took a deep breath. 'It might work, I suppose...' he murmured. 'I understand that the accused speaks fair English too, which may help us…' He paused, rose from his desk once again and turned, with his back to Henry, towards his crowded bookshelves. After what seemed like perpetuity, he let out a long sigh and returned his gaze to his confidant. 'But I fear my influence with His Majesty may be insufficient to get him to agree to such an interview.' Archbold drummed his fingers on the stack of papers before him. 'What to do…?'

At length, his face brightened. 'However, I'm prepared to make an attempt. If not me, I believe I know of someone with greater influence than I who might sway the argument in our favour. But before I approach him, I need to know one thing for certain. Do you know if Woodward is prepared to intervene in the way you suggest? To do so may allow Kittisak to walk free, and this will have consequences.'

'I do. He is as much interested in achieving rightful justice as the two of us here now. Of that I am certain.'

'Very well. I will see what I can do.'

~:~

Albert Woodward was sitting alone on the bungalow veranda when Henry returned, with only the evening chorus of clicking cicadas and whirring beetles to keep him company. The early evening breeze ran through the bamboo like wind amongst the rigging of a schooner at the turning of the tide. As the blood-red sun sank into the western sky, Albert spotted his old friend approaching.

'By all accounts, you had a momentous day in court,' he exclaimed as Henry crossed the lawn. 'Charles' account has been most enlightening. He said he'd never been so shocked by a man's words as he was today. Pray, tell me all. I want to hear every detail.'

After Henry had recounted the full story, Albert, who had been leaning intently towards him the whole time with hands on knees, sat back into his planter's chair and let out a huge laugh.

"Tis nothing to be amused about, Albert...' Henry retorted. 'It was possibly the most difficult conversation of my whole life.' And then, on seeing his friend was still in full mirth, he added with a whimsical smile, 'Apart from the day I asked Caroline to be my mistress, that is!' Now they were both hooting. So much so, that the droning insects, as if taken by fright, seemed to stop their noise for a while. After the jollity had subsided, the pair discussed Henry's idea that Albert be allowed to speak with Kittisak in person. The Excise detective readily agreed.

'If I can be of service, of course I will attend the accused and hear his story. But my mind is troubled at the thought of what Hope will make of it. I think it is his wish that the man be convicted at all costs, thereby confounding the French in their nefarious plans. But I agree, if Kittisak is indeed innocent, we must do all we can to prevent him from meeting his maker before his appointed time.'

'That is good to hear. I have told Archbold as much. He says he knows someone with influence with the king, who may then allow it. I expect we shall hear more in the next few days.' Henry changed the subject. 'And what of you? Are you making progress with the revenue men? Is Luang Phitisak amenable to your suggestions for reform?'

'Oh, 'tis early days, I fear, but I believe our steps are, for the most part, forwards. Phitisak is a strange cove in many ways – unyielding at times, well-disposed at others. We have been discussing the art of covert observation these last few days, and tomorrow Chalke and I will join the Siamese in a drill to demonstrate the practice. I have to say, I am warming to Horatio, despite what we have learned of him. He is a most courteous and intelligent fellow who seems genuinely anxious to assist my programme at every turn.'

'Oh, have a care, Albert...'

'I know...' Woodward replied in exasperation. 'I know that Chalke must be treated with the utmost caution. But something vexes me. I am usually a good judge of character, and I cannot for the life of me see how such a man could be our traitor – I have got to know him so well. In fact, he has asked us to dine with him tomorrow at the Falcks Hotel. I have accepted his invitation. 'Tis an opportunity for you to judge for yourself.'

'Very well, I'd be most happy to join you. Perhaps it will provide an opportunity to proffer Chalke with some specious intelligence to further help our cause. But only if Beaumont sanctions it will I join you. We must consult him first. By the by, has any word been received from Hope? Do we know what course of action he wishes us to pursue against Chalke?'

'Now would seem to be a good time to find out. I expect the latest telegrams have arrived from London. Let's see if we can find His Excellency in his study.'

Ten minutes later, it appeared His Excellency had already been primed to meet them, as Singh ushered the two into his presence.

'I was about to send for you, as a matter of fact. Hurdus has brought me the remarkable news from the Privy Council. Quite a day, by all accounts... Pray be seated. There is much to discuss.' On hearing Henry's report, Beaumont remarked simply, 'If that is the truth of the matter, so be it. We shall have to wear it. I can't disguise my irritation, however, as I expect the French will be utterly delighted...' Then he clapped his hands and added with a profound look of resignation, 'If Archbold can provide you, Mr Woodward, with an opportunity to speak to this fellow, Kittisak, I have no objections. Justice must take precedence over everything – even in this sea of worms we have created. Just keep me informed, would you.'

Henry changed the subject. 'Have you received any further news from Hope regarding Chalke?' he offered tentatively.

'I fear there is no news from London today,' Beaumont replied curtly while straightening his necktie. 'We shall have to wait a while longer before we know how they wish us to tackle the damned traitor. I should have thought it a simple matter. Send the man back in chains and be done with it, but who knows what Hope and his merry band in the War Office might think... For now, we must continue as normal.'

～:～

For Henry, at least, lunch at the Falcks Hotel was an event to look forward to. Despite its rather miserable reputation as a drinking house for gone-astray sea captains and fallen missionaries, the food exceeded passable. Much to his surprise, he had developed a taste for the spicy fare its ramshackle restaurant had to offer. At first, the sting of red chilli had taken him quite aback, but when the initial shock had passed, he found the unfamiliar flavours distinctive and quite to his liking. Ginger was in abundance, as were onions and garlic and a host of other local spices, including a strange scented leaf which he learned was called *pandan*. When mixed with rice and pieces of dried pork or boiled chicken, the result was most agreeable. As he and Albert took their table in the same private room the pigtailed Chinese waiter had offered them just days before, Horatio Chalke arrived, as if on cue, looking larger than life and with a broad smile of welcome.

'An excellent choice, gentlemen,' he beamed, 'I always try to take this room when it's available. Despite all my years in Siam,

I never tire of the view onto the river, and when the wind is in the west, the breeze hereabouts can be most refreshing.'

'I must say, you appear very jovial today, Horatio,' Albert advanced.

'Aha! Maybe 'tis because I bear good tidings for you both. I heard about all the rumpus in court yesterday from young Archbold. In fact, we had a good chuckle about it. Bravo, Mr Gough! By your actions you may have saved the life of an innocent man. There is nothing like witnessing the collapse of a stout party to enliven proceedings, eh?'

As Chalke poured out this effusive declaration of welcome, Henry and Albert exchanged quizzical glances between themselves. This was not the reaction they had expected at all.

'Oh, 'twas all I could do...' Henry said lamely. 'But you say you bring us good news...'

'I do indeed.' At this point the Chinese waiter appeared with a tray of iced beer. Chalke uttered a few words in Siamese, and the man departed. When he was out of earshot, Chalke continued. 'I met the king this morning – as good an excuse for being late at a luncheon as any, I think you'll agree!'

The others nodded, looking slightly bewildered.

'After Archbold told me the whole story and asked for my assistance in the matter of obtaining an audience with your man Kittisak, I went straightway to the palace, and as luck would have it, the king agreed to see me immediately. Furthermore, he had just come out from a meeting with the chairman of the Privy Council, so he was fully appraised of recent events.'

'I see – most fortuitous, I'm sure...' Henry replied, trying to disguise his surprise that it was Chalke who Archbold had asked to intervene with the king.

'At the outset, the king appeared very grave. Your testimony, Mr Gough, seemed to surprise him greatly. You see, he had been assured that Kittisak was the guilty man. His spies had told him as much in no uncertain terms, and all but a few of the king's personal advisors held the same opinion. Even the regent did not demur when the question was put to him. So, you can imagine their shock when they learned of your mysterious man with the snake tattoo.'

"Twas a tiger, Mr Chalke. A leaping tiger.' Henry feigned indignation.

'Oh, forgive me. I meant to say tiger, but in all the excitement, you know...'

'So, what happened then?'

'Well, I did what Archbold had asked and suggested to His Majesty that the matter bore further enquiry. Then I took the bull by the horns and suggested that, given all the apparently false accusations flying about, we might ask an independent person to speak to the accused and hear his story. Much to my relief, this idea did not anger the king at all. Quite the converse, in fact. He muttered something about "confounded spies" – a subject on which I did not press him for that might have been considered impudent, and then he said I could go ahead. I could find someone to interview Kittisak. I told him about you, Mr Woodward, and he replied that he had already heard good reports from the head of his revenue service that you seemed a most professional and trustworthy individual.

'To cut to the quick, he gave the matter his full approval without any further ado. So, you see, you have his blessing. It is all arranged. In two days, you will meet Kittisak. They will bring him from his cell and you can ask all you like. You may recall that Kittisak is a timber merchant by occupation who, for more than twenty years, has had many dealings with the British traders in Chiang Mai. His English is very good, by all accounts, so your meeting will be in private with only the king's guards for company. Should you require it, of course,

I am happy to offer my assistance.' Chalke paused for breath and took a gulp from his cold beer.

In silence, trying to absorb the torrent of words they had just heard, the others followed. The beer tasted wonderful. In that moment, Henry imagined it was better than any he had ever tasted before.

Albert Woodward spoke next. 'You have done us a great service, Horatio. Thank you, and I'll admit your access to His Majesty seems second to none. For him to see you at such short notice speaks to it. The consul general must be mightily grateful for your connections.'

'Ha ha! Albert – there's the rub. Your deduction could not be further from the truth, dear friend. I'm afraid that His Excellency feels quite the opposite. Beaumont is riven with jealousy. Why, he has hardly spoken to Chulalongkorn more than twice these last twelve months, whereas I, on the other hand, am a frequent, and dare I say, in all modesty, welcome visitor to the court. I fear the Fanny Knox affair laid the foundations for the situation. Her father, the former consul general, refused to take my advice on the matter. I could see that enlightened conversation, rather than threats of hostile intent, was the way to solve the crisis. The result of his hasty and portentous diplomacy was a British gunboat steaming, unannounced and unwelcome, up the Chao Phraya. And the inevitable conclusion? Sir Thomas returned in shame to Whitehall to cool his heels. Regrettably, His Majesty sees the freshly arrived Beaumont cut from the same English cloth.

'Trust me, I do not seek to undermine the new consul general. I am not an ambitious man, gentlemen, but I have come to love this country and know its ways better than most. I admit I fear for the future of Siam, too. Although I am a loyal servant of Queen Victoria and a most fervent patriot, if Britain's iron fist descends in conquest, I dread the outcome.

I fear it will end in the most awful tragedy. On this and other matters, the consul general and I do not see eye to eye. And I regret that my close friendship with Chulalongkorn only serves to exacerbate affairs. In truth, I did not tell Beaumont of my meeting with the king today. To have done so would have only provoked his refusal. I imagine he will be incandescent when he hears of it.'

'I see...' Albert looked thoughtful. 'And on the matter of the king's half-brother, Prince Gagananga, has the king ever discussed the matter with you? Particularly concerning his reasons for dispatching the man to London?'

'Ha!' Chalke cried. 'That is a subject he will not speak of – not even to me. I believe he is keeping his own counsel on the matter until the outcome of the trial.'

'So, the purpose of Prince Gagananga's visit to London has not been revealed to you?'

'I regret, it has not, Albert. I raised the matter with the king shortly after the news of his half-brother's brutal murder reached us. But he looked daggers at my impertinence. It seems there are still matters he will not trust me with. Much to my eternal sadness, the king looks like a cornered animal at times – trusting of no one, confiding in no one, and suspicious of everyone. Although we have known and been faithful to each other these many years, I fear the very fact I am *farang*, and British to boot, has created a cloud of mistrust which he cannot ignore. The king is not the carefree man he once was. He is learning that politics can be a deadly game. The manipulations and falsehoods surrounding the Fanny Knox affair have woken him to the ways of the world. It was the turning point; I am certain of it. I fear that Chulalongkorn trusts his spies more than his true friends. And as I'm sure you know, gentlemen, spies can be capricious and false-hearted – malevolent even.'

'And what of the French?' Henry ventured, biting his lip in anticipation of the reply. 'Do you see their hand in any of this?'

'Oh, my God! If anything, the French are worse than anyone – far worse, in fact!' exclaimed Chalke. 'Why, they go about their clandestine business in a most devious and guileful manner. While we British blunder about with gunboats and groundless menaces, they plot and scheme. You ask if I fear the French, sir. My reply is "yes!" – and most forcefully. But what alarms me most of all is a conspiracy between the French and the Bamroongs… the king fears it too.' At that point, Chalke halted, and as if in rueful reflection, he added at length, 'But I have already said too much… I would prefer if you did not repeat my words to old Beaumont. If you do, so be it, I am resigned to it.'

The door to the private room opened, and the Chinese waiter entered carrying a blue-and-white porcelain dish on which was placed an unopened envelope.

'Sir,' the waiter addressed Chalke with a little bow. 'The letter you give me last week. I cannot deliver. I ask many time, but no one know lady. *Khun Kop* not here.'

Horatio Chalke removed the envelope from the outstretched plate and handed it to Albert Woodward. 'This must be yours, if I'm not mistaken. I expect your sailor friend must have got his girls mixed up – ha ha!'

Chapter Seventeen

Henry and Albert's lunch with Horatio Chalke had not gone the way either of them had expected. After their host had ordered food for them all and had followed the waiter out of the room to answer a call of nature, Henry turned to his companion with a look of strange unease and said in a low voice, 'Where do we go from here, Albert? Chalke appears to have confounded us. His eagerness to help us prove Kittisak's innocence, his avowed loathing of Beaumont, his close working with the king himself, all seem to put matters in a very different light.'

'I agree, Henry. It is possible we may have misjudged him. While his words demonstrate a resounding affection for Siam and his wish to protect the country from the great powers could be construed as a form of subversion, when you combine them with his spoken vitriol about the French, it tells us a different story and much about the character of the man, to boot.'

'Not to mention the newly returned letter from our "Jim" – unopened by the look of things,' Henry replied. 'How can this be? Our ruse appears to have failed, after all. Can we have been so wrong about him all this time?'

'With your consent,' Albert was looking decidedly shifty all of a sudden, 'we have one more card to play,' he whispered. 'A final test before we can be certain in our minds that we have been barking up the wrong tree. When Chalke returns, I shall open sailor Jim's letter in his presence, and we shall all read it together. It may require some patience on our part, but in the end, we will surely know for certain if Chalke is our traitor or otherwise. In some ways, this has not come as a surprise. For the last few days, various doubts have crept into my thinking on the matter. You see, it has occurred to me that while Hope's last telegram to Beaumont revealed that Paris had become aware of our fictitious Singapore gunboat sightings, the news alone does not unreservedly incriminate Horatio. I do not recall the name of HMS *Foxhound* being mentioned in Hope's dispatch. Don't you see, the presence of our fantasy gunboats could have been reported by anyone who heard of our account. News travels fast. Maybe one of our fellow passengers – that appalling fellow, Herbert Collins, perhaps – is obliquely responsible. After all, we heard the fool telling all and sundry of our report and with the very greatest of gusto too. Why, even our dear friend, Charles, knew of it! The alleged sighting of British warships could have come from a host of others. If French spies got to hear of it, then Paris would know soon enough. But the singular facts, known only in this letter, include the name of the ship – that is, the *Foxhound* – and that it will shortly be visiting Bangkok.'

'I begin to comprehend.' Henry's eyes lit up. 'If we reveal the letter's contents now, we can be sure Chalke *will* know all. And if he then shares it with the French, we will become aware. Only once the name *Foxhound*, and its itinerary, surfaces in Paris at some later date, will we have our certain proof.'

'You have it, Henry. Until then, I think, we must show our friend the letter and allow matters to take their course. We will reserve our judgement for another day...' At that point, the door from the main hotel opened once again and in walked a beaming Horatio Chalke.

'The food will be along presently. I have to admit, Henry,' Chalke added cheerfully, 'I am most surprised at your choice. That *tom yum* soup is a spicy affair, I'll warrant.'

'It was recommended by Mr Pigtail last time I was here. I think it was a test of some kind. It certainly cleared the cobwebs!' Henry laughed. 'But the flavour was like nothing I could describe. So, I thought I would partake once again, just to be sure I liked it. Important to be sure, don't you think?' Henry asked with a hint of mischief.

'I have an idea,' Albert said suddenly, with a roar of enthusiasm. 'This letter of ours – maybe there is a clue within that will lead old Pigtail to the lady *Kop*. What do you say, gentlemen? Shall we open it to find out?'

'Why not,' cried Henry. "Twill pass the time until I feel my mouth burning with chilli pepper once more.' He laughed.

'I agree, there can be no harm in it, but I suspect it is all written in Siamese,' Chalke advanced.

'Then we shall look forward to hearing you read it to us. I'm sure it will be rather amusing,' Albert replied in an instant. Albert took up the envelope and examined it carefully. "Tis a battered missive, for sure. Pass me that knife, would you, Henry.' A second later the covering was breached, and the contents were laid before them. Chalke picked it up and peered at it with curiosity.

'Oh, very well,' he said at length. 'It might be an amusing diversion. Pray allow me to read it first, and then I'll try to draw out the bare bones from the message. I must admit, it is written in a strange hand.' He tutted. 'You say a sailor gave it to you in Singapore...'tis unlike any Siamese script I have seen before. Er, let's see...' After about twenty seconds of frowned concentration,

Chalke announced. "'Tis as we thought: a love letter from a fellow who goes by the name of "Jim" to his lady-love, a Siamese who possesses the rather amusing moniker of "*Kop*". It appears the aforementioned Jim has suffered some accident of sorts – he fell from his ship – which has laid him low, but then it goes on – "Oh how I love you and miss your embrace"… et cetera… and then some words about a future marriage, et cetera, et cetera…' He halted and peered into the letter once more. 'Aa-ha! Here is something of interest. The writer tells the lady *Kop* that his ship, HMS *Foxhound*, no less, will be returning to Singapore to pick him up in a few weeks, and he has been told his next port of call will be Bangkok, where he asks her to call for him every day, ha ha. Wait… He wishes the lady to visit this very place – quite amusing – outside the Falcks, until his arrival at the end of the month.' After another scan of the missive, he concluded, 'That's about the sum of it.'

'Oh dear, I didn't hear anything that might help us identify the recipient. Did you, Henry?' Albert frowned.

'Nothing at all…'

'But this is quite a revelation, all the same,' Chalke exclaimed. 'I, for one, had not heard that a warship was on its way to us. I do hope this is not a repeat of last year's doleful events, which played out so badly for all concerned. I shall have to show it to Beaumont. If he has a part to play in the arrival of another gunboat – pray God, he has not – I'll know from the look in those sly eyes of his! Would you mind if I took possession of the letter, Albert? I really think the consul general should see it.'

'Not at all. I fancy poor *Kop*, whoever she may be, will be none the wiser. It's probably for the best. Why, exciting times, eh! The Royal Navy is about to call.'

'May I crave your indulgence, gentlemen?' Chalke suddenly looked very grave. 'Please don't tell a soul about this. Not a single person. If word were to get out that the *Foxhound* was about to return to watch over the king's palace once more, there will be all hell to pay. Do you give me your word?'

'I'm sure I speak for both of us when I say, of course we will,' Albert replied solemnly.

'Thank you. I will take this to Beaumont directly, but for now, we must consider this a piece of intelligence strictly to be kept under the coconut matting.'

The Chinese waiter entered carrying a heavily-laden tray of food. 'Very well. Here comes your hot soup, Henry. I wish you well with it.' Albert sniggered. 'After lunch, I believe you have business with the consul general too.' Henry nodded obligingly. 'In that case, why don't you both report to him together? He may get a fuller picture that way, don't you agree?'

'A capital idea, Albert,' Chalke replied. 'Two minds are better than one, and with Henry as a witness at my side, I might even be spared from the worst ravages of Beaumont's tongue. He has avoided me since his return from Chiang Mai. We have not spoken a word together for nearly two weeks, which makes me think he must be displeased with me once again.'

After their lunch at the Falcks Hotel, Henry accompanied Horatio Chalke into the presence of the consul general. Here, Beaumont, looking a little fatigued from his recent travelling, heard the report of Chalke's meeting with the king. Then, without adding further comment, he listened with stony face to the translation of the letter, read aloud to him by Chalke. Much to Henry's relief, Beaumont had not flown into a rage on receiving all the news. Indeed, such was the man's apparent equanimity, that as Chalke spoke, Henry found himself searching in vain for signs of displeasure on His Excellency's face. The complete lack of reaction suggested to Henry that the consul general's emotions were being held in close check.

Even the fact that the new information cast significant doubt on Beaumont's avowed belief that the man now addressing him was none other than a sinful traitor drew only an elusive frown from the great man. Henry's cheerful presence may have been a contributing force for calm, for when Chalke had concluded his revelations, Beaumont seemed to understand instinctively what was required of him. He must play the game a little longer – at least until he could share private words with Messrs Gough and Woodward on the matter.

'If true, this is a shocking revelation,' he said with an air of convincing surprise. 'I know nothing of an impending visit by HMS *Foxhound*... I shall send telegrams to London and Singapore. Damned cheek, what! I'll get to the bottom of it somehow. Thank you both for bringing it to my attention. And on the other matter, concerning the intervention of Mr Woodward with the accused man Kittisak, I have no objections. Justice must be served at all costs. You have done well, Chalke.' Such was Beaumont's dexterity with both words and countenance that no one in the room could perceive the gritted teeth and seething emotions that lay just below the surface of his seemingly effortless diplomatic composure.

～:～

Two days later, Albert Woodward found himself being ushered, by a pair of surprisingly lofty Siamese guards, from the Royal Palace's blazingly adorned portico towards a forbidding citadel structure that lay within its inner walls. Then, passing through a series of winding stone passages, the little detachment arrived at a narrow staircase, where the air felt cooler with each descending step. At the foot of the stairs a small atrium lay; a table and two bamboo stools had been arranged at its centre, amidst a carpet of stained sawdust. The room was heavy with atmosphere – fusty and lit only by a pair of distant skylights, high above, cut into thick fortress walls. After Albert had been invited to sit, the sound of numerous approaching footsteps, clanking and shuffling, could be heard from one of the connecting passageways. When Albert turned his head towards the sound, he was greeted by the dishevelled sight of Kittisak Aromdee, shambling awkwardly towards him, ankles clapped in irons, hands tied in front of him, and with a single guard at his side. Dressed in the same tainted clothes he had worn in court three days earlier, he made a valiant attempt at a *wai* of greeting – his shoulders hunching forwards as he nodded respectfully to his *farang* visitor.

'Take a seat, Khun Kittisak.' Albert tried to sound cheerful. 'Do you speak English?'

'Yes, sir. I learned my English from your countrymen in Chiang Mai.' A wan smile strayed onto Kittisak's face. 'Mr Leonowens used to say I spoke better English than his business partner, who was from Glasgow.'

Albert thought momentarily to inform the chained man that he was in fact Welsh, not English, but he decided against further complicating matters. Instead, he said, 'I should like them to free your hands. Can you tell the sentries I wish it?'

This time the smile in return was broad. Kittisak barked out some words in Siamese, and after a little hesitancy from his captors, he spoke again, sharper this time, as only a man used to giving orders can. One of the guards stepped forward, and soon Kittisak was rubbing his wrists with his swollen hands directly in front of Albert.

'You are my first visitor in three months. They told me this morning someone would come to hear my story, but I didn't believe them. I am overjoyed to see you, sir. But I don't understand your connection with my case.' Kittisak wiped his mouth with the back of his hand. 'I should like some water…'

Woodward put his hand up to the guard, and much to his surprise, managed to conjure up a sentence in Siamese. 'Nam pao derrm. Khun Kittisak au derrm nam pao.' After water was brought and the prisoner had taken a violent swig from the bowl, Woodward continued. 'I should like to ask you some questions. My name is Albert Woodward. I work at the British consulate, and I am a friend of Mr Henry Gough, who testified in your trial.'

Kittisak's eyes widened. 'He saved my life from the wickedness of my enemies.'

'Quite... Now listen. I would like to help you, if I can. If you promise faithfully to answer my questions with the honest truth, I will do what I can to ensure that your reprieve is a permanent one. Do you understand?'

'Completely, sir. Thank you.'

For the next hour, Albert Woodward listened fixedly, only interrupting occasionally to clarify, as Kittisak's story poured out of him like a gushing torrent from the very Mekong itself. The tale was a fascinating one. Kittisak explained that as a Siamese nobleman of low to middling rank – a *muen* – he had been granted teak-logging concessions in the Chiang Mai district by the then King Mongkut, Rama IV, about thirty years ago. His business had prospered, and working with the English, in particular, had proved to be both profitable and agreeable. He had made many *farang* friends over the years. The French, too, had been close at one time, before some disagreements with the English traders had encouraged them to move across the border into the forests of Cambodia, where France had planted King Norodom onto the throne but ruled the country in all but name.

When King Mongkut died in 1868, the teak concessions continued under Chulalongkorn, but as Kittisak's riches grew, he had become aware that a certain hostility was brewing towards him, fermented by the king's regent, Lord Sirrichi Bamroong. Apparently, the regent had started to spread false words that Kittisak was a collaborator with the English and had grown rich on the backs of the poor local peoples. According to the swell of gossip, the regent wanted him stripped of both his position and his land, all to be turned over to his own family. Initially, King Chulalongkorn had resisted these advances, although Kittisak's dwindling supporters feared it was only a matter of time before the regent persuaded the king to cancel the concessions and pass them over to the Bamroong family.

'Very interesting, but we may not have much time. I need to hear the story of your time in London. Why did you go there in February?' Albert, who had been taking copious notes, asked.

'For my business. I had many wholesale hardwood contacts there, given to me by my English friends. This was not my first visit to your fair city,' Kittisak said. 'It was my third; my first was in 1876, and I have travelled there every two years since then.'

'Where did you stay?'

'I always stay at the Crystal Palace Hotel in Bermondsey. Most of my business friends live near the London docks. It is convenient, and the hotel owners have always been kind to me as a foreigner.'

'Did you know the king's half-brother, Gagananga Wararit?'

'I never met him in my life.'

'On the night of his death, on 21st February, where were you?'

'I was dining in the Angel Public House at Cherry Garden Pier. I ate there most nights.'

'Will the landlord vouch for you?'

'I am sure Mr Harman will. He used to call me a Chinaman, but he meant no harm by it. "The only Chinaman who eats roast beef sandwiches", he'd say.'

'Who else can swear you were in Bermondsey that night?'

'Mrs Hardaker at the Crystal Palace Hotel, for sure. I always took a cab to the pub – it was my little luxury. Although most folk in Bermondsey were kindly towards me, some of the young corner-boys, on seeing my complexion and face, could make trouble. So I always rode, not walked. I had a regular hansom driver, a Mr Bert. He took me most nights. I like to eat early, so I would leave the hotel at five-thirty. If I was lucky, I'd get a table overlooking the river. Sometimes an English friend would join me.'

'Can you give me his name?'

'It was a lady friend, actually. Sophie was her name. Sophie Duckworth. She told me she was nineteen. Sometimes she would return with me to my hotel. She said she liked the warmth – as I did… and providing I paid Mrs Hardaker a shilling, she would allow it. Both ladies were very good to me, especially young Sophie. I miss her.' Kittisak suddenly looked whimsical. 'She had red hair, you know – in all her secret places too. I had never seen that before I'd met and witnessed her up close. She seemed not to mind my age or my darker skin, or even my looks, which to her must have appeared quite strange.'

The conversation continued in this way, with Kittisak piling alibi on top of alibi and providing one explanation after another. Eventually, Albert had to bring matters to a conclusion.

'Finally, before I depart, can you tell me why you think you have been falsely accused.'

'That is easy. The regent would have my logging concessions for his own. Until I die or the king approves it, he can do nothing. I was arrested as soon as I arrived in Bangkok by the king's men, but I know they acted on the false information given to the king by the regent. I tried to explain, but no one would listen, not even Khun Chaidee, my lawyer, who is only interested in the easy life. Lord Bamroong is a wicked man who would have me dead in place of the one he himself sent to kill the prince.'

Woodward sat back in his chair in amazement. 'You believe the regent sent an assassin to London?'

'I would expect nothing else from him. He is, without doubt, capable of it,' and then with a downcast expression, he added glumly, 'but I cannot prove it...'

'But why? Why should he want to murder a man of the king's own blood?'

'As for the reason why Prince Gagananga was murdered, I can only offer you what I have been told. The word amongst some is the prince had some message for England which the regent did not wish to arrive.'

'Who told you that?'

'A few days after I was arrested, I received a visit from my cousin, who had a place at court. He told me there were reports that the regent himself had ordered it, and I was just the hapless victim who would lose his head for an act I had no part in. By his actions, the regent will discredit me also, and after my execution, my family will be stripped of their land. After my cousin told me this, I received no further visitors until today. One of my guards told me my lonely confinement was on the direct orders of the regent.'

'Not the king? I was informed you were in the private custody of the king's men, and that it was he who had forbade you any visitors, especially those associated to the regent.'

'Ha. It may look that way; that's what they would have you believe. The king may think he has given the order, but trust me, nothing moves in this palace without the hand of Lord

Bamroong. You have my word on that. I am shocked even that you have found a way to see me.'

'The king agreed it in person.'

'Oh, my Buddah! Maybe there is hope for me yet if the king has heard of my plight and can do such a thing.' Kittisak threw his hands on the table and broke down into floods of tears.

When he had composed himself, Albert asked him softly, 'And your cousin, where can I find him? I should like to speak to him.'

'That will be difficult, sir,' Kittisak blurted. 'My poor cousin is dead, killed by a stray arrow, or so they say. He cannot help me now. Only you can.'

Chapter Eighteen

'I will send a telegram to Hope directly,' Beaumont exclaimed on hearing Albert Woodward's report of his prison visit. 'If this man Kittisak has told you the truth, Scotland Yard will surely get to the bottom of it.' It was three pm and the closet triumvirate had once more assembled to discuss the latest revelations in the privacy of Beaumont's study.

Albert offered up his thoughts immediately. 'Chief Superintendent Grieve has prior knowledge of this matter. He and Hope are close, so with luck, it will not be long before these witnesses are tracked down and their statements taken. It would appear that all centres on the Crystal Palace Hotel and the public house by the river.'

'I know both establishments well,' Henry advanced. 'My work over the years has taken me into Bermondsey on many occasions, and I believe I know the hansom driver, too. Bert Smallpiece, if that is he, is a most trustworthy fellow who keeps stables in the Old Jamaica Road.'

'I shall mention it in my dispatch this afternoon.' Beaumont looked grim. 'God willing, we shall save this man's life after all. But I fear in doing so we are playing into French hands.'

'The question now must be, if Kittisak is innocent, who is the true killer?' Albert asked. "Twas another Siamese, for sure. There cannot have been many of that ilk in London in February. Perhaps we can ask Grieve to put some men on it. To search the records of London hotels and passenger manifests will be a tedious task, but we may learn much from it.'

'I will add that suggestion too. I think it is worth asking the question at least. Now, gentlemen, if you will excuse me, I have a private telegram to write. If I have news from the inbound dispatch, I will inform you.'

Hardly two hours had passed when a message arrived that Beaumont wished to see Henry and Albert once again. Henry had been washing at the time, and after he had hurriedly hauled on a clean shirt and brushed his hair, he joined Albert, and with Singh escorting the pair over the now darkening lawns, they climbed the creaking staircase and returned into the inner sanctum. A most agitated consul general greeted them.

'I sent the telegram to Hope as we agreed. But by return this has arrived. Its content is most startling.'

'I'm guessing that our new theory that Chalke is innocent has been destroyed,' Albert said gloomily. 'I'll be bound the telegram says Hope's spies have learned that Paris have become aware of our ghost ship *Foxhound*, and of its supposed threat to Bangkok.'

'You couldn't be more wrong, sir. I think you should read it yourself.' Beaumont passed the document to Woodward.

ATTEMPT ON GOUGH'S LIFE NOTED <STOP> PARIS SOURCE ADVISES FRENCH ARE AWARE WE KNOW OF MLLE MIELETTE'S GUILT IN THE ATTEMPT INCLUDING DROWNING METHOD USED AGAINST GOUGH <STOP>MIELETTE DESCRIBED AS 'RENARDE' (ENGLISH IS

```
'VIXEN') IN DISPATCH FROM PARIS <STOP>
URGENTLY CONVEY TO ME NAMES OF ALL
THOSE YOU INFORMED OF THE INCIDENT ON
        BANGKOK RIVER <END>
```

'This is most unusual,' Beaumont said steadily after the others had read the telegram. 'For Paris to have learned of your survival so quickly and in so much detail suggests that the Mielette woman cannot be working alone. She must have an accomplice at the consulate. Maybe our traitor has had something to do with this too. When will it cease? We must be truly breached. God save us if the whole French mission are involved and are working hand in glove with *Le Deuxième Bureau* – I shudder to think whether even Corbin himself has knowledge of this ugly business. My God, *Le Corps Diplomatique* used to have standards!' Beaumont slammed his fist on the table. 'True diplomats should never become embroiled in such sordid affairs.'

Henry's eyes widened at the hearing of such fury, but at length he spoke up. 'Listen, as far as we know, apart from Françoise Mielette and her Siamese henchman, only the three of us, now in this room today, knew of the incident, let alone the part she played in it – how she drugged and tried to drown me. We must believe that none of us can have informed the French...'

'And Singh, of course...' Albert muttered.

'But surely not,' Henry cried. 'For want of his bravery I would not be amongst you now. He risked his life to save mine.'

'I will not hear of it,' Beaumont said. 'That man has been a trusted member of our staff for years. He cannot be our skulking traitor.'

Albert looked pensive. 'Well, if not Jasvinder Singh, and not us, who? Do each of us swear we told no one?'

The others nodded in open-eyed agreement.

'Of course, the lady herself could have told old Corbin.' Woodward sighed.

"Tis possible, but my experience of such clandestine matters is that as an agent of *Le Deuxième Bureau*, she will have worked alone, albeit with the force of a paid local accomplice. I truly doubt if Corbin knows of this skulduggery – he's a dyed-in-the-wool diplomat. I may be wrong, of course... My suspicion is this Mielette woman must have a trusted contact, a hidden spy, unknown to even his colleagues at the French consulate, who has access to their telegram system. It is he who passes messages for her. It'll be someone we know; someone we see regularly but who works clandestinely for *Le Deuxième Bureau* while posing as a legitimate member of the French Foreign Service.'

'That seems the most likely solution.' Woodward sucked his lip. 'Such a man would be the natural contact point for our own traitor too.' He paused. 'But, we must examine our own actions, all the same. Is it possible that someone could have overheard one of our private conversations, perhaps?'

'I, for one, have told not a soul.' Beaumont looked drained. 'The only time I have spoken of it has been in this room; on that, I give you my word.'

'And for my part, I can vouch that Henry and I have not discussed it outside this room, not even when alone in our bungalow. I cannot see how we could have been overheard.'

At this point, with the group fallen into a mood of sullen reflection, Henry rose from his seat and walked towards the tall study window. He leaned a shoulder towards the dimming shadows and gazed down past the wooden exterior of the consulate building on either side for as far as he could see. Below him was the veranda, with its teak floorboards under an assortment of scattered chairs and tables. Here the Siamese staff milled, silently adjusting cushions and lighting lanterns with tapers. There was Singh, tall and resplendent, offering soft words of advice and quietly directing the others in their work. Beyond the palms and the expanse of lawn, the ill-lit shapes of boats could be discerned, gliding past on the now black river. As he surveyed the gentle movement of people and craft outside, he realised the impossibility of any discussions within Beaumont's office being overheard from below and began to wrack his brain for a solution. He cast his mind back to the events of the recent few days since the moment he was fished out of the Chao Phraya. In the distance, a stray dog limped past the perimeter fence.

And then it came to him… and with its coming, a terrible feeling of dread started to well in his stomach. He went over it again in his mind. He needed to be certain before he spoke to the others. Eventually, he said, 'I may have the answer, gentlemen.' Henry tried to look positive but his head was reeling. 'But if I am correct, I fear I am to blame.'

'You had better tell us then!' Beaumont had assumed the demeanour of a pompous town councillor.

'If I am correct, I fear we will have another problem to solve. One I dread to undertake. For it will be difficult in the extreme, both in its execution, and doubly so for my soul.'

'Then, sir, the sooner you tell us, the sooner we can find the solution…'

'Very well. While I was in the Privy Council anteroom awaiting the call to give my evidence, I became briefly reacquainted with the woman Françoise Mielette. She was with a party of French diplomats, waiting for her turn to enter the chamber also. On seeing me, she made some excuses and less than a minute later she quit the room – and with her whole entourage, too. I have not seen her since. My deduction is that until that moment she had thought me dead. My appearance, as if from my watery grave, must have been a shock – enough to persuade her to make a speedy departure.'

'Did you speak to her, Henry, before she left?'

'Not a word, although we exchanged glances.'

'Then, if nothing was said, no one would be the wiser. I doubt very much if her French companions knew of her wicked actions that night, in any event – being just simple diplomats,' Beaumont said in a voice of surprising encouragement. 'Trust me, that lady was acting on the instructions of others – bigger and more ugly fish, I'll warrant.'

'But you see,' Henry said softly, 'I did speak of it, after she had gone. I was so incensed by her coolness that I talked to Singh. I told him that I was never more grateful than then for him saving my life. I mentioned the river and commented on the woman's bad character. I called her a vixen, in fact. The very fact that the precise word "vixen" is repeated in Hope's telegram shows us the information must have come from my own lips – from my conversation with Singh.'

'But we agree – Singh cannot be our traitor. And in any event, you did not need a conversation with Singh for him to know the events of that night.'

'No. I agree. But there was another in the room when I spoke so carelessly to Singh.'

'Another?'

'Yes, 'twas Charles Hurdus... Although I spoke directly to Singh, Charles was sitting within earshot, most certainly. Shortly after, he was called into the council chamber, but it is clear to me now that my conversation, thoughtlessly given, was before he left us.' Henry put his head in his hands. 'Oh, what have I done?'

The room fell into a long contemplative silence. At length, Albert said, 'But the vixen herself could have informed Paris, via her contact at the consulate, that you were alive and she had failed in her mission. Your conversation, overheard by Charles, proves nothing.'

'I beg to disagree,' Henry replied with the grimmest of expressions. 'The word "vixen" is the proof – 'tis *renarde* in French. No one heard me say that word other than Charles and Singh, and if we rule out Singh, what have we?'

'But you forget, Charles Hurdus saved your life, also. The episode on the *Verona* speaks to his courage.' Beaumont looked nonplussed.

'That is indeed true, I have no explanation for that at present... Perhaps Charles knew nothing of the plot to kill me. Perhaps his role as spy is to merely eavesdrop and pass on what he hears and reads – a messenger only. In truth, why would the French burden him with the information they had decided to kill me. In the parlance you use so readily, Albert – Charles Hurdus "did not need to know".'

'And there is the business of the gunboats off Singapore,' Beaumont added gravely. 'Hurdus was present when you spoke of your invented sighting, was he not?' Far more likely for him to have shared the intelligence with the French than any stray passenger, I would propose.'

'But, 'tis hard to believe it of him. I feel he has become our friend,' Albert said with a resigned sigh.

'Let me tell you something which I have not disclosed before about my colleague Charles Hurdus,' Beaumont said, winding his fingers together so the knuckles turned white. 'But please keep what I am about to say close. I have never mentioned the facts I will share with you now with others, because it would have been indiscreet. To disclose confidential, private family matters about another is both improper and reprehensible. But under the circumstances, I think you "need to know" – to coin that phrase of yours again, Mr Woodward. You see, Hurdus is not quite the man you see on the surface

– the genial, friendly, helpful individual he appears to many. The actuality is that over his many years here in Siam, he has adopted some local practices that others might consider somewhat wayward. A taste for gambling... and alcohol... and a tendency for the fairer sex – of the native kind, no less. He has three local wives, as far as I can count. I grant he does what he can to support them and his countless children. In the past, his drinking has been a problem, and reports from my predecessors have been quite vivid on the matter, but each time he has been able to pull himself back from the brink and save his position.

'You see, the man adds much value to our work here. Hurdus is intelligent, resourceful, a most competent linguist, and when in the correct disposition, he can be charming too. But aside from his womanising and his drinking, it is his habit of frequenting the Chinese gambling haunts, late at night, that troubles me most. I get reports from time to time, that he has been seen here or there, circulating in one gambling den or another. I have raised it with him – why only last week I did so – but he brushes off my concerns, describing his deeds as harmless sporting activities which he rarely takes part in. I have often wondered how, on his paltry salary, he can get by, especially with all the mouths to feed at home. The tragedy is that without these vices he would have progressed much further in the service. His weaknesses have held him back, and I know at times that makes him bitter. So, maybe you have come up with the solution today, Mr Gough. By your careless actions, you may have uncovered our traitor, after all. Maybe Chalke is indeed an innocent man, as current evidence seems to suggest.'

'But what course shall we take now, if we have two possible turncoats in our sights?' Albert enquired with a weary exhalation. 'I take it we have heard nothing concerning Chalke's *Foxhound* trap from Hope.'

'Nothing has surfaced.'

'If you will allow, I have a suggestion,' Henry said. 'I propose we wait a little while and do precisely nothing until news reaches us from Scotland Yard that corroborates Kittisak's London visit. If we have heard nothing from Hope concerning the *Foxhound* by then, we must presume Chalke is cleared of all accusations. It is my belief we should then bring the man to our side to help us lay a trap for Charles Hurdus. My plan would be to trail Charles at night and see where he frequents and who he meets. You have been discussing the art of surveillance with the Revenue Service, Albert, have you not?'

'I have, and my charges are becoming more proficient each day.'

'Then with Horatio Chalke at our side to ensure your instructions are fully comprehended, why not use these new skills to our advantage and task your new students to track Hurdus around the city after dark. For sure, 'tis not work we could accomplish ourselves with any satisfactory outcome – our faces and frames would be picked out sooner than you could say "Jack Robinson". But your fellows, Albert, will blend like the rest, and with their help we might learn much. Indeed, if Charles is passing our intelligence to the French, let's give him something to share and see where he goes with it – a tasty morsel which might cook his goose. It might help us save Kittisak's life too.'

'I should be most interested to know who he shares our information with. To find out which one of them at the French consulate is a spy…' Beaumont exclaimed, clearly warming to the idea.

'Whoa!' Albert exclaimed. 'Let us not convict a man until we are certain. We have learned as much from our experience of prejudging Chalke – and Kittisak, for that matter. I think your idea has merit though, Henry. We should wait till we get news from Scotland Yard before commencing. I further propose, to be on the safe side, that we keep Singh in our sights too. I concur that his involvement in the affair is most unlikely, but it might be best to be aware of his presence at all times. Are we all agreed?'

'We are!' came back the united chorus.

~:~

It took far less time than any of them imagined before further news was received from Hope. Just four days, in fact. In that time, Henry and Albert had tried to act as ordinarily as possible. Albert's visits with Chalke to the revenue offices continued apace, with a greater emphasis on developing the skills of their eager students with tracking and trailing. Henry, with little else to do, embarked on a few excursions, visiting some of the many exotic sights Bangkok had to offer. Although he took plenty of short trips along the network of *klongs*, he avoided the wide river. For some reason, he felt he could not stomach it. He lunched at the Falcks each day, and as his taste for fish sauce, green peppers and red chillis grew, he was challenged by Mr Pigtail to tackle ever more spicy fare, the latter being more than quietly impressed by the way his newest *farang* customer devoured the choice offerings he presented each day.

Twice during the four days, Henry dined with Charles Hurdus, who always appeared at his unflappable and genial best, and they had passed the hours together in agreeable but inconsequential conversation. Despite his dining companion's longevity in the Orient, Henry was amused to note the man's penchant for hot peppers was much less enthusiastic than his own.

'I cannot abide too much spicy fare,' Charles had announced. 'My old intestines have resisted chilli since the first day I arrived.'

It was Tuesday evening when the next telegram arrived from the War Office Intelligence Branch. Chief Superintendent Grieve had put some of Scotland Yard's best men on the case, and building on what they had already gleaned from the city's hotel records, they were able to produce a list of all those claiming Siamese nationality who had been in London hotels during the week of the Ashburn Place murder. The list was a short one. There were only four, in fact. For good measure, Grieve, displaying not only great initiative but a surprising grasp of Asian geography, had asked his men to add the male names of those who hailed from Burma, Laos, Cambodia and Malaya. That produced another twenty hotel residents – nine Burmese, eight Malays, a pair of Laotians and a single Cambodian. When Henry and Albert examined the catalogue, they were mildly disappointed. The list came with names, ages, occupations, and places of birth, which had been taken down by their hotels from the travel papers presented to them. Albert noted with gloom that all four Siamese, including Kittisak himself, were aged in excess of fifty, two being over sixty. In terms of occupations, all were merchants of some type, either in spices or textiles, with the exception of Kittisak, whose entry, in bold handwriting, announced him as a "Teak Trader".

'Not what I had hoped for...' Albert tutted.

'Nor me, I confess,' Henry replied. 'The tattooed killer was a much younger man. If I had to guess, I'd say he was less than thirty years of age.'

'This may not be conclusive, of course,' Albert continued. 'There may be others who have slipped the net. Some could have found different lodgings, away from the normal round of hotels – with friends or relatives, maybe. The lists of arriving and departing ships' passengers, when Grieve obtains them, will help us discover if there are any strays.'

The other news was much brighter though, as it completely corroborated Kittisak's story.

```
ALL LONDON WITNESSES CONFIRM
KITTISAK'S ACCOUNT <STOP> HARMAN,
DUCKWORTH, HARDAKER AND SMALLPIECE
HAVE GIVEN STATEMENTS WHICH PROVE THE
ACCUSED RESIDED AT CRYSTAL PALACE
HOTEL AND WAS IN ANGEL PUBLIC HOUSE
AT TIME OF MURDER <STOP> WILL FORWARD
STATEMENTS IN DUE COURSE <END>
```

'I take it there was nothing from Hope concerning *Foxhound*...' Albert enquired.

'Still nothing,' replied Beaumont with a deep frown.

'In that case, I believe the moment has come to put our trust in Horatio Chalke. What say you both?' Henry asked. 'Is it now time for us to bring him into our inner circle?'

Beaumont grunted. 'I suppose we have no alternative. I have to speak with him anyway. We must inform Chalke of Kittisak's alibi without delay, so he may speak to His Majesty. If King Chulalongkorn is the enlightened monarch we all think he is, he will put a stop to this wicked spectacle of a trial forthwith – or at least demand the Privy Council defer their judgement until the witness evidence from Scotland Yard arrives. I propose we call Chalke in now. No time like the present, eh?'

'Before we do, what of Archbold? Should we bring him into our confidence also?' asked Henry.

'There is no need at this time,' Albert answered swiftly. 'He will know soon enough. The matter concerning our suspected turncoat is best kept from him.' Then he added with a broad smile, 'After all, he does not *need to know*!' It brought a knowing, head-shaking chuckle from the others.

Singh was sent to fetch Chalke who, as luck would have it, was reading in his office when the giant Sikh knocked on his door. Minutes later, Horatio Chalke was sitting amongst the others in the consul general's study with an expression of profound astonishment as the whole saga was unfolded before him. The account was communicated to him, for the most part, by Beaumont himself, with occasional interjections from Henry and Albert to elucidate when required. In conclusion, Beaumont said simply, 'That is why we should like your help to uncover our conspirator. Are you with us?'

Chalke thought for a moment before replying with a question, 'Pray tell me, did any of you at any time suspect me of these crimes?'

Beaumont's diplomatic mask seemed to slip for a second. He looked suddenly evasive. 'We suspected everyone at one time…' he muttered.

'But me specifically?' Chalke pressed. 'Did you suspect me?'

Beaumont shifted uneasily in his chair. 'I would be lying if I said otherwise, sir. You see, both you and Charles Hurdus have been servants of Great Britain in these parts for longer than anyone. It was only natural for our focus to arrive with you both. But now, I believe we have our proof. If I did not trust you, Horatio, I would not have called for you just now.'

Chalke sucked loudly on his teeth. 'Very well,' he said at length. 'For me to learn that I was once suspected of being a spy is hurtful in the extreme. However, I am grateful for your candour…' He paused and looked directly at the consul general. 'I will do whatever you ask of me.' The words were spoken with an air of resignation. 'But believe me when I say I take no joy in it. Charles has been a valuable friend to me and my wife these many years. If what you say is true, then I must have misjudged him, but in my heart, I cannot see a bad bone in his body.'

'You are aware of his gambling, I take it...' Beaumont asked.

'Why, yes. I think all that know him well are aware of it. He has a weakness for the *thua po* dens. Charles has been attracted to the roll of the dice for as long as I can remember, and I believe he has a liking for the fighting cocks, too.'

'And his wives, do you know of them also?'

'Most certainly. He makes no real secret of it. Why, I have met all three of them myself and, to a woman, they tell me he is a highly devoted husband. His wives and children seem to adore him. For sure, none of them will starve on his account, for I believe him to be a most generous guardian and the founder of all their feasts.'

'We are of similar mind, Horatio,' Albert advanced. 'We find it difficult to grasp that such a kind-hearted gentleman could have fallen into such a caustic abyss. But the evidence, as described to you just now, points to his guilt, and now we must do whatever necessary to finish the matter. Why, our work against him may reveal we have been wrong and have misjudged him... There may be other factors in play of which we are presently unaware. But try we must to get to the bottom of it all. And your help in our future scheme will prove to be invaluable – of that I am certain.'

Horatio Chalke's reply was wearily given, but the message was simple. 'What do you want of me? Tell me, gentlemen, and I will do your bidding.'

Chapter Nineteen

At the following break of day, as the sun rose amongst yet another chorus of competing cockerels and Henry Gough turned in his bed, Horatio Chalke and Albert Woodward stepped onto the now familiar tarred deck of the consular launch for the short journey through the easy morning air. Their destination was the rather grand office of the Head of Revenue, which lay less than a mile upstream. This time, the couple travelled with a new purpose.

Luang Phitisak Rattana, the head of the Siamese Revenue Service, was a gaunt skeleton of a man. He seldom smiled, save when he sipped on a bowl of whisky, and when he did, his skull seemed to explode with teeth, most of which were not his own. A man of indeterminate age but probably in his late fifties, he came from a family of notable landowners and was related by marriage to King Chulalongkorn himself. The moniker *Luang* was a title indicating that Phitisak was a nobleman of approximate equivalence to an English baron. At first meeting, the revenue chief had presented himself as a personage of few words and sullen appearance. He spoke little and grunted a lot. But over recent weeks, both Woodward and

Chalke had got to know the man better. As the ranks of his ill-fitting ivory teeth began to make more regular appearances, so did their association grow. The foreign implants, for which he had invested much and were often mentioned in court circles, had, in effect, become a barometer of their growing union. With each encounter with the *angrit* (the Siamese word for English) the mounting number of Phitisak's toothy smiles became a strange indicator to all who witnessed them that headway was being made.

Phitisak liked to portray himself, particularly to strangers, as an old-school conservative, right down to his traditionally woven sandals, and at the outset, he'd made no attempt to disguise his resentment at the intrusion of the two prying Britons into his domain. But it was the king's wish that he entertain his *farang* advisors and he knew he had no alternative but to obey. It helped enormously that Chalke was of gracious disposition and spoke near-perfect Siamese, for Phitisak had no inclination to learn English, let alone utter a single word of his visitor's alien language. But once the surface of ice had been cracked, which had taken at least five meetings, the discussions became ever more congenial, and by the end of the first week even Albert Woodward had taken up his courage to try out some of his best Siamese phrases on the wizened government official – a few of which were sufficient to create a brief glimpse of their host's famous teeth. Deep down, Phitisak was a good man, proud of his calling, and protective of his staff. When, at length, it was apparent from reports received from his workforce that the *angrit* seemed, for the most part, to be amiably altruistic and desired only to help all to improve the efficiency of his department, the old warrior became increasingly approachable and less resistant to their ideas for change. But still, some days Phitisak could be difficult. Maybe it was his way of ensuring he kept his callers subservient or maybe it was because he was suffering with another toothache – it was never clear.

Unfortunately, Chalke and Woodward were soon to discover that this was such a day, for when Horatio proposed, with his customary winning smile, that he and Woodward take a body of revenue officers to conduct a night-time surveillance exercise around the back streets of Bangkok, the living corpse did not flash his tusks in happy agreement. Instead, he frowned deeply and mumbled, '*Mae dae. Pom mae chop.*' – "Cannot. I don't like the idea." This was uttered in such a scowling, eye-averting way that even Woodward instantly understood it to be a rejection. For his part, Chalke quickly realised these were two short Siamese phrases that he did not need to translate for his companion.

'But, sir,' Chalke countered in his best-pronounced Siamese while doing everything in his power to sound cheerful, 'this would be a fine chance to test your men with the new skills we have imparted to them. Night-time is when most skulduggery is done. The drinking establishments will be full, as will the gambling dens, and it is in these places we can learn much. Why, it will not only be an exercise to assess their skills, but an opportunity to gather information as well.'

There was no verbal reaction from Phitisak, just another low growl.

'Can I ask… what is your objection, sir? I will do my best to put your mind at rest if you have any concerns.'

'Innocent Siamese people will not take kindly to *farangs* following them secretly around the city – least of all at night.'

'But if you have a revenue suspect, sir, a smuggler or a manufacturer of bad whisky, it is the best way to discover their activities.'

'I do not have a suspect for you to follow, Mr Chalke,' was the flat reply. 'When I have one, we can reconsider.'

Chalke translated the words to Woodward with a strained expression, and the two men looked at one another dumbfounded. Clearly Phitisak's department had plenty of suspects to offer up, had he wanted. Perhaps it was the thought that the two *angrit* would be learning more than they needed to know about the way crime worked in Siam that bothered the head man. Or perhaps the earlier qualms had returned. Phitisak had been forced to accept the coaching from the *angrit*. It was a bearable imposition as it had come from the king himself, but it did not involve his officers hounding his own people, whether they be criminals or not.

Woodward seemed to grasp the situation first. He spoke in a low whisper to his colleague. 'Tell him we will choose a fellow Englishman to follow in the exercise. That way, no Siamese can be threatened or impugned.'

When this proposal was made, the Head of Revenue lifted his head abruptly, his dull eyes now lighting up. Suddenly, he was fully engaged once more. 'You will use an Englishman as bait?'

'We will,' Chalke replied firmly. 'And not only that, we will not inform him that we intend to trail him. He will be oblivious to our actions – an Englishman shall be the innocent ferret we shall attempt to track down. That way, the exercise will be completely authentic, and your officers will be fully tested as if the surveillance was real.'

'Do you undertake not to track a Siamese around the city?'

'We do. In fact, you will be able to interrogate your staff on their return, sir. They will tell you the truth of the matter.'

The famous wide grin, full of stained ivory, appeared once more, and Chalke understood they had secured Phitisak's approval.

'How many men will you engage, and for how long will you want to use my officers?' the Siamese elder croaked.

'I will choose six of your most promising men, and the duration will be for three nights only. If it works well, we will choose another six to deliver our skills to next week.'

By nine o'clock the same morning, the two Britons had gathered their class of students, and after a short talk on the relative advantages and pitfalls of recruiting members of the public as their eyes and ears, they set about honing the group's skills on the subject of clandestine surveillance. The emphasis was to teach a series of discreet hand signals that could be used by the company to communicate activity and intentions amongst themselves. By one o'clock, it was too hot to continue, so Woodward dismissed the class for the rest of the day, save a small party of six specially selected by him. These he asked to return at dusk for a special briefing meeting. As the little group finally departed, he put his arm up to stop one of them.

Chalke strolled over to join the pair, and once the others had left, he spoke to the young man. 'We should like you to be the team leader for something special we intend to trial tonight.'

Khun Praew Asnee was a striking muscular rock of a fellow. About thirty years old, he was noticeably taller and better developed than most of his contemporaries. Despite his lack of any familial influence in court circles, he was regarded by superiors and peers alike to be both astute and ambitious – a combination that might have made some of his less able but better connected brethren wary of their own position. But his charismatic character and general enthusiasm for life made to eclipse such fears, and there was little doubt that Asnee was well liked by nearly all his colleagues. To make him head of the small squadron was a simple choice for Woodward, who could see the young Siamese commanded both respect and loyalty. In his judgement, Asnee had emerged as a natural leader of men.

There was another factor that had made Woodward's choice even easier. Asnee had made a concerted effort to learn English, and during his time under the Welshman's tutelage, he'd shown an almost instinctive ability not only to understand the foreign language, but use it to communicate also. So much so that Chalke, having seen the man's potential, had been providing Asnee with separate one-to-one language lessons for an extra hour each evening.

'Thank you, sir. What you like me to do?' came Asnee's immediate and smiling reply.

'We are going to put our trailing training into practice this evening. I want you to use your team to follow an Englishman around the city. Your task is to tell us where he goes, what he does, and who he meets. You must keep a record, which I will check at the end of the evening, of the man's each and every activity, from the moment he leaves his office at six o'clock this evening. I will give you his description and more instructions when we meet later. For now, go home, take rest, and be ready for a long night's work.'

'*Na durnt den!*' Asnee replied instinctively, before adding in slightly halting English, 'Sorry – mean to say, exciting!'

It was nearly dark when Asnee assembled his troops in an empty godown close to the British consulate. It had begun to rain. Albert Woodward had spent the intervening hours in the company of Henry Gough, outlining the plan he and Horatio Chalke had devised. Henry had asked a few questions of clarification, and had wished them good luck on their adventure. They agreed to meet at the Falcks Hotel later in the evening to discuss developments. Now, in the seclusion of the rain-splattered godown, with Chalke translating to the team of men whenever necessary, Albert had reminded the gathering of the basic principles of foot surveillance. When he was satisfied the squad were as prepared as they could be, he provided them with a full description of their quarry. In doing so, neither he nor Chalke could avoid a tinge of guilt by their actions. Charles Hurdus had become a friend to both of them, but equally, they knew they had to perform their duty, and if this meant tracking their old ally through the night-time streets of the ancient city, so be it. The task was not theirs to refuse. The matter had to be resolved one way or another.

The pair of Britons had not given Asnee and his team the name of the man to be tracked, just his description. They'd also decided it would be wise to leave the Siamese to their own devices during the process. It was better not to interfere while the shadowy little band went about their duties. To do so might have caused confusion and would certainly have risked them revealing themselves by accident to Hurdus. The only concession was for Woodward to remain at Asnee's side until Hurdus left the consulate, just to confirm the identity of the man his team were about to follow.

Charles Hurdus was a man of routine, and true to form, on the stroke of six pm, as if on cue, he appeared at the steps of the consulate, adjusted his hat, raised an umbrella against the now heavily falling rain, and hurried across the grounds towards the front gates. From their sheltered vantage point, about fifty yards away in the cluttered godown opposite, Asnee and his team watched in silence as Hurdus turned left, and at a brisk pace, headed south. Woodward nodded his confirmation, and with an encouraging pat on the shoulders, he whispered his protégé good luck. He watched as the line of Siamese revenue officers snaked out of the warehouse and assumed the initial travelling surveillance positions taught to them by their mentors. Woodward and Chalke let them go, and once all were out of sight, they emerged themselves into the downpour.

It was Woodward who spoke first. 'We can do nothing now. It's in their hands alone. I suggest we head straight for the Falcks, as arranged, and wait. I have invited Henry Gough to join us there later for a spot of supper.' Chalke, looking down the line of rustic tiled rooftops and pelting rain, heartily agreed, and the pair strode out on the short march to the riverside hotel. Meanwhile, Praew Asnee had spread his men to both sides of New Road. Using the system they'd learned of spacing and discreet hand signals, and by rotating the officers regularly so that none were closest to their quarry for longer than two minutes, they were soon in gentle unobtrusive pursuit of the tall Englishman with the raised umbrella.

All, bar one, of the ex-patriot consulate staff lived within the shielded confines of the walled compound. In short, it was policy to provide safe housing there for all British personnel, including the consul general himself. Within this sprawling estate, a number of low bungalows, similar to the type Woodward and Chalke now inhabited, had been constructed, dotted amongst the tropical trees and freshly clipped lawns. But Charles Hurdus was the exception that proved the rule. Years before, during the time of Sir Thomas Knox as consul general, he had obtained permission to find private lodgings well away from the goldfish bowl environment of British protection. Hurdus had been in Siam longer than any, and after more than a dozen years of towing the official line, he'd found he couldn't bear the claustrophobic atmosphere of the compound any longer. Everyone seemed to know each other's business. It was insufferable. His initial request to up sticks had been rejected by Knox, but Hurdus was quietly obstinate and after raising the matter for the umpteenth time, the consul general had, in a weak moment, relented, more in hand-washing exasperation than for any other reason.

And now, here was Hurdus hurrying towards the dwelling he had secured for himself, and where he and his muddled family had been living for the last eight years. It was barely a ten-minute walk away. The property was large by Siamese standards, of ancient build and entirely made of wood. Consisting of no fewer than eight rooms, it sat on stilts close to the softly sloping banks of the Chao Phraya and was surrounded by trees bursting with papaya, mango and jackfruit. As he approached, Asnee's team were not far behind – the point man being less than thirty yards away – as Hurdus, grasping the sodden balustrade, scurried up the wooden steps towards his hallway and dry sanctuary. The feeble light and the crashing rain had afforded Asnee and his squad some protection against discovery. The conditions had allowed them to draw much closer to their target than was generally advisable. As Hurdus disappeared into the house, the hushed group encircled the building, took up their positions, and waited. They did their best to find whatever shelter they could against the continuously falling deluge. Some hid under trees, another found a wall to lean into. Two managed to hide in a damp barn, still with eyesight onto Hurdus' front porch. Asnee was one of them. Here they stayed, near motionless, in their respective stations, as the rain pelted down.

Nearly an hour passed without change, save for some lights moving around inside the property. Then, just after the rain had abruptly stopped and the welcome half-moon had appeared, the front door of the house opened, and candlelight flooded onto the raised entrance. The now unmistakeable figure of Charles Hurdus, dressed as before, appeared on the threshold. He halted momentarily and turned as if to speak to someone inside, and then with a wave of his hand and an adjustment of his hat, he tripped lightly down the steps with the gait of a man full of buoyant exuberance. Gingerly avoiding the puddles that lay all around, he reached the road, crossed it, and headed east at a quick-marching pace away from the river – towards the bazaar and its shallow, crowded buildings.

Charles Hurdus was feeling a good deal brighter than he had for a very long time. News had reached him that very day concerning his maiden aunt, a certain Charlotte Agnes Hurdus, who was the last surviving sister of his dead father. Aunt Charlotte had died suddenly, aged eighty-eight, in the sprawling cottage she owned on the outskirts of the village of Storrington, which lay under the rolling hills of the Sussex South Downs. The letter from solicitors Messrs Holt and Blackford, who had been charged with settling the spinster's estate, had informed him that he was the sole benefactor of her will. The brief sense of melancholy felt at the loss of his ancient aunt had soon evaporated when he learned that his inheritance, measured in the value of her property, including some substantial outbuildings and nearly seven acres of land, amounted to the princely sum of no less than five hundred and thirty-five guineas.

Hurdus knew precisely where he was going that night. His was a well-trodden path, but on this night, the spring in his step seemed to make the journey go faster than usual. He turned down a back street, passed a pair of decorative gates sunk into a crenulated temple wall, and then slipped into an even narrower alleyway lit on each side by an assortment of randomly hung lanterns. After another dozen strides, he arrived at an antiquated but solid wooden door, which he rapped with three confident strikes of his knuckles. The door opened after a few seconds, a dim light shone into the passageway, and almost instantly he disappeared into the bowels of the dismal-looking abode.

Praew Asnee and his shadowy little band were not far behind, and the first of their number had managed to glimpse the now familiar coat-tails attached to Hurdus' stout frame as he'd vanished into the premises halfway up the alley. As the officer drew closer, he heard the solid thump of a door closing against the brick wall. The young revenue man knew the place well and knew of its reputation even better. Rather than following his quarry directly inside, he held back and waited for the others to catch up. Asnee was the first to arrive.

'He's gone into that shop,' the officer said, pointing to a spot a few yards down the dim alleyway, 'just ten seconds ago. I heard a knock and he was let in. I know the place.'

'Don't we all...' Asnee replied thoughtfully. 'But I hadn't imagined ever to see a *farang* inside this particular establishment.' The others nodded in laughing agreement. 'You two wait here, Chet,' Asnee said to the officer while pointing to one of the others. 'Take care, both of you, to watch the door. The rest of you, stay here too. I need to speak to Khun Albert. The Falcks is a short run from here. We need to hear what they want us to do.'

Chapter Twenty

Five hard-walking minutes later, Praew Asnee was standing opposite Woodward, Gough, and Chalke as the trio sat drinking whisky at a table overlooking the rippling black river. Aside from the four of them and the Chinese waiter, the hotel was completely deserted. As Asnee delivered his report of the preceding hours' events, the three *farangs* sat in mute silence, nodding and shaking their heads in equal measure, such was their interest in hearing the account. Asnee ended his narrative with a question.

'Do you want us to continue with surveillance, sirs? We have only finished two hours. We very happy to continue, if you like. We hope exercise not stop…'

'Before I answer,' Woodward replied, 'what can you tell me of the place where our English friend now lodges? You say it is well known to you all.'

'Why yes, sir, the shop-house is best *sonng* in city.'

Albert Woodward looked nonplussed and gazed towards Chalke for help. His colleague suppressed a chuckle, grunting loudly instead, and raised a fist to his bushy moustache. At length he said, 'He means to say the place where Charles now lies – a *sonng* – is no more than… well – a bordello.'

'On hearing the translation, Woodward could not disguise a smile. 'I see, I have heard that such places are commonplace hereabouts.'

'Of course, sir,' Asnee replied, 'but Mamasam Malee's house is one of the finest – and certainly the most famous.'

'A woman in charge of such a place, indeed… Is that commonplace?'

Asnee was quick to respond. 'Malee took house after husband died – stab in fight with enemy – was many years ago. She young then, but she now strong and she fear no one. There is drinking and games there too,' he added with a notable air of exuberance. 'I know the place well, as I have visited it many times.'

'You! Asnee… really?'

'Why yes, you see, the truth is… my Uncle Loong works there. He is the enforcer.'

'The enforcer?' Chalke gasped.

'Yes, Mamasam Malee like to have strong and good men around her. Sometimes her customers drink too much. Sometimes they not pay. There are fights.'

Chalke said casually, 'Where there are women and money, there will always be fights.'

'Malee, she keep two or three strong men to help keep house clean from problem. My uncle been there long time. He big boss now.'

Chalke blanched. 'How long?'

'Maybe twenty years, maybe more. Since I could walk, I have never known him not be there. He was royal guard once – under King Mongkut – for many years. Then he start work for husband of Mamasam Malee.'

'Most illuminating.' Albert Woodward leaned forward.

'Now listen... would it be normal for you to be seen inside your uncle's place at this time of night – with a friend, perhaps? Would you both be welcome?'

'Of course! Uncle Loong always happy to see me. Before I drink there often. It nearly two year since I meet my sweetheart, Gaew, at house of Mamasam Malee. I not go back for long time – maybe more than one year.'

'On account of all the other women, I expect?' Woodward enquired with an affable expression.

'Not really...' Asnee said simply. 'Not the girls – they mostly friends of mine. You see, I used to play games, too – but not now. My *teelak*... sorry, I mean to say "my sweetheart"... Gaew kill me now, if she know I give my money on fighting chickens.'

'Cockfights?'

'Yes – of course. There are bird fights one day every week, maybe more. Every day, dice games like *hi-lo*, and *mai mun*, and *duat* too.'

'*Mai mun* is a sort of Siamese roulette,' Chalke advanced with a guilt-ridden clearance of his throat, 'and *duat* is rather akin to backgammon – or so I'm led to believe...'

'I see...' Woodward paused for a moment and then looked at Chalke and Gough with wide eyes and a broad grin. 'I think we might be in luck tonight, gentlemen,' he said quietly.

Then, turning to the youthful messenger, he roared in his very best rolling Welsh tones, 'Well, what's keeping you, young Asnee? You and Chet had better get back down there as fast as you can. Find out what's going on and report back once you know all there is to know. Leave no stone unturned.'

Chalke added in Siamese, for the avoidance of any doubt, 'You have our permission to be prudently resourceful and use whatever cunning you deem necessary in your quest. We'll stay here until midnight. Be back before then with your account. Write it down, if you have to, like we have showed you. And a word of this to no one – not even to Uncle Loong, do you hear? This is our secret. Just find out what you can about our mysterious *farang* and just make sure he doesn't suspect you of watching him, eh!' he thundered, laughing. 'Cut along now…' And then in English, he cried, 'As Mr Shakespeare would have it, we'll be waiting on your return "with bated breath!"'

It mattered not that Praew Asnee had never heard of Shakespeare, *The Merchant of Venice*, or had any idea what "bated breath" meant. All the same, he picked up the gist, and it didn't take him long to return to the corner where Chet and his friend had been waiting discreetly with an unobstructed view of Mamasam Malee's front door. In all, he'd been away less than twenty minutes. He assembled the group at the edge of the alleyway. Chet had nothing of importance to report, save the fact that the Englishman had yet to depart. He still remained inside the celebrated *sonng*.

'The *farangs* want us to continue watching until midnight,' Asnee told the company in lowered tones. 'Chet, you and I are going inside to see what the Englishman is up to. We have been tasked to secretly record everything we see and hear. And I want you to meet my Uncle Loong too.' He smiled. 'You'll like him, I know. The rest of you must wait outside, as invisibly as you can manage, until we return. It will be good training for you all.'

With that, Asnee and Chet turned on their heels and advanced in line abreast along the alley. After a dozen or so strides, as the others watched their every move from a distance, Asnee took an assertive pace forward and rapped boldly three times on the front door. The familiar thud of his knuckles resounding on the ancient teak brought back memories of his past. It felt almost as if he was returning home, and although a tinge of nervous excitement flooded his veins, he was confident he'd receive a warm welcome from his uncle and the rest of the household, some of whom he'd not clapped eyes on for over a year. The door was answered in seconds. It was not his uncle...

Instead, a much younger man, powerfully built, impressively tall, and dark complexioned, stood loftily at the threshold. He was chewing tobacco and holding a smoking oil lamp. Asnee did not recognise him.

'What you want?'

'I am Khun Praew,' Asnee replied with a deliberate air of arrogance. 'My friend and I wish to take whisky and meet the ladies.' He tried to push past the sentry, but the man instantly put up his hands and set his feet apart to block the way. It was clear the fellow was not going to be blustered.

'Whoa,' the doorman cried, 'no one enter without pass.'

'A pass, what do you mean? I have been in this place more times than your mother has sewn stitches into your nappies. I need no pass.' Asnee had never encountered this routine before. The thought occurred to him that this new procedure might be connected to the king's recent pronouncement that he disapproved of gambling and his newly avowed ambition to limit its reach.

'You show me pass. It is simple.' The sentry wiped his mouth and placed a sharp elbow under Asnee's chin. 'This is private house. No pass, no come in.' There was only one thing for it. Asnee would have to pull rank.

'Idiot!' he cried. 'Let me speak to Khun Loong. He is my uncle.'

The sentry slowly dropped his arm and frowned deep into Asnee's eyes. At the same time, he lowered his forehead steadily towards his new visitor until the two men's brows came together with a not so gentle thump. Like rutting stags, antlers entwined, the two glowered into each other. Asnee stood his ground as the opposing skull pressed against him, muscling his own neck forwards and staring back unblinkingly.

At length, the doorman withdrew his head and spat deep into the darkness. Still hooked on the eyes of his new adversary, he snarled, 'Wait one minute. I will come back.' The door slammed shut.

Asnee turned and looked over his shoulder. Chet was wiping the remnants of yellow spittle from his eye. 'This won't take long, trust me...' Asnee muttered, trying to console his friend. But it was clear Chet's earlier swagger had somewhat drained away.

'In the name of Buddha, Chet,' he added as loudly as he dare, 'just stand up straight and look like you own the place!'

After what seemed like an eternity, the heavy portico creaked open once more, and much to Asnee's huge relief, the instantly recognisable shape of Uncle Loong was silhouetted against the interior's orange glow. Uncle Loong peered out and recognised his visitor immediately. An unambiguous smile of welcome lit up his face.

'Why, Praew, my boy. You are the last fellow I expected to see tonight. Arthit says you two have come to drink and meet the women.' The big man looked Chet up and down for a second or two. 'You'd both better come in... I hope you and our beautiful Gaew have not been arguing, young man...' He tutted. 'She's such a lovely girl. Too good for this place, for sure. You did well to take her from here!'

'Oh no, Uncle. We are still much in love.' He changed the subject. 'This is my friend Khun Chet. We work together. I promised him I'd show him a house where he could meet some pretty girls and enjoy a drink or two. It's been a long day. I've talked about Mamasam Malee's many times at my work, and Chet is an inquisitive sort.'

'You are *all* inquisitive fellows in the revenue, young man.' Loong laughed as he ushered them through the door and past the now retreating and cringing doorman. 'Stay by the gate,

Arthit; do your duty,' he barked as they passed into the main rooms.

The interior of Mamasam Mallee's hadn't changed in the year Asnee had been away – perhaps it seemed a little darker than he'd remembered. None amongst the half-dozen huddles of men sitting cross-legged on the floor, blankets and cushions strewn everywhere, looked up as they entered. Asnee cast his head about quickly for sight of the *farang*, but his eyes couldn't focus fast enough and Loong's chivvying was not allowing him to settle. A clatter of dice and yelps of delight accompanied them as they trod their way between the games towards a vacant area and a row of short-legged tables. Loong invited them to sit and heaved a couple of soft fabric bolsters in their direction. A bottle of Siamese whisky and jangling glasses were quickly brought. A young woman, attractively presented, hovered nearby. 'I keep this spot free for my special guests,' Loong announced. 'Now, tell me what you've been up to, young man. You're still with those bastards in the revenue office, it seems.'

'Yes, Uncle, but this is just a friendly visit. I'm sure all your whisky is well accounted for, as is everything else…'

'Ha, of course, Nephew. You have my word on it.' His uncle winked then sat down with a thump between them. He was a bulky, muscular man who, at forty, felt he was in his prime. As he poured out the clear liquid, a bicep emblazoned with black tattoos showed itself to them. Loong was not a man to be messed with. He knew it, and rarely did any of his customers dispute it. 'We miss seeing you,' he declared, 'but we pine for the lovely Gaew even more. Why don't you bring her to meet her old friends?'

'She is too busy taking care of me!' Asnee smirked, preening his hair, and fluttered his eyelids with a look of mock enticement worthy of a courtesan in the king's harem.

'Ha ha ha, now I know you're lying!' Loong replied with a hefty backslap. 'You always was a boy who liked a pretty face.'

Just as the first draft of warm liquor stung the back of his throat, Asnee became aware of a commotion on the other side of the room – the sound of a muffled argument, perhaps. Raised voices could be heard from behind a trembling blood-red curtain in an elevated corner of the den. Asnee knew that at the top of the short flight of wooden steps was the gallery. This was where the principal gamblers played their games in relative privacy. It was here where the biggest wagers were staked, out of sight – and usually the hearing – of the hoi polloi who inhabited the caked-dirt floor below in the main chamber.

A shrill woman's voice screamed out from behind the drapes. 'Loong! I need you. Come quick!'

'If I'm not mistaken, it'll be that damn *farang* again. I've warned him once already tonight – Malee should never have allowed him here in the first place,' Loong growled. 'Will you excuse me for a minute, Nephew.' Loong pulled himself to his feet with an almighty grunt of energy.

'A *farang*, Uncle? Here?' Asnee jumped up too. 'Can I come and see?'

Loong exhaled loudly. 'If you must...' He exhaled again. 'But no meddling from you, do you understand? You're a guest here, you're not on duty. I have a job to do – this is a task I have delayed too long.' Loong reached a heavy arm behind the wide counter, cluttered with platters and half-filled tumblers, and after some fumbling he produced, with a grim flourish, what looked to Asnee like a pair of gnarled blacksmith's tongs. 'If I'm not mistaken, I must put things right once and for all, and I warn you, it won't be a pretty sight.'

Asnee winked at his partner, indicating for him to stay where he was. Chet, who by this time was happily flirting with the loitering girl, nodded back with an easy smile. It was obvious he needed no further encouragement to obey his leader's latest orders.

Seconds later, with the iron pincers firmly in Loong's grasp, the pair had leapt up the little staircase and advanced around the edge of the heavy curtain, where they encountered a group of gamblers standing amongst fallen stools and an upturned table. The gallery floorboards were scattered with half-empty whisky bottles and a disarray of discarded dice and ivory counters. A cat skulked into a corner and a line of candles guttered and spat as the two made their appearance. The occupants of this space were all Siamese, save for one man, who Asnee instantly, and with some relief, established as his *farang* quarry.

It would have been natural for Asnee's eyes to have become fixed on his newly recovered target, but it was immediately clear to all who witnessed it, the principal figure in the chaotic tableau was not the Englishman. Instead, the young revenue officer's gaze became irrevocably transfixed on another figure, one who was impossible to disregard. Asnee recognised her immediately. Like a living bronze of Aphrodite herself, a diminutive yet imperious goddess bestrode the scene. Of indeterminate middle age, she must have been very beautiful once. Angular-framed, rouge-cheeked, red-lipped, she was dressed in a traditional Siamese patterned blouse of crimson, complete with single exposed neck and shoulder. Below her waist, a flowing loin-cloth of black silk trimmed with silver swept around her elegant hips and legs. Jet-glossed hair, parted at the centre and pinned into a neat bun, completed the picture. Asnee knew instantly that she was none other than the lady of the establishment. This was Mamasam Malee, and her dominion over the household was obvious to all in that place.

'Loong,' Malee bellowed, 'you see my English customer, Khun Charles. He's thrown his last dice in my house. His credit has ended, as has my patience. He tells me he no money to pay his debts today. Two hundred and twenty *ticals* of silver is no small amount. I wish you to deal with it.'

'It will be my pleasure, madam. I reminded Khun Charles of the rules of your house less than an hour ago,' Loong yelled back. 'His promises are as worthless to me as his life.'

Charles Hurdus put his hands up in submission. 'Now listen, Khun Loong...' Hurdus spoke in perfect but breathless Siamese as he started to back away. 'I can pay.' As the fearsome enforcer advanced, brandishing the blacksmith's tongs above his head, the others parted, as if in a biblical scene, to allow him to draw ever closer to the now cowering Englishman. 'Please listen,' Hurdus beseeched. 'I have money... I mean, I *will* have your money... soon. I am to be a rich man. I will pay double my account, if you will just give me more time.'

'You made such a promise but a few days ago,' Malee shrieked. 'But instead, you tried to gamble your way out of your debt. Tonight, you have lost once more, and I vow you shall pay for it, if not in money, then I will take something even more precious from you in its place. Loong – see to it!'

'But I have nothing to give!' Hurdus screamed.

'You have plenty enough for me!' Loong cried as he threw himself at Hurdus, who toppled backwards onto the bare boards, arms and legs flying in all directions. 'Come Praew, help me to hold this villain down. I have something to show him.' Asnee hadn't expected such a command. After all, his uncle had only just told him not to interfere. Now he was being asked to participate in something which he truly wished no part in. He hesitated. 'What are you waiting for, my nephew? Help me to hold him while I apply the horse tongs.' At that moment, one of the other customers, a plump, moustachioed man, drew forward.

'He owes me silver too. I will hold him for you, Khun Loong.'

Then another, seeming to gain sudden courage, stepped up. 'I will help too.'

Soon, Charles Hurdus was pinned to the floor, his arms held under the knees and weight of three men. Another straddled his chest. Loong sat on Hurdus' calves, and now trapped under the embrace of nearly the whole room, the struggle abruptly ceased. From above, Mamasam Malee surveyed the scene with a look of implacable hostility.

'Open his clothing, Praew.' Loong nodded towards Hurdus' groin. His nephew winced, but obeyed all the same, doing his best to appear enthusiastic, and with shaking hands, he gingerly started to undo the Englishman's belt and buttons.

'Is this wise, Uncle?' he whispered as he fumbled with the fittings. 'The man is a diplomat, I believe. I have seen him many times at the British consulate. To do such a thing may provoke the wrath of the king.'

Then a muffled cry came up from Hurdus, his face half hidden by the mass of bodies that still trapped him. The cry turned into a scream as he felt warm hands touching his nether regions. 'I can get you the money tonight. I give you my word,' he yelled. 'Just two minutes from here, I have a friend who will give it. Please don't handle me, I beg you,' he sobbed. 'I have wives and many children. Send someone with me to collect the money, if you like. I will return with your *ticals*. If I do not, you can do what you will with me. Just give me one final chance.' Hurdus was blubbing now. A mixture of tears, spittle and sputum dribbled down his cheeks in a veritable torrent.

'A diplomat, you say?' Loong hesitated for a second and looked at Asnee with a quizzical expression. Then, with a vicious tug he pulled Hurdus' undergarments fully down beneath the knees to expose his victim's genitalia. 'Now, hand me those tongs, would you, boy?' he said aloud so all could hear.

'Listen, Uncle, he is no common merchant,' Asnee advanced in a low murmur, while covering his mouth. 'Of that I am utterly certain.'

Loong grabbed Asnee by the scruff of his neck. 'Go speak with Malee, boy, if you must. Tell her what you know, while I tease this fellow a little longer. If she wishes me to remove the *farang's* jewels, she will soon tell you. I will wait for her orders.' Loong rose to his feet and placed his full weight onto the bundle of fabric that now clung around Hurdus' ankles. Then, flourishing the metal pincers so the prone figure, by craning his neck, could see more clearly, he exclaimed, 'Which of your puddings would you like me to crush first? No one can say I am not a fair man. I will give you the choice.'

Praew Asnee bowed his head to his uncle and released his grip on Hurdus' naked thighs. Scrambling up, he took a few short steps towards the only lady in the room. 'Do you remember me?' he said to Malee with a polite gesture to beckon her away from the scene of torture. Malee returned the nodded smile with one of her own and followed him to the other side of the red curtain.

'I will get the money, believe me, please!' Hurdus spluttered as the pair disappeared from sight. 'All I ask is just one hour –' The Englishman had hardly completed his sentence when he felt the unmistakeable caress of cold metal, as the tongs gently grasped his left testicle. He sensed the organ being pulled upwards towards his navel.

'This one?' Loong grunted. 'Or this one?' Now Hurdus could feel the pincer's chill grip around his right appendage as it was stretched away from his scrotum. The sensation was indescribable. The physical discomfiture was scarcely bearable… it was the sense of his abject vulnerability that was truly toe-curling. The anticipation of agony at any second was excruciating in the extreme.

'For God's sake, stop!' Hurdus screamed amid a chorus of hilarity from the spectators. 'I will do anything! I have money. I will pay it tonight. In the name of all that is holy, *stop*! This is madness!'

As the mayhem continued unabated from behind the drapes, Mamasam Malee turned to face Asnee. Calmly looking him up and down and with a curious grin she said, 'How could I forget you? It's Khun Praew, isn't it? I remember you took my best girl. I trust you are taking good care of her?'

'Gaew is fine... but listen,' Asnee declared, 'I think you could be making a grave mistake by harming this Englishman. I happen to know he is well connected – his influence may extend as far as the king himself.'

'You're very impertinent, young man,' she hissed. 'Khun Charles deserves what he gets. I should have never allowed a *farang* into my house. Loong warned me, but what is done is done.'

'But the king himself...' Asnee persisted. 'If he is displeased, it will be the excuse he needs to close you down – to shut down all Bangkok's gambling houses, for that matter. If he does that, you won't be so popular.'

Malee's arched eyebrows seemed to meet in an instant. 'Loong tells me you work for the king now. A revenue officer? Is that correct?'

'Yes, Mamasam Malee. But believe me, I wish you and your business no harm – quite the opposite, in fact, but killing a *farang* of such high standing may not be wise.'

'I don't intend to kill him, boy. I will just squeeze out his manhood. It will be a lesson to all those who would dare to dishonour their debts in my establishment.'

'The *farang* says he has money nearby. Let me go with him,' Asnee offered. 'If he's lying, you'll find out soon enough, and you can do what you will with him. But maybe, by taking the course I propose, you will save your reputation and your business, too. The Englishman has offered to pay double what he owes. Let him try, at least. I will bring him back within the hour. I have a young friend with me tonight, Khun Chet. Between us, we will make sure there is no monkey business. What do you say, Mamasam Malee?'

There was silence for a few seconds while the grand dame chewed on her scarlet lips. From behind the curtain, another penetrating scream broke the spell, followed soon after by further waves of boisterous laughter. At length, Malee placed her hands together as if in prayer and said, 'Very well. I will do as you suggest – but you must understand that I do this only because you still take care of my pretty Gaew. Consider this mercy as a reward for your lasting devotion to her. Buddha protect you if you are lying to me on the subject. You have one hour, Khun Praew. Do not waste it. Be sure to be back here before eleven.'

Chapter Twenty-One

It was nearly ten o'clock by the time Asnee and Chet collected the bruised and battered frame of Charles Hurdus from the side alleyway's mud and detritus. Now reunited with his undergarments, Hurdus had been coarsely discarded seconds before, quite literally flung out on his ear, with Loong's bloodcurdling cry of warning ringing from the *sonng's* entrance.

'Return within the hour or reap the consequences. My men will go with you,' Loong yelled in Siamese, as Hurdus dusted himself down with the back of his hand. 'Do as they say. Do not play the monkey. Just bring the *ticals* back here by eleven and all will be well. If you do not, you will wish you'd never set foot onto the shores of Siam. Trust me, Khun Charles, I can't express how much I shall enjoy squeezing out your precious jewels before I hack your deceitful head from your sallow carcass.'

As Hurdus staggered away with the two foisted bodyguards at his side, he wondered how he'd so badly misread the situation. The events of the last fifteen minutes had come as a huge shock to him. He knew the Siamese could be cruel if the red mist took hold. He had seen their brutality many times. He knew too, that to them the subject of money was no trifling matter. But this ugly and distasteful treatment at their hands had taken him completely by surprise. After all, he was an Englishman! And to boot, he'd been living in their damn pox-ridden country for over twenty years, he could suddenly hear himself saying. He had Siamese wives, for God's sake, he spoke the language to perfection – surely, he had earned some respect. He thought he knew their every trait, each and every one of their vices and peculiarities – clearly, he did not, he reflected ruefully. Perhaps it had been the prospect of his aunt's inheritance that had clouded his mind and given him a sense of false confidence as he'd entered Mamasam Malee's house that night. He shook his head and contemplated his new companions. Whatever the reason for his earlier complacency, he knew he was now in mortal danger – more so than at any time in his life. There was now only one person who could save him.

Charles Hurdus picked up his dented hat, which had been ejected with him and had landed amongst a pile of garbage some feet away. 'You are to be my guards for the rest of the night, I take it,' he said with a sigh, as they started towards the corner and temporary sanctuary.

'We are, sir,' Asnee replied. 'If you do as we instruct, you will come to no harm – you have my word. Now we must hurry. You say you keep money hereabouts. We must fetch it without delay.'

'You'd better follow me then.'

On a discreet instruction from Asnee, Chet ran quickly to the waiting members of their squadron with instructions to remain where they were until they had returned to the *sonng*. On completing his short assignment, Chet rejoined Asnee and following Hurdus' lead, the trio walked together in brisk silence for about three minutes. The route Hurdus chose took them back towards the banks of the Chao Phraya, and soon they were marching along the eastern margin, heading north. The half-full moon had risen high into the night sky, so navigating was none too difficult, despite the road being little more than a rutted track. After another five minutes, they had entered the environs of the city where the river-facing housing was spread more thinly. Each dwelling, without exception, rested atop ancient teak piles driven into the dark mud.

'Khun Charles, you said the money was but two minutes away,' Asnee observed after they had walked for more than five times longer than that.

'A fellow will say anything to save his balls, young man. But never fret, my falsehood was not a great one. We are nearly there. Do you see the house that lies under the rain tree, yonder? That is where we have to go.'

'Is that your home?' Chet piped up unnecessarily and rather unexpectedly.

'No, 'tis the home of a friend. I will need to speak to him. The conversation may take some time. You see, my friend is a very private person. It will not wash if he sees you with me. I require you both to remain outside, and out of sight, while I enter alone.'

On seeing that Chet was about to protest, Asnee quickly intervened. 'Of course. I will give you fifteen minutes – no longer. If you do not return by then, we shall come in to find you, make no mistake of it.'

The house, although of similar design, was much smaller that Hurdus' own residence. There was no sign of light as the Englishman trod his first steps on the stained rungs that led upwards, where an ornately carved wood veranda and the entrance awaited. For the second time that night, Asnee and Chet held back under the foliage of a huge rain tree that dominated the nearby landscape. This time, there was no downpour to accompany their vigil. With the chalk-white moon overhead, and a cooling breeze that fed gently up from the river, their only companions were the sentinel tree frogs who chirruped unseen in the undergrowth. From their vantage point about a hundred feet away, Asnee and Chet watched as Hurdus reached the terrace. After peering through one of the shutters, he raised his fist to strike the front door. The observing couple were too distant to hear the rap, but it was not long before the light of an interior candle could be seen, and shortly afterwards, Hurdus vanished from their sight, presumably taken inside by the unseen occupant.

'I rather like him,' Chet said in a low voice as their target disappeared from view. 'The *farang*, I mean. He has a certain style about him. Do you think he is a friend of Khun Albert and Khun Horatio?'

'More likely, an enemy…' Asnee chuckled. 'I'm not sure what to think. This trailing practice seems more realistic with each passing hour. It's indeed a true test of our skills. This man, whoever he may be, is certainly leading us on a merry dance. But I think it's tremendous sport, don't you?'

'I do,' replied Chet slowly, 'but there is something that nags. You may be correct; this man we are following could indeed be Khun Albert's sworn enemy, but have you thought that we might be just nameless partners in some terrible revenge he and Khun Horatio have planned?'

'Ha ha – you think too much, Chet! This is just a practice operation to test our skills. I grant you, it is more lifelike than I had imagined, and events have taken on some startling turns in the last few hours. They said we could be bold. So, all the more chance for us to impress our tutors with our observations. And anyway, all will be revealed when we meet again at midnight. Then, you can ask whatever questions you want, but for now, we must do as they say. I think they will be mightily surprised by what we shall tell them later tonight.'

Just as Chet had opened his mouth to reply, strange noises from the house could be heard for the first time. The unmistakeable sound of raised voices drifted through the night air – enough to make the two onlookers stare at one another in lowering silence as they craned their ears to make sense of the raucous conversation. The hubbub, which throughout was loud but mostly indecipherable – as the language exchanged was clearly not Siamese – lasted for at least thirty seconds. Then a death-like hush descended amongst the sleeping trees once more. Five further minutes passed in frozen calm, and then, as suddenly as he had vanished, Hurdus appeared on the veranda once more. Asnee and Chet watched, holding their breath, as the Englishman seemed to fly down the line of stairs, such was the pace at which he was now moving. He swivelled on his heels to retrace his footsteps and bolted at near running pace along the banks of the river. The two surveillance officers jumped up and followed at speed. After they had advanced two hundred yards in a brisk dash, and were well out of sight of the house, they finally caught up with their prey.

Asnee slapped his hand on Hurdus' shoulder and pulled him back. 'Do I have good news to tell Khun Loong?' he cried out. Hurdus spun round with the bulging eyes of a robber's horse. He looked an utterly changed man from the one they'd first encountered at six o'clock the same evening. The events of the last few hours had clearly taken their toll. Gone was his swagger and his bluster, now replaced by shaking hands, cold sweat, and a paleness of complexion. The latter appeared all the starker for the crimson stream that fell in constant spurts from his left ear. 'Why, you are cut, sir!' Asnee exclaimed.

Hurdus looked bewildered, as if he felt nothing of his

injury. 'Tis a scratch,' he mumbled, reaching his hand up to the source of blood. 'Just an accident…'

'Let me look. I have a cloth… Here, take it. You must staunch the flow. How did this happen?'

Hurdus pushed the offering away, and with his left hand, took a handkerchief from his coat pocket, which he applied to the gushing wound. With his right, he removed a purse from the other pocket and thrust it towards Asnee. 'There, you have your money. There are five hundred *ticals* inside, more than double the amount I owe. No man, or woman for that matter, can say I am a welsher. Take it to your mistress and leave me alone. Tell her I will not darken her doorstep ever again. I fear this episode has cost me my ear – or part of it, at least. That is quite enough for one evening's entertainment. Be gone, both of you. I never wish to see either of you again.'

Asnee could feel the purse was heavy. He had no reason to doubt what he had been told. 'Mamasam Malee will count it. If it is insufficient, she will call on you.'

'Just go!' Charles Hurdus screamed, looking daggers towards his tormentors.

'Would you like us to send a doctor?' Chet enquired with a look of genuine compassion.

'Leave me! I shall attend to it myself,' Hurdus yelled. He looked as if he were about to erupt.

Asnee and Chet needed no further encouragement and within a few moments, the pair had dissolved into the night. As the solitary Hurdus watched them go, he suddenly became overwhelmed by a feeling of terrible and abject sadness. The emotion arrived uninvited and took him by complete surprise. He gazed towards the distant forest trying to make sense of the last few hours, but found himself struggling to remain upright; his legs felt like sand, as if they would shortly fail him. 'How has it all come to this!' he sobbed, shoulders shaking uncontrollably. Weeping onto the wrist that held the blood-soaked cloth against his ear, he turned his trembling head and blinked towards the slumbering city. A distant *boobook* hooted from the darkness as Hurdus gulped in a lungful of night air. It was time for him to start the long walk home.

⁓:⁓

Henry Gough, Albert Woodward, and Horatio Chalke had occupied the last hours eating stewed duck and rice, and drinking local whisky in the Falcks' timber-panelled private room. The mood had been subdued as they anxiously awaited news of the evening's events. Despite the steady and prolonged ingestion of alcohol, their unease had grown with each passing minute as the clock on the wall steadily tick-tocked towards midnight.

'What did you say to young Asnee as he left us earlier, Horatio?' Henry asked casually as he lit his pipe. 'I couldn't pick out all the words; my Siamese is simply not up to it. It sounded like you were encouraging him. Whatever you said, seemed to have a profound effect.'

'I agree,' Woodward added brightly. 'It must have been a good speech for his eyes positively lit up on hearing what you had to say. My understanding of Siamese is worse than yours, Henry, but at least I could see Khun Asnee looked truly invigorated.'

'To translate my words precisely, I told him to be *prudently resourceful*,' Chalke replied with a droll smile. 'I added that he and his lads should try to use their wits, and apply whatever cunning they could muster in their search for as much information as possible.'

Woodward's cheerful grin turned rapidly into a mope. 'Are you sure that was wise, man? This is supposed to be a mere surveillance exercise – and the first of many, too. You may have given our novices carte blanche to overreach themselves – to take unnecessary risks.'

'I apologise if I have transgressed,' Chalke tapped the table with an ink-stained thumb, 'but it seemed to me that an opportunity had presented itself – one not to miss. Why, you said yourself that we appeared to be in luck tonight. Gentlemen, we may only have this chance, and although you call Asnee and his band "novices", I believe I know these people better than either of you. The Siamese are, almost to a man, naturally resourceful and audacious. As long as Asnee's team acts within their own laws, all will be well. I feel sure of it.'

'Lawfully audacious, eh?' Henry grinned through a haze of pipe smoke. 'Most amusing. I like the sound of that. And I happen to agree with you, Horatio. You are right.' Henry gawked at Albert with a theatrical grimace. 'I think your words of encouragement hit the mark and the moment precisely. We may never have a better opportunity than tonight to discover the truth of the matter. And from what I have seen of Mr Asnee, he is a most impressive young man indeed.'

Albert Woodward grunted. 'Well, it's done now... Can't change it. We'll know soon enough. If they've overplayed their hand, at least we have others to take their place.'

As the clock chimed a quarter to midnight, the door of the chamber suddenly flew open, and as the pigtailed waiter skulked behind them, Asnee and Chet entered. Both were wearing the broadest of smiles, and it was clear to all that they were bursting to deliver their report.

'We came as fast as we could.' Asnee sounded winded, his chest heaving as he closed the door. 'Are you ready to hear our report?' he asked in breathless English. 'Chet is here in case I forget any detail, for we've had no time to write it down.

There have been many events to tell you about tonight, and it is nearly midnight already.'

'Pray, take a seat, both of you,' Albert Woodward said genially. 'Would you like a refreshment? Whisky perhaps?' He signalled to the waiter.

'Just water, sir,' Asnee replied.

'Whisky, please,' announced Chet, moistening his lips.

'Where is the rest of your team?' Albert asked.

'They wait outside for your further instructions.'

'Very well. They must remain there until our business here has ended. Is that understood? Now you may make your report.'

'I will take notes,' Chalke offered, gathering paper and pencil from a leather satchel he'd earlier strung over a chair. "Tis no matter that you have no written account to show us. You appear to have had a hectic night. Just start at the beginning and leave no detail from your narrative, however minor it may appear to you.'

More than thirty minutes passed before their report had been put into writing. At intervals, Woodward and Gough asked questions, and if the response in English was too difficult for Asnee, Chalke translated. By twelve-thirty, Praew Asnee had settled back into his chair, and sipping his water for the first time, he said, 'That is our story. I try to forget nothing. I scared about your friend, sirs. Khun Charles may be hurt. He have big pain and many blood.'

'I see...' Woodward looked sombre. 'We shall make sure Mr Charles is properly taken care of. You have done very well.' Woodward broke off for a moment to speak to Horatio Chalke. 'Please Horatio, what I have to say to them now is of the utmost importance. And I would ask you to translate for the avoidance of doubt.'

Chalke nodded. 'Of course, Albert, I will try to do justice to your words.'

Woodward turned his eyes back to the pair of revenue officers and continued. 'I applaud your work tonight. You have led your men well, Khun Asnee, and I have no doubt you and your little band have the makings to become some of the finest sleuths in the whole kingdom. But I confess that many of the events you have described to us have come as a very great surprise, and much of what you have told us has proven quite shocking to our sensibilities. Therefore, I ask you, as brother investigators, to keep your observations top secret for the time being. Please tell no one. I cannot force this on you. I understand none of us has jurisdiction over you and your actions, here in Siam. But as a courtesy to us, I dare say we are like-minded souls, I ask you to keep your counsel for a day – just a single day – after which time we will release you from your oath of silence. Do you understand?'

On hearing the translation, that appeared to last much longer that the words Woodward had spoken, the two Siamese looked at one another and grinned. It was Asnee who replied.

'We will, sir – but on one condition…'

'Name it.'

With bizarre choreography, the trio of Britons took a deep breath and frowned in unison as they waited for Asnee's answer. It appeared, for all the world, as if with one combined inhalation, they were about to suck the entire volume of air from the room. Chalke translated the reply which, when it came, surprised them all.

'If there is more surveillance training to be undertaken, please include us,' the young Siamese had answered almost instantly. 'We have taken such enjoyment from tonight. The whole team is agreed; it has been the best stretch of work since joining the service, and thanks to you, we have learned much. If you will allow us to continue, we should be most grateful. You have our word that none of what we saw this night will be revealed until you tell us the time is right, whether it be a single day, a week maybe, or even a whole month. Please be assured, we speak with one voice on this.'

'Very well,' Albert replied with a broad smile. 'I'm sure that's a proposition on which we can all agree. But before you depart to your beds, I have one more task for you tonight, young man. Take us to the house where you saw Khun Charles enter just an hour ago…'

Chapter Twenty-Two

It was customary for Lawrence Beaumont to take a solitary stroll at six am each morning, when the soothing zephyrs, rising from the river bank, would assist him to contemplate and plan his future activities for the day. It was Horatio Chalke's knowledge of this intimate habit that had allowed him the opportunity to waylay his master in the act of leaving the residence that morning. Rather than wake the consul general at two am to bring the grave news of the previous night's revelations, an action that would have brought unnecessary angst, and no doubt a sleepless night for all concerned, they'd decided to wait until Beaumont was in full command of his senses before broaching this most delicate of matters. As the consul general took his first steps onto the manicured verdure that surrounded his home, just as the sun's first shafts flashed through the overflowing branches of the encompassing rain trees, Horatio Chalke, accompanied by Henry Gough (as Albert Woodward had declined to rise at that "unearthly" hour), approached him across the dark swathe of clipped grass. Beaumont's initial surprise at seeing his colleagues so early in the morning was quickly replaced by visible horror and utter disgust on hearing the news they brought to him.

'Are we familiar with the house?' he replied, once the full story had been recounted and after they'd retreated into the privacy of his consulate office. 'This place by the river where Hurdus visited last night, is it known to you?'

'It is, sir, we took the trouble of tracking it down in the small hours this morning. Khun Asnee led us to it. The residence is not far from here.'

'And… Speak up, man – who lives there?'

''Tis the residence of Monsieur Pierre Museau, an attaché at the French consulate.'

'Great Scott! I know Museau. He says he's here to promote French trade – been here about a year. Goodness, he was in my office not two days past. A genial fellow for a Frenchie – big chap, mind – wouldn't want to cross him.'

'I suspect his interest in Siam extends well beyond the trade in silks and spices he professes, sir.'

'My God. What a mess this is!' Beaumont shook his head. 'I have further bad news, I'm afraid. I received a telegram from Hope last evening that has kept me awake nearly all night.' The consul general closed his eyes and took a deep breath. 'Hope's contact in Paris is dead.'

'Dead? You mean the agent who we have relied on these last few weeks?' Woodward looked flabbergasted.

'The very same… They fished him out of the River Seine a few days ago. "Accidentally drowned" is the official cause of death, but Hope suspects foul play. He believes his agent must have been discovered and slain. Whether he confessed anything to his executioner before he died is a matter of conjecture, but we must fear the worst. At the very least, Hope has warned me to expect no further corroborations from Paris. Apparently, his man was on the brink of uncovering the names of the French agents in Siam who are active in this matter. But now, I fear, we are on our own, gentlemen.'

The others fell into a long silence as they tried to absorb the terrible news.

'We have unearthed one of them, at least,' Chalke said with strained optimism. 'Monsieur Pierre Museau must be one of 'em. Why, he may be acting alone, for all we know…'

'I doubt that very much,' Henry Gough replied with a shake of his head. 'There will be others higher that Museau, for sure. But I agree, it is at least a start, and in truth, the matter is in our hands now. We need no further evidence of Hurdus' guilt. And between him and Monsieur Museau, we may yet find a way to the bottom of this pit of vipers.'

'You are correct, Mr Gough. We need no further proofs,' Beaumont responded, his eyes blazing. 'We can only draw one conclusion. Hurdus is indeed our damned spy. The way forward is clear,' he thundered. 'We must arrest our turncoat this instant and send him packing, in irons, back to England to face the full force of the law and the consequences of his wicked betrayal. With luck, he'll be a hanged man before the year is out…'

Gough and Chalke shifted on the balls of their feet and remained silent. Beaumont could see that any support they might have had for his proposed course of action was conspicuously lacking. Instead, it seemed the others had another plan. It did not take long before his doubts were confirmed and a new stratagem was offered to him.

Chalke spoke first. "Tis true, sir, our erstwhile friend Hurdus is a scoundrel and deserving of a dreadful and demeaning end to his life, but the reality is, he is worth more to our cause alive than dead – more to us here in Siam than in London, rotting amongst Newgate's vermin.'

Beaumont looked noticeably shocked. 'How so, sir? You

forget this man has betrayed his country and he needs to pay the price.'

'I am with Horatio on this matter.' Henry spoke with a tone of quiet reassurance. 'You see, a man like Charles Hurdus is in possession of material facts that, with the right approach from us, might serve our cause against the French.'

'Sir, our idea is that we reason with Hurdus rather than arrest him. We offer him a way to make amends by turning his connections with Museau and the French to our own use. I am not versed in double deceptions such as this, but I trust Messrs Woodward and Gough. They have the expertise to make something of it. On the face of things, it seems a good plan to me.'

'We would make him *our* informer, sir, against the French, in return for safe passage from here with his family,' Henry advanced. 'If he refuses, then the gallows at Newgate will, for sure, soon have another client. If he agrees to turn, we might yet save this nation of Siam from the lascivious advances of France. Albert Woodward has experience of such matters. Indeed, it is via such means that I was recruited by him to act as his eyes and ears in Whitechapel—'

'This is not Whitechapel, Mr Gough!' Beaumont snapped back, his eyes protruding most alarmingly. 'These are deep waters, indeed. Charles Hurdus is not a mere dockyard thief! Why, by his actions the security of our nation may have been threatened.'

'That is precisely our point, sir.' It was Chalke who spoke. 'We have nothing to lose and much to gain. Permit us, at least, to bring Hurdus into your presence today. You may challenge him yourself on the matters we have witnessed and discussed. Then, if you agree, we can put the proposal to him – to help us against the French or return to London in chains.'

'Hope will want his say in the matter…' came the muttered reply.

Sensing Beaumont was weakening, Henry pressed on. 'I suggest, sir, you dispatch a telegram to London outlining our findings. You must mention our intention to challenge Hurdus later today and our desire to recruit him to our cause. I can help you draft the latter passages if you wish, sir. Meanwhile, the rest of us should take some rest. We have been up the whole night and will need our collective wits about us if we are to get the better of Mr Hurdus… I propose you call him to your office at five this evening, before he departs for his home. You can confront him then, with the facts. It would be advantageous to have Albert Woodward at your side to lay out the full story, if necessary, and to outline our idea for Hurdus' future cooperation. We shall not be far away. It will be interesting to see the man's reaction when confronted with what we know. My guess, knowing the man's sensibilities, he will opt to save his skin and his family's too, but whatever the outcome, we shall have to make arrangements to hold him in custody during the night, maybe longer – at least until Hope's reply is received. Make no mistake, we cannot allow him to wriggle free once we have our blanket over him – he will be *de facto* under your arrest.'

'We have cells here. As part of the Bowring Treaty, we built them to hold British prisoners. Singh can organise his incarceration.' Suddenly Beaumont seemed to be warming to the idea. 'The rat will not escape our clutches. Fear not, Mr Gough.'

'Then it is settled.' Henry had never sounded more decisive. 'We meet again here at four o'clock to make preparations. Do you wish me to stay a while to assist with your telegram, sir?'

'I will not require a hansom driver to help me write a telegram, Mr Gough,' Beaumont spat back with a withering stare. Then, sensing he'd been unduly spiteful, he added more softly, 'Now go and take your rest. You have done well. I will see you all here at four – Mr Woodward included.'

Charles Hurdus had spent twenty minutes bandaging his head after his return home in the wee small hours. What a night it had been – one he'd been lucky to survive. His wife Umkaa had helped him staunch the flow, but in truth, the copious stream of blood caused by the knife that Pierre Museau had wielded against him had rather exaggerated the seriousness of his injury. Things could have been so much worse. The fact was, despite all the brandished tongs and daggers, he'd merely lost an earlobe and a piece of skin from his upper jaw. The tag of flesh had been sliced from his head in an abrupt but mightily deft movement from his attacker, which, despite the Frenchman's obvious rage, he'd failed to anticipate. The mention of money had been the final straw that broke the back of Museau's simmering anger, but it was not the main cause of Hurdus' new-found disfiguration. The root cause for his interlocutor's untamed fury had been the fact that Hurdus had actually called on him in the first place. Hurdus knew his instructions had always been to never look in on his French contact at his home, but he'd reasoned – partly in bruised pain, partly in desperation, and partly in drink – that at that time of night, the coast would be clear, and it would be as safe a time as any to pay an unannounced visit. After all, he'd been in utter distress, and Museau was the only man who could help him. In the end, Hurdus had got what he wanted – the money to pay his debts – but this had come at the cost of an earlobe and a lot of new pledges.

At least, he reflected, the blood had finally congealed, but his latest dilemma was how to explain the wound to those interfering busybodies at the British consulate. They were bound to notice and ask for an explanation. He contemplated passing it off as a shaving accident but rejected that as implausible. Then, he hit on the idea that one of his wives had thrown a knife at him, but that seemed unreasonable too. Finally, he settled on the story that a footpad had attacked him as he was taking a pre-slumber stroll outside his home. The man, a Siamese, naturally, who had wanted to steal his money, had been valiantly fought off, but during the struggle the injury had been sustained. The 'assailant' had scampered off unseen and unrecognised into the night, leaving no clues to his identity. It was just one of those things – only a flesh wound – to be borne with the resilience and British pluck he imagined his Siamese hosts expected of him. If he played his cards right, he might come out of it as a minor hero.

Much to his surprise, when he arrived for work the following day, the bandage to his ear, which had shrunk to about the size of a penny piece by the time repeat dressings had been applied, had hardly been noticed. The office had seemed unusually quiet that morning – no sign of Chalke or the two temporary emissaries either. Only Singh seemed to have spotted the injury, offering his polite sympathy as he'd marched past on his way to the registry. The story of the mystery attacker seemed to work well, and Singh had promised to keep a lookout for suspicious characters patrolling around the grounds.

There was a handwritten memo on Hurdus' desk after lunch, from the consul general, inviting him to drinks in his office at five pm, and although slightly surprised by the nature of the invitation, he wondered idly if the great man would notice his new appearance. At least he'd practised his story if the matter was raised, he thought, and left it at that.

At five minutes to five, he gulped down a couple of shots of the local whisky he kept in his desk to provide a dash of fortitude against what he expected to be a bland encounter with his superior. He locked his drawers, straightened his collar, and examined his scars once more in the looking glass. Then he walked the short distance across the landing to the consul general's mahogany-panelled office. He'd been inside that room more times than he could count. At one period of his career, he'd even harboured ambitions to spread his own papers across its sacred desk, but he knew better nowadays. He knew his place – he'd been reminded of it often enough.

Beaumont greeted him with a fixed expression and invited him to sit down. Hurdus instantly spotted Albert Woodward, who was sitting opposite the consul general and had turned his head to greet him. The Welshman's reception was as warm as ever and soon the two were sitting next to one another. Although there were exchanged smiles, for some reason there were no words. In the silence, Hurdus heard the door latch click behind him, like a clock preparing to strike the hour.

Beaumont broke the spell. 'I have asked Singh to secure us in my office while we have our discussions this evening. He will wait outside until we have concluded. You know Albert, of course. He will be joining us.' Beaumont's words were cold, and for the first time, a pang of dread fluttered into the pit of Hurdus' stomach. This wasn't what he had expected at all…

'I don't usually drink until six, sir, but I'm happy to make an exception tonight… Is there something to celebrate, perchance?' he offered lamely.

Beaumont laid his hands flat on the table. 'I apologise for my little deception in getting you into my office, Hurdus. There will be no drinking this evening. I have something of the utmost importance to discuss. I won't beat about the bush. Pray, tell me what you did last night.'

The organs in Hurdus' abdomen began to turn somersaults. 'Why, I see you have noticed my little wound. 'Tis naught but a scratch. Some wretched villain came at me last night with a dagger. I fought him off, but I fear I have lost some of my ear. It will heal—'

'I know different, sir.' Beaumont's seething anger was evident. 'Pray, do not waste my time with this banal blathering. I have but a simple demand of you. You must tell me why you visited the home of Monsieur Pierre Museau?'

The sight of Hurdus' jaw dropping was plain for all to see. He crossed his legs and folded his arms – then unfolded and uncrossed them a second later. Swallowing hard, he managed to utter, 'Well… I don't know what you are saying—'

'If you do not speak the truth now, I will clap you in irons this instant!' Beaumont shrieked, rising to stand behind his desk. Clearly, his temper had suddenly got the better of him. A fist thumped into the polished teak table and a candlestick toppled to the ground. 'I will not abide it. You, of all people! My God, I wish I could throttle you now!' Beaumont's face was purple with rage, his voice rising to such a pitch it seemed a vessel in his neck might burst at any second. As the consul general rounded his desk to approach Hurdus, his arms waving all about, Hurdus stood to defend himself, and for a moment the "Queensbury fists" of both parties were raised. Albert Woodward quickly got to his feet, put himself into Beaumont's path, and pressed him back. Without this intervention, the two distinguished diplomats would have certainly come to blows.

'Calm, gentlemen, please.' Woodward's Welsh burr rose above the hubbub like a valley preacher upbraiding a wayward member of his flock. 'I'll have none of this. Gentlemen, pray, be seated. We can solve nothing by ranting.' Placing avuncular hands onto the consul general's shoulders, he looked directly into the diplomat's dark eyes and said, 'Permit me, sir, if you please… We must show some restraint. This matter cannot be resolved by fisticuffs. If you will let me, I propose I ask Charles some candid and forthright questions. As a gentleman, I'm sure he will want to provide us with his story, his version of events – for it is his statement which we must all hear.' With a final reassuring shake of Beaumont's trapped arms, Woodward released his grip and enquired, 'Will you allow it, sir?'

Beaumont suddenly appeared to come to his senses. Breathing deeply, he dropped his hands, and at length, he replied, 'That I will… Pray continue. Forgive my outburst, but the moment was too much for me to take. Please, sir, ask what you will. I will give way. I have nothing further to say on the matter.'

'Very well, let us take our seats once more.' Albert Woodward's voice was the epitome of calm resolution. Once the others had obeyed, he joined them around the desk and turned his unyielding gaze onto Charles Hurdus' troubled face.

'My friend…' Woodward said, in a strange, sad, slow tone, 'I am so sorry it has come to this, but before you utter another word of your self-condemning balderdash, I urge you to hear what I have to say.'

Hurdus nodded that he understood. His demeanour was distinctly combatant, but his face was as white as wet ice.

'Your consul general has every reason to be outraged, for we have discovered your secret, Charles, one which I fear you have kept for many a long year.'

Hurdus started to mouth some words in reply, but Woodward put his hand up to stop him in his tracks. Almost in a whisper, and with a single finger raised to his lips, the Welshman said gently, 'Pray, do not speak until you have heard me out. If you do, you may say things you will come to regret. I will give you a chance to tell us the whole truth, but for now, just listen…' This short speech, softly and deliberately delivered, seemed to hit its mark immediately, for Charles Hurdus suddenly looked like a beaten man. The transformation from belligerent denial to abject submission was stunning and took but a few seconds. Pulling on his lower lip, as the faintest of tears glistened on his cheekbone, he replied with a now trembling voice.

'Speak then... I will listen.'

'Charles, you know me...' As he spoke, Woodward gradually raised the pitch and pace of his address. 'You know Henry too. Together, we have been the best of shipmates and fellow travellers these last few months. I believe you know me as a fair man – an honest man. You know also I am an investigator of some standing and many years in the service. You have been informed by Hope of our purpose here in Siam. You understand that Henry Gough is witness to a murder; he is here in Bangkok to give testimony in the matter of the death of the King of Siam's half-brother. You have also been informed I am here to advise the Siamese government in matters concerning revenue. All this is true, but there is more substance to our oriental assignment; there is one matter in particular we have kept from you. Henry and I have a further mission, one we have kept secret until now.

'We are also here, at the behest of the War Office, to uncover a traitor – a man who has betrayed his country. Mr Nathanial Hope believes there is an individual acting clandestinely in Bangkok. It is his view, which is shared by others, that this party has been divulging British intentions and passing sensitive information to our French friends for over a year. He has tasked us with unmasking the person concerned. It has taken us some time to get to the bottom of the matter. Henry and I have encountered many obstacles, some put intentionally in our path, which have swerved us away from our goal, but now we know, with certainty, the truth of the Bangkok betrayal. I will not obfuscate with you,

Charles. You are the man we have been hunting – and you have been in plain sight all along. You are our elusive fox, now run to ground.

'The evidence against you is irrefutable, and being a man of substantial intelligence, you must know already that the charges to be brought against you will be impossible to deny. The events of the last twenty-four hours have been decisive. Your actions have been witnessed and recorded in the minutest detail. Your every movement has been watched. Your visit to Mamasam Malee's establishment and your violent altercation with her henchman, Khun Loong, are known to us; your subsequent headlong fall into the arms of your collaborator for the monies you needed to cover your debts – we have seen it all and at first hand.'

On hearing the words "Mamasam Malee" spoken out loud so all could hear, Hurdus' head sunk to his chest, and he let out a low moan.

'And for clarity,' Woodward pressed on, 'who did you go to for succour in your hour of need? Why, to none other than to your French brother-in-arms, Monsieur Pierre Museau. We know Museau is an undisclosed officer of French military intelligence, who poses in Siam as an honest man of commerce. So, you see, sir, the square is fully circled. I could go on, Charles, but I won't labour on each event of duplicity, save just one, which I believe to be your most heinous crime – the betrayal of your friend, Henry Gough, to Monsieur Museau.'

Another piteous groan came from Hurdus as Henry's name was mentioned once more. As Woodward persisted with his address, his soothing tones had gradually given way, through stages, to a more robust style of speaking, which had now risen to a volley of harshly offered sentences – acid-dry, acerbic, designed to hurt. 'Henry was the man whose life you once saved!' he exclaimed. 'On board the

Verona your act of courage brought you tribute – but what then?' Woodard threw his hands apart and halted for effect. 'Then... in an act of pure vindictiveness, you shared with this Museau an overheard conversation between Henry and Singh. It concerned Henry's near slaying at the hands of that malevolent female emissary they call Françoise Mielette. That very act was, in my book at least, an unspeakable, insufferable deed, which alone will be sufficient to see you swinging from the neck at Newgate – and deserving of a baying mob, too. Your journey into the molten lakes of hell will not be without a jubilant fanfare, sir!'

'I had no wish to harm Henry... I give you my word, I knew nothing of any attempt to kill him,' came the whimpering response.

Woodward ignored the attempt at justification and continued his attack, this time more forcefully than ever. 'As for your motives, I doubt they were even principled... I don't believe you ever held any moral animosity against your country – or its values. Nor do I believe you admire the French doctrine of *Liberté*, *Égalité*, and *Fraternité* any better. If that had been the case, perhaps there would have been some honour in the matter. No, for you, my friend, the goal was driven by pure venality. Money was your only spur; to raise capital to cover your hidden sins. Am I right?'

'I had no intention for it to carry on as long as it did.' Hurdus was weeping now.

'And I suspect you wished to take some revenge for being continuously overlooked for higher office. That is correct also, is it not? Your life became a pathetic travesty of mendacity and deceit, with weekly covenants with the French devil to help pass the time.' Woodward was twisting the knife for all he was worth. Gone was the gentle, understanding, empathetic soul of the earlier exchanges. It had been replaced by a spiteful, intimidating, fire-breathing accuser. The dove had transformed to dragon in a matter of seconds. The effect was dramatic.

'I am so, so sorry...' Hurdus wailed, falling to the floor and slapping the timber boards with his bare hands. 'I wanted to stop,' he yowled. 'I tried to stop – many times – but they wouldn't have it. Even last night, I thought I might break free of his clutches. Oh, 'twas all such an avoidable calamity! My money problems had ended, you see, my inheritance was secured. I am soon to be a wealthy man with an estate in Sussex, but then that damned woman, Malee, tricked me with the dice and... well, then I had no alternative. One final time, I thought. Pierre was the only man I could turn to. For all that is sacred, look what he did to me!' Hurdus screamed, pointing towards his head. 'The bastard cut me before he would give me the money. He made me make further promises, too. It would have been the last time, I give you my word.'

Albert Woodward stood up abruptly. Beaumont, seized by all the drama, found himself copying his colleague, and in an instant, both had risen together and were towering over the grovelling Hurdus.

'Look at me, Charles,' Woodward commanded. 'Get up off the floor, for God's sake, man!'

Hurdus dragged his limp carcass into some semblance of an upright posture. He looked utterly befuddled and bedraggled.

'So, Museau forced you to make further promises, eh?' Woodward advanced. 'What promises?'

Hurdus, decidedly unsteady on his feet and swaying from side to side, replied, 'He wishes me to learn more – it's always more he wants! To tell him more of this, more of that... gunboats and the like... our meetings with the king... anything I can glean from the London dispatches I am privy to. No detail seems irrelevant. If I do not, he threatens to expose me, and I am as good as a dead man.'

Albert Woodward's next words were spoken with the utmost gravity. 'The consul general and I need to know everything, Charles. We will be here all night, if necessary, but if you truly trust me and wish to make what few amends you can, now is the time. I am going to call Henry and Horatio to join us now. Tell your audience everything, and you have my word, I will do everything in my power to protect you.' Woodward glanced towards Beaumont for his sanction, but the consul general seemed to be so totally transfixed by the tableau of drama unfolding before him; he seemed hardly able to muster a response. Such was his state of mental intoxication, he could only nod his consent lamely to the silent question posed.

Woodward lost no time in confirming the signal. 'That is indeed excellent news for you, Charles. We are all in accord. Between us, we will do what we can to save your skin but only on the condition that you play your part. I will now fetch the others while you clear your mind. Pray, start at the beginning – leave nothing out. You can start by telling us how long has this being going on?'

Chapter Twenty-Three

As Hurdus stared blankly ahead, Woodward stepped quietly out of the room. Within less than a minute, Gough and Chalke had entered the office, traipsing through the door in complete silence, and were soon assembled around the table to hear Hurdus' story. The mood in the room was one of stifled tension. It was as if the group had gathered around a condemned man to witness the last rites and hear his final will and testament. Once all were seated, and without any further prompting, Hurdus launched into a long speech.

'My association with the French started at the time of the terrible Knox debacle. The very day Sir Thomas was called back to London, and I learned I was to be overlooked for higher office once more, Museau came to me. How he'd heard of my problems with money I have no idea, but he offered, as a friendly gesture, to help me. He seemed quite genial at the time, if a little dull, although I hardly knew him. He was new to Siam, and I was at a low ebb, especially down at heel on hearing that not even a small promotion was coming my way. Knox and that foolish daughter of his, the precocious Fanny, saw to that, I'm sure of it. You see, I'd always seen her as a flirtatious and headstrong character. She had many suitors and toyed with their affections in a most unsuitable way. I raised it with her father on a number of occasions, but he wouldn't listen. My concerns were that her affairs might damage our relations with the royal court. In the end, I was proved correct. Her actions with the Siamese nobleman, Preecha, were irresponsible and provocative in the extreme, especially to the sensibilities of our hosts. But that's another story for another day...

'So, feeling sorry for myself and more than a little resentful about my position, I saw no harm in Museau's advance. I borrowed a little money from my new-found French friend, which paid off my gambling debts. But later, after a further run of bad luck, I found I could not repay him on time – on the date we'd agreed. Instead, he asked a favour of me. In return for a month's extension of credit, he asked me to let him know immediately when you, Horatio, were next going to visit the king. Please forgive me, sir, but at the time I saw no conflict in his request, and so, obliged.

'Our meetings took place at the Falcks at first, but then he told me he wished to be more discreet about our association. He suggested I leave a note for him in a private place of his choosing whenever I had something to tell him. He passed it off as a perfectly normal arrangement, and I did not think anything was untoward. It was an easy relationship but one, in truth, I was disinclined to tell others about, due to the shadow that my gambling habit cast over things. In fact, Museau warned me against telling others. They would misunderstand, he said. But then, when my wife was ailing with the dysentery, and I was sick with worry, he came to me again and offered to cancel my debt altogether, if I could tell him something of the *substance* of the meetings between you and Chulalongkorn. I always thought we'd got on well together, Horatio,' Hurdus continued in low tones, without once glancing up towards Chalke, who was seated just three feet away. 'So, you see, the task was easy.

'But after I'd obliged a few times, the Frenchman's requests started to get out of hand – more frequent, more strident. In effect, they became demands. I tried to put a halt to it, but I still owed Museau money on the second loan.' He looked up briefly and addressed Lawrence Beaumont. 'He threatened to tell you, sir, as the new consul general, of our little pact.' Once again Hurdus' head lowered to his chest as he spoke. 'I was suddenly scared rigid and realised I'd waded too far into the shallows. I was in veritable deep water now, the waves knocking me sideways. It was not long before the French ultimatums grew even greater; the details Museau wanted became more specific. Then he announced he would give me money, rather than lend it to me. I realise I should have known better, but he always paid me well and I accepted the new arrangement without a murmur and was soon back in funds and enjoying life once more. Thereafter, the matter became much of a routine; things became easier. In truth, I began to quite enjoy our little chats, which would always conclude with him handing me a small stash of local currency. But when the subject turned to the movement of our gunboats, my concerns returned. I told him so. That's when he smashed a full bottle of whisky over my knee as a warning to comply. I could hardly walk for a week.'

Hurdus asked for water and when it was provided, he continued. 'It was around this time that I returned to England on long leave and to conduct certain family business. The trip came as a merciful relief, and I thought that would be an end of it all. But then, one day as I was walking out alone, I was approached in Chancery Lane, no less, by a moustachioed Frenchman with a message from Museau. You can image my horror – in broad daylight too! He'd heard I was returning to Siam with two others and was particularly interested in the names of my travelling companions, the purpose of their voyage, and the itinerary of our passage to Bangkok. I met Museau in Fleet Street the following day and gave him all the details, including all our ports of call. I realise now that my information may have precipitated the attack on you in Marseilles, Henry, for which I am truly sorry, but I swear on my children's lives, I had no concept of their intentions.' He glanced up once more to look at Henry Gough, albeit briefly. 'Luckily, I was able to help you in your hour of need.'

Hurdus resumed his bent forward pose, hardly ever looking at his audience as he spoke. 'When, in due course, we all arrived in Siam, Museau made contact once again – within a day, would you believe! It was as if I had never been away. He told me he wanted to know Henry Gough's every movement while he was in Bangkok. He seemed pleased with my return, and another purse of silver coins was given to me. And here I am. Still in his clutches; a sadder but wiser man. The rest you must know… Yesterday's catastrophe was the last time I saw him. I had intended to end it today and take the consequences of possible exposure, but last night circumstances intervened, and I lost half an ear instead.'

There was a stoney silence for a few moments as the assembly tried to digest the multitude of facts that had poured from the mouth of their once trusted friend.

'To what purpose?' Henry Gough was the first to speak. 'The French must have a reason for all this skulduggery. What has Museau told you about his objectives?'

Hurdus lifted his head from his lap, and for the first time, he looked his accusers directly in the eye.

'Very little – nothing, in fact. I hate him. He will not confide in me. I have ceased asking the bastard.' He paused before adding, 'My only sense is the French must be plotting to overthrow the king, and they wish Britain to be unprepared when they act. My impression is their move will come sooner rather than later. If they decide to strike at Chulalongkorn it will be done quickly at a time when they feel least resistance will be offered and while reinforcements are so far distant to interfere. As a betting man, I'd wager they are merely waiting for Kittisak's trial to conclude, and then use the outcome as some kind of excuse to invade. As they have done in Cambodia, it appears likely they will try to install a puppet – perchance to put the regent, Bamroong, into power, if you can call it that. I know him to be in their pocket already – the regent has always been an ambitious man, despite his age; I don't believe he has devoted feelings for his country or its people.'

'And of the killing in London?' Beaumont spoke for the first time in nearly an hour. 'Do you know who is responsible for the prince's death? Kittisak has been falsely accused, that is clear. But if not him, who?'

'I know nothing of the London killing, sir, I swear it. As much as you – less, most likely. But you see, I only speak to Museau – only him. He is a most unimpressive frog, in truth – no manners to speak of, just a monkey with a vicious streak. No doubt, he has his masters to whom he reports. He's hinted as much. If you think the French are behind the assassination, then Museau will know something. If you can locate the true organ-grinder though, you may yet find the killer. One thing I have gleaned… Your arrival in Bangkok, Henry, has set the cat among the pigeons. The French seem to focus their attention on you above all others. Perhaps 'tis because you were the only man on earth to have actually seen the killer. My guess is the French were frightened of what you would tell the court. *Why* I cannot imagine, but afeared they most surely were – and maybe they still are.'

For over an hour, Hurdus answered questions fired at him by the assembly. Chalke remained largely silent throughout, busying himself by taking notes of the exchanges. When all avenues of interrogation were exhausted, Albert Woodward rose from the group and turned to face them.

"'Tis much as we imagined. To your credit, Charles, you have been candid. Now we must decide our next course of action.'

'I am in your hands, sirs.'

'Now listen to me, Charles… you say you have made further promises to Museau. If so, then you must keep them.' Woodward was smiling all of a sudden. 'You must be a man of your word, Charles, eh! After all, we wouldn't want to dishearten our French *camarade*, would we?'

'There is no need. I can end it all here and now. Trust me, I will end it today. I will go to him tonight and finish it once and for all. I give you my word, on all that is holy.'

Woodward took two paces towards the window and turned to face the group. At length, directing his voice towards Hurdus, he announced with all the gravitas of a high court judge, 'If you want to save yourself from the gallows, sir, you will not be ending anything until I say so. Your meetings with Monsieur Museau will continue. Do you hear?'

A curious look swept over Hurdus' face. 'You actually want me to continue with all my knavish tricks?' He frowned as he wiped his face with the back of his hand. 'I don't understand…'

'You will soon enough,' came the sonorous response, 'but for now, you must remain in our protective custody. Please go with Singh. He will take you to your quarters for the night and bring food and drink. In the morning, we will meet again, by which time we shall have a task for you to perform. You are on the road away from perdition, Charles. We will offer you another path, which will lead you towards redemption. I urge you to take it when it is offered.'

'I don't like the sound of it!' Lawrence Beaumont announced, his brow furrowed from eyebrow to hairline, in answer to the proposal made by Albert Woodward. 'We have our confession – let that be an end to it. Nathaniel Hope will have his man, and we can be left to rebuild our relations with the Siamese. When the king hears we have weeded out the interloper and made an example of Hurdus, the ice preventing us from engaging with His Majesty will melt, and we can engage in civilised conversation once more.'

The others, Henry Gough, Albert Woodward and Horatio Chalke, looked at one another with a look of resignation. Clearly this encounter with Beaumont was going to be more difficult than they'd expected. It was seven am the following day. The meeting had been convened by the consul general to discuss the way forward. The quartet sat around the now familiar antique table drinking hot coffee and nibbling on warm rice cakes. Charles Hurdus was noticeably absent. Instead, he slumbered in a dank cell thirty feet beneath them, deep within the bowels of the building. The shutters of Beaumont's office that overlooked the river had been opened to their widest extremity, drawing in the morning's cool air and all the noises of the garden. A pair of jaunty myna birds danced across the lawn, chirruping to one another, only ceasing their cackle for brief moments to pick at the leaves amongst the tangled roots of an ancient banyan tree.

It was Chalke who answered first. 'Maybe I am best placed to respond, sir, as the only true member of your staff, and one who has known this country, its politics, and its convoluted ways for more than twenty years. I believe I speak for all three of us when I humbly beg to disagree with your assessment. It is our view that the time has come to be bold – audacious, even. The biggest prize at stake today is Siam itself. We may have its destiny in our hands. With the greatest respect, sir, if we merely pack Charles Hurdus back to London on the next ship, it will achieve nothing, save to provide a temporary respite in our relations with Chulalongkorn. All the evidence points towards an imminent French incursion. If we have proof of their intentions, and of those within the secret circle who would do him harm, we can forewarn the king. Between us, Siam and Great Britain can take pre-emptive actions, which may forestall such an attack. The battle is only half won, sir.'

'I have sent a telegram to London with our views on France's intentions. That should be sufficient. If Mr Gladstone decides to take action to resist the threat, so be it. The matter is now in his hands. We have done enough.'

'I beg also to disagree,' Henry Gough said in a bold voice. 'I may be but a humble hansom driver, but equally, I am not used to mincing my words. My view is this…' he said, glaring directly at Beaumont. 'We did, indeed, capture a prize from the French yesterday. But I am certain we must do more – much more. Now is the time to turn our prize; to round its guns on the French and shatter their ambitions to capture Siam. Any support Great Britain can provide in this moment of crisis is limited. Our forces are too far distant. Why, I suspect a couple of gunboats in Singapore may be the most we could call on until a greater fleet arrived. By then, the matter will be settled. The key to extinguishing French ambitions lies within Siam itself. Unfettered, the king is a powerful man. There is still time to save his kingdom, if he acts decisively. Firstly, he must move against the regent; then, he must mobilise his forces to the border with Cambodia. But at present, he knows of no one to trust. His spies tell him one thing; the regent's agents tell him another. We are not trusted, and the French tell him lies. He must be given proof that Regent Bamroong is in cahoots with the lot of them. We, who could be in possession of the true facts, cannot sit idly by and allow matters to take their course.'

'But the king will not meet me – he will not hear me!' Beaumont cried. 'How can I influence him if he refuses to talk to me?'

'I can get you an audience with His Majesty, sir, that is not the problem – this very day, if you wish it,' Chalke replied. 'But for such a meeting to change his thinking, idle gossip will not suffice. You will need to show him irrefutable evidence there is a plot to cause his downfall. If Hurdus can lead us to the true killer of Prince Gagananga, and by doing so, show the hand of France and the regent in the affair, the king will surely come round. His trust in Great Britain will be restored, and he will be open to receive our future advice. It's still not too late to save this land from the tentacles of Paris.'

'But the risk!' Beaumont cried. 'What if Hurdus cannot be trusted, and he leads us into a French trap. The man is an alcohol-dependent womaniser and gambler. His nature is, at best, unpredictable – at worst, he could be hostile to our intent.'

'Hear me out. There is a simple way to resolve this.' Albert Woodward put his hands together as if in prayer. 'It will take but a short time to effect, and there is nothing to lose by attempting it. In short, we ask Charles to give some bogus intelligence of our making, and of apparent high value, to Museau. Then we watch the Frenchman's every move. I have an excellent team at the ready who will do this for us – and do it without exposure. We'll see where he goes, and with luck, he will lead us to our newly monikered "organ-grinder". If he does, we may learn much – enough to persuade the king to treat this danger seriously. If not, we will have lost nothing, and we can send Charles packing, back to the Old Bailey. We will need some enticing bait, of course, the intelligence he shares must be weighty enough to get Museau's heart fluttering and running for help. Sir, pray give us forty-eight hours. If we have not achieved our aim by then, you are free to send Charles wherever you choose. Two days is all I ask…'

All eyes now fell on Lawrence Beaumont. At length, he placed both thumbs under his chin and said in a low tone, 'Very well. You have won the argument. I will give you the forty-eight hours you request, but on one condition. Horatio, get us an audience with the king today. His Majesty must hear our news. If he is to be part of the solution, he must be appraised of our plan – and sanction it, too. For Great Britain to act alone could be construed as an act of war, and I will not be part of it. The stakes are too high for both our countries. If Chulalongkorn insists he needs the proof, we will do our level best to supply it, and you will have your forty-eight hours to act. Only then, may you use Hurdus in whatsoever way you see fit. Meanwhile, see to it that you do not let him escape.'

'And if Hurdus helps us – what then? Will you allow him and his family free passage from Siam?' Henry enquired.

Beaumont shook his head. 'I cannot answer, other than to say I will consider it. I cannot commit to anything. If the blighter plays his part honestly and convincingly, and we manage to turn this dreadful situation to our advantage, I will plead for him with London – maybe more… That's all I will say for now.'

Chapter Twenty-Four

Much to his surprise, and despite his strange surroundings and sparsely furnished accommodation, Charles Hurdus had slept soundly through the night. Singh had been kind and had rustled up some fresh blankets and a duck-feather pillow. He'd also left a bowl of sugared buffalo-milk porridge, two boiled eggs, and a flagon of local beer, all of which Hurdus consumed with relish before retiring to his bunk. Perhaps it was the unburdening of his guilty secret that had somehow cleansed his mind – whatever the reason, whether it was the beer or his conscience, the slumbers came naturally.

A few minutes after eight am, less than twenty minutes after Hurdus had awoken from his inertia, Henry Gough and Albert Woodward came to call. Their arrival was announced by the rattle of Singh's keys and the sound of two bamboo stools being dragged noisily into his cell.

'So we can sit while we talk,' Henry announced with a cheerful smile.

After they had exchanged pleasantries, mostly concerning sleep and breakfast, and Albert had commented about the variance in design between the prison cells of Tower Hill and Hurdus' current bolthole – which was very little, as it transpired – the trio sat to discuss the important business of the day.

Woodward opened the dialogue. 'To speak plainly, Charles, if you are to save your neck, you must help us.'

'I will do as you ask – and do it willingly.'

'Then listen. We have hatched a plan that we hope will reveal all, but first we need the king to approve it. The consul general has insisted on it. Within the last ten minutes, he and Horatio have hurried to the Royal Palace to seek an urgent audience with His Majesty. We should know soon enough, but it would be wise for us to outline our stratagem, as time is of the essence.'

'Tell me what you wish me to do.'

'Very well. We will ask that you take a certain paper to Museau today. You have told us you always leave your initial messages in a secret place – the ones alerting him you have something to impart.'

'That is correct. He tells me at the conclusion of each of our encounters where the next is to be. He has a choice of six places, known to us both.'

'And the next message? Where will you leave it?'

'I am to place it under a particular flat stone at the rear of the temple grounds at Wat Pho, the temple close to the Royal Palace. I have used this location before. Museau will check the location twice daily, between eleven and midday and then between five and six pm. The message is always brief – just enough to tell him to meet me at a place of my choosing at the appointed hour.'

'Where will you choose for your next meeting?'

'It depends on the hour and the urgency. If the matter is pressing, I will choose a place close to where I left the message and simply wait for him. If I drop the message before eleven today, I can tell him to meet me inside the temple itself. I like to meet in temples. They are generally quiet and provide an easy place to linger. Also, by leaving my calling card and holding our meeting in the same area, I save myself two trips.'

'Very well.' Woodward fingered his pocket watch. 'It is nearly half past eight. News of the king's wishes may take some while to reach us, and we have barely enough time to make arrangements to observe your meeting.' He halted to scratch his neck before saying, 'So, it's best we plan for you to leave your note this evening. Shall we say at a quarter to five? Until then, you must be seen to go about your normal business at the consulate. You will not be allowed to go to your home, however, for at least the next two days, and only then if our plan succeeds. Fear not for your family. A message has been sent to your wives that you have had to take a consulate trip upcountry at short notice. They are not expecting you back for a few days. But…' he added most sternly, 'you must not attempt to use your free moments to escape. If you do, you will be discovered, and both you and your family will have to bear the consequences.'

'What will the paper say – the one I am to give to Museau?'

'It will be a telegram, which you'll tell him has just been received from London. You will also take a handwritten copy. The original telegram is merely for show, to reinforce the veracity of the message. You will inform Museau you must return the original to the consulate before it is missed. The copy, which you have transcribed, is for him to keep.'

'What will the message say?'

'We have discussed this at length and believe we have arrived at something that will set the French into a mild panic,' Woodward said with a gleam in his eye. 'The telegram will refer to the highly confidential and classified tour of the

Far East by the Duke of Cambridge. It will say the duke is currently en route to Singapore from Hong Kong and has expressed an interest in visiting Siam before landing in the Crown colony. He wishes a personal audience with King Chulalongkorn as quickly as possible. The message will refer to the tragic murder of the king's half-brother on London streets and offer further condolences. Most importantly, it will indicate that the duke is anxious to hear, *in camera*, the message the king wished Gagananga to impart to him in February – the missive which, due to the aforesaid prince's untimely death, went undelivered. The duke wishes it, as he understands the conversation may concern matters of mutual national security.' Woodward looked pleased with himself. 'In case you didn't know it, Charles, the duke is commander-in-chief of the British Armed Forces.'

A look of whimsy seemed to flood Hurdus' countenance, as if a distant memory had transported him back in time. 'Surprisingly, you may think, I have met his grace,' he said distractedly. 'The duke was both a fine horseman and a keen follower of the sport of kings in his day, as indeed I was... if only in respect of the latter facet. As a young man, I was briefly introduced to him at Royal Ascot. 'Twas back in '53, when "Teddington" won the Gold Cup. I had a decent wager on the horse, I recall...' His voice trailed away. 'It's most interesting that he plans a visit to Siam. He must be a man of advancing years by now...' Hurdus added with a mildly confused look.

Henry tutted as he cuffed Hurdus on the shoulder. 'This is not the time for joking, Charles. I'm told the duke is well over sixty, and make no mistake, he will not be visiting us at any time soon. You must know 'tis but a ruse to smoke out the French!'

'Ahem... Of course. And then?'

'You will have done your work, and we shall observe what happens next. Our guess is Monsieur Museau will have to share the information with others, not least with the regent himself. If, as we suspect, Lord Bamroong is involved in the plot to dethrone the king, he will need to be informed quickly, as the imminent arrival in Siam of such an important British military man may require some rethinking of their joint plans.'

'But who knows?' Albert Woodward advanced. 'We must be prepared for every eventuality.'

⁓

Much to Beaumont's surprise, he and Horatio Chalke were quickly ushered, with utmost reverence, into the gloriously adorned king's antechamber within just a few minutes of announcing their arrival at the Royal Palace.

'Your access here, Chalke, is most impressive,' he commented to the junior man once they were alone. He did his best not to sound sour in the process.

'I have known Chulalongkorn since he was a mere stripling, sir.' Chalke spoke a low whisper. 'At one time, I even had a part in his education. He speaks English more fluently than some of the members inside our House of Lords and is a most intelligent, knowledgeable, and sensitive man in every way. Those who underestimate him do so at their peril. Nowadays, the king and I rarely discuss matters of state when we meet. I deliberately keep our conversations light-hearted and informal, and I make a point of never asking favours of him unless there is the greatest of need. It is precisely for these reasons I believe he trusts me more than most. On being informed that I have arrived with you today, he will know we wish to discuss matters of importance. While we are in this chamber, we might be physically close to the king's presence, but pragmatically speaking, we remain still far away. He may yet keep us waiting. Make no mistake...' his voice lowered even further, 'we are being watched as we sit together and must show no signs of impatience or arrogance as he considers whether to convene with us or not.'

More than an hour passed, during which time various courtiers and attendants entered the room and passed behind the patterned door that led directly into the king's chamber. At the outset, the two Englishmen chattered pleasantly to one another, carefully ensuring never to touch on the topic they wished to discuss with the king. After twenty minutes of idle gossip, there was nothing more to be said, and thereafter, they remained in almost complete silence, only rising occasionally to stretch their limbs. Refreshments, including coffee and sweetmeats, were brought to them every fifteen minutes on gilded trays as they waited.

On the stroke of ten, a courtier, resplendent in a bejewelled tunic of yellow and gold silk, appeared from the other side of the ornamented door. He beckoned them to rise and accompany him. The king was poring over a huge map of Siam when they were announced. As the two stooped in respectful unison, His Majesty looked up briefly to acknowledge their presence and then continued his examination of the chart. Chulalongkorn was a slightly built but erect young man, pleasing to the eye, handsome, and clear skinned. He was dressed simply yet elegantly, in traditional dress of orange and gold silk jacket, belted at the waist; embroidered pantaloons of finest cloth; and patterned slippers. His hair was tidily cut and swept back from his forehead. A dark moustache, trimmed neatly above a pair of full lips, completed the picture.

Beaumont and Chalke knew it was not their place to speak first, so after their bowing, they stooped in awkward silence awaiting a signal from the king to engage in conversation.

When, at length, the monarch spoke for the first time, it was in the form of a question, which surprised them both. 'I need more roads, gentlemen,' he announced in perfect English, 'will you help me to build them?'

It was Beaumont who replied first. As the higher-ranking diplomat it was his place to do so. 'Good roads are most important to the prosperity of your kingdom, Your Majesty.'

'And also, to its defence,' the king flashed back in an instant.

Beaumont gave a sycophantic smile in return. 'For both reasons, I am sure Great Britain would be glad to support Your Majesty's plans. We have some highly experienced engineers we could call on to work on such a project with Your Majesty's own excellent builders. In fact, Your Majesty's observation concerning defence is most apposite, as it is about the defence of Your Majesty's realm we would wish to speak to Your Majesty today.'

The king, with a contemptuous sigh, suddenly looked world-weary. Wincing at this fawning kowtow and irritated by the repeated "Your Majesty's", he turned instead to speak directly to Horatio Chalke. 'Come, take a seat with me. Are your family well, Horatio? Your lovely wife, Kanchana – is she in the best of health? It has been too long since we all dined together; I should like to renew my acquaintance with her and hear all your news. Pray, speak to Phomsak when you leave. He will give you a date when we can sit around the table together.'

'Your Majesty is most kind,' Chalke replied as he and Beaumont settled onto a broad button-backed sofa. 'My wife remains in fine fettle, and I'm certain she will look forward to meeting you and the ladies of the court once again. I agree it has been too long.' Chalke paused briefly and then, before the king could reply, he said, 'Sir, I hope you do not think me presumptuous, but we have grave news to impart to you, if you will hear us out.'

'If you have news for the King of Siam, then speak it, Horatio.'

Chalke glanced towards the consul general, who meekly nodded his acquiescence in return. It was clear that any dialogue between the kingdoms of Great Britain and Siam this day would be carried out between Horatio Chalke and King Chulalongkorn.

'The matter we wish to discuss today is complicated, and for Your Majesty, it may be difficult to bear,' Chalke started tentatively. 'To be direct, it concerns a threat to your life, your throne, and your country.'

The king stared blankly back. 'Then speak directly, and pray leave nothing out.'

It took Chalke nearly fifteen minutes to tell the full story. He commenced his narrative with the killing of Prince Gagananga, then the growing perception that British intentions were being misinterpreted in Siam, the suspicion of a traitor at the consulate, the dispatch from London of Henry Gough and Albert Woodward to expose the culprit, and the various attempts on Henry's life in the process – he listed them all. The idea that Kittisak was a mere scapegoat for the crime of murder brought a knowing smile from Chulalongkorn. The king's eyes widened on hearing of the capture of Charles Hurdus and his admittance of guilt as a spy with treacherous ties to the French. Finally, Chalke reached the most delicate subject of all – namely, the role of the regent, Lord Sirrichi Bamroong, in the whole affair and the British view that he was actively plotting with France against his own monarch.

'To sum up, Your Majesty, it is our assessment that unless it can be forestalled, Siam is shortly to encounter an uprising, sponsored and led by French forces in Cambodia, with the aim of installing your regent as a puppet ruler. Our message to you is one of the greatest import and urgency. We feel it would be wise to take steps quickly to thwart their plans. Great Britain will do all in its limited power to help you deflect any incursions on Siamese sovereignty, but we feel the key to defeating this menace lies largely in your hands, Your Majesty. An attempt to discredit and dislodge the regent before it is too late could prove to be very prudent. Then, to demonstrate your resolve to defend your kingdom, we would urge you to mobilise all your available forces to the border with Cambodia. If you require further proof of the plot, and the regent's alleged complicity, we have a plan to obtain indisputable evidence, but it will require a series of bold moves, and we desire your sanction before we can proceed.'

The king looked visibly stunned. With a deep exhalation, he got to his feet and gazed down on his still seated guests. At length he said, 'You have been my good friend for many years, Horatio. Why, I almost consider you as Siamese, such is the love you have shown for my country and my people. But, to speak plainly, I have little trust for the great power you represent. Between you and the French, your constant machinations and manoeuvrings present a near relentless disquiet for my people. You speak of French conspiracies. But are you not here to represent your own country? How do I know Great Britain, whose history of foreign conquest is second to none, does not have her own designs on Siam? How do I know your gentle words are not orchestrated by others, more powerful than you, who have intentions against my kingdom? I know you mean well, my friend, and in truth, I have suspected something of the kind you have described for many months – some subversion, some scheme or other to dislodge me. That was the reason I sent my half-brother to England to plead directly with your queen. I wished her to hear my concerns in person. But I still have no firm proof of a plot, and neither does Great Britain, by the sounds of what you have just told me. I may be no lawyer, but your account smacks of conjecture based on a scattering of facts and a host of accumulated guesswork. The regent, Lord Bamroong, has been my honest mentor these many years. I cannot strike him down on your hearsay alone.'

'We can give you proof, Your Majesty, if you will allow it. As God is my witness, my motives are honest. The consul general and I may represent our country here today, but for my part, the undeniable love I hold for Siam is my true inspiration. We have a stratagem to uncover the truth, but we will need not only your authority to implement it, but your help to make it work.'

The king walked to the chart table and solemnly ran his index finger down the jagged line that marked the border between Siam and Cambodia. The others watched him in silence, daring not to speak as the monarch weighed up the options.

'Very well,' Chulalongkorn announced after nearly a whole minute had elapsed, 'if you can give me proof of Lord Bamroong's guilt, I will act. I owe it to my people.' He turned to face the others. 'You say you can obtain undeniable evidence. Tell me how you will manage it, and if it is proper, I will approve it. If then you need my assistance to bring the matter to fruition, I will give you whatever you need. I wish an end to this heartbreak – far more than you can possibly imagine...'

Chapter Twenty-Five

On hearing the details of the British ruse to entice Museau into a trap, and following further long discussions between the three, the king finally sanctioned the plan, and all were now in a state of high excitement and anticipation as they worked on the details of the operation. The British proposal may have been straightforward in concept, but they soon realised that its execution was fraught with difficulties and new challenges. Their expectation was that once Hurdus had shown Museau the bogus telegram, purporting to announce the imminent arrival in Bangkok of the commander-in-chief of British forces, Museau would have no alternative but to share the information with his superior, or superiors. On the theory that Museau's master, who all assumed would be a member of the French mission, was in cahoots with the regent, it was considered almost certain that he would want to seek an urgent audience with Sirrichi Bamroong, in order to share the news and allow the conspirators to devise alternative tactics.

The plan was simple: to place a concealed witness, or witnesses, to covertly overhear the anticipated seditious meeting between the regent and the French, thereby delivering the proof the king so needed. It was possible, they all agreed, that Museau had, in fact, no puppet master controlling his actions. It was conceivable he was acting alone, but either way, any imminent meeting between Lord Bamroong and others had to be witnessed. Once the stratagem had been outlined to Chulalongkorn, the king was asked by Chalke if he had any trusted spies within the regent's entourage who might assist their cause.

The king shook his head glumly. 'Only Lord Bamroong's diary secretary, I'm afraid,' he announced with a sigh. 'Somchai is certainly a fine young man, and a cousin of my deceased half-brother, Prince Gagananga. He keeps me informed of his master's future movements, including details of any engagements the regent is scheduled to attend. However,' the king added bleakly, 'I doubt if my little spy has sufficient access to overhear any private conversations or witness any clandestine assignations.'

Thus, there was a very great problem that needed to be solved. How was it possible to place a trusted person, a man directly commanded by the king, in a position to overhear a deeply personal and potentially incriminatory conversation between the two parties? They knew the regent would perforce allow only those of his most trusted coterie into his presence at such critical moments, and the king's reluctant conclusion that his young infiltrator, due to his lowly status, did not belong to such a group was a notable setback.

'There may be something that could help your cause, Horatio,' Chulalongkorn offered, his face brightening. 'I am aware the regent is accustomed to holding his most private gatherings on board his steam yacht. These have included meetings with foreign diplomats, and I know for a fact that members of the French consulate have been recent invitees.

Somchai tells me these are closet affairs from which he and most of the other staff are excluded. Only a few of Lord Bamroong's inner sanctum are permitted to attend. There are no notes taken, apparently, so the subject of their discussions never reaches me. In truth, it is this type of secret meeting that has given rise to some of my suspicions over the years, as while I am aware these assignations take place, I am never informed of the outcome. When I ask the regent about it, he laughs the meetings off as mere diversions, private trysts, and hints there are ladies and whisky involved…'

'I know the vessel well. 'Tis a most delightful design of paddle steamer,' Chalke replied lightly. 'Indeed, I have been a guest on board a number of times over the years.' On hearing this, Lawrence Beaumont raised his eyebrows and pursed his lips. As a man who had never been invited onto the vessel, he was struggling not to appear slighted.

'Yes, the *Rama IV* is the most elegant of all the river craft on the Chao Phraya,' the king advanced. 'As you will be aware, Horatio, it was a gift to my father from your Queen Victoria nearly twenty years ago. I remember the day it arrived so well; it was a most thrilling event for a boy of seven – the craft was brought here on a British warship, all in pieces. I was told it had been first built in a place I thought had a most amusing name – "The Island of Dogs". I watched the boat being reassembled here on the banks of the river. It took just a few short months to restore. My father absolutely loved to sail the river in it. He even took it to sea, on occasion – often to entertain and impress visiting dignitaries. Indeed, it was customary for me to take astronomy and nature lessons in the *grand salon*, and when I was very young, we loved to play hide-and-seek whenever we were allowed.' The king looked melancholy for a few moments, but then his disposition shifted back to one of business. 'A week before my father died, he gifted the vessel to Lord Bamroong as thanks for his loyal support and in anticipation of his future service to me as my regent.'

The room fell into a thoughtful hush before a lonely voice piped up. 'I have an idea!' To everyone's surprise, it was Beaumont, who had broken his long silence. His intervention seemed to startle the king, in particular, who looked at him with a most quizzical expression. Without invitation, the consul general pressed on. 'Your Majesty, if your regent is known to use his paddle steamer to hold clandestine meetings, why do we not smuggle someone aboard ahead of time to overhear the exchanges? I may have never been on board the *Rama IV*, but I have seen it on the river many times, and it is a most substantial craft. Surely, there must be some place, even if it's in the bilges, to hide an agent close to where Lord Bamroong holds his meetings. 'Tis only a thought…'

King Chulalongkorn and Horatio Chalke looked at one another and exchanged smiles. 'I will summon Somchai,' the king said with a respectful nod. 'He will know the answer to your most interesting question.'

※

By four o'clock the same day, all arrangements were in place for Charles Hurdus to lay the trap – to leave his message of invitation in the grounds of the ancient temple of Wat Poh. Much to Albert Woodward's relief, the toothy Head of Revenue, Phitisak Rattana, had raised no objections to his officers, Khun Asnee included, participating in a further "surveillance exercise". Earlier in the day, it had fallen to Woodward to explain the objectives of their latest mission to the assembled teams of revenue officers. In addition to the first band of men who had so brilliantly followed Hurdus from the gambling den two days previously, a further six officers had been seconded to the squad, making a total of a dozen in all. These were divided into two teams of six, with Asnee and his close friend Chet (acting as his deputy) taking command of one team each.

'Gentlemen, today we have a new and even greater challenge for you all,' Albert announced in deep Rhondda tones. 'We have not just one *farang* rabbit for you to chase this evening – but two!' After each sentence, Asnee translated into Siamese for the others – if not Woodward's exact words, the thrust, at least, was conveyed to his little audience. 'Your objective tonight is vital in more ways than you can imagine, and you must see it to its conclusion.' Albert raised his hands as if to emphasise his words. 'You are to witness a coming together of our old rabbit friend from two days ago, the animal with the wounded ear, with a fresh rabbit he shall meet in the temple of Wat Poh this evening. Once you have clapped your sharp eyes on the second rabbit, it will be your job to follow this creature wherever he goes and report his actions back to me. Treat this assignment as if it were a matter of life and death. Do not flinch from your duty. We shall await your regular reports at the Falcks. When there is news to deliver, you must dispatch a messenger to us immediately. We will tell you when your work is complete. It may be a long night, and whatever you do, you must not scare the rabbits at any time. It that clearly understood? Your actions must be the ones of silent stalkers, passive pursuers… Find out all you can in your pursuit, but if our little bunnies detect your motives at any time, all will be lost, and your mission will be a failure.'

At fifteen minutes before five o'clock, Charles Hurdus, the remnants of his left ear still displaying a neatly fixed bandage, passed through the impressive eastern gate of the Wat Poh temple complex. First established nearly two hundred years earlier, in the reign of Rama I, its imposing buildings were laid out on land that extended to over twenty acres. Wat Poh housed one of the most famous statues in all Siam – the legendary Reclining Buddah – and was considered to be one of the most revered royal shrines in all of the city. The amber light from the setting sun, in pursuit of the darkest corners of the temple grounds, angled past the age-old stupas directly into Hurdus' face as he manoeuvred his way through the site. He raised a hand to protect his eyes, but his progress was barely compromised, for he knew exactly where to go. Walking briskly despite the blinding light, he quickly found the spot he was looking for, and without even a backward glance, he placed a crisp white envelope beneath the chosen stone. Within seconds, he'd retreated back into the shade of one of the tall edifices that dominated the sacred ground. The message he left was simple.

Meet Reclining Buddah before six. Important news to impart.

With an ageless wall to conceal him, and from a distance of just thirty yards, Praew Asnee watched and waited. After lingering for nearly ten minutes, he made a surreptitious signal to one of his team. The first rabbit had arrived. He studied the now familiar figure of Charles Hurdus as he moved from the shadow of the stupas towards the grand pavilion, where the colossal figure of Buddah lay. At more than a hundred and fifty feet in length, fully reclined, head propped on a mighty hand, the golden statue seemed to swamp the entire temple. Undoubtedly, it was one of the most striking sights in all of Bangkok. All around the majestic icon, an air of unhurried serenity infiltrated the senses. Chet and the rest of his small team had already spread themselves amongst the nooks and crevasses of the interior. One of them, having once served as an apprentice monk, had donned the saffron robes of his youth to disguise his true motives. The remainder had dispersed outside into the heat, where they loitered amongst the fragrant frangipani, the ribbon-strewn fig trees, and buzzing insects.

A few minutes before five, Hurdus removed his hat and placed his shoes next to an elaborately painted figure of a giant serpent. Then, taking the dozen or so steps towards the wide portico, he entered barefoot, unnoticed save for those within who had been silently anticipating his arrival. A minute later, on finding a tranquil spot, the Englishman lowered himself to sit on the cool stone floor, close to the Buddha's giant feet. It was here, with his back supported by the temple's ancient brickwork and the heady scent of incense in his nostrils, he rested.

Charles Hurdus did not have to wait long. Less than twenty minutes had elapsed before he heard the soft tread of a figure approaching. Raising his gaze from the chill flagstones, he saw the unmistakeably powerful figure of Pierre Museau looming, shoeless and hatless, before him. Hurdus didn't bother to get up. Instead, he nonchalantly patted the stone slabs as an invitation for the Frenchman to sit beside him. As much as anything, this was a deliberately casual gesture designed to soothe the situation – an attempt to psychologically disarm his scary confidant. Hurdus thought Museau looked a little tired, the eyes lacking in sleep perhaps... but nonetheless, the profile before him presented as intimidating as ever. The Frenchman was not a tall individual, but Hurdus had always imagined the man possessed the physique of a pugilist under his elegant Parisian-tailored garments. There was no doubt Monsieur Museau was used to projecting and delivering considerable menace when the need arose – Hurdus' half-chopped ear was testament to that.

Not surprisingly, perhaps, the Frenchman repaid the welcoming advance with a withering sneer and remained mulishly on his feet. 'You have news for me?' he said with the look of a man exhausted with life.

'I have – 'tis a telegram from London – it arrived this afternoon.' Hurdus felt in his jacket and pulled out two folded pieces of paper. 'You may look, you may read, but I must have the first document back. The registry will miss it if I do not return the original.' Museau leaned forward to grasp the papers proffered by the extended fingers of his still squatting collaborator. 'One is a copy for you to keep,' Hurdus continued. 'I think you will find the content most revealing.'

Museau took his time reading the message, looking over his shoulder intermittently to check if the coast was clear. Then, dividing the twin papers between each hand, he appeared to read them simultaneously – checking to see if the transcript agreed with the original. At length, he said, 'This arrived today, you say?'

'At four minutes past three this afternoon. It is timed in the top right-hand corner. I came as soon as I could.'

'Has Mr Beaumont seen it yet?'

'He has indeed, and the news has been shared already amongst those who need to know. The consul general plans to meet the king with Chalke tomorrow morning to make plans for the visit. It's hard to tell, but the duke could be in Siam in less than a week. I expect I will learn more in due course.'

'This Duke of Cambridge – he is a military man, is he not?'

'Most certainly. He is the commander-in-chief of the British Army, no less. He is a cousin of Queen Victoria too. A man of considerable influence, it must be said. I am told he has a reputation for obstinacy and is a lover of the old order. I met him once as a matter of fact—'

'Why do you imagine the duke wishes to meet the king?' Museau said sharply.

'In truth, I have no idea – I can only surmise. The duke is taking an opportunity, perhaps, afforded by his current travels. But I suspect there is more to it – the message speaks of the death in London of the king's half-brother and the duke's wishes to talk with His Majesty on the subject. It may be to offer further condolences, but equally, there could be more substance to their discussions.'

'The telegram tells of the duke's tour of the Orient.' Museau frowned. 'I would have expected to have received some news of it – such a grand undertaking, yet Paris has been silent on the matter.'

'In truth, it has been a surprise to us, also. It seems his journey east is cloaked in secrecy. We can only speculate that affairs in Hong Kong have sparked the expedition, and the British Government is at pains not to aggravate China. The situation in the colony has become tense of late.'

Museau rubbed his chin in a gesture that smacked of disbelief. '*Tres étrange…*' he muttered. 'We should have heard something of this…' Handing the original telegram back, he said coldly, 'I need to know more, Monsieur. You must tell me as soon as you know when the duke will arrive. And I need to know the outcome of the consul general's meeting with Chulalongkorn.'

'Of course. If I read or hear anything, I will let you know. Where shall I leave the next invitation card?'

'Entrust it to the brick wall close to my consulate – in the cavity we have used twice before, under the giant banyan. It is an easier place for me to reach and will save my legs. In view of the importance, I will check the brick three times a day, at least.' Museau paused and offered Hurdus his outstretched hand. His demeanour had changed somewhat, and now the formidable Frenchman was looking positively equable. 'Come, let me help you up. You have done well today. Your ear… are you in pain?' he enquired with unaccustomed tenderness.

'"Tis nothing I cannot manage.'

'You must appreciate I had no alternative. You must never visit my home again, my friend. I'm sure you understand…'

'I do,' Hurdus replied bluntly as he was hauled to his feet by a strong hand, complete with vice-like grip.

'Then, please accept my apologies. I trust your injuries have not created unwanted gossip amongst your colleagues.'

'I have told them I was attacked by a vagrant. They can gossip all they like. I have no fear of them.'

'And the money I gave you? Have you used it well?'

'My debts are all paid. When this is over, I will be a free man to go wherever I please.'

'I'm sure France will thank you for your work.'

'And what does France want from all this?' Hurdus heard himself asking a question he had never dared put before. It was a spontaneous utterance, which he hoped he would not regret.

Museau forced a smile in return. 'Only *la stabilité pour la région*, Monsieur. We merely wish the egalitarian and fraternal values of our country to stretch a little further west – an admirable aim, I'm sure you will agree,' he replied with a strange stilted expression.

Much to his surprise, Hurdus found he could not let the matter lie, and he returned with a further question. 'And pray, sir, what about *liberté*? You have conveniently omitted the most important of all your ideals. What of the freedom of the Siamese? Does this not cause some disquiet for France?'

The mood changed suddenly. In a flash, Museau's manner reverted to type. 'That is not your concern,' he growled, 'nor mine, for that matter. I do as I am asked, and so should you. *Mon Dieu*, you are paid enough for it!' He started to leave, but then, as if an afterthought had struck him, he turned back. 'Why, you hate imperial Britain and its vile conquests as much as I.' He glared. 'You have said as much more times that I can count. France's mission here is simple. We wish to return a certain balance of power to the region. What we do is for *Indochine* and its peoples. Let the matter rest there. Just ensure you inform me when you hear more. This event could transform the plans others are making, and I need to know the instant you learn anything. *Tu comprends, Monsieur?'*

Chapter Twenty-Six

From behind his carved stone concealment, Praew Asnee watched the Frenchman step out of the temple shadows into the golden evening. He observed carefully as the *farang* donned his hat and replaced his shoes. Darkness was descending fast. As his target moved off, Asnee was forced to quicken his pace to close the gap between them. He noticed that his quarry appeared to be crouching slightly as he navigated his way steadily through the grounds. After passing under the eastern entrance of the temple compound, Museau stopped in his tracks and made a signal with an uplifted arm. A straw-hatted rickshaw driver approached, and within seconds, the Frenchman had climbed under the canopy of the twin-wheeled craft. Shortly afterwards, both driver and passenger were trotting away with the near diagonal sun plying its gentle heat to their backs.

Asnee was prepared for this. As he mounted his own rickshaw, procured specifically for this eventuality, he watched with satisfaction to see a second machine, complete with scraggy driver plus an ox-cart, wheel out in front of him. Each contained members of his surveillance squad, and slowly they commenced their unruffled pursuit of the retreating Frenchman. The procession headed south, following the contours of the river in the general direction of the French and British consulates, but the convoy did not last long. After less than half a mile, Museau's rickshaw arrived at a jetty situated directly opposite the city post office. Here he dismounted, handed his wheezing chauffeur a few coins, and walked the short distance to an awaiting ferry boat that lolled lazily against the pier. By this time, Asnee had made sufficient ground to overtake the others and was now in the vanguard once more. From less than twenty yards, he watched as the Frenchman jumped aboard the open boat and took his seat amidships amongst a gaggle of about half a dozen waiting passengers. The little ship rocked violently on receiving the muscularly built *farang*'s added weight.

Asnee had to think fast... After barely a moment's reflection, he leapt instinctively down from his rickshaw and hurried straight to the quay. In less than five seconds, he'd jumped aboard also. Finding a vacant bench in the stern, about six feet away from his adversary, he was able to sit behind Museau and avoid the man's steady gaze. To his relief, Chet managed, at the very last second, to squeeze in alongside him. With a final lunge onto the open decking, he'd landed in the boat just as the ferryman was loosening his lines and pushing the bow out to face the open river. Once free of the shore, the captain lit two oil lamps, which he placed at the bow and stern. Then, he raised a sail and released the tiller. A deckhand, who was no older than seven, came to collect the fares.

Instead of tracking the natural surge of water to the south, as Asnee had expected, the ferry turned at right angles and headed directly west across the wide coffee-coloured expanse. Clearly the boat was aiming for the other bank, and the journey would be a short one. Once the course was set and the light winds had filled its canvas, the little craft, bobbing and dipping all the while as its passengers sat in mute silence, started to make steady progress. It was nearly dark by the time they reached the jetty on the west bank of the Chao Phraya. As soon as the bow nudged the weed-incrusted beams of the foreign pier, the passengers, who clearly knew the routine, clambered to go ashore. Asnee and Chet waited until the others, including their target, had stepped on dry land before disembarking. Asnee was confident that Museau had not suspected either of them during their brief expedition. The Frenchman's eyes had been fixed directly ahead at all times, and as the passengers mounted the jetty steps, he took not even the slightest look about himself. On the single occasion when Asnee had caught a glimpse of Museau's face, his quarry appeared to be in serious thought, with eyes pinched, outwardly unaware of his environment or even of those who circled around him.

'Chet, you go ahead. Stay with him. I'll hang back for a while,' Asnee said in a low whisper. 'I fear it is just the two of us remaining now. The others must be stuck on the other side.'

Chet was more optimistic. 'They have seen us depart. They will find a way to get to us soon enough. I'll go first, as you ask, my friend.' Then, with a broad grin, he added, 'This is more fun than watching our wives feed the children at home, don't you think?'

It was nearly an hour before Asnee and Chet were reunited with the rest of their fellow revenue officers. As Chet had predicted, a few of the group had seen them board the ferry, and on learning its destination, they had usurped an empty vessel, inducing its captain to carry them all over the river in pursuit. The boat owner had been reluctant at first, but a reminder of what the king's treasury could do to disrupt his business proved a sufficient incentive. The pair who had carried out the initial surveillance in the temple had managed to link up with the others, and by the time they all reached the west bank, the teams were back to full strength. Their subsequent rendezvous with Asnee and Chet took a little luck, and some good judgement, to achieve.

Within two hundred paces of the pier sat a small settlement, and the chasing group made for it, knowing all other tracks merely led back to the river.

The tiny village of Ban Nam Suaay lay astride Klong Somdet, a prominent canal which snaked in a south-westerly direction away from the Chao Phraya, towards the wilderness of rice farms and towering bamboo beyond. After questioning some of the locals in the act of closing their rather paltry market stalls, it was revealed that a *farang* had been seen entering the village at sundown. The man had purchased a chargrilled chicken thigh and a banana leaf containing a handful of cooked rice from one of them. From another, he had bought a jug of beer. The stranger, whose Siamese was good but strongly accented, apparently, had headed away to the south, following the *klong* path towards the next rural village. With the waxing moon now to guide them, and by using bird calls to keep in contact, the group had set off in pursuit. They eventually encountered Asnee and Chet sheltering inside a dilapidated outbuilding, less than half a mile along the *klong* path.

Asnee could not disguise his exhilaration at seeing his band of brothers once more. 'He's gone into that farmhouse,' he whispered the second they were reunited. 'It's the only habitable place I can see around here.'

Asnee pointed towards a dark structure that lay about sixty yards distant, its high-pitched roof reaching upwards into the silver moonlight. The house was half hidden by the towering clumps of bamboo that pressed in from all sides. Its interior was softly lit by a pale-orange glow, and lighted oil lamps had been hung from the outside beams. It was clear to all – the property was occupied.

'He's been inside for nearly half an hour,' Asnee offered. 'There must be others in the house, too. Earlier, when I drew a little closer, I overheard people talking, but I couldn't decipher anything. It was too dangerous to venture any nearer, but for sure, it wasn't a language I recognised.' Turning to Chet, he said, 'I don't think our rabbit will move again at this late hour. We need to split our forces. I wish you to take command here. I'm going to take one man and return to the Falcks to make my report. The *farangs* may have further instructions for us. If the rabbit does move in the night, take two of your men to follow him. If others appear, you must do your best with the men you have. I will return as soon as I have news. You must be prepared to wait until dawn, if necessary.'

'We have a boat waiting for us at the river, Khun Asnee,' Ong, one of the men, piped up. 'The captain can take you directly to the city pier, if you wish.'

'Fine, then you will accompany me, Ong. Lead me to the boat. The sooner I can make our report, the better for all of us. Come, we must hurry.'

By the time the two reached the river, the half-moon was high in the night sky. To Asnee's relief, the craft that had carried over his reinforcements earlier in the night was still waiting at the pier, just as he'd been promised. As they approached, the skipper, who was slumped against the stern rail, raised a bottle-filled hand towards them. 'I'll need to see your money if you wish me to take you back,' he blurted in drunken Siamese. 'I am a poor man who will do your bidding, but only for a price, this time.'

'Don't be foolish, man. Don't let the drink do the speaking for you.' As they shinnied into the boat, Ong snatched the half-empty whisky bottle from his grasp. 'You will do as we say, or you will regret it.'

'But I need money to feed my children,' the skipper cried. 'You both look like important men – I am but a poor fisherman.' As if to emphasise his point, he made a fruitless attempt to stand in the boat. Within seconds, his balance had failed him, and narrowly missing the tiller, he'd collapsed back into the bilges.

Praew Asnee fumbled in his pockets and withdrew a handful of coins. 'This will suffice. If you do not accept this as payment, I will put you ashore now and we shall sail across ourselves. I know these boats and the river well enough. Take the money or remain here amongst the mud and weeds – all night, for all I care.'

The boatman snatched the offering and then spat back, 'Give me five more and we have a deal.'

Suddenly, as if from nowhere, the deep voice of man could be heard. 'I have money. I have five.' The declaration, in heavily accented Siamese, came from the jetty above their heads. Asnee swivelled his neck to see the broad and muscular shape of a *farang* standing over them. 'Look, see, I have money...' the interloper repeated.

To Asnee's utter horror, the intruder who now stood before them, hand outstretched with what looked like a bag of coins dangling from it, was none other than their night-time quarry. Although Asnee did not know it, the *farang* leaning over the landing stage was one of the most dangerous foreigners in all Siam – Monsieur Pierre Museau.

The boatman made a lunge for the purse, but Museau hastily withdrew it before it could be snatched. 'You want five. I have ten,' he said in deliberate but accurate Siamese. He put his fingers into the pouch and withdrew a neat stack of silver coins. '*Voila*, here is ten.' As the skipper grabbed the money, Museau clambered aboard. 'Before you cross the river, I wish you to take me to the landing stage at the regent's canal.' The boatman understood immediately and bowed his head respectfully to his new passenger, and together they started to cast off.

'Wait!' Asnee cried. 'He is my boatman, sir! We wish to go to the other bank. I have given him my money already.' Asnee knew he was taking a risk by remonstrating in the way he had. Suddenly, the man he'd been trailing all evening had fallen into his lap – quite literally. But an instinct told him he could turn the situation to his advantage. What would a fellow passenger do when provoked by the hijacking of the boat he'd just hired, he asked himself. Why, such a man would protest, of course, and by playing his part correctly, Asnee realised he might learn something also, some facts about his adversary – something to report back to those who now waited for him at the Falcks.

At first, Museau just scowled back, but after a few seconds his nature seemed to change. An ingratiating smile magically appeared. 'I am so sorry... You see, I have important business. I will pay your fare if you will let me take my journey first. Then you will be able to cross. The delay will cost you less than twenty minutes. Would ten silver coins be enough to make you happy?'

Asnee's outward expression spoke of a mighty insult, while his inner self was in turmoil just trying to stay calm. He calculated he could afford one last roll of the dice. 'I have business too – important work awaits us,' he said indignantly.

'Please, sir, forgive me. I am but a lonely Frenchman in your country. I do not wish to upset you, but my business is with the regent himself. I have to be there before the hour of nine, at the latest. Will twenty suffice to ease your inconvenience?'

Asnee did his best to look sulky. He put out his hand and took the pile of coins offered. 'Very well,' he replied. 'You must be a most important man indeed, to be seeing the Regent of Siam at this hour…'

The large spoonful of scepticism was not missed by his opponent, but this time, the remark failed to glean a response. Museau merely smiled back and said nothing. With everyone apparently satisfied with the new arrangement, the craft turned north, and after leaving the shallow waters, they started to make steady advancement, with the now changed tide moderately helping their progress. Nothing more was spoken on the short journey, which continued in an uneasy armistice until they had passed the imposing stupa of Wat Arun, which rose from the banks of the river like a brooding behemoth. That night, it appeared particularly mystical, silhouetted as it was against a backdrop of distant stars. It was the Frenchman who eventually broke the silence. 'Thank you, gentlemen. I am nearly at my destination – and in good time, too. If our paths cross once more, I'd be happy to talk with you again. You are men of business, I take it…?' he added, with a large question mark in his voice.

Asnee nodded. He'd been expecting the enquiry for some time. 'You are very perceptive, sir. We are involved in the business of import and export,' he replied coolly. 'My name is Asnee – Praew Asnee.'

'*Excellente*,' Museau gushed as the boat pulled alongside the jetty. 'Pray, call on me at the French consulate one day. I am the trade representative for the Republic of France in Siam. If there is anything I can do for you, please tell me. Trade is a matter of great importance to France. I'm sure we could do some mutual business.' And then he was gone, disappeared up the steps into the night. The skipper turned the boat away from the pier, and twenty minutes later, the two revenue officers had reached the west bank and were bumping along in a pair of rickshaws en route to the Falcks, where a meeting with Henry Gough and Albert Woodward awaited them. Asnee's heart raced at the thought of the encounter. There was such a lot to tell them. He hoped they would be pleased.

⁓:⁓

Although Somchai Rattana was a distant relative of the king, he had, more importantly, become one of his favourites. A studious, bespectacled wisp of a man, practically the same age as his monarch, he'd shared school lessons with the then crown prince in his youth and had entered full royal service two years previously. Such was Somchai's prodigious ability with languages, his cousin, the since murdered Prince Gagananga, had invited him into court to act as a translator and interpreter. Bookish and scholarly since the day he could talk, Somchai was fluent in six languages: Mandarin-Chinese, Burmese, English, Japanese, German, and French. In addition, he spoke passable Spanish and could read Latin. The king had always liked his studious relative, and it was not long after his court appointment before Chulalongkorn had brought Somchai into his full confidence. It was the king himself who, six months previously, had induced the regent to take on the "bright young man" as a member of his own staff, a proposal Lord Bamroong had felt impossible to refuse.

'It will give him much-needed experience. Somchai has great potential, and one day he will serve his country with distinction,' the king had effused, with a genial gesture of his hand.

But the king's motives in proposing Somchai were not entirely altruistic. For the most part, they were driven by his own self-preservation. Beginning to suspect a conspiracy might be mounting against him from the other bank of the Chao Phraya, he had secretly tasked Somchai with reporting back all he could learn from the regent's inner circle. It was a mission that had nearly scared the young man to death, such was Somchai's halting demeanour and shy character. But Somchai Rattana had no choice. He had to accept the king's trust, and with it, this clandestine assignment. He knew he was not born to be a spy, and the thought of being uncovered by one of Bamroong's henchmen gave him constant sleepless nights. For his part, the regent, being a wise old bird, knew that even he could not refuse the king's munificence. But always cautious of infiltrators, he gave his new recruit only the most menial of positions – that of his junior diary secretary. Consequently, Somchai, much to his eternal relief, was excluded from attending any of his new master's meetings, his personal interactions with the regent being limited to just the ordinary exchanges of greeting that opened and ended every working day.

So, when early that morning, Somchai received news that the king wished to see him, his stomach turned slightly in nervous anticipation. He loved and admired Chulalongkorn, but he was always terrified by what His Majesty might ask of him next. He also knew that in the king's eyes, he'd been an abject failure as a spy. The previous six months of his so-called "covert intelligence-gathering" had produced nothing, save a dull list of places and people the regent was slated to visit.

'Ah, Somchai – it is so good of you to come.' King Chulalongkorn looked genuinely pleased to be welcoming his "little mole" back into court. Somchai smiled graciously back, but it was not long before his worst fears had been realised.

'I have a most important task for you to perform.'

'Your Majesty is most kind…' came the rather flaccid reply.

The king took Somchai to one side and said, 'Fear not, I only ask that you inform me directly of my regent's diary plans for the next few days.'

'I am at your command, Your Majesty, but it occurs to me I do this for you already. You receive my list every week, as you have instructed. Is there something else Your Majesty wishes?'

'Not in substance, Somchai. Only in frequency. Weekly reports are not sufficient at this time. I need to know twice daily, for the next three days, where Lord Bamroong intends to go and who he plans to meet. I wish you to report to me at ten am and three pm every day, until the week is out. I will provide a boat each morning and afternoon for your convenience. It will be your personal transport across the river. If you are asked by others where you are going, you will say I have called you to translate some German for me – or some Japanese – whatever you choose… You can tell whosoever enquires that my personal translators are indisposed. Just until Saturday, you understand. I doubt if I will need such information after that.'

'Very well, Your Majesty. It will be an honour to do your bidding.' Somchai made a little bow before adding, 'Would Your Majesty like to know the details of Lord Bamroong's diary for the rest of today and tomorrow? I have brought the information with me.'

Chulalongkorn's eyes widened as he nodded his assent.

'The regent has no plans to travel this morning. He has a meeting with the head of the armed forces, General Pravat, at eleven. After which, he will dine with the general, plus three colonels and other members of the general's entourage. Another general from the army will be attending the lunch also – the head of the household cavalry, General Saelim.'

'That's a lot of military men in a single morning.' Chulalongkorn looked disbelieving. 'And the rest of the day? What are the regent's plans?'

'This very morning, the regent asked for his steam vessel to be prepared for his personal use tonight. All must be arranged before six pm. I'm informed he has plans to meet others on board for dinner.'

'Who? Which others?' the king fired back.

'I regret, I have no names or numbers – there is only an order to prepare the boat for sailing at seven. As I have reported to you many times, sir, Lord Bamroong likes to hold his most private gatherings on board the *Rama IV*. It is customary for only his personal bodyguard and closest family to be involved.'

'You have done well in disclosing this to me, Somchai. Now tell me, how might I put someone on board the ship before it sails?'

'Put someone aboard?'

'Yes, in a secret fashion, as a stowaway might. You see, I wish to know who Lord Bamroong entertains tonight, and if possible, all of what he says.'

Somchai could not hide his surprise at this startling line of questioning. 'Why,' he stammered, 'I imagine it would not be too difficult – if you had a mind to do it, Your Majesty...' And then, after a moment's reflection, he added, 'Like you, I know the ship well. You will recall sometimes your father allowed us to take special study classes on board when we were younger. I am still permitted access to the vessel, of course, but I always have to depart before the regent and his party arrive. What exactly did Your Majesty have in mind?'

Chapter Twenty-Seven

'Khun Praew Asnee is the man for the job, Your Majesty,' exclaimed Horatio Chalke, who had been ushered into the king's presence just moments earlier. 'He is bold and resourceful, but above all, I believe him to be loyal.'

'Have I met this man?' King Chulalongkorn looked bemused. 'If I have, I do not recollect him.'

'He is one of your revenue officers, sir, currently under special training from Mr Albert Woodward, the new British envoy. I have been assisting him, sir. You may recall you gave your authority some weeks before the trial...'

The king's eyes widened. 'Yes, of course, but why this man Asnee? Surely a pair of my personal bodyguards could fulfil the role. After all, we need only two men to accomplish the task.'

'Asnee has shown a remarkable aptitude, Your Majesty. He is highly suitable, in our opinion, and has been involved from the start. But I agree, two men would be better than one, if room on board the vessel will allow it. In which case, we would propose Henry Gough to accompany Asnee. Mr Gough is acquainted with the art of surveillance and such clandestine challenges. He and Asnee know one another well. Together, they have an excellent rapport and both have seen Monsieur Museau at close quarters.'

The king appeared to acquiesce, but there was one final question. 'What of your Mr Woodward? You have told me he is the true master of the art of surveillance. Should not he take the lead?'

'Albert Woodward is not a young man anymore – he is not as nimble as he once was. He feels he should step aside and has personally recommended both Asnee and Gough for the task.'

'I see… Very well, you may have your wish. You appear to know more of these things than I. When this is over, please bring both of your recruits to see me. If they are successful in their bold assignment, I will wish to thank them personally.'

'Your Majesty, I'm sure both would be delighted to accept your kind invitation.' As Chalke spoke the words, he wondered absent-mindedly what the king might say if the two were ultimately defeated by their task. He dismissed this as unthinkable and moved on. 'You say Your Majesty knows the ship. I take it there will be some place for our agents to conceal themselves.'

'Indeed, there are such places. My emissary, Somchai, will explain. I have summoned him here to speak with you and do as you command. I do not wish to know all the details of your plan, but I vouch he knows the *Rama IV* as well as I and can gain access on board this very day. Pray, wait outside for Somchai. Treat him well, Horatio. He is of nervous disposition, but you will find him trustworthy and accommodating. Together, you will make your dispositions, set your stratagem in motion, and bring me news as soon as you have it.' And with that, the king rose abruptly; it was time for Horatio Chalke to depart. The audience had ended as suddenly as it had begun. Genuflecting as he withdrew, it was not long before he found himself within the privacy of the outer chamber, where he took a seat and waited for Khun Somchai.

When the slim figure of Somchai eventually appeared ten minutes later, he put up a self-effacing *wai* on seeing the seated Chalke. Closing the door silently behind him, the young man approached the waiting *farang* in a series of short, hesitant steps across the patterned carpet, while all the time polishing his spectacles earnestly on a scrap of yellow silk.

'You must be Khun Somchai. The king speaks very highly of you.' Chalke got to his feet, and with both hands raised courteously, he made a *wai* in return.

'And you too, Mr Chalke,' Somchai replied with a bashful smile. 'We do not have long, sir. The king says you require my help to get aboard the *Rama IV* today. How can I be of assistance to you?'

Over the next twenty minutes, Chalke outlined his proposal, and between them, they talked in a series of whispered questions and answers. Appropriately, given the subject under discussion, they sat in huddled conversation under a tall portrait of the watchful and resplendent King Mongkut as Somchai revealed his knowledge of the *Rama IV*. This proved to be extensive in all respects, and no doubt, benefited from his many years playing aboard as a child. He told Chalke that the salon, used by the regent for gatherings, was situated on the upper deck towards the stern of the craft, behind the giant paddle-wheel housing and the single smokestack amidships. The boiler room and steam engine were positioned below. Somchai added proudly that on a flat calm river, these were capable of propelling the vessel at more than a roaring twelve knots.

The *Rama IV* was not a leviathan, being only ninety-nine feet from stem to stern – precisely one and a half times the length of a cricket pitch, Chalke recollected. She was perfectly formed in every way. Flat-bottomed, with a broad beam for increased stability, her interior was beautifully appointed too. Gleaming brass-work, shining black and gilt paint abounded, and the sumptuously decorated cabins were a marvel to behold. From the plush aft-facing salon, a broad view of the river pressed in from both starboard and port sides, interrupted only by a narrow companionway that surrounded the salon on all but the amidships boundary. This margin fronted onto a stowage cabin with attached wheelhouse, forwards of the lofty funnel. The stowage area was extensive and set over two decks. It included a coal bunker, an engineering workshop, and an area for ship's stores.

According to Somchai, there was an inspection void directly under the salon decking, between it and the workshop ceiling beneath. It was easy to access, robust, and deep enough to conceal five men, if necessary, as long as they were prepared to crawl in and lie flat. With a wistful smile, he told Chalke how he'd used the concealment many times as a child in games of hide-and-seek.

'On the instructions of His Majesty, I have just returned from visiting the ship at its berth.' Somchai suddenly looked animated. 'The king asked me to check whether the hidey-hole still existed.' Somchai, his confidence growing fast, beamed at Chalke as he reported that indeed it did, and the recess would provide a perfect spot to overhear any tête-à-têtes taking place in the salon above. 'Unless the full force of the engines drowns out the sound of conversation…' he added with a thoughtful frown.

'How can we get two men aboard today without being seen?' Chalke asked, once he'd informed Somchai that Praew Asnee and Henry Gough were slated to perform the role of peeping Toms.

'The vessel is now alongside the regent's pier. Tell your men to meet me there at six o'clock. It will be nearly dark at that time, but tell them to dress as river traders and to bring a large bag of mangoes and two boxes of beer between them. Your Mr Gough will have to dress as a Siamese peasant, of course – I trust he will not object. I will see them on board and guide them to their hiding place. At that time, the regent's bodyguard will not be present, and the ship will be almost empty. It will be easy for me to conceal them before I depart. Can that be arranged?'

'And what of the engines? You speak of noise. If the paddles are turning when the meeting takes place, what then?'

'You will have to trust to luck. My understanding is that the *Rama IV* will sail soon after seven. Only the regent and his closet circle will be on board. If Lord Bamroong is to meet others, he will have to sail to meet them. Hopefully, your moles will know who he meets when the visitors board. If then the regent decides to take a cruise, it may be your bad luck, as I fear the steam pistons could drown out all other sounds...'

∽:∽

On the stroke of six, with the light fading fast, a small open boat approached one of the makeshift jetties that scattered the western banks of the Chao Phraya River. On board were three straw-hatted forms, one of whom was noticeably taller than the others. Henry Gough's bulkier physique was disguised, in part, by a sable-coloured cloth that draped over his naked upper body and around his neck. Gough's face and skin had been masked by the application of a crushed charcoal paste, recommended and applied by Asnee and Chet an hour earlier, amidst much jollity from all concerned. A belt around his waist contained his pocket watch and a few personal items. In a holster on Henry's hip rested his Webley – the British Bull Dog double-action revolver – with five cartridges preloaded into its cylinder. He wasn't going to make the same mistake. He'd made certain it would accompany him this time. Below their waists, each of the bogus boatmen wore a set of baggy pantaloons. Simple sandals sheathed their feet.

From the boat, Praew Asnee and Henry Gough lifted a bag bulging with ripe-smelling fruit and two wooden boxes clanking with bottles of Siamese beer. Chet helped Henry to lift the beer onto each of his shoulders, while Asnee slung the mangoes over his back. Like this, with the boxes hiding most of Henry's face, the pair approached the regent's landing stage, which was less than a hundred yards distant. The splendid *Rama IV*, its interior lamps burning brightly, slipped gently on her lines alongside. Much to their relief, it was not long before they identified the single figure of Somchai Rattana hovering by the gangplank. Chalke's description of a slightly built bespectacled young man made their job easy.

'I have provisions for the boat,' Asnee called out loudly in Siamese as they approached the narrow gangway.

'Follow me,' Somchai replied almost instantly, in a most assured Siamese tone. 'Bring them into the store.' As they took their first steps on deck, a liveried crew member, a set of keys jingling in one hand, seemed to appear from nowhere. After a dismissive glance at the sweating intruders with their close-clutched supplies, he gave way to allow them to pass into the bowels of the ship. A few turns later, and after taking a short flight of downward steps, the trio arrived at a white-painted cabin door, which their leader threw open. After they had entered, he closed the door and announced, 'Leave the bags here. I will arrange them once you are all set.'

The cabin, which appeared to extend across the full beam of the vessel, was clearly used as a storeroom. Apart from a series of stacked boxes and an array of workshop tools, there was a scattering of black char dusted on the deck, which Henry realised must have spilled from the adjoining coal bunker. Henry could see three metal steps that led up to what looked like the boiler room, from which a distinct heat emanated. Inside, he glimpsed an array of greased machinery gently hissing. His love of steam engines flooded back to him, and for a split second, he was transported to the sidings at Euston Station and the smell of the goliath locomotives of his youth.

Henry's reverie was short-lived. Pointing to an iron ladder embedded in the far bulkhead, Somchai, in surprisingly loud Siamese, cried, 'Quick – go up there. Do you see the hole at the top? I have opened the entrance. Once you are in, I will close the hatch.'

Asnee went first. There was more room than had appeared from the outside, and it was not long, by squeezing in head first, that he had disappeared into the ceiling cavity. Henry scrambled up next, and despite his greater bulk, he managed to push his body inside too. Within seconds, they were both lying flat on their backs, staring at the underside of wooden decking, which lay less than eighteen inches above their heads. Then, a sharp clunk declared that the entrance portal had been sealed.

From the top of the ladder, a soft voice could be heard. Realising that Henry was the closest, Somchai spoke this time in whispered English. 'When you need to escape, just push the panel – it will swing open. The hatch is not fastened. I have to leave soon. The regent's party will start arriving aboard shortly. Good luck in your work!'

The sound of retreating steps down the ladder announced Somchai's departure, and shortly after, Asnee and Henry heard the final thump of the cabin door. Then there was a near pure silence – save only for the faint release of air from the paddle steamer's giant boiler, which lay just a dozen or so feet away in the next cabin. The two stowaways lay motionless for a few minutes, hardly daring to breathe. The only light entering their shallow tomb came from small fissures in the decking, which allowed dust-speckled shafts to glow onto their faces. It was not long before their eyes had adjusted to the fragmented light, and they found they could see one another passably well.

Suddenly, there was some shuffling from above as a figure entered the salon. This was soon followed by the scratching sound of candles being lit. By raising his head slightly, and inching a little to the right, Henry found a crack, wider than the others, that gave him a tolerable view into the salon. As the soft-treading servant departed, Henry glimpsed she was a young woman, discernibly pretty, wearing the costume of the regent's household. The door clicked shut, and the salon fell quiet once more; now only the ghostly sounds of the ship itself could be heard – its creaking timbers, and lines being stretched from their moorings.

Henry turned his head towards Asnee, and with a mixture of silent hand and head movements, signalled to ask if he was comfortable. Asnee motioned back that all was fine, and that he, too, had found a peephole large enough to view at least some of the proceedings. There they waited, but it was not long before the chatter of voices could be heard…

Shortly afterwards, the cabin above them became full of noise. A group of servants had arrived, making busy to dress the salon ready for its guests. Chairs scraped across the floor. There was a clatter of cutlery, a chink of glasses. Further candles were ignited, and the fibres of a broom could be seen darting above their heads. For a second, Henry was forced to put his hand over his mouth to prevent him inhaling fragments of the tiny dust storm that fell through the cracks. Henry checked his pocket watch. It was ten minutes before seven. As he pressed the timepiece back into his belt, the salon door swung open once more and a party of men entered. From his vantage point, Henry counted five in all, and from their fine clothes, they were all patricians. One of them, the eldest of the group, he recognised instantly, in all his pomp, as Lord Bamroong, the Regent of Siam.

The group repositioned the chairs and took their seats around the lengthy oblong table, thus obscuring their faces from view. Henry counted the ankles. There were ten in all, the regent's being the closest. Almost immediately, a loud exchange ensued of which Henry could understand just a few words, one of which was repeated often – *farang* was easy to identify. He recognised *ghin khow* which meant they were speaking about eating, and there was a burst of ill-ordered numbers – *nueng, jedt, sawng, sip*, et cetera, but none made any sense in the context of a sentence. He looked over at Asnee who returned his glance with a broad smile, and a thumb signal that all was well, and he could understand everything. Then Henry picked up another word which he knew well enough. It made his heart race – *frangses*. It meant "French". In that moment, the gentle heartbeat that had earlier emanated from the engine room changed also. Rising in volume and vibration, the sound of wheels spinning and gears engaging had become all-pervading, and the steady thumping and crashing was carried through the whole vessel. There was movement too, as the *Rama IV* loosened her lines and offered herself to the dark river.

Henry nudged his partner's elbow as soon as he realised that Somchai's worst fears had materialised. The dialogue taking place above them had been all but drowned out by the churn and knocks from the pumping engine and the huge paddle wheels spinning less than twenty feet away. Voices could still be heard inside the salon, but the substance was largely indecipherable. Although the departure of the vessel had not prevented conversation, the content, to those hiding under the floor, was virtually impossible to comprehend. Asnee's furrowed brow and tilted head told its own story. It was clear that even the young Siamese could not pick out the details of the discussions. The only blessing was that their view of proceedings, obstructed as it was, told them that the occupants of the room, all five of them, had not moved. Neither had the original company of Siamese dignitaries been joined by others, save for the regular entrance and departure of retainers carrying salvers of food and bottles of refreshment. The number of ankles around the table had remained the same, and this gave Henry confidence that the main business had not yet begun.

After about thirty minutes of noisy churning, the note from the engine room noticeably changed, and the paddles seemed to slow their pace. Then there was a sudden jolt, followed by a gentle scraping and the sound of voices calling out from the superstructure above. It was obvious to both Henry and Asnee that the fenders of the *Rama IV* had bumped themselves against the pylons of a pontoon further along the river, and now the vessel had come to a full stop. This fact was confirmed when the pistons finally fell silent, and the paddle wheels ceased their thrashing.

Instinctively, Henry knew this was the moment they had been waiting for. The alighting of the steamer on another stretch of shoreline proclaimed that the important encounter of the evening was yet to take place. He knew he had to act fast if he was going to save the day. Somehow, the now silent machinery had to remain that way – even if only temporarily – just enough time to allow the underground moles to overhear the next conversations in clarity. He elbowed Asnee once more and indicated he was going to break out. With a finger-slicing action across his neck, and by putting his hands to his ears, he indicated what he was going to attempt. Somehow, he had to find a way to sabotage the steam pumps, and he had an idea how to do it.

Henry judged that any attempt to turn and face the hatch by which they'd entered would have caused a subterranean scrabbling that might have been detected by their opponents. Instead, he prodded the panel with his toe, and to his relief, it opened easily and swung back soundlessly on its greased hinges. Gingerly at first, he shuffled backwards and lowered his long legs towards the cabin below. The coast appeared to be clear. By engaging his feet on the rungs, he thus dropped down and was soon standing on the storeroom floor once again. In the corner nearest to him, he spied an oil-stained bench on which were scattered an array of workshop tools; others hung, like a butcher's display, from metal hooks on the cabin bulkhead. He quickly found what he was looking for and lifted the item silently off the bench. It felt heavy in his hands. With the adjustable spanner gripped in his right hand, he peered up the short flight into the boiler compartment and towards the sweltering machinery. Mercifully, this area appeared to be empty too – perhaps, on closing down the valves, the ship's engineer had decided to take a short breath of evening air. Like a jungle cat silently stalking its prey, Henry mounted the first of three shallow steps. He knew precisely what he was looking for – the actuator for the steam regulator. This controlled the delivery of steam to the piston. When it was closed shut, the engine could not be engaged, with any pent-up steam destined to escape from the boiler through exhaust pipes into the outside air. But, with a simple turn of the actuator, and the fire-box fully stoked, the bursting force of the steam could be directed to drive the pistons. With pistons moving, via a system of drive rods, the paddles themselves could then be made to turn. If Henry could just remove the actuator, it might buy sufficient time before the crew devised an alternative way to regulate and control the pent-up boiling air – a few minutes might make all the difference.

The actuator took him just seconds to identify; the twelve-inch iron wheel attached to the boiler mechanism presented itself almost instantly, complete with stained cloth draped between the spars. Taking the spanner in both hands, he placed it over the single pin that sat at the centre of the actuator wheel. His hands were shaking, but after a period of fumbling that seemed like an eternity, he managed to manipulate the wrench to the correct size so it fitted precisely over the bolt. There was the sudden noise of footsteps on the deck above. Laughter could be heard as members of the crew shared a joke and talked amongst themselves, barely fifteen feet away. With an anxious glance around, he tugged at the pin with all his force. To his dismay, the damnable thing would not budge. It may have been the first time since its installation that anyone had tried to withdraw it, and with the encrustation of time, it stubbornly resisted. Another giant heave only produced a sharp pain, as the shaft of the spanner shredded skin from his hands. As the tool slipped through his fingers, he was fortunate to recapture it before it tumbled noisily onto the deck. Reaching for the filthy rag, he wrapped it around his palms, and after taking a gasp of air, he attempted a third heroic wrench. At last, there was movement – just half an inch, but enough to lift his spirits, and soon the rod of iron was peeling away anticlockwise towards him. A few more revolutions and it was loose enough to be manipulated by hand. Henry's swollen fingers twirled frantically to lift it away from the block. Time seemed to stand still...

On and on the bolt turned never-endingly upwards. Now he was using his stinging palms to spin the metal, which by this time, was at least six inches proud of the centre of the actuator. Then, suddenly and unannounced, the pin broke free. Henry grabbed the actuator wheel, which came away without any difficulty, and in a few seconds, breathing more heavily than he wished, he was able to retrace his steps back into the storeroom. Here, he replaced the adjustable spanner exactly on the bench where he'd found it, and with the iron wheel, now reunited with its obstinate bolt and clutched in one hand, he mounted the bulkhead ladder back towards his secret hiding place and the awaiting Asnee.

Reminding himself that he had to suppress all unavoidable clatter, Henry took another deep breath, slid the actuator gently ahead of him, and scrambled back into the hole, managing, after some little exertion, to pull the hatch shut behind him. Once inside, he gave a thumbs up, followed by a smiling cut-throat signal to his companion and resumed his place, flat on his back, beside him. Asnee responded with a brief but slightly bewildered smile, and without a sound, the two recommenced their eavesdropping.

Chapter Twenty-Eight

Overhead, as far as Henry could tell, the regent's quintet appeared to be still chattering amiably amongst themselves. It seemed just as he'd left them, four minutes earlier. The embroidered sandals of Lord Bamroong were in exactly the same spot, planted onto the polished deck just yards away from Henry's prone position. Presently there was a rap, and a servant entered. A few words were exchanged, and seconds later two further figures entered the room. Henry felt his heart thump against his ribcage. The visitors were dressed entirely differently. The first, a Siamese, wore traditional patterned pantaloons and simple leather sandals; the second must have been a *farang*, for he paraded European-style trousers of dark material and a pair of polished black boots. The regent remained seated as the new arrivals approached the table. One amongst the regent's company spoke some words of Siamese, which Henry recognised to be of greeting, to which the first of the pair responded in the same language. Two chairs were drawn to the table. Now Henry counted fourteen ankles and seven sets of footwear.

Until this moment, Henry Gough, despite all his exertions, had managed to keep his breathing in check; by utilising shallow inhalations and almost inaudible exhalations, both he and Asnee had been able to remain completely unheard. But when the second of the regent's guests spoke for the first time, Henry thought he might suddenly choke. He could hardly believe his ears. The instant he caught the first sweetly spoken sentence, his gullet caught with the shock, and it was all he could do to avoid revealing himself with a jarring clearance of the throat. For the person who addressed the regent was not a man. Despite the heavy boots and masculine trousers, the voice was unmistakeably that of a woman – and a woman who he instantly recognised. It was none other than the vixen herself – Françoise Mielette.

'Thank you for seeing us tonight, sir. *Merci bien.*' The very sound of her voice sent shivers down Henry's spine.

'You wish to speak with us, madam. Your fellow, Museau, has told me as much. I am a busy man, but I have agreed to meet you tonight only at his urging. I hope you have something of value to say.' The regent's pomposity was evident, even to Henry, who barely comprehended any of the words the great man had uttered.

'I come with important news,' Françoise said gravely in perfect Siamese. 'You know of our infiltrator at the British consulate, of course.'

'I do, madam,' Lord Bamroong replied steadily. 'I hear he has been in some trouble lately.'

'Precisely. But his recent adventures have borne us fruit. We paid him money to solve his little problem, and he has returned the compliment with some information which we must discuss tonight. It affects us all…'

Just then, there was another knock on the door. This time it was the skipper of the *Rama IV* who entered, splendidly dressed in the tropical uniform of a captain of the Royal Siamese Navy – medal ribbons and all.

Bowing profusely, the captain said hesitantly, 'I beg your indulgence, sir, but I wish to report we are encountering some difficulties in getting underway. It may take a little while before we can raise steam – maybe another thirty minutes or so...'

Lord Bamroong sounded irritated by the interruption. 'That is no concern of mine at this time, Captain,' he said dismissively. 'Pray, do what you can to remedy the situation and report back to me as soon as you are in a position to depart. My guests may be ready to go ashore by the time you have made your repairs, so your incompetence may actually suit their forward plans.' The regent nodded at his guests for confirmation.

'Our business will not detain you long, sir,' Françoise could be heard to say. 'Thirty minutes will be more than enough for us to conclude our meeting, and if we are forced to return ashore from here, we should not be inconvenienced.'

The regent stared at the much-decorated interloper. 'There you have it, Captain. Now leave us – by the sound of things, you have some work to do.'

'Very well, sir,' the captain fawned. 'I will inform you as soon as we are able to cast off.'

'Just make sure you have me back at the palace before ten,' Bamroong barked as the man retreated. 'I do not wish to spend a night on board unless I absolutely have to. Is that understood?'

'Quite clearly, sir.'

When he had departed, Françoise resumed her speech. Addressing the regent directly, she said, 'Sir, we believe the British may have uncovered our scheme, and are taking steps to thwart it. We have learned that the commander-in-chief of British forces, the Duke of Cambridge, will visit Siam very soon. He has asked to meet with the king. He wishes to discuss the killing of Prince Gagananga, and we have fears this might alert the king to our intentions.

'As you know, our plan has always been to orchestrate a transfer of power after the guilty verdict against Khun Kittisak has been announced. It was our intention to exploit the bad feeling against His Majesty that would have surely stemmed from it, once you had made it clear that Kittisak was an innocent man in your employ and the judgement of guilt was an act of manipulation and revenge by the king. But now, since Henry Gough's wretched testimony, which has created confusion within the Privy Council, the outcome of the trial is in doubt.

'It is my view, considering the impending visit of the duke, we should not delay any further. We must make preparations to bring our actions forward and forestall the British before they intervene to blight our plans. The king may already have some shapeless suspicions of our intent, but currently he has no proof. If the British provide him with the evidence, and offer their military support, it will turn Chulalongkorn's head, and our business will become all the more difficult to settle. Our intelligence tells us the British duke will be in Bangkok before the month is out, so we need to act fast.'

The regent looked thoughtful. 'And what do you propose I do?' he said at length.

'You will do what we have already agreed you will do,' was Françoise's uncompromising reply, 'but you must do it now. You must set the ground for our attack. You have to mobilise your people, your supporters, the factions in the army who will follow you. You must spread the word that the king is no longer fit for his role. You will say Chulalongkorn is in league with other powers to change Siam forever; he is too young to be a strong king, too headstrong to be a wise one. You will speak of his false accusations against the blameless Kittisak to prove how vindictive and cruel Chulalongkorn is. You will provide some proof of Kittisak's innocence for all to hear, and you will publicly call for the prisoner's release. This will throw the forces who support the king into confusion, and it is in this moment we can strike.

'I can have a combined French and Cambodian force prepared to cross the border within three weeks. Your objective must be to make our onward progress from the frontier to Bangkok as smooth and bloodless as possible. We have no wish to harm a single Siamese if it can be avoided. We do not wish your people to suffer. If you agree, I will leave for Phnom Penh this very night and make the necessary preparations. If you do not, the consequences may be very grave. No one likes a war, and if the British intervene, there can be only one loser – that will be Siam herself.'

'And the king? What of him? What of Kittisak too? As a free man he can only do us damage.' It was one of the regent's entourage who spoke.

'We shall say the king committed suicide,' Françoise replied coolly. 'But in truth, Zhang will see to him – won't you, my darling?' Françoise turned to look at her companion, and from his hiding place three feet below, Henry could see her hand clutch the knee of the man seated next to her. 'As for the pious teak farmer, Kittisak,' Françoise hissed, the malice resonant in her voice, 'Zhang will silence him too – before the maggot can wriggle free from his cell.' The feminine hand under the table slid up Zhang's inner thigh towards his crotch.

It was Françoise's accomplice, Zhang, who spoke next. 'I will do what is necessary to save the Kingdom of Siam from the ruthless Chulalongkorn,' he announced in a strange mechanical tone. 'My brothers and sisters in Cambodia wish our two peoples to be united once more, and only France can help us in our holy endeavour. If you wish me to kill Chulalongkorn, I will do it – it would be an honour.' Zhang's short intervention, replete with its chilling words, caused the room to fall into a morbid paralysis, so much so, that Henry had to hold his breath while the uncomfortable stasis persisted.

'Very well. I will do as you ask…' At length, it was the regent's distinctive gruff tone that broke the inertia. 'But it will take time – a few days, at least. I will need to know your plan in more detail. We must agree dates and times before you depart.'

As Françoise commenced her reply, Henry found he could hardly believe what he was hearing. Although he understood just a few of the words that had been uttered, he'd picked up enough of them to understand that a conspiracy of the hugest proportions was being discussed in the brightly lit salon above their heads. Asnee, who had clearly understood every word, returned Henry's look of amazement with an eye-bulging stare that betrayed the deep disquiet that both of them now felt.

There was the sound of knocking, some raised voices, and a mild commotion from above as a pair servants entered the room carrying a tray of delicacies. The distraction was the opportunity Henry needed. He motioned to Asnee that he had heard enough. It was time to leave and get the news of their adventure back to the king as soon as possible. Asnee nodded his agreement and Henry pushed the hatch open with another silent movement of his foot. As before, it swung soundlessly back on its hinges. But this time, the pair could hear a clamour from the level below. The sound of aggravated exchanges amongst the crew resonated upwards towards them. The commotion appeared to come from the engine room. Henry removed the Bull Dog revolver from its holster as quietly as he could manage. This time, he had to be prepared for anything. Without making any discernible noise, the two descended the iron ladder, one after the other.

The storeroom beneath was still empty by the time Praew Asnee had joined Henry on the wooden deck, but just as they turned towards the exit, one of the matelots from the engine room started to descend the shallow flight of steps towards them. The pair froze for a second and looked around. The workbench before them offered some cover, and in unison, they dropped to their haunches and hid the best they could. Henry raised his gun, and together they waited.

The new entrant appeared quickly, looking more like a cook than a sailor. Of middling age, with a pronounced girth, short stubby legs, and a face florid with exertion, he seemed to arrive in the room more by rolling than walking. Naked from the waist up, his hairless chest gleamed with honest sweat, as did his brow, which he hastily wiped with what might have been the very same discoloured cloth that had earlier helped Henry dislodge the bolt from the actuator. There was no doubt in Henry's mind that the cause of the man's exhausted appearance had much to do with his efforts to return steam into the pistons of the *Rama IV*. Unfortunately for Henry and Asnee, the crewman walked straight towards the workbench where they were hiding, and as he picked up a claw hammer, he caught a glimpse of the two intruders. His immediate reaction was of complete amazement, and he seemed to wobble backwards on his heels. Seizing the initiative, Henry stood up, put the finger of silence to his lips, and with the other hand, he pointed the Bull Dog directly at the sailor's head. A second later, the claw hammer fell onto the bench with a dull thud.

Asnee rose to stand alongside Henry, and put his finger to his lips in a signal to the astonished matelot that exactly mimicked the Englishman's. If anything, the sight of a fellow Siamese alongside the *farang* seemed to make the sailor's eyes widen still further. There was no mistaking it – there was genuine fear in his face. As Asnee backed towards the exit, Henry lowered one hand and tugged at the purse that hung from his belt. Staring directly at the sailor and pointing his revolver all the while, he put the purse onto the workbench and shook out some of the contents. Half a dozen bright-red stones fell onto the coal-grimed surface, looking for all the world like undiscovered jewels in a mine. Henry replaced the pouch onto his belt and indicated to his prisoner that the rubies were his if he wanted them.

He and Asnee edged closer towards their escape route. With a flick of his wrist, Asnee jerked open the door, and then spoke for the first time. 'Take them,' he whispered. 'They are yours. If you let us leave without calling out, we will give you all of them.'

The portly sailor, his shoulders sagging, reached out and picked up the nearest gemstone. As he brought it closer towards his heavy chin, there was the sound of movement from the engine room.

'*Yute!* Stop where you are!' a voice called out in Siamese. 'I have a gun. Drop yours.'

At that moment, in the centre of the cabin, the solitary mariner, single ruby between his chubby fingers, made a sudden lunge for the remainder of the gems, and in the process, dislodged the claw hammer from the table. It toppled downwards and struck one of the fat toes that protruded from his sandals. He let out a shriek like a stuck pig.

In the confusion, Henry and Asnee seized their chance. Bolting through the open doorway towards the outer decking, they arrived at pace on the companionway, legs pumping, and turned to face the jetty. From here, the gangplank, the shore, and safety seemed just a few yards distant. Just as they rounded the wheelhouse, a shot rang out. Asnee doubled up and crashed onto the deck. Henry glared upwards, trying desperately to spot the origin of the missile. Frustrated, he raised his revolver and discharged two bullets into the night air, the intention being to warn the sniper that he, too, was armed. Asnee made a desperate effort to stand but quickly fell back again, clutching his hip. Another blast boomed out; the shot narrowly missed them as it thudded into the side of the wheelhouse. Henry bent down, and with a supreme effort, he managed to lift Asnee to his waist. 'Can you walk a little?' he asked, panting. 'I'll try to hold you up.'

'I will do my best,' came the stricken reply.

Henry emptied two more chambers into the darkness, more in hope than expectation, and holding fast to his companion, the pair made a dart for the gangway. Another shot pinged past his head and imbedded into the superstructure. The conjoined pair collapsed back onto the deck. It was obvious now they were completely trapped. Quailing in unison, like a pair of wounded Christmas geese, they awaited the final strike from their lofty executioner. Instead, as the pair cowered, holding fast to one another, a woman's voice called out to them from the upper companionway. Henry recognised it instantly.

'You are surrounded, Henry Gough,' Françoise cried out in bold English. Her voice was strident, yet to him, he could detect some surprising tenderness too. 'Put your pistol down, pick yourself up, and we shall tend to your friend. Your situation is hopeless. We are many, you are few. There is no need for your foolish Anglo-Saxon heroics.'

At first, Henry could not see her. There was a group of men assembled close to the funnel. He could see one of the company was slenderly dressed as a *farang* – hat, boots and all. But then, after squinting closer, he comprehended it was Françoise. It had to be. Her exquisite face, even from this distance and partly obscured by a felt *chapeau*, was impossible to mistake.

'Oh these?' she called out with a wide grin, while pulling at the broad lapels of her coat. 'I can explain my unusual uniform. Come, be sensible, Henry dear. Let us talk a while. I want to hear all you have been up to since we last met. And besides… you look like you need a glass of whisky.'

Henry Gough placed the Bull Dog revolver carefully onto the deck, got to his feet, and with an apologetic smile to Asnee, he raised his hands in submission.

Chapter Twenty-Nine

Henry scanned the long lines of decking boards as he was escorted at gunpoint by Françoise's powerfully built co-conspirator towards the stern of the ship, and from there back into the grand cabin. Less than five minutes previously, Henry and Asnee had been lurking, dark and unseen, under exactly the same floor on which he now, so shakily, stood. But, as he arrived in the salon, the place looked as unfamiliar to Henry as if he was seeing it for the very first time. With an air of morose finality, he realised his situation above deck, despite the bright candles and gay colours, was by far the more hazardous of the two. Françoise's first words left him in no doubt that she meant to exploit his predicament for all it was worth. There was no mistaking it – she held the upper hand now.

'*Touché!*' She greeted him with a gleaming smile, as she removed her hat and shook out her raven locks. 'I see you have dressed for the occasion also, Henry. Your borrowed Siamese garments are most remarkable. Bravo! And your face! Just look at it... Why, it appears you have been digging up coal this evening! Ha ha ha,' she trilled. 'Mind you, I do believe your near nakedness suits you. I've never liked a man who hides his skin – especially a *farang*.' She stroked her hips with both hands. 'As for my own attire… by way of explanation, all I'll say is that sometimes it's better for a woman to go about unrecognised. This old shirt and jacket have served me well whenever I have felt the need to venture out into the light. Some hold the view that it's a man's world. I disagree, but it pays to play the game when it suits my cause.'

The figure that stood erect and self-assured at Françoise's side was a man of about thirty, surprisingly tall for a Siamese, fine-looking and powerfully built. He wore the clothes and accoutrements of an aristocrat; his silk shirt was high-collared, swathed in bejewelled chains and buttoned to the neck. There were gold rings on every finger. Henry spotted the surrendered Bull Dog wedged into his captor's belt, resting under the line of a muscular chest. In his right hand, the man held his own pistol, which pointed straight at Henry's heart. For a brief moment, Henry had a strange feeling of distant recognition, as if he had encountered the Siamese before in some past life. It was the way the man walked and presented himself that seemed to ring bells in Henry's head. There was no doubt this was the collaborator who'd sat so amorously close to Françoise during their earlier meeting with the regent, but something about his posture nagged… To Henry's surprise there was no sign of the regent at all – or any of his entourage. It was as if the lot of them had vanished into thin air.

'Where is my friend, the man you shot?' Henry asked quietly.

'*I* did not shoot him,' Françoise replied almost instantly. 'Zhang did… didn't you, my sweet?' She touched her accomplice's high cheekbone for a second, in a gesture of unabashed adoration. 'Fear not, your little friend is safe. He's being attended to, as I promised. He has a bullet in his pelvis, I'm told. He may walk with a limp in future – that is all.'

'What do you want of me?'

She laughed aloud. 'That should be obvious! I want to know why you have been spying on me? What brought you to this boat today?' she cried. 'What were your intentions, Mister Henry Gough?'

Henry had to think fast. He had to work on the basis that Françoise was unaware he had overheard her earlier discussions with the regent. If she knew what he had learned in the past few minutes, he would surely be a dead man. He needed a plausible reason for his furtive presence on board that evening.

'Is a man not entitled to seek revenge?' Henry spoke with defiance in his voice. 'You tried to kill me once, or had you forgotten? Despite your disguises, your continued presence in Siam has been noted by others. Your face, the fair countenance that was once your friend, has become your enemy. I have my spies too. I was told you would be at the pier tonight. I merely came to investigate. I wanted to be sure the reports were true. But when I saw what I thought were two men on the shoreline, I became confused. My friend and I moved closer and sneaked aboard when the coast was clear. I needed to have a closer look. My friend is an innocent Siamese, by the by, and one of Mr Woodward's revenue students, so I insist you do not touch a hair on his head. He only agreed to help me in my quest to find you. It was, for him, an adventure of sorts...'

Henry paused and looked directly at Françoise. Indeed, she cut a most extraordinary figure, dressed as she was. 'And here you are, in the very flesh!' he continued coolly. 'Looking much like a music hall villain from Drury Lane. It appears my sources haven't lied, after all.' As Françoise returned a disdainful smile, the thought occurred to Henry that in order to survive the night, he had to change tack, be bolder – brazen even. While it was true the tactic might rile the woman further, it could tilt the balance; if she felt vulnerable, she might just make a mistake. He knew, at the very least, he had to show the vixen he held the moral high ground. Whatever – he had to do something… Suddenly he heard himself blurting, 'And now, mademoiselle, I must ask you to accompany me back to the British consulate, where we wish to interrogate you on the matter of my attempted murder.'

The shriek of laughter that followed made the birds on the river gather their wings and flutter upwards into the night.

'Ha! *You* give orders to *me?*' she cried. 'Damn your impudence. Why, you English are *all* so arrogant, and for what? I have tried to show you some compassion, but all you can muster in return is your absurd pride. I should have known you were no different.' Françoise took three menacing strides towards Henry. Glowering, with suddenly coal-black eyes, she spat into his face, 'I have no further need for this foolishness. If you have come tonight to find me, then you have succeeded!' She clapped her hands mockingly. 'But your quest for revenge will cost you dear. I have a mind to order Zhang to cut you down now, as you skulk before me… but there is something you should know first.' She stepped back and turned towards the swarthy Siamese by her side. With fingers pointing at Zhang's chest she cried, 'Show him, my darling. Let Mister Gough choke on the knowledge of who you truly are…'

Zhang snarled a few words of indecipherable Siamese and with his free hand, and much to Henry's astonishment, he started to rip open the buttons of his shirt. As the catches fell away, a glistening, sweating, sculpted torso was revealed. Henry understood the next word the man uttered easily enough. It simply meant "Look!"

'*Du!*' Zhang cried, '*Du!*' as he exposed his body and the now naked pectoral muscles.

Never in his lifetime had the full force of sudden recognition been so horrifyingly displayed. Henry just gaped in amazement at the half-stripped man that strutted so aggressively before him. In an instant, the harrying thought that he may have known the fellow once before was transformed into a solid realisation. Zhang was none other than the Ashburn Place assassin. Here was living proof and vindication that Henry's account of the murder of Prince Gagananga was authentic in every way. That leaping, dancing tiger tattoo that pranced across Zhang's manly chest was all the evidence Henry needed. He knew he was in the presence of the true killer, the man he had been seeking all these months had finally been run to ground and uncovered – quite literally, as events aptly showed. Poor Kittisak was indeed just an innocent pawn in a vicious high-stakes game played between powerful people – the prize being dominion over Siam, a country the size of Great Britain.

Henry's elation at knowing the truth of the matter was short-lived, however. His situation, perilous as it was already, had now become markedly more dangerous. The fact that Françoise had been prepared to reveal Zhang as the prince killer, and thus by the process of simple extrapolation, demonstrate both their parts in a much larger plot to dethrone King Chulalongkorn, was chilling. For Henry's personal safety, it meant only one thing. He now knew too much… and the chance to share his secret knowledge with others would not be given willingly. His very existence hung on a thread. He knew he had to say something to counter the situation – but what? The truth was he had no reason to feign naivety any longer. But for a few further seconds, he remained utterly dumbstruck. And then, as before, the words that eventually escaped stuttering from his mouth only served to further inflame the situation.

'At last,' he exclaimed, with Zhang's pistol trained inexorably at his sternum, 'I have all the information I need to ensure justice is served – not only for my attempted murder, but for a far greater crime – that of the brutal and premediated assassination of a member of the Siamese royal family. I must ask you both now to lay down your arms and allow me to escort you to the king, who shall want to hear of it...'

Françoise's reaction to Henry's absurd, almost comedic, instruction was very different this time. The chameleon transformation from fiendish sorceress to fairy princess was remarkable. Gone, suddenly, were the ranting outbursts and vitriolic insults. It was as if, in confessing her sins, the unsheathed anger had subsided and simply faded away. In its place returned the ruthless and calculating, yet beguiling disposition most had come to know of her so well.

'Bravo, Henry,' she returned with a dazzling smile. 'You have all the evidence you need – much good it will do you! As now, I fear, you are of no further use to me whatsoever – any ideas that I might have had to preserve your life are wrecked. It will be a shame to kill you, Henry Gough, as I have grown fond of your face and even of some of your asinine English ways. But before Zhang adds another scratch mark to his sword, I have another idea. Instead, your gullible partner in crime will make some sport for us – an appetising *hors d'oeuvre* for *le plat du jour*, perhaps. Zhang, go fetch the miserable worm – we shall hear what he has to tell us.'

As Henry watched, horrified, Zhang barked out some Siamese words in the direction of the portal and the companionway outside. Twenty seconds later, poor Asnee, still bleeding from his hip, was dragged by two of the regent's uniformed flunkies into the cabin and flung unceremoniously towards the spot where Henry stood. The young man made a pitiful cry of pain as his body slid to a halt at Henry's side.

Henry crouched down to whisper to his comrade, 'Hold fast, old friend. We are not done for yet.'

'What is your name?' Françoise breathed in gentle Siamese tones.

'Praew Asnee. I am a servant of the king – a revenue officer.' The words were spoken through gritted teeth as Asnee held his side with a bloodstained cloth. Clearly the young man was in extreme pain.

'How do you know this *farang*?' Françoise pointed straight at Henry.

'He is my English teacher, madam.'

'What brings you to the boat tonight?'

Henry, understanding the gist, looked anxiously at Asnee, and even though the cat was largely out of the bag, he found himself praying that his Siamese student would not reveal the history of their evening's exertions; but he need not have worried. Perhaps Asnee had overheard Henry's earlier concocted explanation, or maybe, and typically for him, he was thinking on his feet and realised that to divulge the truth of their mission would have meant certain death.

'Khun Henry asked me to come as his interpreter,' he answered. 'His Siamese is not so good that he can understand every word. He wanted me to help. He is my English teacher, and I wanted to be his friend.' Asnee's response was spoken with humility but showed an inner strength that belied the hurt he must have been enduring.

'What else did he tell you?'

'Khun Henry said he was looking for a woman who spoke English, French and Siamese.'

'I see…' Françoise sighed. 'Well, now you have found her…' she added, this time in English and accompanied by a languid smile. 'But here it must end, I fear. I am bored by this performance.' She gave an exaggerated yawn and fluttered her hands as if she was fanning invisible flies away. 'It's time to bring down the curtain on you both – Zhang, do your worst. Kill them now for me, would you, my darling. Kill the pretty young man first,' she added, pointing contemptuously at Asnee.

Instinctively, Henry knew what was coming. He felt the sinews in his thighs flicker but to his horror, he could not engage a single muscle. Unbelievably, he found himself rooted to the spot and unable to move as Zhang slowly raised the revolver, and from a distance of about four yards, aimed it directly at Praew Asnee's heart. *Where's the adrenaline when I need it?* Henry thought. He'd acted unfalteringly in Ashburn Place – why not now? Perhaps it was because the gun had yet to turn on him. Time and space seemed to pass in slow motion – a single second felt like six. It was as if all his limbs were frozen in ice, as rigid as death itself; yet he could do nothing. His friend was about be slaughtered, he would soon follow; together they would meet their separate makers like gentle lambs; quietly, without reproach or even a single cry of anguish.

Zhang brought his left hand up to meet the other and gripped the handle. He lowered his head slightly, looked the incapacitated Asnee directly in the eye and coolly squeezed the trigger. Henry waited for the explosion but none came – instead, there was a clicking sound as the pistol misfired. Suddenly, Henry's impulses kicked in, and while Zhang turned the revolver over in his hands to inspect for a fault, astonishment written large on his face, Henry sprang forwards, and like a rugby player diving for a touchdown, he threw his hands out and grabbed one of Zhang's ankles. The Siamese wobbled at first and tried to regain his balance. The pistol slipped out of his hand, only to be gathered safely by the other. But, at six foot tall and weighing nearly thirteen stones, Henry could pack a punch, and the force of his lunge was not to be denied. Slowly at first, one ankle tightly wedged in Henry's grasp, Zhang started to topple. Impulsively, he threw up his arms in a last effort to prevent a fall, and the pistol flew from his grasp and clattered to the deck. As it hit the solid wood, the bullet that should have been released a few seconds earlier decided it was time to perform, and with a loud report that went singing around the cabin, it exploded from the barrel.

At that very instant, Zhang hit the deck and transformed into a half-naked squirming mass of scrunched arms and legs. Fully expecting his adversary to pick himself up quickly, Henry raised his bare fists in the proper Queensbury tradition, but instead of rising up, the writhing and moaning continued. It was in that moment Henry realised the stray bullet must have hit Zhang in some part of his body, and the deduction was soon confirmed when a thick pool of blood started to form under Zhang's groaning and breathless form. Henry saw he had to push home his advantage and act fast. He leapt forwards once again just as Françoise flung herself towards her injured lover, but with one sweep of his hand, Henry brushed her aside. He knew, at all costs, he had to be reunited with the Bull Dog, and nothing was going to prevent it. As Françoise crumpled and slid across the floor, Zhang howled out once more in pain. Henry reached him first, uncovered the pistol and swiftly withdrew it from the wounded man's belt. As he rose to his feet, one of the two guards drew a dagger and advanced ominously towards him. Henry needed no further invitation and fired directly into the man's temple, felling him like a collapsed horse.

'I will shoot anyone who moves,' Henry cried. 'Everyone, stay where you are.'

The second guard backed dutifully towards the door, hands aloft, but Françoise didn't seem to hear the command. She gathered herself together once more and hurried to Zhang's side. There was a lot of blood. From what Henry could see, the stray bullet must have struck close to Zhang's heart. Françoise hurriedly removed her clumsy jacket to reveal a feminine blouse of white lace beneath, and with the divested garment crunched into a ball, she did her best to stem the flow. But it was clear, Zhang was failing fast – his breathing had become erratic, and he gasped and gurgled horribly, unable to speak.

'Oh, my love,' she wailed, 'please don't leave me. I have staunched the wound… just stay with me. I have bandages, the doctor will be here. Please don't close your eyes,' she implored. And drawing him to her soft bosom, she cradled him in her arms. But to the other onlookers, the situation appeared to be hopeless. Zhang stared fixedly ahead as he struggled to focus his bulging eyes on her. The sight was truly pitiful, and even for a man of his supposed wickedness, all present must have felt a degree of compassion for his plight. As Zhang's face turned a ghastly white, he reached out, imploring, for his sweetheart. He surely knew he was slipping into the abyss. The eyelids blinked hopelessly one more time. As if on cue, and with a ghastly gush of drowning blood, a final eruption bubbled out of Zhang's yawning mouth. The discharge spewed onto Françoise's cotton chemise and fell between the half-exposed breasts that pressed against her lover's cheek. And then, just as a clock might grind steadily to a halt and eventually cease its ticking, Zhang's whole body arched up from the cabin floor, quivered briefly, froze for a second, and then fell back, forever silent. The torrent of blood ceased. With his black eyes still fixed at the ceiling, his very being had finally drained away. Zhang was dead – there was no mistaking it.

Françoise, hot blood dripping from her pretty blouse, let out such a shriek the like of which can never have been heard by any of the assembled company. Contained within it was an utter wretchedness, a vile anger, and an abject melancholy, all wrapped into one deafening heave of her lungs.

At that moment, the cabin door flew open, and two sabre-carrying bodyguards stood at the threshold. Positioned between them was the imperious form of the regent himself, Lord Bamroong.

'Seize them!' Bamroong shouted. 'I have heard enough screeching for one night.' On this order, the two bodyguards picked up their sabres and advanced towards Henry and the stricken Asnee. Their progress hesitated briefly as the Englishman raised his pistol to fire. But, for the second time in as many minutes, the sound of a vacant clunk resounded around the salon. 'Damn!' The five bullets in the Bull Dog's chamber had been expended... It was Henry's turn to rue his luck; how he wished he'd not wasted his ammunition trying to kill thin air. There was no time to reload, and he instantly realised there was nothing for it but to submit once more. He put up his hands in capitulation and threw down the empty revolver, which slithered under the regent's patterned feet.

The armed guards advanced still further, but just as they arrived to within feet of his upstretched arms, the terrifying sound of a barrage of gunfire met their ears. The fearsome noise drowned out all other sounds in the cabin in an instant. The whole assembly instinctively ducked to the salon deck as, with all heads now lowered, a second broadside razed the upper deck of the *Rama IV*. A scrambling panic ensued as one and all took cover as best they could. Then followed a curious stillness as the whole assembly held their collective breath. When he felt it was safe to move, Henry lifted his head and squinted past the cabin transom, towards the outer companionway. His eyes were greeted by the daunting sight of a horde of men swarming over the decks. Voices were raised as shouts were exchanged, but there was no further gunfire, only the sound of a ship's horn, its loud blasts repeating every few seconds. From his vantage point, it appeared to Henry the vessel was being boarded by a gang of armed men, and the ship's crew was in the process of surrendering the vessel to the intruders.

When, after a few further seconds, the regent picked himself up from the deck and peered out too, his demeanour changed in an instant. A distinct look of fear now replaced the haughty bearing that had marked his entrance into the salon. He appeared markedly agitated as he shouted instructions to his still-cowering bodyguards. Urging his men to join him, he turned towards the exit. It was clear to Henry that Bamroong wanted to make a speedy escape, but his flight was interrupted by the sound of a high-pitched trumpet that suddenly blasted through the ship. This was followed, shortly after, by a booming voice from yonder that bellowed in thundering Siamese.

'Make way for His Majesty, King Rama the Fifth!'

Seconds later, the salon door flew open once more, and a party of six splendidly liveried retainers crowded in, each presenting a gleaming sword ahead of them and marching in brisk single file. On forming a guard of honour, they kneeled as King Chulalongkorn entered, his countenance appearing most grave and majestic. All those standing in the room, including Henry Gough, dropped instantly to the floor, endeavouring to keep their skulls below the height of the reigning monarch's sacred head. Directly behind the king was the familiar figure of Lawrence Beaumont. On seeing the consul general, Henry touched his forelock in recognition and respect. Beaumont, looking drained and sombre, managed a wan smile in return. Chulalongkorn cast his eyes imperiously about the grand salon and maintained a stately silence for at least ten seconds. When, at length, he broke into the hushed mood, it was to the kowtowing regent the king said his first words.

'It appears there have been some events that have taken place here about which I require some explanation. Will you apprise me, Lord Bamroong? We can see a lot of blood, and at least one of my subjects appears to be in need of medical assistance. We heard the gunshots as we progressed upriver, and we have come to investigate. Pray inform us what has occurred here tonight.'

The regent, hands flat on the deck, lifted his head a few inches and stared back. 'Your Majesty, of course. I have much to tell you, but I humbly request I give you my confidential report in private. There are *farangs* amongst us. It would not do well for them to hear my story.'

'Very well,' the king replied without a hint of affection. 'My guards will escort you to my barge, which is alongside. I will join you there when I have completed my business here.' The king clapped his hands. Two of his men hurried forward, and the regent, humiliation writ large across his face, was led away in embarrassed silence. Chulalongkorn trained his finger at the weeping Françoise, who slouched in a bloodstained heap on the floor, still embracing the limp body of her dead lover. 'Take her away – give the woman some fresh clothes and keep her secure. I have much to ask you, mademoiselle.' Another pair of guards stepped forward, and soon the distraught Frenchwoman was being dragged away from the blood-soaked corpse at her side. At first, she resisted, but strong arms eventually disentangled her, and Zhang's skull thudded irreverently onto hard planks as her grasp was finally released.

When she was gone, and her weeping could be heard no

more, the king turned his attention to the wounded man who lay prone on the deck while pressing a bloody cloth to his side. 'And you, young man... What is your name?'

'I am Revenue Officer Praew Asnee, Your Majesty,' came the self-assured reply.

'We are pleased to meet you, at last.' The king nodded benignly. 'We are told we are in your debt, sir. My ladies will see to your wounds, and we shall speak again very soon.'

As Asnee received attention from two young women, who had appeared as if from nowhere, the king turned his head to speak to Lawrence Beaumont. 'Thank you for inviting me tonight, Mr Beaumont. It has been most illuminating – dare I say exciting – indeed. You know, it does a sovereign a power of good to see his citizens up close from time to time. And I must say, your man Mr Gough looks for all the world like he *is* one of my own subjects,' the king said with a broad smile. 'Ha ha, our national costume seems to suit him very well. Perhaps you can ask him to accompany us to my barge. I would speak with you both before I confront my regent. There is much to discuss, and I want to know everything.'

The consul general returned the smile. 'Of course, Your Majesty. I will see to it immediately.'

∽:∽

It was nearly midnight before Henry Gough and Lawrence Beaumont reached the bar of the Falcks Hotel and their awaiting colleagues, Albert Woodward and Horatio Chalke.

'Come, sit! We have food. We have imported whisky,' the waiting pair effused as they pulled up chairs and fumbled with glasses and bottles. Their questions came thick and fast... 'What news do you bring? We had almost given up hope. Thank God you are safe, Henry. Was there any danger? Do you have a story to tell us? Where is Khun Asnee? Pray, tell us – we are desperate to hear all.'

'Do I have a story?' Henry winked at Beaumont as he cradled his first Scotch… 'I should say so!'

Epilogue

King Chulalongkorn ordered troop reinforcements to be sent to bolster defences at the Cambodian border the following day. This signal of defensive intent had the desired effect, and any French plans to invade and depose him from the throne of Siam were finally thwarted. As a result, Siam has remained the only country in South East Asia uncolonised by western powers to this day. Chulalongkorn continued to rule over his people for the next thirty years, until his death in 1910. Unfettered from his regent, the king became one of the most admired and venerated monarchs in the history of Siam. In 1939 the Kingdom of Siam became known as Thailand or "land of the free". The descendants of King Chulalongkorn, part of the Chakri dynasty, still rule the country to this day.

Henry Gough and **Albert Woodward** sailed to London on the next available boat, less than two weeks later. King Chulalongkorn held a reception in their honour the day before the ship departed and presented each of them with the Order of the White Elephant for their role in helping his country defeat the threat of invasion.

Henry Gough returned to his wife and children in Marylebone, where he continued his work as a cab proprietor and driver. He went on to have twelve children with Caroline. Called on regularly by London's law enforcement community to assist their enquiries, he had many more adventures.

Albert Woodward became Head of the Excise Detective Branch a month after he disembarked at Millwall docks and served the Crown until his retirement in 1890. He moved to Pentyrch in south Wales with his wife and spent his pensionable years in the pursuits of birdwatching, growing leeks, and telling tall stories about his many exploits as an international spy.

Lord Bamroong was stripped of his title as regent. The king showed him mercy for his treason, largely out of political expediency, and for the rest of his life, Bamroong was held under palace arrest. His family were divested of half their land, and their power in Siam faded over time. He died of diarrhoeal disease in 1885.

Françoise Mielette was held in custody and questioned in the Royal Palace gaol for nearly three months. She refused to cooperate with her interrogators, denying her part in any plot to topple the king. As a condition of a new treaty and settlement with France, she returned to Cambodia. British intelligence sources indicated she continued to work for *Le Deuxième Bureau*, and shared her time between Paris and the French territories of Indo-China. She never married.

Zhang was identified as Zhang Chen, a Cambodian national. Based on Henry Gough's identification and testimony, he was posthumously convicted of murdering the king's half-brother, and his body was buried in an unmarked grave on the outskirts of Bangkok. To add further, if unnecessary, proof of Zhang's guilt, shipping records in London showed him to have been in England at the time of Prince Gagananga's killing.

He'd left England for Calais on 24th February on the same vessel as the French agent Henriques D'Argent. The pistol Zhang carried in Bangkok, which jammed just before his death, was identified as a French-made MAS 1875 of calibre 11mm. Using the bullet that had lodged in Henry Gough's cab for comparison, ballistics experts at Scotland Yard later determined the revolver to have been the murder weapon.

Pierre Museau was arrested a week later as he tried to cross the border into Cambodia dressed as a local farmer. Like Françoise Mielette, he was interrogated for nearly three months. Unlike her, the Siamese agencies found a way to extract his confession. As part of a new settlement with France, he was beheaded in Bangkok, some said as a diplomatic scapegoat, for his admitted role in the unsanctioned (according to the French) plot to overthrow the king.

Lawrence Beaumont was knighted for his services in Siam on behalf of Great Britain. He left his position as Bangkok's consul general in 1884 and returned to London, from where he was posted to Paris as Her Britannic Majesty's Ambassador to France.

Horatio Chalke was made deputy consul general a week later, and his relationship and reputation with the Siamese court grew still further. He was appointed consul general in Bangkok, succeeding Sir Lawrence Beaumont, in 1884. He lived in Siam until his death from stomach disease in 1909.

Charles Hurdus left Siam secretly with his entire household two days later. He was never charged with any offence, nor was his part in the extraordinary events of 1880 ever divulged officially. He gave instructions to sell his newly acquired Sussex estate, and with the funds, he purchased a farm in the Moluccas, where he lived and worked as a spice trader with his family and a fourth wife. He died in 1901 of an aortic aneurism, brought on by chronic syphilis.

Frederick Archbold remained in Siam for a further three years. At thirty-one, he returned to London's Inns of Court with his new wife, Somsri, the pretty sister of fellow lawyer, Boon Nam Chaidee. The momentous acquittal of Kittisak Aromdee much enhanced Archbold's reputation, and although he never fully shook off the burden of his illustrious father, his career flourished. Over the years, he returned to Siam regularly with his wife and family, where he made many friends and continued to be a source of legal advice at the court of King Chulalongkorn.

Jasvinder Singh remained in the service of the consul general until 1900, when he retired and returned to his home in Chandigarh, Punjab. A statue was erected to him on his death in 1908, which now stands within the grounds of the Viceroy's Palace in New Delhi, India.

Nathanial Hope, having earlier refused a knighthood, was made Viscount Tring in 1882. Until his untimely death in 1901, after suffering a heart attack during Queen Victoria's funeral, he sat nearly every day in the House of Lords.

Chief Superintendent Jack Grieve left the service of the Metropolitan Police as a commander in 1896. He bought a public house in the village of West Chiltington, Sussex, which he renamed *The Peccavi Plot*.

Praew Asnee recovered from his wounds and married his sweetheart, Gaew Saelim. His Uncle Loong gave the bride away. As predicted by Françoise Mielette, Asnee would walk with a limp for the rest of his life. Together, he and Gaew went on to have six children. His heroism was rewarded by the king with a junior appointment in His Majesty's Ministry of Foreign Affairs. In the summer of 1915, he became its leader.

Mamasam Malee became a rich and respected lady of business, continuing to run Bangkok's favourite *sonng* until her death in 1919. On hearing of her unwitting part in helping to uncover the plot to depose him, the king granted her a special licence to open three further establishments in Charoen Krung Road, which still thrive to this day. She drowned, aged 81, during her customary morning dip in the Chao Phraya River, and her passing was mourned by many.

Kittisak Aromdee was released immediately from custody at the king's command. He received no apology or compensation for his incarceration and treatment at the hands of the Siamese authorities. He returned to work in Chiang Mai where he became rich and influential as a timber merchant. He remained a staunch supporter of the king and an avid Anglophile. In 1898, he became a founding member of the Chiang Mai Gymkhana Club, where, for many years, he could be found at sundown sipping Siamese whisky and soda, and playing card games with the other members.

Historical Note

In 1893, thirteen years after the fictitious events of this book had been brought to a close, war actually broke out between France and Siam.

The conflict was sparked by France's desire to bring Siamese territory east of the Mekong River in Laos under French rule. The government in Bangkok, mistakenly believing they would be supported by Great Britain, refused to concede the area demanded by France. When, in 1892, the Siamese expelled French merchants for opium smuggling from the middle Mekong region, matters came to a head. The French sent two gunboats, *Inconstant* and *Comète*, uninvited into the Chao Phraya River, Bangkok where, on 13th July 1893, they came under Siamese fire. This became known as "the Paknam incident". Returning fire, the French then trained their guns on the Royal Palace and blockaded the Siamese coast. After their initial ultimatums were rejected by the Siamese, and in the absence of any support from Great Britain, the Siamese were forced to submit to all French conditions, including the surrender of the disputed eastern Mekong territory. The Franco-Siamese Treaty of 3rd October 1893 was the result.

THE FRENCH WOLF AND THE SIAMESE LAMB.

Punch Magazine in London published the above cartoon on August 5th 1893.

Acknowledgements

My thanks go once again to Clive Woodward MBE for his constant support, encouragement and inventive plot ideas, to Lauren Dennington – https://lcdediting.com – for her professionalism, dedication and creative suggestions while leading the editing process, to Helen Thurlow for her scrupulous proofreading, and to Murray Bealby for his superb work in building and maintaining my social media presence – www.frankhurst.com.

Finally, and most importantly, I would like to offer my sincere gratitude to all those friends in Thailand, past and present, who inspired me to write this historical novel, grounded in the Siam of their ancestors.

FH
Chiang Mai
November 2023

About the Author

Frank Hurst, who writes under a pseudonym, was born in south London and spent thirty-six years as an investigator and intelligence officer for HM Customs, Scotland Yard and the British Foreign Office. He travelled widely in his career, including many years living in India, Thailand and the eastern Caribbean, tracking down some of the biggest traffickers in the world of drugs smuggling. He received the Outstanding Law Enforcement Award from the US Department of Justice for his work against Howard Marks, aka 'Mr Nice' and has been a contributor to the recently published *Drug War – The Secret History* by Peter Walsh. After leaving the service of the Crown, Frank has devoted his time to writing novels. His *Golden Triangle Trilogy*, set in the Far East, has received wide acclaim and won literary awards.

Frank has retained his appetite for travelling and when he's not living the quiet life in West Sussex, he loves nothing better than to return to his old haunts and visit stirring new places around the globe – hopefully stumbling into new adventures in the process.